Libby Purves

Libby Purves is a broadcaster and journalist, who has presented the talk programme *Midweek* on Radio 4 since 1984 and formerly presented *Today*. She is also a columnist on *The Times*.

Her books *How Not to Be a Perfect Mother* and *How Not to Raise a Perfect Child* have been widely translated; *How Not to Be a Perfect Family* appeared in 1994 to complete the trilogy. She also wrote *One Summer's Grace*, an account of a voyage around mainland Britain with her husband and two small children in 1988. She lives in Suffolk with her husband, the broadcaster and writer Paul Heiney, and their two children.

Libby Purves's previous novels, *Casting Off* and *A Long Walk in Wintertime*, are also available as Sceptre paperbacks.

SCEPTRE

Also by Libby Purves

Home
Leave

LIBBY PURVES

SCEPTRE

Copyright © 1997 Libby Purves

First published in 1997 by Hodder and Stoughton
First published in paperback in 1998 by Hodder and Stoughton
A division of Hodder Headline PLC
A Sceptre Paperback

10 9 8 7 6 5 4 3 2

A CIP catalogue record for this title is available
from the British Library.

ISBN 0 340 68041 5

Typeset by Palimpsest Book Production Limited,
Polmont, Stirlingshire
Printed and bound in Great Britain by
Clays Ltd, St Ives plc

Hodder and Stoughton
A division of Hodder Headline PLC
338 Euston Road
London NW1 3BH

To Dorothy Bednarowska
with love and gratitude

AUTHOR'S NOTE

It would be idle to deny my family background, as a travelling diplomat's child and one of four siblings. I have pillaged our common past for all manner of details and foreign postings: however, every character and significant incident in this book is purely fictitious. I am not in there, and nor are any of my relatives!

PROLOGUE ∫

1950–1996

At the mid-point of the twentieth century, amid the stiff gilding and blowsy classical façades of Vienna, Robert Gratton met his only and enduring love.

It happened at a New Year's Eve ball given by a group of city merchants to impress upon foreign visitors and officials that post-war austerity and humiliation would not for long keep Austria down. The once private ballroom, though tatty, still wore its operatic gilding with a swagger, and enough pressure had been put on rural apiarists for the candles to be of soft beeswax. Between their scented flickering and an emotional rendering of the "Gold and Silver Waltz" by a scratch orchestra, a pleasing illusion of unruffled nineteenth-century splendour was maintained.

Nobody noticed the shaky state of the great hall's stairway, floor and above all its drains; certainly not a tipsy young British diplomat on his first posting and wearing his first tail-coat. As the evening wore on, gatecrashers swelled the crowd: students in improvised evening-dress, old men with white hair over their collars and coats of greenish antiquity, ladies of not much virtue and musicians released from the opera house and seeking – not champagne, for that had more or less dried up by ten o'clock – but conviviality.

Most of the diplomats left early, oppressed by the romantic atmosphere and the shortage of drink. But Robert Gratton stayed

1 •

on, wandering alone but quite happy through the jostling crowd. Just before the stroke of midnight, he came face to face with a tall fair girl in a white dress. Around them, emotional Viennese embraced and seized one another's hands. Without thinking he seized hers.

"I am Diana," she said.

"Yes," he replied. "I can see that."

And that, more or less, was that. Diana Martin, daughter of a Hartlepool doctor, unpromising music student, had no need to play the huntress. Robert Gratton hunted her thereafter with concentrated care, and six weeks later central Europe had one fewer bad violinist, and one more bride.

Back at the Embassy this caused some consternation. The Ambassador was not impressed by this haste and his wife – who saw herself as a mother to all the young men of the mission, particularly the handsome ones – remonstrated most strongly with him on the day before his brief civil marriage.

"You know so little about her – about one another," said Lady Ford, plaintively.

"I know everything," said Robert firmly. Faced with his dark good looks and romantic determination, she fluttered a little, gave in, and made the Ambassador buy the young couple an unsuitably expensive silver tray.

They honeymooned at an inn near the Czech border, where Robert borrowed langlauf skis and Diana would trudge up through the snow to watch him sliding erratically along the high forest tracks. In the evening they ate their way through a dozen local variants on potato and sausage, drank steins of pale beer, watched the snow falling and marvelled at their luck.

Despite Lady Ford's misgivings, Diana proved to be the very model of a young diplomatic wife: unambitious for herself, deferential to the senior wives, eminently teachable when it came to the decorous conventions of entertaining and being entertained. "Never worry about *placement*," an elderly French chargé d'affaires told her in a comforting aside one day. "Diplomats are like circus horses. They always find their own places." Best of all, she was unhampered by any unfortunate tendency to attach herself emotionally to hearth and home. Moving on was never a problem to Diana as it was to other wives; almost alone among her peers she would greet each new posting with escapist glee, and regarded packing up house every two or three years to cross the world as a positive perk of the job.

Hartlepool, after all, had been dull: so dull she had frequently wept with rage and frustration from the age of thirteen onwards. The Martin parents, GP and district nurse, had been unswervingly dedicated to their humane callings, and baffled and irritated by their only child. At first they had seen her as a successor, and plied her from childhood with Little Nurse kits and books full of colourful cross-sections of intestines and diagrams explaining the Miracle of Skin. Diana had ignored these and crayoned dresses, flounced and princessy, on every blank end-paper. She demanded dance classes and saved her pocket-money for big, stiff wire curlers.

The child's delicate, fair prettiness seemed to annoy her mother in particular every bit as much as Diana's open dislike of the messy and arduous parental professions. It was with a certain guilty relief that the Martins sent her out of the vulnerable port area to spend the war on a Pennine smallholding with some cousins. Here Diana learnt that there was indeed a life worse than being a provincial doctor's daughter: a life spent farming. Here too, however, through a village schoolteacher's gramophone she encountered good music: a discipline so blissfully unconnected with either bandages or pig pens that she begged prettily for lessons. To her parents' further bewilderment, she showed enough swift shallow talent on the violin to win a place at Leeds, and to cap it, by November 1949, with a six months' exchange scholarship to Vienna. Of which, as we now know, she served only one month before New Year's night revealed her true vocation as a diplomatic wife.

Robert Gratton, still dizzy at his luck in love, struck lucky again in 1952 with a posting to Venice. It was not customary for diplomats always to come home between postings, and he took the pregnant and excited Diana by the night sleeper through the Alps, waking her with a kiss as the train trundled across the causeway towards the towers of Venice in the morning mist. Here Diana wandered for two blissful months through churches and galleries and piazze, determined to feed her unborn on beauty, on Bellini madonnas and Canaletto views. Here, at the height of Carnival, the first Gratton baby opened her eyes on the white apron, blue habit and pendent rosary of a midwife nun.

"I shall call her Catherine," said Diana dreamily. "She is going to be beautiful. My Venetian baby."

Soon, however, Catherine was merely Cat, and not particularly beautiful either. A stout, fair, stolid, practical child, she was very different from the dark elfin Venetian babies around her. Diana was almost embarrassed by her offspring's smiling pudding face and lack of mystery. Catherine grew fast, was never ill, turned the pages of her rag books with plump concentration, adored her father and merely tolerated her increasingly edgy mother. It is hard to know how these mismatches occur: how a baby not yet two can have a personality dangerously at odds with its own mother's. But it can happen. Somehow the practical, doctorly, Hartlepool inheritance had forced its way through Diana's defences. Hijacked by her own genes, she looked on her small daughter – already so painfully, obviously suitable to be a district nurse – with something like distaste. The grave, quirky, flaking romantic beauty of Venice was a daily reproof, a contrast to the child's blandly grinning fat pink Anglo-Saxon face.

An early onward posting moved the three Grattons to Tel Aviv in the newborn state of Israel. For Robert it was an important promotion, and the young nation's birth pangs excited and fascinated him. His reports to the FO were widely noticed and praised, his network of acquaintances and contacts discreet and effective. He was marked for stardom and knew it. To Diana, after Venice's dim velvet glamour, Tel Aviv was an atrocity: the buildings were concrete slabs, the landscape alien, alternately dusty and overbrightly green. Life within the diplomatic corps was tolerable but the intrusive, noisy, plain-speaking, prickly warmth of the Israelis offended both her natural reserve and recently acquired diplomatic poise.

However, she still worshipped Robert, despite the dough-faced baby girl he had so inconsiderately given her. Eventually, Diana resigned herself to making the best of it. She thankfully handed Cat over to Rachel, a stout teenager with a faint moustache. Cat's first whole sentence was "Rachie gimme Torah story", and her first naughtiness was cutting off, with craft scissors, the hair of a very expensive doll that Robert had ordered from Harrods for her second Tel Aviv Christmas. "Dat doll was *Samson*," she explained indignantly. "Dat doll was getting *too strong.*"

Diana's doldrum ended in 1954 with the birth of Toby. This son, dark and saturnine like his father, provided all the romantic mystery and infant glamour which Cat so woefully lacked. He rarely slept but never cried; his black glittering eyes were everywhere, his smile devastatingly crooked, his demands on her breasts constant and strangely flattering. Cat had sucked happily but dully, eyes closed, so easily satisfied that she often fell asleep with her mouth open halfway through a feed, dribbling. Toby hung on Diana's breast as purposeful as a little vampire, feeding every two hours, punching her with his small perfect fists and watching, always watching her face through open, long-lashed dark eyes. At night, giddy and euphoric with sleeplessness and the released hormones of frequent feeding, Diana would gaze at her baby mesmerized, and wish she had not let Robert name him so boringly after a recently dead uncle. Toby! Bah! This baby should be a Giovanni, a Maximilian, or an Horatio; not that dull jug of a name. But never mind. He was here. She was, at last, complete.

It never occurred to placid Cat to be jealous. She adored Toby with baby passion, watched over him with care, and endlessly picked up the toys he hurled from the pram when Rachel – who was rather less enamoured – grew bored of his demands. Two years later, when the family was posted back into the heart of old Europe, to Berne, it was the four-year-old Cat who packed Toby's toys and worried whether there would be enough clean nappies for the long journey by ship and train. This time, Robert flew home for briefing at the Foreign Office and Diana was left alone, with a weeping Rachel, to pack up the Tel Aviv house.

She had the grace to be fleetingly glad of Cat's stolid helpfulness, and to call her a "good girl". The departure itself was rushed. Cat looked back at Rachel as the overloaded taxi drew away from the gate, but said nothing beyond "Bye-bye". She was not quite sure, and did not like to ask her mother, but expected Rachel would probably come on later. Nobody had explained the permanence of the separation.

"They just accept it, at that age," the Ambassador's wife had sagely told Diana. "The rule is, don't for heaven's sake make a big thing about the children saying goodbye to local help. They soon settle in the new post, and forget. Dimpy never even talks about his old ayah, though he had her for three years when we were on the Viceroy's staff."

Berne is no Venice. But the buildings are old, satisfyingly ornate and richly permanent, surrounded by a fine city wall. On each hour strutting figurines march out of the Zeitglocke in the centre of town and bang hammers for the chimes. There are parks, not deserts or irrigated plantations. Other wives at the Berne embassy grumbled about the stodginess of Swiss society, but for Diana, back from the horrid brash sandiness of the Bible lands, it was something to be revelled in: formal, safe, understated, *European*. Best of all, from Cat and Toby's points of view, there was a great concrete pit on the edge of the city with trees growing up the middle and real, live brown bears in it who served as the patrons and symbols of Berne. Sometimes they had baby bears with them, who crept from the caves below the roadway to glare up at the ring of visitors' faces above. Sometimes they climbed the biggest tree, and glared across the pit from eye level. Any level of good behaviour – in Cat, at least – could be instantly summoned up by a promise to go on the tram and see the bears; any bad behaviour quelled in a second by a threat to withhold this joy.

After a few months of settling in, a nanny-governess was engaged to teach Cat to read and keep Toby from falling into the bear-pit. The day of her arrival found Cat oddly excited, up early in her best dress, waiting. When Helge came, fair and formal and obviously not Rachel, she made no complaint but picked up Toby, hugged him briefly, then unaccountably went upstairs and changed into an everyday dress before returning dry-eyed to greet her new attendant.

"Cat could go home to school," said Diana, two years later and grumpily pregnant for the third time. "Most families do send children home to board. That's what the allowances are there for. It's stupid not to take the chance."

"Poor Pussy, she's only six," said Robert, who had a particular tenderness for his tubby little daughter, and loved to see her politely handing round bridge rolls and vol-au-vents at the compulsory cocktail parties. "Home is here. She's never even been in England, come to think of it."

"But she really ought to go to school. If we put her in school here, she'd have to do lessons in German. Switzedeutsch, too, not even real German."

"Other children do. I think it's rather broadening for them. She actually speaks it quite a lot, with Helge, I can't understand a word either of them are saying. It is a villainous accent, I grant you."

"You're changing the subject."

For the first time, a rift seemed to be opening between the two elder Grattons; but in the nick of time, just as Cat was about to be shown glossy prospectus photographs of a convent school in Wiltshire, Robert was posted to Washington. It was another showy promotion, second-in-command to a distinguished Ambassador. Accordingly, he flew to London for more prolonged and deeper briefings than before, then briefly back to Berne for Diana's confinement.

The baby was too late for the exigencies of the posting, however, and Robert was already on the train to Geneva airport at the moment when Mark was born, with some difficulty, in a spotless Swiss nursing home. Cat and Toby stayed for a week with Helge and her family in the mountains while Diana and the baby recovered from the long and frightening labour; the house was already relet and the family furniture and baggage crated in Pickfords' store, awaiting a freight 'plane. "Poor you," said the Vice-Consul's wife to Diana. "Isn't it hell, really, this life!" But Diana did not care at all about the furniture or her limbo of homelessness; only about Robert's not being there nor – apparently – much wanting to be.

So Cat went to school in Washington DC, and learnt to spell *color* and *labor* American style at school and English style at home, to salute the Stars and Stripes and – to Diana's dismay – to chew gum. At seven, even under the liberal regime of the chic private prep Diana chose, she was painfully aware of lagging behind her well-drilled contemporaries from Ivy League families. Toby, at four, was initially indignant at leaving the bears but before long found himself revelling in the American atmosphere of carefree wealth, TV cartoons, and the curious acceptability of cheekiness in small children. When his father, helpless with laughter, tried to check some of his wilder excesses of Yankee lip he would say, "I'm not a children now. I'm a kid."

Diana desultorily cared for Mark (another stolid, fair, dull sleepy baby) with much help from a Mexican maid, and longed for Europe. At one stage – Cat always remembered, with an uneasy sinking at her heart – there were many afternoon visits from one particular European, in a sitting room banned to children. Toby, smaller and less censorious and more in his mother's confidence, told Cat this visitor was a real live Count, like in fairy stories, from the Bavarian forests. "It's called a Graf, in Germany." The Graf had shot actual boars, with a blunderbuss. Cat would hear raised voices echoing up the broad stairway of their tall, brownish-yellow house on the rare evenings that Robert and Diana were not going out in cocktail party clothes. Eventually the Graf no longer came. Perhaps the raised voices were only because Robert's starry diplomatic career seemed unaccountably to have stalled in the New World. Or perhaps the career stalled because of his wife's too visible indiscretions. At any rate, he no longer felt himself to be inevitably on the fast track to Ambassador. Those who had described him as "brilliant" in Tel Aviv and Berne had scaled it down to "sound enough". When a posting to the industrial city of Lille in Northern France came, it was seen by his colleagues as a demotion. To Robert, who saw Diana's joy and relief at leaving the brash New World, it was equally a relief.

Europe did indeed seem to cure whatever malaise had affected Diana. As for the children, at nine years old Cat was at last free of the bewildering informality of American education, taken out of unflattering blue jeans and safely enwrapped in a dark-blue pinafore ("No, *tablier*, Dad, it's different"). Enrolled with the nuns of the Sacré-Coeur on the Rue Royale, joyfully she forgot her faltering Swiss-German and learned French at a speed which impressed even her mother. So did Toby, in the junior class and looking prettier than ever in a little pale-blue pinafore of his own. At four, Mark went into the *jardin d'enfants* and in his very first term was awarded a *prix de politesse* for his ps and qs.

Convent life, impeccably orderly behind the great oaken street door, brought Cat to a deep contentment she had not known since parting so many lands ago from Rachel. *Tenue*, manners, the look of things were respected; teachers greeted their class with a formal *"Bonjour mesdemoiselles"*, expected a *"Bonjour Madame"*, or *"Bonjour, ma mère"* in the corridors. The world of "Hi!" and "Hey, kids!" and acres of bare leg was safely an ocean away. There were dark-blue tunics for gymnastics and white ones for eurythmic dancing, homework about exports of the Côte d'Ivoire, lists of *Départements de France* with *chefs-lieux* and *sous-préfectures* to learn parrot-fashion, and La Fontaine's fables about crows and cheeses and foxes to memorize nightly. There were gold stars and linen napkins at lunch and a white-gloved ceremony on Saturdays in which you curtseyed to the Reverend Mother and received your "note" of whether you had been *très bien*, just *bien*, *assez bien* (a yellow card and a bit of a disgrace) or *médiocre*.

This latter, a white card, was given only once in Cat's three years at the convent, to one Marie-Claire Lapomelle. Her crime was only whispered, but had something to do with something *sale* she had done. All her life, Cat regretted that since this came early in her Rue Royale career, she never found out exactly what sort of dirtiness Marie-Claire had performed. She wanted to know; not least because she suspected that in America it would not even have been remarked upon.

Diana too loved France. The house that went with the consul's job was part of a palatial old merchant house ten minutes' walk from the Place Général de Gaulle; it overlooked a cobbled courtyard with worn stone lions and a wilderness which had once been an ornamental garden. The *grand salon* was shabby but widely gilded, and furnished in the style Robert described as "Ministry of Works Louis Quinze". Chopin had once played there. There was a small cosy sitting room beside the salon, a sweeping wrought-iron banister on the staircase, dusty shuttered bedrooms and half an acre of assorted attics in which to lay out Toby's train set and Mark's doll's house. Social life was easy and lively, less frighteningly smart than Paris would have been; Diana made close friends among the wives in the Dutch and Italian consulates. There were walks in the Bois, long Sunday lunches with prosperous banking families at their country seats, and for the children, countless tea parties for which bourgeois parents sent out neat copperplate invitations, in the third person. The Catholicism of the children's education did not bother Diana for a moment: their convent seemed to her to have considerably more *ton* than the *lycée*, and she thoroughly approved of Cat's formal little friends with their aprons and neat hair ribbons.

Robert did not repine at coming so suddenly from Washington to such a backwater, but took to consular work with vigour and humour and discovered in himself a taste for rescuing Distressed British Subjects. Sometimes he would bring them home for the night; once, a sailor who had followed a girl onto the train from Calais slept in the spare room before being returned to the Mission to Seamen on the coast; once Cat shared her bedroom with an indignant stripper from Manchester who had been lured to France under false pretences and found she was expected to provide services beyond mere dancing. Diana – who was in London on a shopping trip with the Dutch vice-consul's wife – made heavy weather of this incident on her return, but Robert only laughed.

"I don't think she'll have corrupted Cat into wanting to dance naked with a python," he said. "Toby, now that might have been a worry. But not Cat." Diana pressed her lips together, but said no more.

Cat continued to love the Sacré-Coeur with cosy passion, Mark was reading in French and English and even Toby appeared to be kept under reasonable control by soft-voiced nunly sternness. It was agreed by envious friends that the Gratton policy of keeping the children in local schools was paying off; so when, out of the blue, the news came of his posting to Johannesburg, Robert persuaded Diana that even now, with Cat twelve and Toby ten, all three children might just as well travel out there and find schools instead of being shipped home.

Listlessly, his wife agreed; she was pregnant again, and depressed at the thought of another brash, new, difficult, chippy, cheeky country after the emollient *politesses* of provincial French life. Toby, growing up and wriggling free from his mother's romantic devotion, was no longer the constant delight he had been. She had had a most difficult interview with Révérende Mère after he had stolen one of the litre bottles of beer which was served between each table of eight schoolchildren, hidden it in the shrubbery and absconded from a game of *ballon prisonnier* to down the lot and arrive, visibly drunk, for Benediction. He bit the nun who carried him out, although she shrugged this off with a promise to pray for his soul. At least Mark, a prosaic child rising five, was little trouble and spent most of his home-time in the attic with scissors and cardboard and a hundred battered toy aeroplanes, designing airports.

So the whole family sailed south, by Union Castle mailship, and arrived under Table Mountain at the end of 1964.

In later years, Johannesburg was one of the few things Cat and Diana and Robert all agreed about: the worst post ever. Despite the fact that Robert was fully in charge as Consul-General, despite the swimming-pool, tennis court and pomegranate trees in their Northern Suburb garden, despite the fascination of their holidays in the game reserve, a pall of fear and unhappiness hung over the Grattons during their brief sojourn in South Africa. Cat went to another convent, but her French education placed her at twelve in a class with fifteen-year-olds. Their teenage preoccupations mystified her, their bullying filled her with terror, and her emerging naïve sense of justice was affronted by the casually brutal racial attitudes of both her classmates and – more shockingly – the nuns. "Until you have heard a Reverend Mother referring to 'kaffirs'," she used to say in later life when arguments blew up about ANC terror tactics, "you can't understand what it was like, having to live there."

Toby, meanwhile, said little about his boys' school but returned most days with new red weals across his hands or the back of his calves; his monks, Cat suspected, were as free with the wooden ruler as her nuns.

Mark could not be found a school, and so stayed at home with Diana and became violently possessive of her. This did not make for harmony when Caroline was born. Toby later used to drive Mark into furies by taunting him that he had sulked for a whole year. He himself merely took advantage of the disruption to run away from school one lunch-time on his roller-skates and remain missing for twenty-four hours, which nearly killed his mother.

He was found in Alexandra Township, so grubby that with his dark hair he had passed for a "Cape Coloured". He was playing with a goat, and reluctant to leave. A few months later Cat was beaten and kicked by a group of bigger girls at her school. Robert, preoccupied by a prolonged visit from some troublemaking British MPs, seemed unaware of all but the very worst crises in his family, and would leave home hastily in the morning saying to Cat, "Look after the madhouse, darling, we all rely on you." Cat took him at his word, forged letters from her mother about medical appointments, and ducked out of school on average one day in three to help with the babies. Diana accepted this, and eventually wrote some of the letters herself, but banned her from telling Robert. "They're not teaching you a damn thing, anyway, darling," she said. "You know you'll have to go home to board, soon, don't you?"

"Yes," said Cat. "Let's carry on like this for a bit, anyway. Better for Toby and Mark." So they did.

Yet Diana was not entirely unhappy. Caroline, born in Jo'burg, made up for all its shortcomings. The mother knew, from the first moment she saw the exquisite baby with her soft swathe of gold hair, that this frail, small, and last infant was all she could want. Practice, it seemed, had made perfect. Where Cat had been strapping this baby was delicate, with long, elegant legs; she was as beautiful and long-lashed as Toby, but fairer and less fierce; as tractable as Mark but less dull.

Gazing at her in the hospital, Diana said dreamily to Robert. "I'm going to call her . . . Catherine. I always wanted a daughter called Catherine." The silent beat of horror which followed this, the universal turning of eyes toward stout, pink Cat at the bed's foot, made her instantly colour and babble: "I mean, I meant to say, *Caroline*." The incident became a family joke. It was better that way. And, after all, in 1964, hospitals were still very heavy-handed with the pethidine: there was every excuse to be fuddled. And Cat was not usually present when, in further unguarded moments, Diana would coo to women friends about the pleasure of having "a girl at last".

In the English autumn, with her father to escort her, Cat came "home" to the country she had only ever fleetingly visited. Everything looked like a film about England, an Ealing comedy: the square black taxi from Heathrow airport, the policemen's helmets, the serge-grey London buildings trimmed with red buses, the small, mean fields and woodland vistas melting through the raindrops on the train window as they travelled down into Sussex. Robert handed her to Miss Ilton, the Senior Mistress, and hurried away, head down, tears in his eyes, to pick up Toby from his sister's house in Highgate and take him in his turn to prep school deep in Devon. Three thousand miles away in Johannesburg, Diana lay beside the pool and watched Mark flabbily kicking around in his water wings and Caroline cooing on white cushions under a lace parasol.

"You be missing dem," said her maid, Mariona, who tempered deference with kindness. "Madam, I miss my kids too, off in de Township." She put down a tray with iced lemonade and biscuits, and stood half-expecting a reply.

But Diana ignored the girl's remark entirely, as a white Madam may do. The truth – which she had no intention of sharing with Mariona – was that she was not missing either of them, not at all.

Cat boarded at Abbey Grange for four years. Once she went home to Johannesburg for the holidays; then it was home to Venice while Robert was seconded to an arm of the UN. She never forgot those journeys from school, crossing Europe on the rattling, whistling night train with Toby. Then the kaleidoscope was shaken, and home became Los Angeles: Robert Gratton's last post.

This time, Diana loved America. She had reached a time of life when sunshine meant much to her: she loved the wide, easy Spanish-style house in Las Palmas Avenue, with its bougainvillea and lemon tree outside. Its marble and polished wood floors soothed and delighted her. She walked with her small beautiful daughter in Hancock Park and drifted coolly around the LA County Museum of Art. She shopped at Saks and, for the first time, became a relaxed and easy driver in her air-conditioned automatic.

It was to LA that Cat travelled in her first university vacation, gaining great credibility among her peers for this (although San Francisco would have been even better). By then Mark had joined Toby at Radley, after two unforgettably terrible years alone at Toby's old prep school.

They were not schoolmates for long, however. Toby was

expelled from the Lower Sixth for driving a master's car into the river. Caroline, golden Caroline, the image of her mother only more beautiful, polished to a bright sheen by a harmonious and cultured childhood in Venice, was never sent home to board. She stayed with her parents and attended a Californian progressive school where she covered herself with glory at the age of eight by invariably recognizing the old master reproductions pinned up on the wall to encourage Positive Attitudes. "She's the Madonna of San Giobbe," she would say. "Only they've cut off the arch bit that should go over her head. We used to go and see her quite a lot."

Her beauty, tractability and gentle manners made her an envied and adored child in their circle, diplomatic and local; which did much to make up to Robert and Diana for the spiky embarrassment of Toby's permanent presence in the area. For a senior diplomat's son to be working illegally in a Long Beach beach burger stand run by an equally illegal immigrant Mexican family was, to say the least, awkward. Still, as the family saying went, that was Toby. "I've found him much easier to bear," said Robert wistfully once, "since I gave up hope."

Surprisingly, Toby was not the first child to plunge the Gratton parents into real shock. In 1973, out of the blue, Cat wrote home from Bristol to say that she had married Tim Lorrimer, a fellow student, and was living with him in a squat and expecting his baby. She was sorry, she said, not to have organized the kind of wedding her parents would have liked to fly home for; but everything happened so quickly. The great thing, she wrote, was that Toby had turned up the night before just by chance. Moreover, he had borrowed a motorbike and nipped up to Radley to get Mark – ("A hundred miles at least! Each way!" moaned Diana. "And we thought he was on the burger stand – where did he get the money to fly home? That boy, that boy!"). So both brothers, continued Cat, were there and had bopped all night at the wedding; and they all sent all love to Caroline, and hoped to see her soon. There was masses of room at the squat.

The suggestion that their ten-year-old princess, their perfect golden Caroline, should go anywhere near the shambles of their elder children's lives filled both elder Grattons with horror. They need not have worried. Although in the following year Robert retired and brought his wife and younger daughter home to damp little England, by that time there was no squat and no marriage either. The unseen son-in-law Lorrimer had vanished from the scene leaving Cat with twin babies. He left them nothing more useful than the names he had chosen to have them registered by: Daybreak and Mooncloud. Cat left the squat to move in with her husband's mother Noreen in Hounslow, and refused steadfastly to join her parents in their retirement cottage in Sussex for more than the occasional weekend. "There's no room, and besides, Mum, you've had enough babies."

She did, however, make some acknowledgement of her return to their world by referring to her children always as Dave and Marianne. Caroline, by now an uncomfortable pupil at a Sussex comprehensive (the boarding allowances no longer applied) rather wished her nephew and niece had kept their exotic names. Mooncloud, in particular, she thought very beautiful. Mark, starting at business school, entirely approved of his elder sister's discarding of embarrassing names and hippie ways.

Diana lived for eight years of retirement; long enough to see Cat remarried to a young gentleman farmer called Gervase Hartley, Mark launched on a career in supermarketing ("A *grocer*, darling? Gosh!"), Toby in and out of successive curious occupations including the writing of punk rock lyrics, and Robert unexpectedly emerging as the author of an acclaimed political treatise on the state of Britain in the world.

This book proved so remarkable, so powerfully analytical and (it turned out) prophetic that it won him a worldwide reputation, an international lecture tour and; in 1987, a life peerage at the request of the Leader of the Opposition. Toby at this time was at his peak as a lyricist: the press had considerable fun with the ennoblement of the man who had fathered the author of "Snot Hard Rock I want its Hard On, Baybee" and "Jack and Jill they kill for thrill".

But Diana knew nothing of that. She was only Lady Gratton of Kilmore for three days before her death: she faded fast and unexpectedly before her sixtieth birthday. Her lord sat by her side in the hospice during those last days and nights, talking gently, vaguely, sorrowfully about the past. Sometimes he would feel the squeeze of her claw-like hand when she too remembered scenes and countries they had known together.

But her last look, her final struggling smile, was directed towards the other side of the bed where Caroline sat in a soft blue jumper, her pale beautiful face inclined, merging for Diana at that last moment into every Bellini Madonna and idealized maiden in every gallery, church and glowing city of the past.

1996

Catherine knew how tired she was when, looking towards the exit from Great Portland Street underground station at dusk, she mistook a bus for a building. London these days! she thought hazily. Imagine painting a whole façade as bright a red as that!

Upon which the building drove away and no longer filled the dingy frame of the Tube station's exit. Catherine shook herself, gave an embarrassed inward laugh and trudged with her overnight bag onto the winter street whose buildings were not red at all, but streaky London grey. Ahead of her, high overhead through the drizzle, she could see the illuminated name of her hotel. Eden Central. Its starburst logo proclaimed it an outpost of the Eden empire, and Catherine Hartley had seen that starburst often enough on cheques for its very shape to cheer her. Good old, boring old, Eden PLC.

She walked towards the misty glow, and turned left as the drizzle intensified. Her coat was wet across the shoulders before she reached the shelter of the hotel's concrete canopy. She dodged the puddles along the ramp where taxis with beating engines stopped to disgorge their cargoes of tourists and business travellers, and stepped thankfully through the smoked-glass doors. Holding the flap of her soft old leather shoulder bag open with her teeth, she dug distractedly in its messy interior in search of the Eden hotel voucher (*Accommodation only, not including breakfast, dinner, telephone services or minibar*). She did not stop walking towards reception as she rummaged. Catherine rarely did fewer than two things at a time. She had been known to correct page proofs in the dentist's chair, rather to his annoyance. Sometimes, she was so anxious to get ahead of herself that she would pull out her entry card to Eden Headquarters before she reached its glass doors, and have tidily put it away again before she got near the commissionaires' desk. So she would have to get it out all over again.

"Mrs Hartley," she said to the girl behind the desk. Her voice was muffled by the flap of handbag between her teeth as she hauled out the crumpled voucher. She dropped the flap and pushed the paper across. "It's a courtesy booking, head office, OK? Non-smoking—"

"One moment please," chirped the receptionist. She leaned forward, jabbing at a computer, her glossy blonde chignon wobbling slightly. "I'm sorree, Mrs Hartlee, we have no record of a booking—"

"Every Wednesday," said Catherine, tiredly. "I come every Wednesday. I have a meeting at Eden head office on Thursday mornings. I'm a freelance. I work for your company magazine and internal staff communications. They put me up here. Every week since last June."

There was, had anybody been there to appreciate it, a note of half-shameful triumph in the guest's voice when she said this. Even though the chain owned nine London hotels in addition to its shops and insurance business, it had been hard work to get Staff Communications to persuade Eden's tight financial establishment that if they insisted on a 7.30 a.m. London meeting every Thursday with a freelance who lived on a Northamptonshire farm, they owed that worker a bed for the night. It had been almost as hard for Catherine to persuade her husband Gervase that she would function better in every way, and come home sweeter, if she did not have to drive twenty miles to catch the Northampton milk train on winter Thursday mornings.

He had finally agreed, with his usual controlled politeness but without enthusiasm. At first, so as not to disrupt his day, she made a habit of postponing her Wednesday departure until after the six o'clock communal supper with the farm boys.

Recently, pleading the uncertainties of winter travel, she had taken to putting a large macaroni cheese in the oven and leaving, shamefacedly, in the afternoon before the chickens were even shut up for the night. Amongst themselves in the barn, the boys would josh about this.

"Mrs Hartley's off on the tiles again, up 'n London," Gary would say, and Duane would chortle, "Good on 'er, p'raps there is a bit of life in the old boiler." Luckily, perhaps, no such coarse suspicion occurred to Gervase. He would merely see her from the fields, and straighten up from his task to raise a hand in solemn farewell as she passed in her old blue Renault. Guiltily, Catherine would raise her hand in return and drive on.

On the train, she would read through the papers Eden PLC had sent, note down a few ideas which might sound convincing at the 7.30 meeting, and fall into a deep refreshing sleep in anticipation – not of any dissipation such as Gary and Duane might dream of – but merely of the bland, blessed anonymity of a hotel bath and a night in a featureless room, alone and responsible for nobody.

Today, however, she had not slept on the train, even though she much needed sleep. The tension of a long day was on her. Just before dawn sixty-three ewes, restless in the late stages of their pregnancy, had broken out of the field through a badly fastened gate and begun bleating stupidly under the bedroom window. Catherine lifted her head, soggy with fatigue: she had been up until two, answering letters and going over accounts. She remembered that Gervase was away addressing a social work conference in Bedford, and Gary staying the night with his mother in Midmarsham village. There was nobody there on that black winter morning but herself, inefficiently assisted by Duane, to get them back. In nightdress and waxed jacket, Catherine routed out the aged sheepdog and chivvied the foaming, bounding mass of sheep back down the lane into their field. There had been a heart-stopping moment when it seemed that the flock, under her inexpert guidance, would veer right instead of left and break onto the fast dual carriageway, but the old dog had reached the corner just in time to turn them.

Afterwards, heart pounding at the thought of the catastrophe averted, she could not sleep. How did people ever think that counting sheep could be soporific? The smell of lanolin and panic was still strong in her nostrils, and each time she nearly drifted off to sleep she would jerk awake to escape a vision of stupid faces and bulky, fleecy bodies, a jostling river of sheep flowing towards the headlights of the main road.

She was up early, to telephone for a replacement part for the electric fence; Gervase was not back until the afternoon, which left only time to tell him briefly of the crisis before she hurried out of the house to a later train than usual. She was by then too tired to relax on the journey. Now, at the hotel reception, Catherine's back and neck ached and a sniffle of self-pity rose in her as she leaned on the imitation marble desk amid the sleek business customers checking in. *Show me*, she thought savagely, *show me just one of these sodding corporate smuggos who could round up a flock of sheep in the dark with a half-dead dog and a drooling moron . . .*

The receptionist, who had a long, worried face not unlike a sheep herself, was prodding the computer console under the desk. "Sorree, we're in fact fully booked at the moment . . . we are implementing a refurbishment programme, which could be the reason . . . did you reconfirm under our SureBook system?"

"No," said Catherine shortly. "I never have before."

"It's a new system, if you look at your voucher – see—"

And indeed, printed in the corner of the voucher was a notification of booking condition alterations as from 13.12.96. Today was the fifteenth.

"It's not very big," said Catherine grumpily. "I couldn't be expected to see that."

"Ye-hes," said the girl, stretching the syllable out sympathetically. "We have had some misunderstandings previously, since the implementation date—"

"So there's really no room?"

"I can try and rebook you at our Islington hotel," offered the girl. "That's on the same grade as this. Or—" she consulted a leaflet. "The Eden Dockland."

"Oh, hell," said Catherine angrily. "Just forget it. I'll go to my sister's."

"Sorree for any inconvenience," said the girl automatically, to Catherine's retreating back. And to her colleague: "That's another of the SureBook ones, Nadine."

"Oh," said Nadine blankly, as if she didn't very much care.

Catherine trudged back into the Underground station, stood shivering on the platform for a while, then caught the Circle Line train to Notting Hill Gate. Her tiredness, briefly dispelled by fury at the hotel, returned as she walked on southwards through the rain towards the overgrown but exclusive square where her sister lived in a tall, imposing townhouse with her tall, imposing town husband. A husband who, pray God, by some glorious chance would be out. She might have visited Caroline more often on these London nights if she could only have been sure that Alan would not be there. Caroline asked her to, often enough. But Alan was always stressful company. So was Caroline, come to that, but she was family.

It suddenly occurred to Catherine as she turned into Moreton Square Gardens that Caroline herself might be out. She should have telephoned. But no: the light was on. Better, it was on in her sister's small studio, not in the long and formal sitting room favoured by her husband. Catherine, her hair streaming wet now, lying in brown rats' tails down her back, pressed the bell, rested her forehead on the stained-glass panel beside the door, and waited.

"Cat! Oh, Cat, come in – poor you – soaking – how lovely!" The wet visitor slid thankfully inside, gingerly kissed her sister's smooth cheek, and dropped her shoulder bag on the marble flagstones of the hallway.

"Can I stay? There's a cock-up with the hotel, and I got furious and flounced out. I should have rung."

"Oh yes – yes – that's wonderful," said Caroline, sweeping the wet coat away to a curly rococo hook on the marbled wall. "Alan's away, we can have a really good chat!"

Catherine flinched, hoping Caroline did not see her do so. She longed more than anything to sleep. Now, straight away, without food or even tea. Just to lie down in a dark room and drift away in the blessed urban night, where there was no risk whatsoever of sheep alerts. If her sister had been closer, a more familiar confidante, she might have said so. But there were twelve years between them and the older woman still felt a certain responsibility for not upsetting the younger.

"For a bit," she compromised. "I have an early meeting, so not late. Where is Alan, anyway?"

"Brussels. No, Stockholm. Drumming up co-production money. Or something."

Catherine looked sharply at her sister, wondering at the tone of her voice, but only said: "You're looking wonderful. Suits you, being pregnant. I looked terrible."

"Well, yours *was* twins," said Caroline graciously, leading the way into the small studio, ignoring the panelled door of the big sitting room on the far side of the hall. "How *are* my niece and nephew?"

"Horrifyingly adult," said Catherine. "Marianne got her psychiatric nursing ticket, you know – she's staying on at the London for a bit, though. She's on her way."

"And Dave? Did he get his postgraduate place? Brilliant. You are lucky, they're so marvellous, your children – come on, sit down. I'm in the snug, much nicer. Food? No? I've got a surprise for you—"

Caroline walked across the little room. She was graceful despite her pregnancy and her fair hair swung forward in a perfect bell as she bent to pick up a video cassette and put it momentarily on an angled drawing-board by the window.

"We can watch this. I taped it. On the news magazine thing, the new six o'clock. They did a report from the National Social Forum Workshop or whatever it's called, and guess who—"

"Oh God. I know what you're going to say."

"—Gervase was on! Yes! He was so, so good, honestly Cat. I just dived, hit the button and got all of it more or less, because luckily there was a long bit at the beginning and they said his name in that. So I *hit* the button, obviously. I think I've wiped Alan's rugby."

Catherine smiled a little crookedly. "That was really sweet, Caro. Thanks."

"So it's just right that you turned up. Isn't it?"

Catherine looked at her sister with affection. So kind, so beautiful, so anxious to please, so apparently unspoilt by a lifetime of being treated like precious porcelain. There was always an effortless air about Caroline, a comfortable sense of privilege. You could tell that she had been accustomed to being held as a rare and wonderful thing: first by their parents, then by a series of mentors at art college and the Courtauld Institute, and lately by doting generally elderly and often gay – gallery owners in her various jobs. Now presumably the rich and influential Alan had taken over the role of curator of the porcelain. Nobody, thought Cat as she watched her, would leave Caroline to bring up newborn twins alone, or expect her to round up sheep, or turn up at 7.30 in the morning in ghastly boardrooms to write reams of rubbish about prioritizing interpersonal communication strategies. Nobody would expect Caroline to read stupid little notices in the corner of hotel vouchers, or indeed to check into a hotel alone.

This might have made other women – including her sister – resent Caroline; but strangely, it hardly ever did. Cat, although she was tired and conscious of her own worn, dishevelled, lined, workaday appearance, looked at the smooth lovely face and smiled. Dear little Caroline. Fancy her recording Gervase on the news.

Caroline bent again, grunting a little, and pushed the tape into the slot. Returning to a chair next to her sister's with the remote control, she said anxiously:

"But would you like tea, first? Or a drink?"

"Scotch. No, on second thoughts, don't bother going through to raid Alan's stuff. You've got a bottle of wine open."

Caroline took a glass from the shelf and poured white wine into it from a bottle which – Catherine noticed with a slight twinge of concern – was half-empty. Her sister caught her eye as she turned, and gave something like a laugh.

"I do normally stick to one glass a day, like the books say," she said, "only . . . with Alan away . . ."

"Anyway," said the older woman, breaking into the awkward moment. "I'll need most of the other half, if I've got to watch Gervase."

The programme was a chatty news round-up, the second half-hour of it devoted to the softer magazine stories. Caroline's tape began half-way through an item on young offenders.

"—told the conference that there are other ways to return these troubled young men to a valuable life in the community. On his small organic farm in Northamptonshire, ex-offenders work and live for six

*months as part of a family, and, for the first time, get a chance to develop
a real relationship with the natural environment. This, says Mr Hartley,
can change their lives. Like the old song they plough and sow and reap
and mow – using old-fashioned carthorses. Netta Harkess reports.*

The scene changed to a long shot of green fields and a red-tiled
farmhouse, with two horses plodding across the foreground
pulling a plough. The tune of "To be a Farmer's Boy" swelled
on the soundtrack.

"God," said Catherine. "I forgot they did that filming. They
were there on Monday. Someone picked up on the advance text
of Gervase's conference speech. They kept Gary for two bloody
hours, so Gervase had to ring up Mr Badsley to come and help
load the pigs."

The music was faded. *"Seventeen-year-old Gary – we can't give
his surname or show his face – has been in and out of trouble since he
was thirteen,"* said Netta Harkess sententiously on the television,
over a picture of Gary, his head turned from the camera, hauling
a bale out of the barn in a self-consciously manly fashion.

"I wondered why there were two bloody bales left out in the
rain in the middle of nowhere," said Catherine, swigging from
her glass. "Props, of course."

"Sssh!" said her sister. "Gervase is on now!"

*"But – as Gervase Hartley told the conference – Gary's six months
at Knoll Farm, living in a purpose-built bunkhouse but sharing meals
and work with the farming family, will give him, as it has dozens of
others, a chance to learn a different set of attitudes."*

Now the screen filled with Gervase: a strong, weathered but
refined face, greying temples, broad shoulders, a keen eye: the
very model of a leader and philanthropist. He was speaking:

*"There are three things they learn straight away, and these are
things which society has failed to teach them elsewhere."* He began
to tick off points on his fingers. *"One: they learn that work is
something necessary, something basic: the animals obviously must be
fed, the weeds must be kept down, or there will be no food for any
of us. Two: they learn what responsibility is: if they don't feed the
horses and the sheep, those animals will suffer and the suffering will
be their fault. Three: most important of all, they learn that they have
the capacity to be useful, and respected, and loved. Out in their own
communities people may fear them and brand them as young thugs*

*and tearaways to be punished, but here they are trusted and relied on,
both by the animals and the people they work with. The animals don't
know they're young offenders. They just know they've brought the food."*
"But there must be risk," interrupted the reporter. *"These are young
men who have been convicted of serious offences."*

"Well, they've been burglars," said Gervase, frowning judicially.
*"And they've been in fights and affrays outside pubs, and usually stolen
a car or two. But we don't take sex offenders, or kids involved in serious
violence, because I have had my own family to think of. I wish we could
take the challenge of more serious former offenders, and perhaps one
day we will."*

"Super," said Catherine, with an edge of sarcasm that made
her sister turn, in silent wondering query, before looking back
at the screen.

"I don't want to sound precious," Gervase was saying, with a
slight self-deprecating laugh. *"But I seriously believe that there is
a healing element in the way we farm here. We respect and nurture
the soil and the animals, and in return they feed and nurture us. It's
an ancient cycle of birth and death and regeneration, and a lot of the
problems we have in society stem from the fact that most people have
lost touch with that reality. Here, we help the worst casualties of that
disjointed society to come right back to the centre – to the root of all our
being, if you like."*

The scene cut again to Gary, pulling out another bale of
straw. Netta Harkess spoke in the background, this time more
reverently.

*"The Prince of Wales has expressed an interest in visiting Knoll Farm
to see its work. Meanwhile, for Gary – it's time to feed the stock."*

"On *rye straw*?" said Catherine. "Give me strength."

"I thought it was hay," said Caroline. "For the, you know,
sheep and things."

"So did the reporter," said her sister. "No, it's actually wet
straw. What's more, it's still there. I fell over that bale at four
o'clock this morning." She reached forward and snapped the
television off.

"Anyway, it's amazing about the Prince of Wales," said
Caroline. "Is that true?"

"I dunno," said Catherine morosely. "Might be. Gervase met
him at some organic conference, got introduced, he's really into

young offenders, isn't he? The Prince's Trust, all that? Except
they're not offenders, most of them. Besides, I can't see Gary
starting a business. Not a legal business, anyway." She lost
the thread of her thoughts, took a slug of her drink and
yawned.

"It's *wonderful* work," said Caroline warmly, her beautiful,
calm face lit up like a saint in a Renaissance painting. "I love
the way he talks about it. It's so unassuming, so ordinary, but
really valuable. Do most of the boys do OK afterwards?"

"Yes, actually," said Catherine. "I have to admit, they do.
Gervase quite often finds them local work, and gives them ref-
erences. There's one working at Harkeston Zoo, in the elephant
house. A model citizen."

"Well, there you arc!" said Caroline. "And" – suddenly the
Madonna vanished and she took on a coquettish tone: "Didn't
your husband look seriously dishy?"

Catherine laughed and poured the rest of the wine into her
glass. "Oh God, yes, all right. I admit it. Gervase is wonderful.
He's a saint." She swigged it, without refinement. "Have you
ever tried being married to a saint?"

"No."

There was an odd moment of silence, and Catherine glanced
sharply across at her younger sister. Caroline sat absolutely still,
looking down at the swell of her pregnancy but not touching her
stomach, her hands in her lap, her lips pressed tightly together.
Again she said: "No, I haven't tried that. Being married to a saint
is not something I know much about."

Catherine shifted in her chair, drained her second glass of
wine, and asked gently, "Alan's at a sales thing, you said?"

Caroline continued looking bleakly at her belly.

"I don't know," she began slowly. "And it's disloyal to say,
but . . ."

"But I have started the ball rolling by casting doubt on
Gervase's canonization," said Catherine comfortingly. "So . . . ?"

The words began to tumble, the lovely face to distort, tears to
roll down Caroline's cheeks. She was talking, sniffing, wiping
her nose on her sleeve, out of control.

"I don't think he's on his own, I think he's been seeing an old
girlfriend again, I'm sure of it, actually."

"Quite sure? I mean, everyone imagines disasters when they're pregnant, it doesn't usually mean a thing."

Another brief, awkward silence fell as both women became conscious of the infelicity of this remark. Catherine's first husband did, after all, walk out on her without warning when her twins were six weeks old. Therefore any premonitions she might have had during pregnancy would have been totally accurate. Caroline avoided her sister's eye as she said: "Quite sure. I asked him, weeks ago. He said—"

She could not go on, but bowed her head so that her beautiful pale hair swung forward over her face and parted, leaving the nape of her neck white and defenceless. Catherine looked at it with pity and affection.

"Go on. What did he say?"

"He thinks – it doesn't count."

"Why?"

"Ex-girlfriends. He said it wasn't as if it was someone new. Cat—" She stopped, and kicked out viciously with her foot so that the glass by her chair fell over and spilt an unregarded rivulet of white wine across the floor. "—Cat, he really thinks that. I suspect he's been sleeping with two or three of his old girlfriends ever since we got married. As a matter of course."

Catherine was silent. Her sister straightened up and stared at her for a moment, her face reddening.

"Cat, you're – not surprised, are you? You're not even surprised."

"No," agreed Catherine. Suddenly a great wave of fatigue overcame her. This, she thought suddenly, this was why she had avoided staying or lunching or even talking privately with Caroline in the year since the wedding. She had seen her only at wider family parties. The last had been at Easter, and a difficult gathering it was, too. Caroline's husband was anathema to Cat, and even more loathsome to the upright Gervase. Alan Halliday was handsome, charming, devious and cold. He had probably, the family concurred, married Caroline as a trophy: a beautiful, well-spoken, sweet-natured girl whose father sat in the House of Lords. Any child could see that Alan was an out-and-out pig. Only Caroline, apparently, couldn't. Nor was her sister close enough to challenge her on the subject.

So now she was in Alan's power, in his house, about to have his baby; and there was nothing anybody could do to save her from the acres of approaching pain. And all Catherine could do, could not help herself doing, was yawn.

"I'm really, really sorry. But I've got to get some sleep. Last night, we had the sheep out—"

Strangely, this change of tack seemed not to affront the stricken Caroline, but to come to her as a relief. She swung abruptly into another social gear, sprang to her feet and smoothed down her skirt.

"Of course, poor you – and there I am going on about all this nonsense, there's probably nothing in it – you do imagine things when you're pregnant, don't you? Anyway, poppet – hot-water-bottle?"

"No thanks." Catherine now felt inadequate: lumpen and boorish and ungrateful and ungraceful. It was an old, familiar feeling. Her younger sister led the way upstairs, smoothed already immaculate pillows, chattered brightly, and left her alone in a chaste, restful white room smelling faintly of lavender. Sadly, with a sleepy sensation of shame, Catherine set her pocket alarm for 6.30, shrugged off her clothes and fell into bed.

2 ∫

Under the window, in the afternoon sunshine, Gervase and Gary were bringing in the sheep. When he heard about Tuesday night's escape Gervase had decided that they should come in until their January lambing a few weeks away; he had set the boys to strawing the yard after breakfast and now was ushering a huddled woolly mass of ewes out of the home paddock and along the rough track below the front lawn. Cat looked out from her attic study as her husband, with measured step, followed his flock towards the sagging metal gate and the end of the red brick barn.

On the cork board above her desk, half-obscured by an untidy jumble of papers and sticky notes, was a sketch-map of it all: the track, the barn, the home paddock and the rest of the farm beyond. In a frame on the wall, fading slightly, hung an aerial photograph of the whole fifty acres. Years before, newly married and in love equally with Gervase and a new life, Cat had guiltily paid twenty pounds for this picture when an amiable young photographer came to the door on a cold autumn day. He had, he explained, hired a pilot friend, and from his plane had taken speculative pictures at the height of summer.

Gervase was a little shocked at such waste – the farm, after all, was where he had always lived, he needed no pictures of it, it was in every fibre of his body – but he had laughed at her enthusiasm and paid her back the money.

In the picture, the trees and hedgerows were in full buoyant leaf, the grass green. The pale, trodden-down ring in the meadow, made by the horses' cantering, stood out as clear and incongruous as a corn circle. The house and barns looked like toys, their shabbinesses hidden by distance: sheep were peacefully grazing, the flock scattered into white blobs. With a magnifying glass (provided by the salesman that day on the doorstep) Cat could just make out one of the black-and-white sows, snoozing outside her tin-roofed arc with a suggestion of piglets around her. Her favourite among the cows, redpoll Molly, was clearly visible next to a hedge, the others hidden by branches as they rested in the shade of an oak-tree. There was a half-built June haystack, where Gervase, Catherine and one of the boys of the moment (Jerry? Leroy? a decade on, their sharp young faces blurred in her memory) were forking sweet yellow bundles of hay off a waggon.

This tranquil moment, caught from high above, as perfect as a child's toy farm in a Christmas stocking, had hung imprisoned behind glass by Cat's desk for over ten years now. She no longer noticed or even saw it. Turning back now to her dusty old Amstrad 8256 word processor, Cat focused on the more immediate problem of concocting a lively, appealing, 750-word read on the subject of *Eden PLC and the Challenge of Portable Qualifications*.

"TRAINING DIVISION," typed Cat. "COPY FOR JAN 97, ex CJ HARTLEY."

That was the easy bit. She looked dispiritedly down at the notepad she had brought back that morning from the 7.30 meeting, picking out the words "National Vocational Quali-fication", "NB Transferable" and "Take risks\Win Loyalty".

What the hell had that been about? And why had she done the slash backwards in her notes? Usually, it was a device to remind her of something. She closed her eyes, and visualized the keen young personnel officer in the dark suit, his woman divisional boss in a cherry-red one, and the pale-grey decor of the conference room. She hated writing copy for the Training and Personnel divisions. It was far easier to be snappily convincing about new hotel construction, or the importance of diversifying into high-street life assurance outlets, or the future of retail display. Next to "the challenge of Europe" her most difficult pieces were the ones about middle-management motivation or assisted creative career planning. Having had a chaotically unplanned and unassisted career herself – prize scholar, single mother on benefit, school library assistant earning undeclared income from toshy magazine stories, freelance copywriter – Cat found it hard to throw herself into these corporate lives with any enthusiasm.

Still, the stuff had to be in by Monday. She flicked over the page. "Junior staff, sense of belonging" she read. That would do. Sighing, she began to address her invisible reader, yawning in some Eden staff canteen: *Eden PLC is where you work. Sure. But is it where you belong?*

Outside the window, some kind of commotion was brewing. There were shouts, and more baa-ing on a wider range of notes than was usual for minor stock movements. Cat looked out of the window on her left, and saw Gary running and Gervase trying to get the old sheepdog to head the flock off from the gateway. Voices floated up to her.

"Duane, shut the other gate – the OTHER one."

Ah. That must be it. Duane, the elder of the teenage ex-offenders currently in residence, must have left the far gate open, so that the first flood of sheep could flow straight into the yard and out again onto the barley stubble. Oh dear.

Cat had a fondness for Duane: he was so terribly dim that all his past misdemeanours could be, had to be, forgiven him. The joy-ride which had landed him in custody had ended ignominiously when he drove up a cul-de-sac and could not manage to get the unfamiliar car into reverse gear in order to get out again. Then he had locked himself in with the remote-control key, and could not get out without setting off the car alarm. The police had been laughing when they picked him up. He was a sweet boy, Duane, touchingly unconfident and anxious to please. They were not, under Gervase's rules, supposed to talk about their convictions ("it only makes them brag, and normalizes bad behaviour") but he had privately told Cat over the washing-up one night that he only nicked the motor for a friend who'd been "a bit down, like. To give him a laugh". Dear boy. Gervase would try and find him a mentally untaxing job for low pay, and he would most likely go straight. Especially if he could find an equally dim, good-natured girl to go with.

She had more problems with young men like Gary: bright wide-boys who had, it seemed to Catherine in her more unforgiving moods, played the system deliberately from the start.

Garys exploited their mothers' weakness, idled at school, got girls pregnant and ignored them, got jobs because they were bright and lost them because they stole or lied or never turned up. Then – being bright – they made the most of their family problems in successive courtrooms. Gary knew how to be angelic when it suited him, and how to sound like an inarticulate victim, worsening his syntax to show that he "never had no chance". He knew when to speak, and how haltingly, about his disrupted and fatherless family.

Cat, however, had met his mother often enough to have a shrewd idea of how much of that disruption Gary had himself caused, and how very unkind were his hints at a childhood maltreated by a succession of brutal "uncles". Poor, meek, buck-toothed Mrs Bird, so Cat knew from her innocent chatter while she waited for Gary on Friday evenings, had only achieved one boyfriend since her husband's departure. By that time Gary was fifteen, six foot two, and up for his second burglary. Try as she might (and usually she succeeded in seeing the good or at least the funny side of what Gervase's mother called his "pet thugs") Cat could not like Gary. She was grateful that he was in the fourth month of his stint at Knoll Farm.

He would be gone by February, and there would be another boy. Winston somebody: cannabis, was it? Gervase had been on the phone to the probation service about it. Then Duane would be off in summer, and some other lad would turn up, sullen and defensive, in a tattered t-shirt and baseball cap and trainers quite unsuited to farmwork; and Gervase would talk to him, and Cat would find him boots and feed him up, and on it would go for another half-year of all their lives.

Sometimes, Cat wished there could be girls just for a change. But girls did not seem to commit the kind of crimes which made probation officers think that six months' simple farmwork would tone them up morally. Girls just got pregnant, perhaps? With a twinge of misery, she thought of Caroline.

Beneath the window the sheep, penned in a tight knot by the dog, had begun to move towards the end of the barn again, and turn through the gateway. She watched Gervase walk behind them, whacking the occasional fleecy back gently with his crook, and thought what a good, what a very good man he was. She turned back, with a sigh, to the computer screen, and so missed seeing him glance up at her window and hesitantly raise his stick in greeting.

At Eden Personnel, Jack Hardacre would like to know. As Senior Director with Board responsibility for Onward Training, so would Joanna Raschid—

Or was it Rashid? Cat had not been at her best, during that morning meeting. She had yawned several times. Not a good move. At Eden PLC HQ nobody dared yawn. One disaffected departing secretary had been heard to remark, as she viciously stuffed her possessions into a carrier bag in the corner of an office where Cat was waiting for an appointment, "Talk about tight-arsed. Eden makes Marks & Spencers look like San Francisco in 1975." Anyway. *Joanna Raschid (sp?)* it would have to be. The great thing about filling a corporation with frightened, neurotic, obsessive people in a strict and nervous hierarchy was that after a while nobody in such an organization was any longer capable of writing clear, cheerful, upbeat prose. So they had to hire freelances, and pay them, and let them work at home not far from their stoves and families.

Which, in turn, could lead to unsuspected social good, balancing the social evils perpetrated elsewhere by the company. In this case, thought Cat benevolently, stabbing at her keyboard, the absurdities of Eden meant that a man with an idealistic but unremunerative mission could follow his calling and do good in the world without a moment's anxiety about how to finance his own family life. For although Knoll Farm was Gervase's inheritance, and the boys' keep was notionally covered by £25 a week from a rehabilitation charity which also paid them a low wage, there were costs of seed and feed, of vets and transport to be met. Farm produce sales could only just cover farm costs in a good year; no nett income whatsoever had resulted from Gervase's long, arduous working days since 1990.

That was the year when Gervase's mother sold off an adjoining, and profitable, hundred acres in order to recoup her Lloyds' losses. That this hundred acres represented Gervase's income did not occur to Artemis Hartley at the time.

As a result the widely unrecognized fact was that for nearly seven years – despite the patrician and philanthropic appearance of Gervase and the general knowledge that he had taken on "poor little Catherine" as a divorcee with two children – Cat had supported him. The daily spending of the Hartley household, their council tax and petrol and food and clothes and reading matter, was met entirely by what Catherine earned alone in that scruffy study high over the lawn. Her income derived mainly from the profitable if unedifying task of writing – for the staff paper and a dozen departmental newsletters – some semblance of a human face onto the stiff corporate mask of Eden PLC. It was, in its way, a good joke.

Catherine looked out of the window again, to where Duane and Gary were engaged in acrimonious arm-waving debate over the matter of who told whom to open which gate, when. Gervase stood by the gate, looking back at the sheep. Unhurriedly he turned, walked over to the boys and said something. Cat did not need to hear. It would be "Cut it out, fellers", and an instruction. Sulkily, the two moved away, Duane towards the feed store and Gary to the stable barrow. Gervase looked up again at the window, and this time Catherine leaned sideways from her desk, and waved. A smile broke across her husband's face, and he carefully kissed his hand and blew the kiss up to her. Laughing, she drew back into the room and ran her hand across the static crackle of the green computer screen, chasing a veil of dust.

For what the neighbours, and most of the family, would not have understood was that Cat did not mind being the lone financial support of this absurdly quixotic enterprise. It seemed to her, and had always seemed, a central part of Gervase's nature: a brave stab at social cohesion and natural healing. It was a small gallant struggling plant with its roots in all the most deeply held beliefs of the decaying gentry class he came from: in guilt and pride and patriotic philanthropy and inarticulate public-school idealism. It had nothing to do with the worlds of Eden PLC or Alan Halliday. Nor with the elderly socialite world of Artemis, the hippy world of Cat's first husband Tim, or the argumentative Westminster world in which her own father seemed increasingly to live. Keeping Gary and Duane off the streets and usefully employed and smelling of dung instead of lager for six months might be ultimately pointless, given that there were not that many jobs for them to go to when they left. It might be true that, as her brother Mark had once argued at a difficult Christmas dinner, big international business deals and the chasing of profit did more for jobs and therefore for youth than toy farms could ever do.

But when the barricades were up, Cat said at the time, she would rather be on the losing side with Gervase at Knoll Farm than out there winning with the others. So when the money dried up in that same year, Catherine had said to Gervase that of course the farm and the work with the boys must go on. They could manage. That was the only conversation they had ever had on the subject. Catherine paid her Eden earnings into the joint account; most years she made between ten and twelve thousand pounds after tax. Without holidays or indulgences, and with her own children now grown, it proved enough. Just.

The sun had gone behind a low black cloud on the horizon. After a last glance out of the window at the suddenly grey and spiritless scene, Cat turned back with a sigh to the screen.

Joanna Raschid (sp?). The three letters on her mind at the moment are NVQ – National Vocational Qualification. "Its important," she says, "that young staff know we care enough to offer them not just internal progress, but a portable qualification—"

"Mrs H!" called a voice up the attic stairs. "Is there any bandages? Only Gary's cut his hand on the barrer."

3 ∫

"I'm not happy with the island SKUs," said Mark Gratton, for the third time since the meeting began. "To some extent yes, you do gain space. But I think psychologically—"

"*Psychologically*," chimed in Dean Harwood, with a ghost of a sneer. Mark pressed on, pretending not to notice.

"—there's a sense of unease, of disorientation. And shoppers lose sight of children, and anxiety levels rise. It isn't like aisle-end display, where there's a natural flow-past."

"It's geometrically more efficient than aisle-end," said Melanie Hayes, tapping her reading-glasses menacingly on her leather-bound folder. "In Esher we've proved that on the computer simulation."

"With the EasiTroll data fed in. How many R2 stores are going to get EasiTroll this year?" Suddenly, mysteriously, the treacherous Dean Harwood seemed to be batting on Mark's side. Some private feud with Hayes, probably. Mark seized the advantage.

"As you know, I've got doubts about EasiTroll too. The whole point of the traditional trolley design is shopper-pace degradation—"

"What?" This was the PR Director, newly arrived from the Hotels division. Mark smiled, to show that he did not despise this ignorance (although he did, rather) and smoothly said: "A bit of unwieldiness, not too much, obviously – slows the shopper down and gives her time to notice the mid-stack premium product."

"Peaches in brandy," said Harwood, sneering again. Mark winced at this direct hit, and unwisely let his foe see it. He flushed.

"So – we all make mistakes. The price was bloody good, and as a promotion—"

"As a promotion, cheapo Romanian bottled fruit that ends up by *fizzing* and getting exposed in the *Daily Mirror*," said Melanie Hayes scathingly, "is not ideal."

"We were talking about insular and peninsular stock-keeping unit trials," said Mark, recovering himself. He caught the Chairman's eye and thought he detected a ghost of an approving nod. So did the ever-vigilant Dean Harwood, who swung once again, effortlessly, to Mark's camp.

"Yes – *peninsular* – we ought to remember that's included in the trial. Perhaps if we compromised—"

Mark smiled, and relaxed a little. Though not much. It did not do to relax too much at EdenFoods inter-regional liaison meetings. The business of supermarketing today, as he often told his smiling admiring wife Lindy, was not just a matter of hiring people to stack up tins and waiting for other people to come and buy them. Customers were fickle and spoilt for choice. You had to pull 'em in, treat 'em clever, light and decorate and entertain and soothe and flatter, all so you could sell, sell, sell, and stay alive yourself. It was more than salesmanship: it was showbiz, it was bloodsport, it was – when you thought about Tesco, always out to wipe you off the map – yes, Lindy, it was war! Lindy would smile, and admire, and massage Mark's shoulders.

He thought of her now, with a pang of needy affection. The meeting wound through its circuitous course: underlying the discussion of display and branding, bakery aroma-reach and chill-area temperatures, there moved other shapes, other themes. Like monsters beneath ice, the half-visible politics of a large mistrustful corporation writhed: alliances and betrayals, rivalries and revenges all seething below the bland businesslike surface. Mark left the meeting at 12.22 to walk back to his own office for a 12.25 briefing concerning loyalty cards. He had compromised on insular shelving, won a tactical victory over trollies, and been badly caught out in the matter of the Romanian peaches in brandy. Fifteen all. Not bad.

Except that the humiliating small moment of the peaches would not leave him. Two years ago, dammit! He sat at the round marble table in his office and talked rapidly and clearly to his three immediate subordinates about the problem of computer-wise and cunningly fraudulent customers fiddling the barcode on their smart loyalty cards. He was well-briefed and succinct and usually a friendly enough manager to deal with; but today Mark cut short their questions and shooed them out faster than they had expected. Suddenly, uncharacteristically, he needed ten minutes to himself before facing a lunch-time meeting with a group of discontented suppliers.

Ten minutes, not much to ask. He stabbed the privacy button on his intercom so that there should be no calls, and moved round to the far side of the desk. Here he would be out of the line of sight of anybody passing the glass panel in his office door. Mark sat down in his heavy leather chair, shrugged off his jacket, and folded his thin arms on the desk. His head sagged forwards onto his forearms and he exhaled a long, self-pitying sigh. Peaches! For God's sake! It had been a bloody good idea, a bloody good price, an experimental way in to the new Eastern Bloc markets. Not his fault the quality control was crooked. Old Manders had never blamed him. Deering didn't, either, he was sure. Why Harwood and Hayes had ganged up in that brief exchange, when they normally avoided one another – why it had taken a snipe against *him* to unite them – why they did it so publicly, felt so safe doing it, in the middle of a discussion about bloody *trollies* . . .

His eyes were shut now, pressed against his arms on the desk, his floppy brown hair trailing forwards onto the neatly aligned leather-framed blotter. Old Manders had liked his senior executives to have gentlemanly-looking desks, and even if they never used a fountain pen from one year's end to the next, each had had a blotter. Mark had kept his when Eden – not a leather-blotter corporation, not gentlemanly at all in its instincts – absorbed the supermarket chain into its diverse empire. Normally its presence comforted him in a tiny, unacknowledged way. It showed that a small part of him was secretly resisting Eden, holding out against new sods like Harwood and syco-phantic bitches like Melanie Hayes. When office life oppressed him, Mark would, without really noticing what he did, stroke the soft leather edges of the blotter, running his finger over the old gold logo of M35derFoods.

Now, however, a stronger discontent than usual seized hold of him and he shuddered, clenching his shoulders, digging his forehead savagely into the flesh of his forearms. Bastards! Always the same – any chance to make him feel small. All of them. Just like Toby, telling Révérende Mère about the *pain-chocolat*. Just like when Piet the gardener called him – that word – and Caroline laughed, stupid baby, and said it again and Mum thought he had taught her the word, as if he bloody knew bloody Afrikaner obscenities – and sent him to his room – just like Purvis at school about the underpants – and what Toby said to the housemaster, trying to be so funny – and *"a grocer, darling? Gosh!"* – from Mum, cocking her head on one side, big-eyed, flirting as usual. But not, never, with him. And Toby's poem that Christmas about Grocer Gratton—

Knotted up, angry, head down on his big desk, Mark Gratton hunched his shoulders against the torrent of confused memory. He did not know why, nor want to, but it happened quite often these days: this sudden and total recall of every humiliation of his life.

Of life until Lindy. Mark raised his head from his shirt-sleeves, which were damp with tears or perspiration, and glanced at the clock. Ten to one. He could ring home and still be down in the marble reception hall on time to meet his lunch guests. Lindy! He picked up the private line and dialled rapidly. It was the only number he ever dialled himself, by hand, without the secretary's intercession. Nor was the number of their home stored in the machine's memory.

She was home. He could picture her straight away, her pale hair springing away from her vivid little face, leaning on the bright-red kitchen worktop against the bright yellow paint, one hip out, in her little high-heeled red boots, perhaps looking at her bright fingernails as she answered. He sighed with relief as Lindy's high enthusiastic Birmingham voice rang down the line.

"Marky! Ooh, lovely! You never ring at lunch-time, lovely to hear you!" And as an afterthought, for she was not a morbid girl but a naturally blithe one – "Is everything all right?"

"Yes," said Mark. The venomous cloud of humiliation receded, like smoke sucked through an unseen extractor-fan. It left the air around him clear. He blinked, and looked around the office. It was a big office, an important man's office, with a solid desk and walnut panelling. The very blotter showed him to be no corporate tool but an individual, with his own views and his own history.

"I just rang to see how your day was going." Against her vivid warm accents, his own voice sounded to him a bloodless and chilly thing, an effete and piping public-school whine.

"S'going lovely, thanks. Aerobics, shopping, library – I'm doing citizens advice this lunch-time, there's a meeting." He smiled, loving the hard g she sounded on the end of *meeting*, loving her upward inflection for its optimism. He was going to speak again, but could not think what to say, only wishing to hear her and bask in her unselfconscious enthusiasms. Before he could think what to say to prompt her, Lindy rushed on.

"Oooh . . . actually it's good you rang. Your sister's been on."

"Which sister?" Mark sounded defensive. "Why?"

"Catherine. She wanted to know about Christmas."

"Oh God. Did you tell her, no?"

"Well, no. Don't be cross, Marky—"

"Never cross, Lindy-Lin. Never ever. But you mean, you said yes? We have to go there for Christmas?"

"Well, I really like Catherine, she's not—"

"Not snooty like the rest of my bloody family?"

"Oooh, don't be chippy. They're all right. Only, it's your Dad. She just worked out he's going to be seventy, on Christmas Eve, OK? Seven Oh, the big one! Three score and thingy! So Catherine thought it would be really, really nice if we were all there, all his kids and that. I think it's a really nice thought!"

Mark smiled, in spite of his dismay. Lindy moved through a world of nice thoughts and kind people and fun ideas. Life to her was a laugh. It was what had first drawn him to her three years ago across a crowded supermarket: her laugh. Shrill, some would say; vulgar, unrefined, unsubtle; but it cut like a school bell through the tangled unhappiness of his first thirty-five years, and let Mark out, at last, to play.

"Oh, all right," he said now. "Who's going to be there? How much of the dreaded tribe?"

"Well, your Dad, obviously. And Catherine and Ger – Gervis,

her old man. And your other sister, the one I've hardly met,
cos you didn't want to go to her wedding, you old misery –
Caroline, that's it. So I suppose her hubby'll be there. And Dave
and Marianne. And she's got both her mothers-in-law, she said.
Would that be her mother-in-law from the first time, I thought
that was years ago?"

Mark glanced at the clock. Two minutes, and he must go.
Trying to keep his voice inconsequential, he said: "Well, it was,
but old Cat's ever so faithful. She has the old trout every year.
That's all, is it? She didn't say anything about Toby?"

"She's trying to get him. Only he's not in Glasgow any more,
apparently. That's why it's good you rang. She thought you
might know where he's staying."

"Doesn't Dad know?"

"He's in Zag – Zagreb, she said. Doing a fact-finding thingy. So
shall I tell her you don't know where Toby is?"

"No. I do know. I'll call her tonight. Sweetie, I must go—"

"Kiss kiss."

Lindy made loud, chirruping kisses down the wire. Mark
returned the endearment more cautiously, put the receiver
down and went to lay down the law to his suppliers over an
unappetizing, low-fat salad in the boardroom. It was a nasty
lunch for a dank December day, and left him hungry and
irritable; but the menu was as much company policy as the
hard deal he had struck with them. These were suppliers of
cheesecakes, microwaveable deep-fried Brie balls, Kievs, cream
pastries, and a whole range of "dairy-enhanced" luxury products;
so naturally, they got served salad and fresh fruit. Had they been
domestic greengrocery suppliers the menu would have been rich,
fatty and full of obvious imports. At EdenFoods, it was policy to
make suppliers feel insecure. The idea had come from Melanie
Hayes. Let the bastards know that they need you more than you
need them.

Later that night, properly fed and steadied by Lindy, Mark did
ring his elder sister.

"I can tell you where Toby is, because he rang me from the
police station."

"Oh God. Not again."

"Yes, again. Nothing much. Some party in Glasgow."

"Why doesn't he ever ring Gervase? He's used to it. He's always being rung by police stations."

"Probably terrified Gervase'll sign him on for some muck-forking with all the other young offenders."

"He's not a young offender. He's forty-three. And he'd be useless with a muck-fork. He's safe enough, the silly sod. But it isn't fair for him to call you at the office. We're more used to all that stuff. You're busy."

"Anyway," said Mark, his tone softened with sudden regard for this sister who appreciated his importance in the world of business affairs, "he did ring you, apparently, but there wasn't anybody in. Anyway, I sorted it out. Twenty pounds' fine for breach of the peace. That was on Tuesday. He said he was through with Scotland anyway, and going to stay with Topsy for a few days."

"Oh God," said Catherine once more. "That's on again, is it?"

"Sort of. I got the impression. You got the number?"

"Think so. I'll ring her. See if she's got him."

Brother and sister exchanged brief farewells. Putting the receiver down, Mark glanced through the doorway to his red-and-yellow kitchen, and saw Lindy, oblivious to the conversation, washing up the dishes. Her broad, comforting rump was encased in tight shiny leopard-print leggings, and a crop-top showed her bare midriff and nipped-in waist. Lindy had grown up in tiny houses, and always kept the central heating on high so that she could dress in December as if it were July. Mark walked up behind her and put his arms around her bare waist, breathing in comfort from her warm, scented flesh. Sixty miles away, Cat put down the telephone in the icy hallway of Knoll Farm and went back to her study, alone.

4

High over the Tottenham Court Road, three frowsty storeys above the Gimmix computer-game shop, Topsy Tanner was sitting on a kitchen chair varnishing her toenails. She was also, intermittently, varnishing quite large areas of her toes since the man lying on the unmade bed kept making her laugh, and when she laughed she shook, and the kitchen chair – the only chair in the flat, apart from bean-bags – wobbled violently. It had one leg shorter than the other three.

"Oh, stoppit, Toby!" she cried at last. "I'm getting red blotches everywhere!"

The man on the bed, remorselessly, continued his story.

"So anyway, Dunkie pulls the big chair away, and the copper sees the hole in the floor and thinks that must be where the stuff was hidden, so he gets down on all fours, right, and peers down and the rat—"

Another carmine blotch appeared on Topsy's left big toe as she erupted with mirth.

"—the rat shoots out, and the guy falls over backwards getting away from it, and Dunkie says, 'Sorry, officer, he must have eaten it all, that's why he's a bit high!'"

The girl recovered herself a little, put down the bottle of varnish and asked interestedly:

"And was there any stuff?"

"Nah," said Toby Gratton. "Dunkie doesn't do any drugs now. It was just a laugh. Only the cop got really serious, and tried to catch the rat so they could look in its stomach and see if it really had eaten a stash—"

Topsy was giggling again now, and Toby sat up, black hair

flopping forward over his high, fine brow, his eyes sparkling as he finished the story of the Glasgow constabulary, the supposedly high rat, and the disruptive Duncan. When they had both finished snorting with mirth, Topsy stretched and wiggled her drying right toes and asked in a marginally more serious tone:

"So what'cha doing here, anyway? I thought you were in Scotland for a bit. Didn't expect you hanging around here."

"Ah. Well, the booking we had in the pub ended."

"Was that the fake Irish pub you told me about?"

"Yep. Mucky Murphy's. Anyway, Dunkie got offered a bit of work for the winter, teaching schoolgirls woodwind up near Fort William, so he could stay with his Ma."

"Teaching *schoolgirls*? Dunkie?" Another blob of nail varnish flew from the brush and lodged stickily between her toes.

"Lolitas of the Lochs. Good luck to them. Then there was a bit of a row about the flat because of a party the guys had, and I ran spang bang out of money anyway, and had to get my supermarket supremo brother to pay my fine. So I came south. To you, my turtledove, my queen of hoofers, my long-leggedy beastie."

Topsy stopped twiddling her toes and fixed him with a cold stare which did not suit her snub and freckled face. She pushed back her tousled platinum-white hair with a defiant little gesture and said: "You're not staying, you know. I can lend you a bit if you want, and you might talk me into it now and again, but you're not moving in."

"Perish the thought! I said I ran out of money, but that was in Scotland. This is England."

"You've got money here?"

"Sort of. When I went up north last year I never gave my royalties agent my address, because he was a bit of an arsehole about some business with his stupid sister. And I know he's got royalties I'm owed, because the songs keep on going. So I'll go round and get the cheque, then I'm going to get a job."

"There's a bit of backstage work going at the theatre," said Topsy. "Non-union, on the quiet, sort of stuff. The show's got an extra month."

"No, a real job."

"A real job?" The girl sounded incredulous. "Ten years I've known you, you've never had a real job."

"I was a gorillagram," said Toby with studied dignity. "For six months."

"Your poor Dad," said Topsy scathingly. "All that education, and him a Lord, and the best you can do is gorillagram."

"Perhaps I should have been a Lord-o-gram. I'd be really good: burst in to the party in ermine and coronet and silk stockings, strip off the robes, introduce myself as Lord Loveaduck, do a number in suspenders—"

Topsy began to laugh again, and flung herself onto the lounging figure on the bed. Together they rolled among the tangled bedding shrieking, "Suspenders!" and "Ooh, Sir Jasper!" and "End of the peer show!" By the time they had finished what Toby called their victory roll, Topsy was late for her call and had to summon up all her dancer's fitness to run, shoes in hand, down through Covent Garden piazza to the stage door of the Imperial Theatre. Toby followed, panting, with her dressing-case.

There was an illuminated cut-out, above the shabby canopy and below the theatre's name, of a row of Topsies high-kicking in black stockings, their toes resting on giant letters spelling out THE PARIS PACK. ("A joyous knockout" – *Evening Standard*). Toby looked at it with pleasure. Looking down, he noticed that he had no shoes on, and so decided to sit on the doorstep of Gimmix Computer-Game Centre until the show ended and Topsy came home.

He did not repine. He pulled a tin whistle, in two pieces, out of his trouser pocket, fitted its sections together and busked. Between 7.00 and 10.30 he made sixteen pounds and twenty-two pence, which they spent on a large sticky pizza and a bottle of Japanese whisky. When they got upstairs with these spoils, there was a message on Topsy's answering machine about Christmas at Knoll Farm.

"She doesn't sound a bit like you, your sister," said Topsy, biting into the pizza.

"Ah, but she is like me," said Toby, wrenching off the top of the whisky bottle. "Deep, deep down." He swigged, straight from the bottle, sitting deep in one of the beanbags. "You'll see.

We're going there for Christmas, me and you." Topsy's mouth was too full of pizza to contradict him.

In the serene, humming quiet of an airline cabin high over the Alps, Lord Martindown of Ashe, a Labour peer, turned to his friend Lord Gratton of Kilmore as they put aside their papers to address their plastic dishes of dinner.

"Not a bad trip. I'm quite impressed with some of these companies that are moving into the new countries. You've got a boy with Eden, haven't you?"

"Yes. Mark. He's in the supermarkets now, but who knows."

"Your other boy in business, is he? Haven't seen him since he was a nipper when you were in Venice."

"Hmm," said Lord Gratton, taking a sudden close interest in the tinfoil cover of his *sole bonne femme*. "No, not exactly. He's a pop songwriter by trade, and he works around a lot, here and there, in the entertainment business." The foil ripped as he pulled it off, spilling sauce on to the tray. A sudden compulsion to honesty made him add: "Raffish, you might say."

"Well," said Lord Martindown, pulling the cover off his own sole in one piece with rather more grace. "We've all got one in the family, eh? My daughter's with Channel 4."

"Not bad, this fish," said his noble companion, closing the subject with natural diplomatic authority.

It was late, past eleven o'clock, when the door creaked open. Gervase looked up from his desk and smiled, a little hesitantly, at his wife. Cat crossed the faded carpet and put her hand on his shoulder with a passionless, threadbare affection. "Christmas," she said. "I worked it out. We could end up with thirteen at table, if it isn't fifteen. Does that matter?"

Gervase screwed up his face and began to count on his fingers.

"Mama, your father, Noreen – two of us, Mark and Lindy, Caroline and Alan, Toby obviously—"

"I've counted Toby as maybe two. He used to bring Topsy, didn't he? Last time round. And Mark says he's back on her phone number now, so . . ."

Gervase looked up at her, a grin suddenly transforming his

serious, ascetic's face into something almost puckish, lively in its mischief.

"I always liked Topsy."

"It's the stage-door Johnny in your blood coming out. Your father probably used to hang around theatres in the 'thirties with bunches of flowers, twirling his moustachios and waiting to have his way with Topsies."

Gervase laughed. "He wouldn't have to wait long." Cat sat on the edge of his desk, suddenly more relaxed. She smiled back at him.

"Do you remember the first time Toby brought Topsy down for the weekend?"

"She went out for a walk, and got so excited at the sight of blackberries actually growing, free on bushes, that she decided to bring some home for a surprise," said Gervase. "Only, she hadn't got a basket so—"

"She wriggled out of her bra, pulled it up through her polo-neck and brought them back in that. Said two C-cups should be enough for a pie." Cat giggled. "Then there was the business with the spiders in the bathroom."

"God, yes. Rushing round the house screaming, in a teeny towel like something in a Donald McGill postcard. Mother took days to get over it."

"She was good fun. I wish, in a way—"

"You think Toby should have married her?"

"Oh, I don't know. I mean, neither of them was remotely faithful, as far as I could tell from the conversation."

"Generally in front of my mother and poor Noreen."

"Don't remind me. But there was," Cat continued thoughtfully, "something about those two. You could see Mark was jealous of the way they were together. He never got anywhere with girls before he met Lindy. And Tobe's gone back to stay with her now Glasgow's folded up on him. They've obviously stayed friends. It might be a goer."

But Gervase seemed to have tired of discussing his brothers-in-law and their love lives, and looked meaningly down at the pile of letters on his desk. None were personal, except for a few in illiterate handwriting and oddly-coloured inks: the rest were a scatter of charity letterheads and logos. The Soil Association,

Countryside Commission, Country Landowners' Association, National Council for the Care and Resettlement of Offenders, Northamptonshire Wildlife Trust, Projects In Probation, Rare Breeds Society, Third World First. Gervase gave unstintingly of his time and energy to a dozen good causes, even apart from the boys on the farm. There was not one of these that Catherine could fault, not one pointless or undeserving labour among them. Gervase was, undoubtedly, a very good man.

She sighed, took the hint and got off the desk to begin counting on her fingers again in a businesslike way. She too was furthering a good cause, that of a united family Christmas.

"So Dad, Artemis, Noreen, Mark and Lindy, Caroline and Alan, you and me, Toby and perhaps Topsy. The kids. Then Duane makes it fourteen, or thirteen, but I've assumed the American should be here by then?"

"The WWOOFer, yes. Martin Szowalski," said Gervase, glancing down at the letters in front of him. "Coming next Friday."

"Woofer," said Cat. "That's a terrible word!"

"Working Weekends On Organic Farms," said Gervase automatically.

"I know." She was irritated now. How dare he tell her something she already knew! In that teacherly voice too, as if she were Duane. Sometimes she wondered if he remembered the difference between her and the boys. "It's just that the ones who come to us are always here for much longer than weekends, and it might be more dignified to call them just volunteers."

"As you wish." He turned back to his papers. Cat went towards the door, then turned and said: "I take it Gary *is* going to his mother for Christmas?"

"Apparently. I wish Duane would go home to his family, but he says he'd rather spend Christmas on the streets." He hesitated a moment, looking at her with a kind of appeal in his eyes, although she had already begun to turn away. "Do you mind him being here?" he said to her back. "Your Dad's birthday party and everything?"

"No," said Cat wearily. "I like my family much better when it's diluted a bit. He can have a fling with Topsy. Make a man of him."

On that small unregarded victory she withdrew, and left Gervase to his midnight oil. There was, at least, enough hot water left for a long – if spidery – bath.

5

"So we could be thirteen at table," said Lady Artemis Hartley, in her high disapproving voice. "You're not superstitious, then, Catherine dear?"

"'Course she's not," said Catherine's father with decision. He raised his glass to his daughter. "She grew up in so many different countries that if she took on one lot of superstitions she'd have to take on the lot. She'd be warding off the evil eye like a Venetian, keeping Hebrew festivals, believing in the *Krampus*—"

"Burying bits of meat in the garden tied up with elephant grass to cure warts," said Mark, "stamping on pomegranate seeds to abort babies—"

"That is disgusting," said Cat, reaching up to tuck a stray end of tinsel under an ivy branch on a beam. "I don't remember that one, from anywhere."

"Jo'burg," said Mark. "Mariona taught it me, in the servants' quarters. I got a lot of home voodoo lessons you never knew about. Actually, Caro—" he looked across at his younger sister – "I had a damn good go at doing it to you. I took a pomegranate seed up to my bedroom and danced round it chanting, then I stamped on you so you wouldn't be born. I didn't want a new baby."

Caroline, heavily pregnant and not in the best of tempers, glared at her brother for a moment before accepting the joke without much grace.

"It's still disgusting. Horrible little boy, you must have been."

"I was," said Mark complacently. He had arrived still rattled from the Eden directorate Christmas party the night before. Santa hats and foam reindeer horns had been handed out at the

door, and he had been given horns only to find that everybody
else from the Executive Two floor was wearing a Santa hat. These
things mattered. Then the drive had been slow and frustrating,
and ever since he and Lindy had arrived at lunch-time he had
been refilling his glass from Cat's traditional welcoming saucepan
of mulled wine. The glass was now horribly sticky from the sugar
and his last refill was growing cold, but he sucked noisily at it
and outfaced his beautiful younger sister with a stare to match
her own.

Lady Artemis, curled in the better of the two fireside chairs,
looked across at Caroline with condescending sympathy. Of all
her son's in-laws, this beautiful cool creature was most to her
taste. Boorish Mark, fey disruptive Toby, and their unspeakably
common womenfolk were, in Artemis' view, not at all desir-
able connexions. She had originally had great hopes of Robert
Gratton – a peer, albeit a mere life peer unlike her late father
– and a diplomat, very nearly an ambassador. How suitable,
how amusing it would have been if he as a widower, she as a
widow, could have entertained a flirtation. It would have been
appropriate and graceful, considering that her son rescued his
daughter from the unfortunate status of deserted and penniless
mother.

Yet not only, reflected the lady sourly, was the man inclined
to left-wing views, but he appeared not to have the slightest gift
for civilized dalliance either. So Artemis had never been such a
fool as to show her hand. Now she sat a good distance from him
at the Easter and Christmas gatherings around Gervase's table,
suppressed her kittenish side and cultivated instead a refined
aloofness. Now, gently to underline the crassness of *his* son's
remark, she merely said in a cool sweet tone:

"Well, never mind the thirteen. We shall throw salt over our
shoulders, as my old nanny taught me."

"It won't be thirteen, anyway," said Robert, who had been
counting on his fingers. "Not if Toby brings his girlfriend and
Alan gets back on time."

Artemis ignored him, to turn on the other old woman present.
"Noreen, dear, you look cold. Have you had some of Catherine's
hot wine?"

Mrs Noreen Lorrimer, looking older than her seventy years,

darted a terrified look at the imperious little figure at the fireside. Where Lady Artemis' hair was shining silver, hers was a dead, dirty, thinning grey; where the other woman had shrunk to a slender, aristocratic boniness, Noreen had merely sagged from middle-aged podge into elderly flab. Neither in body nor in mind could she compete; she knew that in every possible sense, when placed next to Artemis she lacked class. There was not even a moral high ground to which she could retreat. Her son, after all, had callously abandoned poor little Cathy with two babies. Lady Artemis' son was the white knight who had rescued them all three and brought them to this solid farmhouse and a life of landed security.

No, Noreen had no defence whatever against the cruel little creature in Chanel. It was a matter of unending wonder to her, indeed, that Cathy still included her in these family gatherings and wrote all year as well. Taking them in, after all, had been her plain duty when bad, bad Timothy ran off. And it had been, in addition, a pleasure. To have those children close for those precious years – her eyes filled with tears, now, when she thought of their first Christmases.

"I shouldn't really," she quavered now, but Artemis waved her objections aside.

"Mark, dear, do fill a glass for Catherine's – ah—"

This was another game that she played. She could not say "Catherine's mother-in-law", for was that not her own, Artemis', rightful title now? She could have said "the twins' grandmother" – indeed, could have asked Dave to get the drink, and said "your grandmother". Or she could just have said, to any of them, "Get Noreen a drink". Instead, she chose the small cruel barb of calling the humbler woman "Catherine's – ah." and finishing the sentence with a tinkling, silly-me laugh.

Noreen understood all this, and flushed, and accepted the sticky glass which Mark put in her hand as she had, all her life, accepted bitter cupfuls of humiliation.

But then Dave and Marianne, so long ago christened Daybreak and Mooncloud by her unspeakable betraying son, came over to Noreen as if drawn by her unspoken distress. They were fond of their grandmother: how could they not be, when from birth to the age of six they had lived in her minute house, crammed in the tiny boxroom in home-made bunks, with their mother in the only proper bedroom and Noreen on a sofa bed in the front room? The four of them had lived thus in the tiny gardenless house in Hounslow, hugger-mugger and defiantly, unjustifiably happy as the airport traffic thundered past outside and the aircraft screamed overhead taking luckier people to luckier places.

Nanna Noreen meant home to them, giggles and baking and first days at nursery and school, and Hallowe'en games involving apple peelings and Co-op marshmallows on strings and grabbing a fivepenny piece out of a mound of flour with your teeth. Of course Gervase and Knoll Farm and the animals and the green fields were an adventure, the springboard for growing independence; but the imprint of their first home was strong in both their happy, uncomplicated young hearts. The two of them bounced across to Nanna Noreen now, lapping her in welcome warmth. They had, in fact, very little to talk to her about these days; their determined careers had not much in common with her modest retired life of church and housework. But it did not matter: the warmth transmitted itself through the blandest of conversations.

"So, Nanna, give us the dirt," began Dave. "What's going on? Which evening class is it this year?"

"Upholstery," said Noreen, her smile reviving. "Oh, my, you are big! Aren't you ever going to stop growing?"

"I have stopped growing," said Dave. "Years ago. It's you, you're shrinking. But you did upholstery last year! Time you moved on!"

"Why should she?" said Marianne, who was almost as tall and broad-shouldered and simple-hearted as her brother. "You can't keep moving on all the time, you know. Some people have staying power. Perseverance. They master things." She smiled at Noreen, and gave her arm a little shake. "Don't get pushed around by these fly-by-night types, Nan. Their unhealthy sense of competition at family occasions is just another manifestation of what we psychiatric nurses call Christmas Rage. All rooted in personal inadequacy."

She looked at Dave in comic hostility, but the gibe was so plainly aimed at Lady Artemis that the latter flushed slightly, and poked a log at the edge of the big fire with a brown alligator-patterned toe. Cat was in the kitchen, hauling a shepherd's pie out of the oven and gossiping with Lindy, and Mark was too slurred to be of any social assistance. Robert Gratton, still the diplomat, weighed in with weary skill.

"Tell you something, that supper smells pretty damn good. Are we waiting for Toby and Topsy?"

"Certainly not," said Cat, reappearing. "We'll wait five minutes while Gervase and the boys check the ewes, then we'll start. Toby said he might stop off at a friend's."

"I don't get it," said Lindy, bouncing through the door behind her, a tea cloth thrown over her shoulder and her face flushed, "I thought lambs came in spring."

"They do, normally," said Cat. "But Dorsets can lamb at any time of year, and it suits Gervase to do his lambing now. That way there's plenty of work for the boys through the winter, and he's clear of it for the spring ploughing. Which he needs to be because that takes ages using horses; and we get a good price for the lamb because it's early."

Lindy listened without much understanding to this agricultural explanation. "It's just like *The Archers*, innit?" she said. "Will there be baby lambs tonight?"

"Could be. Martin reckoned one of the ewes was at it, when he went out at five o'clock."

"Brilliant," said Lindy. "I like lambs. You could have a cuddle of one for practice, eh, Caroline?"

Caroline gave a pale grimace. "I shouldn't, should I Cat?"

"Certainly not. There's a zoonosis, a disease you can catch off the animals. Enzootic abortion. Even if you don't know it's in the flock, pregnant women shouldn't go near lambing."

"Really?" Lady Artemis gave a silly, tinkling laugh. "Just as well you never had that trouble once you became a farmer's wife, Catherine dear." She had never quite forgiven Catherine for bearing healthy twins to some ghastly runaway hippy, then producing nothing at all with the impeccable Hartley genes.

"Yes, maybe," said Cat, determined not to rise to this, still less betray her own and Gervase's long-standing sorrow at that very fact. "But everyone wants to cuddle lambs, and it's always terribly embarrassing when visitors come at lambing time. You have to ask every woman of remotely likely age whether there's any risk she might be pregnant."

"Must be tricky," said Robert, intrigued. "That would challenge even a consummate diplomatic wife like your mother. Imagine asking one's middle-aged ambassadress. Or the Saudi consul-general's teenage daughter."

"You never ask me," said Marianne, demurely, twirling the ice in the gin-and-tonic she had somehow acquired in the face of the prevailing mulled wine policy.

"I *trust* you would know better, after growing up on a farm," said her mother tartly. "And it makes a useful test, every Christmas. All I have to do is say 'Marianne darling, just help Gervase in the lambing-shed' and if you won't, I'd know you're in the club. A lot of mothers would be grateful for a discreet little test like that."

Lindy, who was now perched on Mark's knee, giggled suddenly. "So if there's any chance at all . . . what do you think, Marky? Let's count back—" Mark shifted uneasily. Joyously impervious to his hinting, Lindy gushed on. "Wun't it be lovely, though? We've been trying for ever so long . . . well, six months."

"Terrific," said Dave politely. Lady Artemis made a moue of distaste for the whole subject, and rose gracefully from her fireside chair.

"Well, if dinner really is imminent, I will just withdraw for a moment or two—"

In the hall, she met Gervase, pulling off a pair of yellow rubber gloves on his way to the utility room sink.

"All well, Mother?" he asked. "Cat can dish up in a minute. Duane and Martin won't be long."

"Darling," said his mother, "are we eating with the farm boys?"

Gervase looked at her with weary resignation. Every year they had this conversation, at this time, in this hallway.

"Mother, don't be feudal. Martin is a college student taking a year out before he does a PhD in sustainable farm economics, and Duane—"

"Is Duane the one who looks mental?"

"Duane," said her son firmly, "has nowhere else to go. It's Christmas."

*   *   *

The *placement* was as tricky as any that their parents could have faced at a diplomatic dinner. With a brown envelope plucked from Gervase's desk and a stub of pencil, Cat frowned over the problem in the moments before she called them all through. It would have been natural to sit Lady Artemis Hartley next to Lord Gratton of Kilmore – clumping up the elderly nobs at one end of the table – but given their tendency to political animosity and unresolved sexual tension, Cat decided against it. Noreen must at all costs be protected from Artemis; so she was flanked by Dave, who loved her, and Robert Gratton, who had good manners. Opposite she put Martin Szowalski, the woofer, and Marianne; a distinct attraction had made itself obvious when the two first met earlier on Christmas Eve, and Cat had come to like the big young American and feel that such an attraction, however fleeting, was no bad thing for her daughter. Marianne's last boyfriend had been a sour young houseman with the appearance of an underfed and cynical rat.

Caroline, the other family member whose manners were beyond reproach, could entertain Lady Artemis at the far end of the table, with Mark on her other side. If Toby turned up he and Topsy could fit in next to Cat, near the kitchen door. Duane could sit next to Gervase, who had his mother on his other hand, and Lindy could talk at him. She never noticed whether anybody was listening or understanding. And *really* – Cat threw down her pencil in sudden exasperation – really, that was the best she could do. If Toby failed to turn up in time to eat, she herself would be a little isolated at the far end of the table, but nothing could be done about that. At this stage of the festivities she might rather enjoy a silent meal. Tomorrow, the Christmas Dinner preceded by the Christmas Morning Walk, would be time enough for bonhomous sociability. Tonight, by family tradition, a simple meal was eaten and those who were not inclined for Midnight Mass could go to bed early.

Beds. She ran through it in her mind again. The boys and Dave would sleep in the farm bunkhouse, Marianne and Noreen in Dave's old room, Robert in Marianne's, Mark and Lindy on the folding sofa in her study, Artemis down the lane with her old sparring partner the Rector. Caroline and Alan – if, as promised, he turned up later that night – would sleep in the best guest room. "Not because of Alan," she guiltily told Lindy as they drained the vegetables. "I only put them there because she's so pregnant. Normally nothing would please me more than to make bloody Alan sleep on the fold-up."

Toby and Topsy, she had resolved, could damn well doss in sleeping bags on the downstairs sofas. It would give her a certain savage sisterly satisfaction to rout them out in the morning, maybe by very loud Hoovering. Looking along the table now, enjoying the brief isolation imposed by their empty chairs on either side of her, Cat stifled a yawn and hoped that most of the party would disperse early to bed so that she could sit quietly through the Christmas midnight with her own twin children, catching up on their lives while Gervase tended the labouring sheep.

She was not left alone at her end of the table for long. Toby and Topsy arrived at nine o'clock, just as the shepherd's pie was about to be breached. They were heralded by a series of crashes, giggles and delighted squeals from the direction of the farmyard. Gervase looked up sharply at the first noises, frowned at the chorus of baas and bleats, and leapt to his feet at the unmistakable sound of a metal gate crashing to the ground and toppling a series of hurdles with it. Martin hesitated, then grinned apologetically at Marianne and followed him out. She glanced around, then muttered, "I'll give them a hand, my boots are in the hall." Dave, on a warning glance from his mother, stayed next to Noreen.

"Something escaped?" said Robert. "A farmer's work is never done, eh?"

"D'ju think I oughter go?" said Duane blankly. "Only, Mr Hartley says I aren't to go in the yard in indoor clothes."

"No, you stay. Help with the plates." Cat went through to the kitchen for the vegetables, and moved to the window to listen. From the yard came high girlish laughter, too shrill to be Marianne's, and the sound of Gervase quietly remonstrating with somebody. Metal hurdles clashed and scraped as they were reassembled to form the outdoor pen for the ewes which had not lambed. The dish of green beans in her hands grew cooler as Cat listened; at last, Toby's unmistakable drawl was heard, saying: ". . . wanted to see some Christmas animals, that's all. See if they could talk."

Gervase's voice, lower and more level, seemed to be enjoining him to come indoors. Topsy's high voice rang out again, "Woooh!" Mark came through and stood beside Cat, a lopsided smile on his face but looking less drunk – or anyway, less sullen – than he had before dinner.

"Sounds as if my big brother made it," he said. "And the amazing chorus girl."

"It's funny, isn't it," said Cat thoughtfully, handing him the dish of beans. "Fifty years out of date. These days chorus dancers are serious, superfit, ambitious, multiskilled professionals. Could turn into Sarah Brightman any day. But Toby somehow manages to find the last of the old-time high-kicking chorus girls, just when you thought they were extinct."

Mark was in no mood for cultural nostalgia. "Bloody bad manners. What are they doing coming in through the farmyard anyway?" He stumped off with the vegetables, just in time to create a distraction and abort another of Artemis' attempts to torpedo Noreen's confidence with a pointed lecture on the failure of overindulgent modern mothers to instil responsibility in their sons. "I always took great care that Gervase understood the concept of duty."

Mark's grumpy question was answered – not that he wanted an answer – minutes later when Toby came into the room flushed and grinning, pushing Topsy before him with his hands on her wriggling waist. She was wearing a very short skirt but no stockings or shoes ("Covered in sheep-shit, she fell over," said Dave under his breath to his grandmother) and giggling.

"We knew there'd be lambs," said Toby. "Wanted to salute New Life. Christmas. Congratulate a sheep, cuddle a slimy wee lamb. Very into New Life, are me and Topsy. Guess what, Dad? The long grandchild famine has become a feast. It's not just Caroline who's set to pop any day."

All eyes turned, drawn irresistibly to the girl's small waist and flat belly in the red stretch skirt, framed absurdly small between Toby's hands. He gave her midriff a shake, "Yes indeedy. A small but pukka Gratton lies within." He widened his eyes and wagged his head comically at his brother. "Bet you never thought I'd beat you to it, Grocer!"

Mark flushed to the roots of his sandy hair. "How," he asked coldly in the silence that followed this announcement, "do you know it's yours?"

Before anybody could answer, Lindy gave a piercing squeal of horror. "You never touched the lambs, did you? You'll get antibiotic abortion!"

"Enzootic," said Cat automatically.

"Boys, really," expostulated Robert.

At the end of the table Duane choked on an undercooked piece of carrot and had to be thumped, repeatedly, on the back.

Cat's hope of a quiet evening's talk with her son and daughter was dashed when Dave, Marianne and Martin announced that they were going for a "starwalk". The expression, however, made her smile. Dave had invented Christmas starwalks when he was seven, during his first winter at Knoll Farm. It had been a cold clear Christmas night like this one, and although church at Midmarsham was never at midnight, Dave had begged his mother to let him stay up, just to be outdoors under a skyful of pinpoint stars as midnight struck.

"Then if the animals speak I'll hear them, and if Father Christmas flies over, I'll see him." After that, starwalks had taken place for years, even on wet and cloudy Christmas Eves, with the result that a heavy-eyed mother had had to stay up until two o'clock to make sure the children were fast enough asleep not to see who filled their stockings.

The custom had lapsed, but at the end of a difficult dinner, with Toby and Topsy manic, Mark sulky, Lindy chattering nervously and Caroline picking at her food and jumping at every car engine noise from the lane, Dave's suggestion: "Starwalk? Marianne? Martin?" rang so blithe and natural over the washing-up that it lightened the whole atmosphere. The three young people went outside, with much laughing and stamping and shivering and coming back in for scarves. Duane retired with obvious thankfulness to the bunkhouse by the farmyard, and Mark and Lindy with equal relief to their attic. Toby and Topsy appropriated the chairs on either side of the dying log fire and promptly fell asleep, their mouths open, legs sprawled. With weary chivalry Robert offered to walk Lady Artemis down to the rectory, thus inadvertently rekindling certain old hopes. She had drunk quite a lot of wine, and he *was*, though left-wing, a very handsome man still. Noreen had crept up to bed clutching a hot-water bottle as soon as her drying-up duties were fulfilled. So Cat and Caroline were left alone together, both their heads swimming a little with wine and emotion, to drink a last cup of tea at the kitchen table while Gervase checked the sheep.

Cat would have begun discussing Toby's bombshell, or what on earth could be wrong with Mark to make him so chippy, but Caroline could focus only on her own baby and her own torment.

"He promised he'd be here tonight," she began immediately they were alone. "The bastard, he promised. It's Christmas Eve, there's no meeting in the world that happens on Christmas Eve. He's with that bloody woman, I know he is."

"He might still come," said Cat. "It's only eleven." She was tired, and did not want to discuss Alan any more, being far more intrigued with her brother's remarkable new status as a father-to-be. But her sister's distressful, beautiful face reproached her. Caroline's manner had subtly changed over the weeks since the night when she had first confided Alan's infidelity. She had always been too serene, too well-bred to talk of private matters in a frank, female way; but now the enthusiasm of the convert gripped her and she sought the relief of confidential chat at all hours, unconscious of her sister's busyness. The smooth veneer of her self-possession once broken, she had rung Cat incessantly, saying "it's such a relief to talk!" repeating her distress again and again, talking in circles, deciding nothing, just emanating pain and affront. Cat had listened, sympathized, and offered the most banal of reassurances; something dim but powerful prevented her from expressing to her sister anything other than platitudes. Now, reluctantly, she repeated those reassurances.

"You know he doesn't like these family gatherings. Lots of men don't when they marry into big noisy families. He's probably just holding off so he can sneak in late, get up late, have lunch and whisk you home. It's probably no more sinister than that. Do you think Dad's looking well?"

Caroline frowned, as if trying to remember who this "Dad" was who had nothing to do with her own trouble. Then distractedly she said: "Yes . . . never better . . . wonderful, really, for his age. Cat, the thing is, I've been thinking a lot, about me and the baby. It might be better for us just to admit it, mightn't it? Strike out on our own? Alan doesn't seem to care about it at all, and he was really horrible the other night when I asked him again if he was seeing Yasmin. He said I was hysterical and frigid and who could blame him if he *was* seeing her? Cat, he doesn't love me! I don't know if he ever did!"

"Maybe you're right," said Catherine heavily. "But it's too late now, isn't it?"

"Why? Why is it too late? I can see it's not going to work, it never was, he's a bastard – I'll cut my losses." She was rattling on now, on the verge of losing control, hugging herself, her teeth chattering a little despite the heat from the coal stove in the corner.

"Caroline," said Cat. "It *is* too late. The reason it is too late is sticking out from your front. You have no idea, *no idea whatsoever*, what it is like bringing up babies without their father."

"You did! Dave and Marianne are great, look at them tonight, anybody would be proud of them! And Gervase came along, and look how well you've all got on. It could be like that for me and the baby, too," said Caroline hopefully. "God knows I don't envisage any other man, right now, but people do. Meet new people. We could have another chance." She looked exalted for a moment, a woman with a high and noble destiny, a painting of Joan of Arc.

"Cat, I've thought and thought, and it's the best thing for all three of us, however hard it is. I'm going to tell him, tonight. Or" – she concluded rather lamely – "whenever he arrives."

Cat looked at her sister with irritation. Her head was beginning to ache on the left side, where her migraines always started. She felt the dim, strong inhibition within her crumble and began speaking in a low rapid voice, turning her mug of tea in her hands with nervous clicking precision on the scrubbed table-top.

"You think we were all right on our own? You really think Dave and Marianne didn't need their Dad? You think they didn't look around for their Dad, wonder about him every single bloody day? If it hadn't been for Noreen we'd have gone under."

Caroline frowned. "Yes, but you wouldn't let Mum and Dad

help you, so staying with Noreen was all you could do – I'm not saying it'll be anywhere near as hard for me, I mean financially, Alan would have to look after us—"

"It wasn't just the roof over our heads! Don't bring everything back to money!" burst out Cat. "I stayed because Noreen is Tim's *mother*. She was ashamed of what he did, but she's his mother. The twins had a right to that half of their genes. To have a life with someone who was part of their father. Noreen used to tell them about when Tim was a little boy, and she'd tell me when they did things or made faces like he used to do. When Dave built that circuit board, she told us about Tim's old crystal set. When Marianne was scared of the dark, she had stories about how her father had a nightlight till he was eleven."

Cat paused, and took a swig of tea. Her hands were shaking now. "And neither of us ever told them he was a bastard who left them. I used to fudge over why he was in America. I showed them pictures. I told them when they made the sort of jokes he liked and I didn't. We made a sort of legend of him. What I'm saying to you is that I didn't want bloody Tim back. Not for myself, not for a minute, after the first shock. But for their sake I had to pretend to think well of him and act like a grieving widow. It was hard work."

She drew a long shuddering breath and glared at her sister. "Children need a father. Preferably their real father. Your baby's got one, so hang on to him. Fuck what you need or want! Fuck all that feminist crap! That baby ought to have a chance to know its father, even if he is a bastard. Who knows? He might stop being one."

Catherine rarely made such long speeches, and generally spared her sister the strong language which came naturally after a decade of eating supper with young offenders. Caroline pouted, the wine still fogging her brain, her own trouble puffing and spreading to fill every corner of her awareness. She began again:

"But with Alan it's more of a betrayal . . . I mean, you and Tim, you were virtually students – I know I never met him, but I saw the wedding picture – you were living in a squat, there was all that impermanent seventies thing . . . you must have sort of expected—"

She checked herself as she glimpsed the expression on her sister's face.

Cat snapped down her empty mug and looked steadily across the table.

"You art restorers do learn to look at the outsides of things first, don't you?" she said slowly. "What you mean is that Tim was a student revolutionary and an anarchist and had hair down to his waist. Whereas Alan is a rich smoothie with a Saab and a big house in Kensington. You think that having pink silk knicker-blinds makes it different. It's *not* different. One louse is much like another. Tim should have behaved like a decent father and a decent human being, and so should Alan. I had a right to expect my children's father to stay around, and a duty to put up with him if he did. So do you."

She picked up her cup again and drained it. "The real difference is that Alan is still in earshot, and you have a chance to persuade him that he's got to stay with his baby and treat you halfway reasonably until it's grown up. I didn't have that chance. Tim left me a letter, in the night, and no address."

"Well, that's what I mean. They're not the same. Alan's much more guilty, 'cos he's older."

"Nah. Long-haired left-wing student louse, 1974; right-wing louse in a Kenzo suit, 1997. Same model, different trim. We were both had. The difference is, you can still fight."

"I didn't mean –" began Caroline placatingly.

"Yes you did. You've always thought I was some stupid girl who married an unsuitable sort of man and got what was coming to me, and that you were a wise virgin who made a good catch. That's what Mum would have thought. But there isn't any difference, you know. We were both stupid cows with no judgement. But you can fight. You can change things. You don't have to be a single mother."

"Well, at any rate," said Caroline, "Gervase came along, for you."

"Yes?" said Cat. "And?"

"Well, that was lucky."

"It doesn't ever occur to you that *he* was bloody lucky?" Cat stood up, and took the two mugs to the sink. "No, I suppose not."

"Well, the twins were lucky. To get a new father, and such a nice one."

"Not theirs, though. No genetic link, no tug of understanding, none of that recognition, that ability to deal with each other. Even Dad and Mark are closer than Dave and Gervase can ever be. Dad even understands Toby, though he'd rather not admit it. It's biology."

"I never knew you felt that strongly about it," said Caroline sulkily.

"Well, I do," said her sister shortly, rinsing the mugs under a jet so powerful that water spurted up and hit her in the eye. "And don't say what about adoption, what about AID babies, donor embryos, all that. I know. Lots of people make the best of it and make good families. But it isn't the same. Not the same magic." She put the mugs down to drain, and turned to dry her hands and face on the kitchen roller towel.

"Why," said Caroline, shaken out of self-absorption by her sister's strange vehemence on this unexpected subject. "Why do you feel like that?"

"Because Gervase does," said Cat, her back still turned to the table and her voice muffled, though whether by emotion or the roller towel it was hard to tell. "Because he couldn't have babies. Zero sperm count. Don't you ever tell a soul, or I'll kill you. We found out years ago. Gervase came back from the test and walked for miles, on his own with the sheepdog. Then came back and told me he didn't want donor stuff out of a test-tube. He said he'd rather be honest about it, and not even adopt. He said he'd get his stake in the next generation by using the farm and the land and the horses to help kids whose real fathers were no bloody good."

"And you agreed?" Caroline was startled out of her self-absorption. Cat tossed her head and looked steadily at her sister.

"I said yes, fine. I'd got two children already. It's not the kind of thing you argue about. We've never discussed it since. We have sheep and young offenders instead of children. Dave and Marianne have been great fun for him, but they never called him Dad. End of story, end of line for distinguished Northamptonshire landed gentry family. We let Artemis assume it's my fault for having fucked-up fallopian tubes or something. That sounds like Alan's car. Make him some tea. I'm going to bed."

When Alan Halliday came into the kitchen, shivering from the cold and anticipating a string of reproofs from his wife, he found Caroline sitting at the table, looking white and slightly shocked. But she smiled tentatively up at him. "Bad journey, darling?" she said. "Would you like some tea before bed? Nearly Christmas Day!" Bemused, he bent and cautiously, with an indefinable qualm of distaste, kissed the top of her golden head.

7

Toby woke in the armchair, cold and stiff, and saw by the grandfather clock in the firelight that Christmas midnight had passed. The house was silent but the fire had been made up again to warm the big room with its faded carpet and long beams where ivy and tinsel were wound together between years-old nails. Someone – Cat, presumably – had left two sleeping-bags and pillows on the sofa. He glanced across at Topsy. Her floss of yellow hair stood comically on end in tufts and fans of blonde exuberance as she sprawled in the other chair as relaxed as a cat.

His own body felt dense and stiff and middle-aged. He had been waking in the night quite often these past months with a sense of ageing upon him. Tentatively, he moved a leg. It creaked, he could swear it. Not yet forty-five, he was creaking. Would he ever again swarm over a backyard wall in a nightclub raid? Or drink all night, sleep on a hot beach and wake up ready to run into the sea? This ageing thing might not matter to Mark, him with his business suit and his executive villa, but he, Toby, had suited youth. He had made good use of it and enjoyed every minute. At least, since school was over and his parents ceased pestering him to be otherwise than he was

But what he was now . . . that was not so easy to deny or discard. He wriggled in the chair, aware in the midnight chill of stale neglected muscles and the slow treacherous growth, below his belt, of a paunch.

A log fell sideways in the iron fire-basket with a small cracking noise, flaring a brighter light across the room. Topsy yawned,

showing a pink mouth and sharp little white teeth like a kit-
ten's. He roused himself from his chair and went over to her.
"Bedtime," he said, and picked up her light firm dancer's body
in his arms to deposit her on the bigger of the two sofas. She clung
sleepily to his neck for a moment, then flopped like a rag doll, her
arm dangling over the side. He picked it up, put it carefully on
her chest, eased a pillow under her head and threw the better of
the two sleeping-bags over her. A satisfied "mmmph!" rewarded
him, as she drifted down into deeper sleep again.

He knelt for a moment, looking down at her. The only
symptom of Topsy's pregnancy, in the weeks since she had
revealed it gigglingly to him in a pizza bar after the show, had
been this increasing sleepiness. Always a girl who fell asleep
easily, she now slept even later than usual in the mornings,
and had taken to dozing off backstage in a costume-hamper
after her first routine, with a Post-It note on her chest saying
"WAKE FOR ACT II". Sometimes, she told him with shrieks of
laughter, she woke up covered in other Post-It notes written by
the rest of the chorus saying "PRIME PORK", "THIS WEEK'S
SPECIAL OFFER", and "THIS SIDE UP".

She also fell asleep in his arms straight after they made love.
Lovemaking had been strange lately: gentler and more – more
reverent, thought Toby, surprising himself, ever since he had
known about the baby ("Definitely yours, made in Glasgow,
remember – when I came up during the electricians' strike at
the Imperial, and I left my sponge bag on the train"). She was
no longer just another old mate, a bit of happy familiar fun,
one of a dozen male and female companions of his revels in
the loose world of second-string rock musicals and near-miss
showbiz. Toby had been surprised by the strength of his own
reaction to her news, and by its nature: no resentment, no panic,
not even shock. She had told him across the glutinous pizza in
the neon glare of that late-night supper, and he had taken her
hand and impulsively kissed it.

"So you want it?" she had said, a little breathlessly.

"Don't you?"

"Yes, yes – I was going to say, I'm having it, whatever the girls
say – sure thing." She pouted. "But I wouldn't chase you with
the CSA or maintenance and stuff. Def'nitely not. Because it was

my fault leaving the spongebag on the train." He had smiled then, and smiled now in the firelight, at her sturdy sense of justice.

"It's yours and mine," he said, still holding her hand. "What shall we call it?"

"I think of it as Amber. Dunno why. It's my favourite stone."

"Could be a boy. Ambrose?"

"Do me a favour!"

They had talked endlessly about it since, always in the same bantering tone, never raising such practical issues as whether they would live together, or where. Certainly not in Topsy's terrible bedsitting room over the Tottenham Court Road with the tarts down one flight of stairs and the computer games below. Nor did they discuss what any of them would live on. Toby had found £500 owed to him at his agent's, and was writing three crude songs for an aspiring boy band whose managers thought that punk aggression should make a comeback, and had turned to the old master of the genre for inspiration. It was more money than Toby usually had, and steadier work too.

But tonight, as he knelt by Topsy's side in the firelight wondering when her belly would begin to swell with his child and she would have to stop dancing, he felt the stiffening and ageing of his own body and was suddenly, unaccountably, afraid. This, he recognized, was the moment in his life to consider reversing all the decisions he took back in 1969, when he deliberately made it impossible for Radley College to house or teach him one minute longer. He would have to drop back in: but back, he saw now, into a new world which might not want to afford him a steady, income-bearing, paternal sort of job. Even if he could stand it.

He sighed, and looked at the other sleeping-bag. It was khaki and limp, and probably left over from Gervase's schooldays at army cadet camps.

"Come on, chaps!" he mimicked under his breath, pulling it over his feet as he sat on the smaller sofa. "Bivvy down, we've a five o'clock start!" He stretched out his long legs, putting his feet up on the arm rest. The sleeping-bag had a faint smell of boy scout about it, he thought as he drifted off to sleep. Poor old Cat: she might have burnt her fingers with the hairy poet Tim (Toby remembered that wedding, and the interminable readings from fake Hindu scriptures written by the groom) and he could see she wouldn't want another of those drifters. But it was a bit much to rebound onto a worthy old stiff like Gervase, and end up supporting his good works and organic sheep by boiling potatoes for sullen jailbirds and writing puling PR drivel for Eden. Poor old Cat. Toby yawned, glanced across once more at Topsy's hair sticking out from under the quilted nylon bag, and fell asleep.

Out in the farmyard, where the clean straw glimmered under brilliant stars, Gervase was on his knees beside a panting ewe. One hand was twined in the thick oily fleece of her back, and the other lifting her bloodied tail. He could see a leg, a foreleg by the look of it, just protruding from the swollen gap beneath the tail. But only the one leg. She was straining now, her flanks rock-hard with muscular effort, then relaxing into more hopeless panting. He would have to help. He let go the tail for a moment, and dipped his hand into the jar of antiseptic lubricant beside him.

Gently, he pushed the leg back, and slid the hand into the sheep. He closed his eyes, so as to feel more sensitively, and threw his head back: yes, the leg, and ah! – the other leg. Inside the warm pulsing birth canal his searching fingers could identify the head. Good. Definitely forelegs. He grasped both, waited for a contraction, and firmly but gently tugged. Both legs appeared, then a large head, eyes closed and gummy, streaked with blood and yellow mucus. With a rush of liquid, the whole lamb plopped to the ground, Gervase still holding its forelegs. The ewe was straining again now, but he turned from her to the dead-looking thing on the straw. Gently he tickled its nose with a wisp of straw, but there was no response. He lifted it and blew into its slimy mouth, to no avail. Then he stood up, wiped his hand on his trousers and picked the lamb up again, this time by the hind legs. With some violence he whirled it around his head, its forelegs and gummy head describing great circles against the stars. It worked. The little animal coughed, took a deep giddy breath, and gave a loud indignant bleat. Gervase pulled it to him, holding it against his chest, inspecting it, feeling the strengthening heartbeat in its wet woolly chest.

"Good boy! Good baby! Go on, live, live!" This moment of kindling life always moved him unbearably, even at two o'clock in the morning, even in his deepest secret depressions.

Sometimes the lamb would die hours or even minutes later, overwhelmed with delayed shock at the trauma of its coming. But this one had the mark of life on it: already its head was turning, searching blindly for its mother. He set it down on its legs and it stood, wobbling, and continued to peer around. The ewe had moved two paces away and – he saw with amused gratification – delivered the twin lamb on her own. She was licking it enthusiastically where it lay, clearly breathing, on the straw.

"Come on, girl," he said, putting the elder lamb beside her, and watching it grope, then latch on with determined greed to her teat. "You've got two. Just check –" he felt once more inside the ewe but, satisfied there was no triplet, knelt back and watched the second lamb teeter to its feet and find the other nipple.

A sound behind him made him turn his head. It was Dave, with a mug in his hand.

"Brought you tea, Gerv," he said. "Martin's still explaining the meaning of life to Marianne in the bunkhouse, and Duane's out like a light, so I thought I'd get tactfully out of the way."

"Thanks." Gervase sucked gratefully at the hot tea, tiredness welling up in him.

"How's it going?"

"Nice twins, just born."

Dave looked fondly at the lambs. "Isn't it amazing how quick they dry off, and start getting fluffy? I used to hate the slimy ones when I was seven. I thought they were really disgusting."

"You were good, though. Remember holding the torch for me, that first winter? Inside the barn, when we had all that snow?"

"I was so knocked out to be allowed to stay up, I was prepared to put up with the slime and the bloody bit round their bums. You were good, too. Couple of Hounslow kids who'd never even seen a farm animal up close, and you pretended we were a great help."

"You were." There was a definite note of finality in Gervase's voice: he was ending the conversation. Dave recognized the tone of old, and took the empty mug back from him in silence. Gervase glanced around the yard, looked through the barn door at the ewe which had lambed earlier, her sleeping young warm against her flanks, and said: "Night then. Happy Christmas."

"Happy Christmas. Shall I do the early turn?"

"No. Martin's having a look at six. That'll do. I wasn't really expecting any till Boxing Day, so this could be it for the moment."

When he had discarded his overalls and washed, Gervase eased himself into bed – his parents' old, vast, four-poster bed with springs which sagged beneath the new mattress he had bought in Cat's honour many years ago. His wife was sleeping soundly, curled in her corner. He edged close to her without touching, to feel the warmth which radiated from her evenly breathing body. He closed his eyes and pictured again the lambs rising shakily to their feet. He smiled, and relaxed into sleep.

8

The clear skies of Christmas night had clouded over by morning, and Martin's early round of the animals was done in cold mizzling rain. There were no more lambs, but he replenished the sheep's fodder, checked the three newborns, fed the horses and turned them into their own yard for the day, and carried two buckets of barley meal and water up to the pigs above the house. He could have woken Duane to help him, but decided not to bother. He liked moving about the farm, alone with his thoughts, and besides Duane might appreciate a morning in bed before he had to face Christmas dinner. Poor kid was obviously out of his depth with these people, not like that sharp-arsed Gary.

Martin Szowalski, working his way round Europe at twenty-one, had had plenty of opportunity for quiet observation of families on the various farms he helped on, and found Knoll Farm particularly striking. He admired Gervase Hartley's mission to help boys like Duane with regular work and contact with nature and self-respect and all that – but Gary, in his view, was a lost cause, a waste of space. Martin had all the unsentimental brutality of youth, about youth. Gary was a selfish asshole, and feeding pigs would teach him nothing. You could see he despised the whole thing, and Mr Hartley most of all.

Which was, in Martin's view, very unfair. Gervase seemed to him a man of high principle and an understated kindness which – as Mrs Szowalski back home would have exclaimed – was just so British it drove you wild. Martin, who had grown up amid volatile Polish-American overstatement of virtually everything, found being with Gervase a revelation. He believed in all the organic thing, he believed in social justice, but he didn't preach on about it. Just did his small bit, in his own home. Like Marianne. That was a hell of a girl: nursing mad people, obviously really into it, really caring, but laughing about it too. He hoped Marianne would stay for more of Christmas, and come back before his own time was up. He wondered whether a British family would think it presumptuous if he asked for her phone number. He might take a day or two in London.

Mrs Hartley, he was sure, wouldn't mind. Hefting the pig bucket over the electric fence, Martin reflected that Mrs H., as Gary insisted on calling her, was a hell of a lady herself. She was not much in evidence around the farm, but obviously knew a good bit; whatever she did upstairs in that study clearly preoccupied her, as did the businesslike telephone calls she took in the corner of the kitchen. But the telephone was within arm's reach of the big shabby stove, and he would watch fascinated as she stirred soup or tossed onions in oil with the receiver wedged between shoulder and chin, saying "Yes – fine – if you fax me through the layout I'll fit the copy for the NVQ piece by ten tomorrow." Or "If you need it on a floppy, you'll have to send a bike. If you can wait till Wednesday, I'll Red Star it from Northampton, and Tanya can get it printed up before the meeting. That's my best offer. OK? Great." Sometimes the calls came during the early, communal supper which the Hartleys took with the boys and any volunteers or visitors to the farm, and Gervase would frown if she answered them. But if she didn't, Martin would see her straining to hear the answering machine pick up the call in the living room next door. At times when she heard a high whining voice saying, "It's Tanya, only the DH is worried, there's a problem with the copee . . ." Cat would tend to abandon the table despite Gervase's pained look, run through, interrupt the machine and sort out the problem on the spot. Then she would come back and smile and say "Sorry!" and Gervase would press his lips together and Duane would gape stupidly, as usual, and Gary would go on eating as if there was no bad atmosphere.

So Martin would make a point of bringing up a new subject, with enthusiasm, in his relaxed Kentucky drawl. Cat would glance at him gratefully, take up his thread, and together they would cover the moment of strain with a bright web of talk.

Great lady. Martin thought – though he could not be sure – that whatever her work was, Gervase found some moral problem with it. Or at least, a problem of aesthetics or taste. He did not really want to know more: admiring Gervase, admiring his wife, the idea of such a shadow of principle between them was something he preferred to push aside. Instead, as he watched the sow and her litter splashing their noses greedily into the heavy iron feeding-ring, he let his mind wander over the equally fascinating matter of the other siblings.

What a gang! They did not seem to him to be related at all: a crazy songwriter, a cool Duchess-type, then that bad-tempered, corporate exec guy between them. And the Lord, their father, looking kind of bewildered, as if he wondered what they had to do with him. Martin's own father would never have put up with that kind of yelling-the-odds at table, even though his three brothers were all grown up and married. But Lord Gratton just sat there, with that British face. Stiff upper lip. Weird.

Cat woke at eight to find Gervase sitting on the side of the bed, stretching. Outside, the rain ran down the window-pane and the sky was leaden grey.

"Happy Christmas," she said sleepily, and he turned and kissed her on the forehead.

"Happy Christmas. Twin lambs in the night, good 'uns."

"Lovely. Did you have to help?"

"Mmmm," said Gervase. He yawned. "Martin did the early morning. I said he needn't, but he wanted to. I like that boy."

"Me too," said Cat. "Oh God."

"What?"

"I've just remembered who's in the house. Noreen, Dad, Caroline, bloody Alan, Toby, Topsy-and-a-half, the twins, Mark and Lindy with hangovers, and Artemis heading up from the Vicarage like a smart missile any minute."

"You'll cope. You do a good Christmas, I always said so."

"Aaargh." Cat winced, but it was not her houseful of guests. nor even the dankness of the unheated bedroom, which made her shudder at that moment. She had remembered the conversation, too bibulous and intimate a conversation, with Caroline. She had talked about Gervase, and fatherhood. Christ, how could she have been so stupid? Years of never letting on why they were childless, half-pretending to all her local friends that it was her, or that it was by choice. Now she had gone and told Caroline the truth, just out of irritation and to make her pull herself together about bloody Alan and the new baby. In the chill of dawn, Cat cared far less about her sister's next move. Let her go blinding off into some neurotic Kensington version of single motherhood if she insisted. She could sort her own life out.

"Oh God," she said aloud, for a second time. Stupid, rash, tipsy indiscretion! She pulled herself together and managed to smile at her husband.

"Lunch is sorted, anyway. Martin did the potatoes and sprouts, all I have to do is put them on and the pudding on. Starters are done, and the turkey's been in the slow oven all night, just needs half an hour to crisp it."

"Crackers?" said Gervase. "Nuts?"

"You can do the nuts, they're in bags in the larder. Crackers are in two big boxes in the china cupboard. Big, sealed boxes."

Gervase laughed, a more open and natural laugh than she had heard for a while. He was pulling on a sweater, but said through the wool: "Toby wouldn't do that again. He never repeats himself, I'll say that for him."

"Hmmm," said Cat. "Some things do get dreadfully familiar. When he was a little boy the whoopee cushion was never out of use for long."

"Did they have whoopee cushions in Israel?"

"It wasn't Israel, he wasn't big enough. It was Berne."

"Do they have whoopee cushions in Switzerland?"

"Is the Pope a Catholic? You have no idea how coarse the German Swiss can be. Huge hairy rubber hands. Warty latex feet. Our landlady's son Dieter gave the whoopee cushion to Toby as a goodbye present, and it was in frequent use in Washington. You can imagine how it went down with the prissy American lunch ladies."

"Not an ideal icebreaker. What happened to it? He hasn't still got it, has he?"

"Could have got a new one."

The reference to crackers went back to a time years ago, soon after Cat's marriage to Gervase, when Toby, arriving on

Christmas Eve with every intention, he said, of being "helpful", had gone to the supper table early and privately doctored the crackers, inserting mottoes of the most unlikely nature into the cardboard tube, drawn from the *Communist Manifesto*, the lyrics of Sid Vicious and the *Kama Sutra*. Worse, he had inserted his own choice of gifts. Lady Artemis, unfortunately, got the condom. Gervase (who got the pepper sweet) had been inclined to a tolerant, boys-will-be-boys attitude but Cat (who got a chocolate penis and only just managed to conceal it from Noreen) had been mortified and forcibly made the point that her brother was not a boy, but of an age to show some decent consideration for the older generation. Mark (who got the packet labelled *"powdered rhino horn, oh all right, sherbert, but a man can dream"*) had growled, irritated. Caroline had looked coolly down her nose at her brash brother and her awkward one.

Toby had merely grinned, having achieved all he set out to do by fracturing the brittle veneer of family bonhomie to bring out a pleasingly raw, salty set of emotions. Robert would have exploded with wrath but Diana, already weakening with what would be her final illness, had merely given her warring children a gentle, indulgent smile and said, "It is Christmas, dears, so let's not any of us be nasty. Cat darling, lovely stuffing."

Cat remembered that Christmas, her mother's last, and grinned in spite of herself. Bloody Toby! Still, the announcement about the baby had been a startling change of tune: and he seemed to look at Topsy with something in his eyes she had not seen before. Or not since he was a very little boy indeed, one who had to be held up by a devoted sister to see over the parapet of the Berne bear-pit when the cubs were born in spring.

She suddenly had a vivid picture of herself, too tired to hold him up any longer, plumping him down rather crossly and expecting an outcry. And Toby turning to face her, uncomplaining, eyes still shining from the wonder of the little living teddy bears, to give her a rare hug. When, she wondered vaguely, fumbling for her clothes, had the cynicism, the sharpness, the defensive manic joking set in? With prep school? Or, before that, when Mark was born and he went to that horrible American school? In France he was a tiresome brat, indeed, but she remembered an ebullient, cheerful brat who wanted you to

enjoy each awful joke as much as he did. The time in South
Africa – well, never mind. It was a stupid thing to wonder about.
Toby had to grow up, and pray God, with this baby on the way
he finally would. She gathered up a bundle of clothes and made
for the comparative warmth of the bathroom.

Noreen was just leaving it, creeping apologetically down the
corridor in an ancient pink candlewick dressing gown which Cat
remembered from her early days in Hounslow. She smiled at the
older woman, pierced by another sudden Christmas memory: of
that same candlewick with one of her own babies flopped against
it, flailing little fists, whimpering grumpily while Cat struggled
to get a stiff terry nappy on the other twin. How dare Artemis,
who had never done a thing for anybody else unless there was
a lavish charity ball involved, patronize Noreen?

Noreen was a heroine. Just when she might have been enjoying some freedom as a lively middle-aged single woman with a
tiny but unencumbered house, she had willingly and without
reproach taken in her son's abandoned wife and baby grandchildren. She had lived a cramped and devoted life with them
for six years, then without rancour or selfishness given those
children up. "Don't worry about me, dear," she had said to
Cat, when matters became serious with Gervase. "They'll have
a much better life, out in the country. You know we're all getting
too big for this poor little house, and I can visit, can't I? I'll have
time to start those evening classes again!" Cat knew what it had
cost Noreen, the children's second mother almost, and honoured
her for it.

"Happy Christmas, Noreen," she said fondly. "Sleep well?"

"Not too bad, duckie," said her mother-in-law. She had not, in
fact, slept well at all. On Christmas Eve she always remembered
Tim's childhood: the few years when his father had been alive,
and the years after that when she alone saved and planned for
the surprises in his stocking, and crept alone to his room in the
small hours to lay a heavy, gorgeously lumpy red woollen bag on
the end of the bed. She had done her best all those years; yet she
had done wrong. Must have done, to produce a son who would
walk out on his new wife, his babies, his mother and his debts
and only send one letter – a poor thing, too – explaining about
his "new life" in America. Noreen did not see herself as any sort

of heroine. The removal of the six-year-old twins to this distant, rather alarming place was not something of which she had ever felt entitled to complain. No, the only child she had a right to was Tim: bad, lost Tim. He was her burden, for life.

The old woman sighed, and drew the pink candlewick around her more closely as she moved down the chilly corridor.

Passing the window she looked out to see the piglets in the orchard – dear little things! – and was startled to notice amongst them, apparently dancing, two figures with tinsel and ivy twisted around their heads, presumably stolen from the living-room beams. One wore a robe improvised out of a big red linen Christmas tablecloth. That would need ironing! Noreen opened the window a fraction to see better, and the sound of singing came up to her on the cold air, one voice deep and another shrill:

> *There was a pig, went out to dig,*
> *On Chriss-um-us Day, on Chriss-um-us Day*
> *There was a pig, went out to dig*
> *On Chriss-um-uss day in the morning!*
> *We are the spirit of Christmas Present!*

As she watched, an ungainly figure walked out of the kitchen doorway and towards the orchard, a piece of bread-and-jam dripping in its hand.

"Oy!" shouted Duane. "Mrs H. says she wawnt that tablecloth back, right now!" Toby turned, rather too sharply, and caught his robe on a fence post in mid-pirouette. It whipped off and flew down the orchard on the biting wind. A tide of black piglets surged joyfully over it.

9

Cat forbade Noreen to spend the festive morning washing and ironing the muddied red tablecloth, so the Christmas table was finally adorned with a plain white one. However, so much additional holly, ivy and fir had been gathered by the penitent Toby and Topsy to make "a stunning centrepiece, I promise" and so many plates and dishes and candles covered the rest of the extended table that the colour did not matter overmuch. The errant pair, spurred by an explosion of plain speaking from Cat, had also washed up everybody's breakfast, shaken out the sofa cushions, cleaned the fireplace and put the tinsel back up on the living-room ceiling. Except for one piece which still clung to Topsy's riotous backcombed hair.

It rained too heavily, as the morning went on, for the traditional walk. Only Gervase set off heavily clothed to walk the farm and check the stock. By the time Lady Artemis arrived from church, the rest of the family were gathered in the long sitting room. Even Cat had left the supervision of the Brussels sprouts to Martin and Duane and joined her brothers and sister. The four siblings were kneeling at the hearth, drinking red wine and laughing in a rare moment of unity over some joke from a past Christmas. Alan stood a little aloof, talking international affairs with his father-in-law and studiedly ignoring the cackles and whoops from the fireside. Noreen was on the sofa, safe between the twins.

The general air of festive comfort was rapidly dispelled by the arrival of the newcomer. Artemis always liked to stand in a doorway, letting in cold air, widening her eyes so they sparkled at the company and (Toby always swore, to Cat's scandalized amusement) simultaneously clenching her pelvic floor muscles and silently saying "Brush!" to produce a hellish combination of Jackie Collins allure with a Nancy Mitford social smile. She did it now, studiously ignored by everyone present except her dutiful daughter-in-law.

"There wouldn't be a gin-and-tonic, I suppose, dear?" she chirped as Cat rose to her feet to hand her a glass of wine from the tray. "Since it *is* Christmas?" The old lady gave a little shrug and a pouting pussycat smile. "I know I'm a silly girl, but there aren't many of these modern wines I can drink without food to – er – mask them." Cat, well aware of the roughness of her supermarket dozen, tried to suppress her irritation and replied as sweetly as she could: "Oh, Artemis, I'm terribly sorry, we're out of gin."

"I drank it," said Marianne, not looking sorry at all. She had been terrified of Lady Artemis when she was a six-year-old alien from Hounslow, and now drew genuine pleasure from the fact that she no longer feared her at all. "There's some whisky. And beer."

Ignoring this suggestion, Artemis took a glass from the tray and sipped fastidiously. She glanced at Robert, but he was deep in conversation with Alan Halliday about Eastern Europe. Grimacing at the wine and setting down her glass perilously on the arm of the small sofa, she next swivelled her big, slightly protruding eyes toward Noreen and opened her mouth to speak. Cat saw this move and clapped her hands commandingly.

"I can hear Gervase at the back door!" she lied. "We're all here now! Come on, let's go through, or we'll never have finished eating in time for the Queen!"

"The Queen," murmured Artemis, foiled. "I'm glad *some* old traditions still carry on in my son's house."

"Oh, Gervase doesn't give a monkey's," said Cat, her resolve to be a peacemaker breaking down under the temptation of vengefulness. "It's me that insists on having the Queen after Christmas dinner. And Dad. And all of us. It's the old Foreign Office tradition, wiping away a tear for the Queen in far-flung climes." She held out a hand to pull Noreen off the sofa. "Remember, we expats are always the most patriotic. Ever since we were babies, home wasn't home without the Queen's picture on the wall in robes, and a certificate personally signed, saying Dad was her trusty and well-beloved Robert John Adrian Gratton." She was leading the way to the dining room now, and delivered this message over her shoulder.

"It's true," quavered Toby piously, moving to the table and pulling back a chair for Lady Artemis with rudely exaggerated courtesy. "When Mrs Queen used to say 'God bless you all' we really thought it meant *us*. Personally. We loved her. We knew that if any foreigner got on our wick she would get her Secretary of State for Foreign Affairs to request and require that Johnny Dago afford us assistance without let or hindrance or she'd have a gunboat round. It said so in our passports." He pretended to wipe away a tear and turned towards the American volunteer, who had come in rather flushed with a dishful of potatoes. "And Martin, you Yankee invader, it was a terrible thing to us when they sent us to school in Washington DC, Cat and me. They made us salute the Stars and Stripes. We felt like traitors. We were *traumatized*. You treacherous colonists, how could you have done it to nice King George?"

"That's enough!" said Robert, amused in spite of himself. "The truth is, Martin, that Toby was never remotely reluctant to embrace American culture. It was Cat who found that school a bit much. My elder son turned into the worst kind of cartoon Yankee brat in two days."

"It was a particularly awful school," said Cat hastily, feeling that her father had lacked in diplomacy. "Not because it was in America but because Mum was always a lousy picker of schools. She did it all on how good the headmistress's clothes were. Our only lucky break was when she decided nuns were chic."

"Did Mark go to school in the States?" asked Martin.

"Too little," said Cat. "He only got to suck a Popeye toy. His first school was – oh, nursery in Lille, I think."

"'*Sur le pont d'Avignon.*' '*Meunier, ton moulin va trop vite,*'" said Mark dreamily. "Then I did lessons with Mum, then a year in Venice but I couldn't learn Italian fast enough so they threw me to the wolves of Haddington Hall."

"And you?" said Martin politely to Caroline, who was next to him this time.

"Oh, I wasn't born," she said in her sweet voice. "I only got born in Johannesburg. I had my first school in Venice."

"I *never* got to go to school on a *vaporetto*," said Toby resentfully. "I do not forgive you that. You and Mark got to be *bambini*, while Cat and I were beaten up by deranged Afrikaner clerics and then stuck in England eating mashed potatoes and getting rained on and having our characters formed by assorted sexual inadequates."

"You could have come out to UCLA, though," said Caroline. "When I was at school in LA I used to dream of us all being there together. I didn't have anyone to talk to but Mum, in term-time. But Cat wanted to do English university, and Toby was all over the place, and Mark was home doing 'O' levels and sending me letters about how terrible the American system was."

"Gee," said Martin. "It's like you all grew up in different worlds." Worried at the brief silence that followed this, he added: "It's a really neat way to learn about life, I bet. There's a new name for it, in corporate America when families have to relocate worldwide. They call them global nomad children, and apparently they're famous for growing up real gifted."

"We," drawled Toby, "were just common or garden diplo-brats. Who are famous for never growing up at all."

"They did warn us it might be hard for you to settle down in later life," said Robert. "But I always thought that was nonsense. Cat settled beautifully, hence this exceedingly fine meal."

"And I have settled," said Mark stiffly. Another brief silence fell, as the family looked at him without particular admiration.

Lindy chimed in: "Lovely turkey, Cath. Yum-yum!" She dug her elbow playfully into Alan, who was jammed rather too close to her in order to avoid having his legs trapped on either side of the table extension. "Innit lovely turkey, Alex?"

"Excellent," said Alan sulkily. He was furious at being seated so far from his potentially useful father-in-law. Caroline glanced pleadingly across the table at him, but met only a stony stare. She had been annoying him all morning with brightly playful but disastrously misguided attempts to please. She might as well, thought Alan sourly, spearing a sprout, have worn a t-shirt with SAINTLY FORGIVING WIFE printed on it. He turned to talk business to Mark, who was soon enthusing about his company's new in-service GNVQ training: "Not just offering staff internal progress," he said, "but a portable qualification. There was a fascinating piece in the pan-organization newsletter. Ms Raschid, at our HQ—"

Cat looked suddenly, unaccountably terrified, and Toby caught her eye and grinned. He was the only member of the family who actually knew which company she did all this lucrative copywriting for, simply because he was the only one who had ever asked.

He mouthed silently "Yours?" and Cat nodded, warily watching Mark as he quoted with reverence the words she had flung, so crossly and without commitment, onto paper earlier in the month. Toby made a zipping motion across his lips, and she smiled gratefully. He might like causing ructions, she thought through the welcome fog of wine, but he had a good heart really.

Toby had had no hand in the crackers this year, so the hats and mottoes and plastic puzzles fell from them without surprises except for Topsy going into peals of hysterical tipsy mirth on getting the motto *May all your troubles be little ones* and Gervase, who was very quiet today, getting a red plastic nose on elastic and being harassed into putting it on by a mildly inebriated Lindy. The pudding was on the table and the Queen a mere twenty minutes away when the phone rang. Gervase stood up, gravely pulling off his plastic nose.

"Sorry," he said. "I'd better. Nobody rings on Christmas Day unless it's important."

He took the call in the kitchen, learning on the stove picking absently at the turkey carcass. He listened, asked a couple of questions, said "Don't worry, I'll be over," grimaced, nodded, and hung up. For a moment he stared unseeingly at the turkey, then sighed and went back into the dining room, where somebody had tried to light an indoor firework, and in the process dripped red candlewax all over the ruins of the pudding.

"I'm *very* sorry," he said. "But I have to go to Midmarsham. That was Gary's mother. He hasn't been home since yesterday, and the police are round there searching for something. They think he might have hidden some drugs in her cottage."

"Darling, do you have to?" said his mother plaintively. "You're not these ghastly boys' *keeper*, you know." Cat flashed a warning look at her, nodding towards Duane, but he had no idea of being offended, having other things on his mind. With difficulty, beet-faced and choking down his pudding, the boy emerged from his accustomed heavy silence to say:

"Mister H.! I got to tell you—"

"Yes, Duane?" said Gervase, looking hard at him.

"Gary. I din' want to grass on 'im, but he tried to stash some stuff away in the bunkhouse."

"And did he?"

"I wun't let 'im," said Duane. "Told him that wawn't fair on you and Mrs H."

"Good man," said Gervase approvingly, and Duane glowed sheepishly. "I'm bigger'n he is," he confided to the rest of the table. "So it wawn't hero stuff." He guffawed, and picked up his glass of unfamiliar wine.

"All the same, well done," said Gervase. "But I do have to go. Gary's mother is in a bit of a state. He's probably just round at a girlfriend's, but you know . . ."

"Of course you ought to look after Mrs Bird," said Cat, briskly. "Come on, we'll go and watch the Queen."

Alan Halliday, by this time, had run out of tolerance for family life. He begged to be excused the Queen's broadcast because he and Caroline had social commitments in London. Caroline began, "Wha –?" but was silenced by a hard glare from her husband. Martin volunteered himself and Duane to start the washing-up, and the twins ("not being emotionally crippled by a diplomatic background," said Dave sweetly) abandoned the Queen to take Noreen out for a walk round the farm in the drying afternoon air. The rest moved back to the sitting room and arranged themselves around the small TV set in a silence broken by hiccups and the occasional burp.

Robert, from the end of the sofa, looked consideringly at his children. Cat looked tired, but composed; Toby, his dark hair curling untidily over his collar, as dissolute as usual but with something new about him his father could not place. It could be, thought Robert wonderingly, that this unlikely showgirl of his was going to be the woman who, at last, made his elder son grow up.

His eye rested on Mark, not altogether easily. He hoped the boy was happy: that wife of his with the ferocious Birmingham accent seemed to have made a difference. But there was always something angry about him, a lurking aggression, and the way he talked about his work had an intensity which made his father wince. In a lifetime concerned with the relations between great nations, the movements of trade and the crises of exiled individuals, he had seldom encountered the nervy passion with which Mark routinely spoke of in-service staff training modules or the importance of aisle width in supermarkets. Maybe if he had been posted to Libya, or Cuba, he would have felt more familiar with this kind of passion.

He felt sorry that Caroline had gone. She tugged at his heart, so like Diana, so likely to fall into the same traps. That husband of hers was clever enough, but clearly a bit of a shit in business. Robert hoped, staring unseeingly at the Queen's crumpled royal features, that he was not a shit in private, too.

". . . Wish you all, a happy Christmas," concluded the Queen on the screen. Toby, Mark, Robert, Artemis, Cat and Lindy rose to their feet for the National Anthem, Toby removing his paper hat with gravity. Topsy had fallen asleep. She woke, however, when Dave burst into the room saying: "Cat! Emergency! The sheep are out all over the road! What do we do? The front ones are right near the end of the lane!"

"Hell!" said Cat with feeling, and ran from the midst of her family towards the back door and the farmyard drive. She snatched the keys of the old farm LandRover from the hook above the lintel. Gervase must have taken her car to Midmarsham. Fair enough. Wrenching open the door of the sheepdog's run, she hustled the sleepy old dog into the LandRover and jumped up herself. Dave jumped in beside her.

"Top of the lane," he said, alarmed, as she shot out of the other end of the drive.

"I know," said Cat. "But I can't drive through them, can I? I'll go up the far end, along the main road, head them off."

"You've done this before, Ma," said Dave admiringly.

"Too bloody right I have. But never," Cat said with a quaver in her voice, "never this close to lambing. Christ, some of them must be virtually in labour. I hate this bloody thing, the steering's all over the place."

She was speeding down the lane now, the old vehicle leaping and juddering on the potholes, and barely slowed to swing into the main road. Dave could see ahead the half-hidden opening which marked the far end of the Knoll Farm lane, for the farmhouse lay midway on a narrow loop which left this main road and rejoined it. As Cat had predicted the first sheep were just visible, off-white noses edging forward under their woolly Dorset quiffs, hooves pattering on the damp lane. She slammed her foot down on the accelerator and shot forward, reaching the lane just ahead of the flock. Leaping out, she dragged the rear door open to release the old dog.

The flock paused, while its leaders stupidly looked at the dog and the LandRover skewed sideways across their path. For one heart-stopping moment it seemed that one bold ewe had decided to slither down into the nearside ditch, which would have given her and her followers a clear path out onto the main road. But Dave threw himself ahead of her, shouting "Gaaah!" and the ewe turned and fled back, jostling through her peers, away from the young man and the stick-waving woman and the sheepdog.

The rest of the flock took their cue from this, and fled precipitately after her, back down the lane. Cat screamed, "Come by!" at the dog, put on a burst of speed, overtook the leaders, and headed them off ("Howaaay!" yelled Cat) to the right and into the Knoll Farm front yard. She ran up the lane after them, but Duane and Martin had heard the commotion and taken up their posts. She saw them shut and secure the gates with the milling, panting flock inside.

Cat sank to her knees. "Thank Christ!" she said without a scintilla of blasphemous intent. Her heart was pounding and she drew her breath in long shuddering gasps. As Dave caught up with her he put his hand reassuringly on her shoulder.

"I'm sorry. Can't help it. It isn't just that they're about to lamb, it always gets me like this. It's the – the panic of it."

"The hysteria. The lack of control. The plain bloody barminess of them," said Dave. "I know. I always felt it, when we were little. Can you *catch* panic, off sheep? Like enzootic whatsit?"

"Gervase doesn't. He's always calm as a tree in this sort of crisis."

"Well, I know what you mean anyway. It's different with cows."

"Yes," said Cat. "When cows are running around out of control, you feel it's the exception and they'd rather be grazing quietly back on the farm. When horses go crazy, you know that *they* know they shouldn't. With sheep—!"

"They just go back to their primitive state. Brainless, aimless, suicidal panic," finished Dave. "'*The ancient panic which abides deep in all creatures*'. The great god Pan, who drives men and beasts to frenzy."

Cat recovered herself. "Are we really kneeling on a wet grass verge on Christmas Day, philosophizing about Pan?" She stood up, and rubbed her damp knees. One of her tidy Christmas-day shoes was lying near the LandRover with the heel wrenched off. She hobbled back towards it and flung it into the cab.

"I'll walk," said Dave. "Need the air. Clear my head."

Cat nodded, and started the engine. Reversing into the road, talking to herself ("Bugger this steering, Gervase'll have to have it seen to, it's really loose") she crashed the machine into first gear and proceeded slowly towards the far lane entrance. Her eyes well accustomed to the growing dusk, she did not bother to switch the lights on for the two-minute journey home.

PC Adcock and Sgt Flower were driving along the main road to pursue further enquiries into the whereabouts of Gary Bird, whose pathetically small but damning stash of Ecstasy and cannabis had been found at his mother's cottage following an anonymous telephone call from a vengeful young woman. He was, they realized, probably miles away in the company of some other young woman, and hardly likely to be tucked up in Mr Hartley's Knoll Farm bunkhouse. Nonethless, checks must be made. Ahead of them, a LandRover was turning, in rather too wide an arc, thought PC Adcock, into the farm lane. It had no lights on.

"Look at that," he said to his senior colleague. "You don't suppose—" Sgt Flower grunted. "Funny bit of driving," he said. "Christmas Day. Come on. No point wasting the whole journey."

His colleague pulled something out from the pocket in front of him, and fitted it with a tube from a sealed pack.

"Why not?" he said.

Cat had barely pulled up outside the farmhouse when the police car crunched on the stones behind her. Startled, she jumped out and found herself facing two uniformed officers, the younger of them carrying what looked like a portable telephone. Then she saw the breathing tube, which made it clear it was something else entirely. Woolly panic surged through her like a hundred stampeding sheep, as she realized for the first time that she, who never drank a drop if she were likely to drive that day, had just been in the driving seat of a vehicle on the Queen's highway with three-quarters of a bottle of Australian red inside her.

10

"The light on the box went red," said Cat, hours later. The remnants of the family were around the kitchen table, picking distractedly at the remnants of the Christmas dinner. "It went bright bloody red. And they took me to the station in Midholt, and I did another test, and that was just as positive, which I could have told them it would be." She swigged viciously at the dregs of her wine. "The young one gave me a lift back, because we couldn't get any of the taxi firms to answer. He was quite sweet. At least" – she pulled a dark brown piece off the turkey carcass, looked at it with sudden loathing, and dropped it on the dish – "one good thing is that they didn't pounce till I was on the drive. So the Landy's here, not stuck beside some road."

"Poor Cat," said Gervase sympathetically. "Did you tell them why you had to drive?"

"No. Dave did, but they repeated all the stuff about requiring me to accompany them to the police station. They were just like robots – the sergeant wasn't local, he was filling in for Christmas while the Midholt lot had leave. And then Toby banged on the roof of the police car and said they should be ashamed of themselves."

"Which didn't help," said Robert.

"Solidarity, Dad!" said Toby. "I mean, Cat was only saving the lives of woolly sheep. It's not like my pal Dunkie, in Glasgow, who does it all the time and always carries a bottle of Scotch in the side pocket and if he gets stopped, he pulls in and knocks it back so they can't prove he was drunk before."

"Does that work?" asked Cat, diverted for a moment from her trouble.

"No," admitted Toby. "He still gets banned. Actually, he only ever drives for about a month before the next ban. But there you go."

"Well," said Gervase. "I doubt you'll get banned. We'll get a decent barrister to argue that it was life and death for the sheep."

"Gordon Japhet-Menzies," said Robert, decisively. "I'll call him at home."

"Yes, he'll be good," said Gervase. "Sound, not flashy. He's got a house round here, hasn't he? The court will take the sheep into account."

Cat sucked noisily at her wine, put the glass down, drew her sleeve across her eyes and gave a long, shuddering sniff.

"No," she said loudly. "Stop organizing my defence. I'm not at all sure I *want* a defence."

The group round the messy table looked at her, waiting for more.

"I don't believe in all that," she said. "When Dave and Marianne were little and we were all living in Hounslow with the lorries going by, I was bloody glad of the breathalyser law. I think there ought to be a zero limit. I've always thought that. People who drink and drive don't deserve any sympathy at all. They kill children."

"But you were saving the sheep. You had to," said Gervase gently. "I respect what you're saying, Cat, but you weren't a danger, and you have got an excuse. Like someone going to hospital with a casualty."

"All the same, it was wrong," said Cat grumpily, "and I don't like people who wriggle out with smarmy double-barrelled barristers. I don't like excuses. I'm not bloody Gary."

"Well, I think we have to respect that," said Gervase heavily.

"I don't," said Toby. "I think you're bats."

"Don't be so rude," said Topsy abruptly, turning on him. "I reckon Cat can do what she wants."

"She was always a bit Joan of Arc," said Toby. "Father, I cannot tell a lie."

"That was George Washington" said Topsy, even more surprisingly. "And shut up. You're no help. You're all mouth, you."

"Whatever," said Cat stiffly. "I'm not defending the case. I'm pleading guilty. It'll be awkward, obviously, being banned and living here—"

"Awkward?" said Gervase under his breath. Without an extra driver, he saw in clear dismay, it would be a logistical nightmare to run the farm, and the boys' lives too. Cat did the recreational runs into town without which they grew restless, and took them to their appointments with probation officers. For a non-driver even to shop for food and farm essentials with the village two miles away and the town fifteen would be impossible. At present, the farm and the boys took all his time and more; if he had to replace her on all these runs it would be almost catastrophic.

All this chaos, a whole year of it, could perhaps be averted if Cat were to defend herself. She had only driven for a few minutes, on empty Christmas Day roads, to prevent danger both to animals and human drivers. It was not fair. Even when he turned his mind away from the coming difficulties, his head and heart throbbed with indignation for his wife's humiliation, and he longed to defend her, personally and loudly.

But he could not bring himself to argue about it. These last few years, he admitted with further silent dismay, he had been tired and she had been irritable. They had not had a holiday since the Lloyds' crash and his mother's land sale; they had not talked together relaxedly, in depth, for longer than he dared remember. When Dave and Marianne left home they had taken much of the laughter out of daily life, and now the Hartleys were scarcely more than decently behaved partners, neither lovers nor parents nor even very close friends. They respected one another's endeavours, but left each other space. Acres of empty space lay around each of them. He knew that she was equivocal about some of his human projects, like Gary: she knew, without his needing to express it, how much distaste he felt for corporations like Eden PLC, and for crafts of puffery like hers.

Yet their whole complicated, bothersome, altruistic, financially precarious life now rested on Cat's talent. Her uninspiring trade, he thought sadly, had come about because of his idealism. She churned out platitudinous copy for an aggressive and rapacious commercial empire so that he could do good for the soil and for animal welfare, and bring hope to lost and disaffected young offenders. He, Gervase, wanted to be good: Cat backed him up daily, uncomplainingly, subordinating her gifts to the production of profitable tripe. Now for once the tables were turned, and she was demanding a turn on the moral high ground. How could he argue?

Robert glanced at his son-in-law sharply, aware of something wrong. There was no colour in Gervase's face and he looked tired, worried, and oddly distant. Mark stirred uneasily and grimaced at his wife, who sat open-mouthed watching this family confrontation. Cat blundered on, determined, drunk and tired:

"Martin's with us till April. Supposing the case gets heard within about a month, it's quite quick at the magistrates' court – and suppose I get a twelve-month ban, that gives us three months of the ban reasonably covered, and when he goes we'll just have to get another volunteer who can drive. And Gervase'll have to do more, and I'm really sorry—"

Tears overcame her now, and the sleeve crossed her eyes and nose again. "Oh, sod it. I'm going to bed." Her husband looked helplessly after her, but did not move. Noreen, coming back into the kitchen with Marianne a few minutes later, found the rest of them still sitting in comparative silence, dragging streaks of ever less attractive meat from the turkey carcass. She began to clear and wash up. Gervase went outside to the lambing-yard, and the others dispersed.

When Gervase came upstairs Cat was asleep, or seemed to be. He slid quietly between the sheets and lay for a long time, his hands behind his head, staring at the low dark beams. There was not, after all, likely to be much comfort in counting sheep.

Toby and Topsy, mindful of the dreadful example made of Cat, stayed Christmas night and left sober on the morning of Boxing Day. Toby was rolled off his sofa earlier than he would have liked, because Topsy had to put in some work ahead of a rehearsal of her next high-kick musical, *Mademoiselle from Armentières*. "Nostalgia stuff," she said, "which is really lucky. No high-cut costumes. Just little skirts and awful slow choreography by that old piss-artist Mogadan. It's not like *Cats*. With a show like that I can do three months before the bulge starts to show."

"Didn't your friend Daisy dance till she was seven months

gone?" said Toby, throwing his tattered backpack into her little car.

"Yah. But she was one of the brothers' wives in *Joseph*. She only had to sway a bit."

"Nothing like Bible-wear to disguise an unwanted bump," said Toby. "Bye, then, Catto. Fine Christmas. Shame about the Old Bill."

His sister, watching from the step, smiled and raised her hand. He paused, looking at her.

"Are you going upstairs to write more scripts for Mark?" he said.

"Shh!" Cat heard Lindy, bumping down the stairs with a suitcase, and raised her finger to her lips. "Look, of course I'm going to tell him, it's just awkward finding the moment. It's his world, and you know Mark. Much better if I'm the humble rural sister who knows nothing of the big corporate jungle."

Toby laughed. "You all make things so bloody complicated, you diplomats. Me, I just get pissed and blurt everything out. Then everyone knows where they are."

"Goodbye," said Cat firmly, but smiled at him. "Topsy, look after yourself. Get some rest. It's not that easy, you know." Turning with another wave as Topsy's little car puttered into life she added in a lower voice, "Any of it." Dave and Marianne had left early, bearing Noreen off for a day out in London and one of the big musicals she loved. Without them Cat felt bereft and old and flat. Still, Marianne had looked at young Martin in a way which promised a visit sooner than usual. Who knows? thought Cat, heavily climbing the stairs to her dusty office. If that little romance went well, Martin might even stay through the summer instead of backpacking off round Europe, and her driving ban could be covered for a little longer.

The weeks after Christmas passed in the usual atmosphere of dull endurance that marked lambing-time. It was bitterly cold, and the ice had to be broken on the animals' drinking-troughs three times a day. Each night Cat did the 2.00 a.m. check of the ewes, shuddering from her bed to wrap herself in an old coat and tour the yard with a torch, peering under tails for signs of problematic labours and rounding up any lambs which had been born unattended and mislaid their mothers. Sometimes she would find one dead, drowned in a puddle or strangled by a difficult birth in the brief two hours since the last check. She would lift the small dead body and throw it beyond the fence to be dealt with in the morning. Once, a fox had killed newborn twins, and the ewe bleated over their bodies in uncomprehending distress. Often there were labour problems and she had to trudge back to the house and call Gervase; if that happened she would get up to do the pre-dawn inspection herself, and hope she did not have to wake him again.

Even so, since Martin was inexperienced Gervase worked long, taxing hours and would fall into an exhausted doze whenever he sat in a chair indoors. There was little sun, and no snow or hoar frost to throw back the paltry light from a sky which remained day after day the pale dull grey of a Tupperware lid. Cat worked upstairs for Eden and other clients, wrote a pamphlet about self-assembly furniture, a chatty exhortation about private breast screening, and a paean to a new "Time Organizer" system involving interlocking cork boards and pegs. *"Why strain your eyes peering into a computer screen?"* she wrote one morning, peering into the glowing green eye of hers. *"When you could have your whole year in front of you in vibrant optimistic colour and enhance your home decoration at the same time?"* She paused, looked at this with disfavour, and put her finger on the delete button until it vanished as far as *"Why stra"*. That, she thought, looked a bit Nordic. Perhaps it was Shetland dialect or balladeer's Scots for something. *Why stra the sheepie, quoth my luve* . . . Her head fell forward and her eyes closed.

The door behind her opened, and Gervase came in and stood hesitantly, wondering whether she were deep in thought. Cat heaved her head upright, swung round, and managed a smile.

"Hi. I'm writing about cork pegboards."

"This came," he said. "I opened it." Cat looked at the paper in his hand. It was the court summons for her drunken driving offence. It was imminent. "Good," she said. "Get it over with." Gervase stood for a moment, looking at her. She looked back at him, steadily.

"You know I feel the same as I did," she said. "Guilty, m'lud."

"Yes," said Gervase. "Fine. It's your decision."

"Martin will be here. He said the other day he might like to stay till summer."

"Can we afford him? The loop, I mean? He is useful. This new lad who's coming, the Ecstasy case, is only seventeen. The probation officer says he's nervous of animals."

Cat winced. "Ee, they do pick 'em for us," she said. "Anyway, yes, we can't afford *not* to have Martin. And think of all the money we'll save on petrol. I've told Eden I'll sometimes work by phone. I sort of pretended I was being headhunted. They were terribly co-operative then. They're wondering about putting in a teleconference videophone. Prats."

She gave a sudden bark of reluctant laughter, throwing her head back and looking more directly into her husband's eyes than she had for some time. Gervase moved towards her, put a hand on her shoulder and kissed the top of her head.

"I don't ever tell you how grateful I am," he said. "Do I?"

"No need," said Cat. She turned to her screen and read *Why stra.* "Before Lloyds," she said without looking at him, "you looked after me and the twins pretty well, for years. We owe you. And it is good, what you do. It is worthwhile. It is a bright light in a naughty world. I don't ever tell you that, do I?"

Gervase moved away, as if embarrassed. Cat wished she could summon up the eloquence she squandered every day on copywriting, could turn and stand up and take him by the shoulders and shake him and say, *"Look, I don't mind keeping us going, you work as hard as I do, just because I bring in more money doesn't mean you're worth less. Truly, truly, the more of this meretricious cheap rubbish I write for these crummy PR liars, the more I realize that even the smallest gesture towards human values is always going to be worth making. Believe me, it's true . . ."*

But she could no more have said such things to Gervase these days than fly around the room. "Talking of naughty worlds," she said, "do you have any ideas about what might make a cork board and some coloured pins into an exciting concept?"

Caroline went into hospital with high blood pressure on the same cold January day that her sister was banned from driving for twelve months. Two days later, after an exhausting and dangerous labour, Maria Annunciata Halliday was born. Alan was in Dortmund, sewing up a European broadcasting deal in the company of his former girlfriend Madeleine Minton. He received the news by fax from his father-in-law in the Whips' office at the House of Lords. It was pushed under the door of his hotel room, and he waved it towards the girl who was dressing, silhouetted prettily against the window.

"We are a father," he said. "Girl, eight pounds three ounces. You'd think they'd have metricated it by now, wouldn't you?"

"Caroline all right?" said the girl, who knew Caroline quite well.

"Oh God, yes. She's in the Portland, no expense spared."

"You flying back?"

"No, we've got to see Hauptmann again. Annie's organized some flowers, and my father-in-law's been round there, and all her mad bloody brothers and sisters are bound to pitch up. I'll fly tomorrow night as per. The baby'll be asleep, anyway. That's mainly what they do for weeks, isn't it?"

"Search me," said Madeleine, throwing on a red cashmere serape. "OK, ready."

High over Great Portland Street, in a bright private room, Caroline woke from a drugged nightmare sleep. She lay and wept for an hour, not ringing for the nurse, gazing helplessly through the clear aquarium sides of the little cot beside her where a humped, wrinkled shape lay quietly breathing under a light green blanket. "Mummy," she whispered. "Mum, I want you." At last the nurse came in, blonde and bright, with a tray of breakfast.

"All right, Mrs Halliday? Your sister's come, isn't that lovely?"

But it was not Cat, who had no lift to the station because there was a cow in labour and Martin could not be spared from the anxiety and hauling. The visitor was Lindy, bearing a florist's bunch of roses in a violent chemical pink. Caroline, who was not close to Mark and who had certainly never thought of his wife as a sister, was caught off-guard, wiping her eyes furiously on the silk sleeve of her robe and scrabbling to reclaim her perfect social manner from the snivelling ruins of the morning.

But it did not matter how Caroline looked. Lindy's eyes were all for the baby, wriggling a little now under the sterile coverings of the cot.

"Ooh, in't she gorgeous," she breathed. "Oh, Caroline, you are lucky. Oh, I do hope – I wish Mark—"

And she, in turn, burst into tears, leaving Caroline to mop her own face, dab her nose with powder and sit looking in helpless perplexity at this unexpected result of her childbearing. Robert had left the country again briefly; it was another day before Alan first called for a brief look at his daughter and two before Mark arrived, bearing perfume and bluff congratulations. It was Thursday when Cat managed to escape from Northamptonshire and fit in a visit after an Eden meeting.

"She's lovely," said Cat. "But I don't suppose by the look of you that *you* feel all that lovely yet."

There was at least some comfort for Caroline in Cat's dour matter-of-fact acceptance of her misery. None of the others, she reflected, brought any comfort at all. She would have liked to see Toby, just for the jokes, but for some reason he could not be contacted anywhere by Robert's faxes or Cat's telephone calls.

"Still, he always looks in at his agent's in the end," said Cat comfortingly. "He'll be in touch."

In the flurry of their daily lives, topped by the excitement of the birth, none of the family noticed a small item in the *Evening Standard*, later repeated in few words in the side-bars of the morning papers. It merely stated that a chorus dancer had been killed outright in a freak accident at a dress rehearsal, when her skull was shattered by a falling hammer. The tool was apparently left, said the newspaper, balanced on the overhead grid by a stagehand who had walked out in an earlier dispute. The man was a casual worker who could not be traced. The theatre was making no comment pending legal advice. The dead girl was named as Miss Teresa Tanner.

But none of them had ever known Topsy's surname, still less that she was a Teresa, named twenty years before by a sentimental Liverpool Catholic father in honour of the Little Flower of Lisieux.

Toby lay on the narrow, sagging bed high above the Gimmix
computer-game shop, his hands behind his head, staring at
the ceiling. He had not left the flat for three days. Two of
Topsy's friends from the chorus had arrived, red-eyed, and
collected some of her personal things to take up to her parents
in Liverpool. They had offered Toby a lift up there in Topsy's car,
for the funeral. He had lain unmoving on the bed and said: "I'm
not too good at funerals. Not my thing."

He could tell they were disgusted. It did not matter. Nothing
mattered. Sometimes he got up and used the lavatory in
Topsy's tiny shower room. Sometimes he ate a piece of stale
cheese or a biscuit from the scuffed cupboard which acted
as her larder. He knew he would not be there for ever, and
that he lacked the will to lie there and die. Eventually he
would get off the bed and leave the flat to find more food.
At that stage it was pretty certain that Topsy's landlord –
who knocked occasionally and shouted through the door –
would have the locks changed before he could get back up
the stairs again.

That didn't matter either. A curious white blankness filled his
head. He identified the texture of it: it was, quite obviously,
milk of magnesia. His mother used to give him milk of magnesia
when she judged his stomach to be upset. He would spit it
out in long, viscous white streaks across the room, and laugh.
Usually she would give up after that, though sometimes Cat
would make him take it and he would obey. The other kids,
in Washington and in France, had never heard of the stuff.
Diana had seemed to lose faith in it later, and on holidays

from prep school he never observed Mark or Caroline being dosed with it.

Anyway, here it was, in his head. Milk of magnesia, white and bland and viscous. Toby shuddered, tasting it in his throat.

Maria Annunciata Halliday fed at her mother's breast for only three sticky, hostile days. Caroline, deeply appalled by the ungainliness, the splitting and stretching and humiliating windy mess of her childbirth, wanted only to be healed, to be virginally gowned once more in crisp pure white cotton from neck to ankle. She did not want, she told the nurse hysterically, any more of this undressing and sagging and leaking. The nurse was calm and professional, and offered Caroline an opportunity to talk to a counsellor and reconsider.

"Breast-feeding really is proven to be best, you know," she said almost apologetically. "It needn't be for long, just a few weeks." But Caroline wept and stormed so that Alan flinched and sharply ordered the hospital to do as it was told. He was, after all, paying. So the nurse took Maria Annunciata away and fed her carefully and professionally from a hygienic bottle of scientifically formulated baby milk. Caroline was given neat pills on a clean tray to dry up her swollen, leaking breasts. By the time the two of them went home to the house in Kensington and a discreet, professional, careful maternity nurse, Caroline seemed her old calm self, her fair hair in a girlish Alice-band above her perfect Madonna's face.

Visiting them, Cat found Caroline alone in her studio, drawing. "Baby asleep?" she asked lightly. Her sister glanced up at her, and it seemed to Cat that the beautiful face looked sharper, the eyes unaccustomedly hostile.

"I don't know," she said. "She's with nurse. Go up if you want." She made no move to accompany Cat, but turned back to the drawing board. The older woman hesitated, then turned on her heel and went upstairs towards the sounds of activity, where firm footsteps moved to and fro and drawers were being pulled in and out in the former guest room. She found a neat round-faced woman engaged in putting away soft piles of terry and muslin nappies, and a baby with a quiff of white-blonde hair lying in a smart mahogany cradle.

"I'm Caroline's sister," she said. "You're, er—?"

"Alison Harper," said the nurse. "I'm glad to have a chance to meet you."

Cat looked away from the baby which had irresistibly drawn her attention with a small, beguilingly flailing fist and a wide pink yawn.

"Why?" she asked baldly. The nurse pressed her lips together in a dry humourless smile, acknowledging the challenge.

"I'm only here another week," she said. "I'm booked for another lady. Mrs Halliday has asked *me*" – she emphasized the pronoun, incredulously – "to interview nannies for Maria. She has asked me to make the appointment without reference to herself."

"Oh," said Cat. "Like that, is it? I thought perhaps it was just today. I hoped it was just that she was busy drawing when I arrived."

"Mrs Halliday spends a great deal of time at her drawing," said Miss Harper, with the air of one who hopes that her point will not be missed.

"And Mr Halliday?"

"It is not my place to pass comment."

Cat tired of this Kensingtonian discretion, and felt a strong impulse to shake the woman.

"Are you telling me that you think my sister has not bonded with this baby? That she doesn't like it? That she's depressed?"

The nurse made a movement of revulsion from this frankness, but fell into a more relaxed posture as Cat continued: "—because I know that already. I think she's in trouble. I thought so in hospital, and seeing her now, I know perfectly well that she is. I'm going to try and take her home with me for a while."

The professional demeanour of the nurse crumbled, and suddenly she became just a kind, smiling, confiding middle-aged woman who put down the folded nappies in a careless heap, moved impulsively to the cot and drew a finger lovingly across the baby's soft cheek. "Oh, she's a lovely baby. Really lovely. I've been so upset, I really didn't know what to do. Mr Halliday got quite annoyed when I – oh, dear."

"Mr Halliday is a bit of a bastard," said Cat conversationally. "I think that's probably part of the trouble. If she comes home with me for a while it might be better. Although I do live in a freezing tip of a farmhouse, and I am too busy to act as a full-time nanny so she'll have to pull her finger out."

"The main thing," said the woman, picking up the baby and handing her, without being asked, to her aunt, "is to get mum and baby together. To get baby properly loved. That's the main thing, isn't it? Not a pretty nursery."

"How did you ever end up as a high society nurse?" enquired Cat, nuzzling Maria Annunciata's warm floppiness.

"It's very good money," said Nurse Harper.

Lindy stood alone in her bright, primary-coloured kitchen, leaning on the smooth top of an island unit and puzzling over the calendar. The brief moment in the hospital when Caroline's baby lay in her arms, moulded to her breast and shoulder, seemed to have left her with a permanent burning imprint. The smell of newborn skin was in her nostrils and a raging unappeasable need tightened her chest until she felt she could hardly breathe. Lindy had known she wanted a baby, but not how much. Now she was counting days since her last period, not because she had reason to think herself pregnant but to find out how many more days it would be before she could allow herself the luxury of suspecting that it might be so.

The telephone rang. It was Mark.

"Cat rang me earlier, on her way in to London," he said. "She was wondering where Toby is, to see if she could drop in and tell him about Caroline's baby. She left some messages at his agent's and in Scotland, but he hasn't rung. She said to ask you if you'd been in touch with Topsy or anything, since you two seemed to be getting on well over Christmas."

"No," said Lindy, with a sharpness in her voice which made Mark, alone too at his desk, feel unhappy without knowing why. "I wouldn't know where to get hold of her."

Nor want to, she thought, replacing the phone with a snap. Topsy, stupid name anyway, was pregnant and not even *married*. Hadn't even had to *try*. No fellow-feeling there, definitely not.

When Cat came downstairs from her conversation with Nurse

Alison Harper, she was prepared to take a firm line, to bully her younger sister until she admitted that something was wrong and agreed to come and stay at Knoll Farm for a spell with the baby. She was prepared to combat any amount of bright pretence, social hauteur and plain reluctance: the sight of the baby, unloved in that sterile smart nursery, had stirred her profoundly. In the event, she did not have to make any effort. By the time she reached the little studio Caroline was crumpled over the drawing-board, sobbing her heart out.

"Oh Cat, it's Alan. He didn't ever love me, you know. I was just a trophy, I know it now. He says I'm frigid."

"Bastard," said Cat. "Oldest line in the book, the adulterer's standard excuse."

"No, but the thing is, I *am* frigid. I can't stand—"

"For God's sake, you've only just had a baby. Nobody fancies making love for weeks, months sometimes."

"I didn't much, before," said Caroline, sniffing. "Not all the long drawn out goings-on, anyway. Maybe I didn't love him, either."

"Oh God," said Cat, sitting down on the arm of a chair. This was a confidence too far. She was not up to it. Caroline turned to her, tearfully appealing.

"I know what you're going to say, I do know, Maria Annunciata needs her father and me, I have to do my duty. I will, honestly, when I can *bear* it, but every time I see her I just feel—"

She burst into a passion of tears. Cat looked steadily at her, with a mixture of weariness and compassion which was becoming all too familiar.

"Feel what?"

"Feel *raped*," burst out Caroline. "Oh Christ, it's all so disgusting!"

Cat sat looking sadly at her sister. Once, she had burned with envy of that fragile beauty, that quivering aesthetic sensibility. Even at eight years old Caroline had made her, at twenty, feel like a cart-horse, lumpish and jealous and coarse. Not any more. The tables were turned, and it was Caroline who patently could not cope with real life. Maybe, thought Cat, looking like a Renaissance statue and studying Renaissance paintings was a rather poor preparation for the actual experience of mating and motherhood. Maybe poor Caroline would have done better at both if she had specialized in Hieronymus Bosch and the postcard art of Donald McGill. Now she merely looked broken. Lucretia, raped.

But at least there was to be no trouble in transporting this marble Lucretia to the muddy world of Knoll Farm. All Cat had to do was say "Come and stay. Just while Alan's away so much, and Maria's so little. For a month or two, perhaps. It's not an imposition, you can give me the odd lift in for the shopping while I'm banned. Gervase would love it, too. He likes baby creatures."

Caroline gratefully agreed, too whelmed in her own emotion even to remember that part of the Christmas night conversation which concerned Gervase and babies, let alone notice the oddness and the generosity of her sister's making that particular remark.

They arranged for Caroline to be driven up at the weekend by the nurse, who would spend her last few days' employment settling the baby into a routine in the alien surroundings of Knoll Farm. Before she left, Cat asked: "You haven't heard from Toby?" And absently, Caroline said, "No . . . I suppose he might be abroad with one of those pop groups."

In the end, it was Mark who found the clue to Toby's silence. In his office, tapping his pen on the leather-framed blotter, he sat chilled for a moment by the unease which Lindy's sharp "No!" about Topsy had given him. The unease transferred itself to the question of Toby. His mercurial elder brother had always been more of a tormentor than a friend to slow, careful Mark. But all the same, Cat sounded worried and Cat was – in the schoolboy slang he inwardly used to himself – a good egg. Of all the family, only she was ever really nice to Lindy. And he, Mark, was efficient. He was better placed than any of his extended family (except perhaps Alan, who would never bother) to find things out. He lifted the phone and pressed the button for his secretary.

"*Mademoiselle from Arminteers*?" she said, when Mark had spoken. "Ooh, yes, I heard. It opened last night. About the war, with a lot of dancing. My friend was saying something about it being unlucky, like *Macbeth*. I'll ring the theatre. My friend knows people there."

Within ten minutes Mark knew that there had been a death, that the dead girl was blonde, young, christened Teresa but known universally as Topsy. When Cat got back to Knoll Farm (by train, long chilly wait at the station, slow local bus and two-mile walk) she found a message in Gervase's flowing italic handwriting telling her to ring Mark at home. The house was empty: Gervase was out at a Country Landowners' Association meeting, Martin was walking round the farm in the dusk checking gates and stock, and the racket from the bunkhouse suggested that Duane and the new boy Winston were comparing tastes in hard rock music. She stood by the telephone and dialled Mark's number, but when he had been speaking for a moment she sat down, suddenly, on the floor and put her head against the warm stove for support.

"Oh God, how awful. And Toby?"

"My secretary rang another friend of Topsy's, and she said he wouldn't go to the funeral but he'd been living in Topsy's flat. The phone's cut off. She gave me the address."

"I'd go there," said Cat helplessly, "only it takes half a day to get to the station at the moment, and I've got Caroline coming up with the baby for a bit because she's not feeling too good, and I'm up all hours working on some new rubbish for – for someone I work for. Oh, Mark – do you think . . . ?"

"I might not be the best person," said Mark. "You know me and Toby. Shall I tell Dad?"

"He's in Croatia," said Cat. "Caroline would be better, but she's not exactly up to much right now."

"I'll go," said Mark. "I'll come up to town early tomorrow. If there's any time Toby's bound to be in, it's early morning. Don't blame me if he bites my head off."

In the event, any of them could equally well have made the visit. The flat was empty, and the landlord, a thin seedy-looking man who inhabited the first floor alone, was volubly thankful to be rid of his unofficial tenant. "He left yesterday morning," he said, distractedly smoothing back his thinning hair as he led the visitor up the stairs to view the property. "I don't expect him back, no. He wasn't paying rent, and

Miss Tanner was two weeks behind when the tragedy happened. I wouldn't think of pursuing any claim against her
family."

Mark paid, without hesitation, a hundred and fifty pounds for
two weeks' outstanding rental on the bedsitter. Something about
its shabbiness, exotically relieved with tattered theatre posters
and a luminous orange bean-bag, touched him at a deep level
he rarely acknowledged. Poor little Topsy. He did not, despite
the landlord's continued hinting, offer any rent for the further
fortnight that Toby had spent alone there.

That night, Mark reported back to Cat on what he had and
had not found. The call was cut short by the wailing, bustling,
nervously chattering arrival at Knoll Farm of Caroline, the baby,
and the nurse.

Toby, meanwhile, was walking slowly through the sodium half-
light of a London street, a chip-bag open in his hand. Sometimes
he paused to look in a shop window, absent-mindedly pull a long
greasy flopping strip of pale potato from the bag, and put it in his
mouth.

As he came along the side-street near what was once Topsy's
flat, he stopped in front of a grimy grocery where he and she
had picked up random ingredients for their meals together.
The owner was an affable Cypriot, nicknamed "Ataturk" by
Topsy. On his counter was a collecting-box for change marked,
in felt pen, with the words "COMUNITY FUND; HELP TAKE
LEAKAEUMIA KIDS TO DISNEYLAND PARIS". Toby approved
of Disneylands, having served briefly as Wild West Goofy in
Anaheim in 1972. He also approved of the scruffy unofficial
look of the tin, and the spelling. He had often put his change
in it.

The shop's front door was locked already, and the Venetian
blinds half-closed. As he watched idly through the gaps, Toby
saw Ataturk clearing and wiping the freezer tops and the counter.
He had emptied the till into a large leather bag and now, with a
practised and routine gesture, he picked up the tin, twisted off
its base and without looking at its contents poured them into
the same bag. He set the tin back neatly on the counter in its old
place, drew the string of the leather bag tight and put it inside

his padded nylon jacket before pulling down the burglar-alarm switch and vanishing through the side door.

Toby saw this from the pavement, and for the first time in the weeks since the accident he began to weep.

12

Duane and Winston, to the surprise of their probation officer Mr Willetts, would talk of nothing but the baby when they went for their March appointment. They saw him in his cramped office one after the other, their times being fixed so as not to inconvenience the Hartleys overmuch, given their transport problem. Mr Willetts privately thought it quite diabolical that the court should have disqualified Mrs Hartley, who was so careful and pleasant and had been so tolerant of generations of his troublesome young clients. That woman, he thought grimly, sacrificed her home life to a social project in a way that few wives, even farmers' wives, would consider. He burned with indignation when he thought of her driving ban and its circumstances; but the only way a probation officer could properly express such rebellious thoughts was by making it easy for her to bring the boys in for their appointments and, on occasion, offering to drive them back.

He had had many conversations, over the years, with youths who were working their time at Knoll Farm supported by Gervase and the charity. Some of his more advanced colleagues sniffed at the scheme, but Mr Willetts thought that by and large the experience – a good old-fashioned kind of social philanthropy – seemed to do young men good. Some of the town-bred boys in particular had softened into real enthusiasm for the animals and the land, chattering about it, boasting of their new dexterity with sheep-shears or piglets like the children they had never been allowed to be. Others, he admitted to himself, showed no noticeable improvement; but nonetheless they emerged with more muscle on them, and brighter eyes and less pasty faces as an effect of working long hours out of doors and eating proper food. One, to Gervase's visible horror and Mr Willetts' amusement, had become so handsome after six months' plain home cooking and fresh air that he now earned a respectable living out of modelling leisurewear for mail-order catalogues.

Only a very few, like Gary (now serving two years for dealing in prohibited substances), remained utterly unchanged and unimproved in any way by Knoll Farm, and as sullen as ever. It was a pity, a terrible pity, thought Mr Willetts, half-listening to Winston, that it had to be Gary who was filmed for that television report. Still, with luck the programme wouldn't think to follow him up a year later. If they did, it would reflect most unfairly on the record of Knoll Farm. The project, on balance, was a modest success.

Never before, though, had two successive clients spent their time in the probation officer's presence speaking exclusively of the beauty, cleverness, charm and rapid growth-rate of a baby. Duane became almost articulate in his praise of "Mary-Annie" as she now seemed to be called.

"She's really cute, yeah? She's got this little quiff of gold hair, and she's smiling all the time, big grins wiv no teeth, she's ace. Me and Winse, we do her bottle when Mrs Hartley lets us. Sometimes she gobs all over us, but we dun' mind. An' the shit is just *revolutionary*. Wicked. It's yeller, an' it actually smells OK."

Winston was more scientific in his approach. "It's ever so clever, how they learn things. Stick your tongue out, they stick theirs out back. First time Mary-Annie heard that cow mooin' out, she jumps out of her skin, all right? Next time the cow moos, she don't do nuffin. We worked out that she's learnt the score, OK? She knows it din't hurt last time, so it won't hurt this time. S'like a computer. An' she can grab things now. Just about, anyway. She can swipe."

Mr Willetts listened to this in wonderment, and later walked down with Winston to meet Cat and Caroline in the car park. The back of the little car was jammed with bags and boxes of food, and Caroline was sitting at the wheel reading the *Daily Mail*. Cat was a few yards away, studying a noticeboard about an imminent Midholt Choral Society rendering of Monteverdi's *Vespers* in the Corn Exchange. He joined her.

"This baby seems to have got the boys going," he said. "They wouldn't talk about anything else."

Cat laughed. "Yes, isn't it amazing? Martin started it, giving her a bottle on the first night while he ate his supper with the other hand. Seems he's got a little sister at home he helped bring up. The younger ones then decided on the spot that Real Men *can* play with babies, and that was it."

"It isn't too much strain, for you? Having your sister and the baby and the boys and Martin too? It's a very full house for a working lady."

She looked gratefully at the big, moon-faced, kind man she had known officially for so long.

"No," she said. "Thanks for asking. But really, the house hasn't run so well for years. I'm secretly enjoying the holiday from driving, you know. We all love Mary-Annie, she's the easiest baby there ever was, and I think it's doing my sister good to be in a busy house. She was very much on her own in London."

Mr Willetts glanced at Caroline, sitting passively at the wheel, still reading her newspaper although Duane and Winston had climbed in behind her and were laughing and pointing at something beyond the car park. She was wearing dark glasses in defiance of the season, and her smooth face had a shuttered, emotionless look.

"Good, good," he said vaguely. "Well, any problems, remember we're here. We appreciate you, you can make calls on us. And with Duane, perhaps, particularly, it might be wise . . ."

". . . not to rely on him as a babysitter," said Cat. "Oh, indeed. Still less Winston. Duane might panic, or stick a pin in her by accident, but he's restful. Winston would keep her awake all evening doing hand-eye co-ordination experiments. He thinks she's a computer game. Anyway, Martin babysits like mad, and he's practically a Norland nanny, he's so good. He's taught Winston all about zinc and castor-oil cream. We're in clover."

"And Mr Hartley, how's he taking the extended family?" said Mr Willetts.

"Oh, Gervase is a saint. We all know that," said Gervase's wife lightly, and took her leave.

When Robert Gratton came back from Croatia with much

achieved and much to think of, he found the answering machine in his London flat crowded with messages from his children. Mark's and Cat's ordered him to ring them as soon as he got back, and both asked, had he heard from Toby?

Caroline's said she was staying with Catherine and if Alan rang, please to let her know, because he was travelling a lot and calls could be difficult and her answerphone didn't seem to be working very well on the remote control.

Alan's, which followed, made no mention of Caroline or his baby or indeed of being abroad, but asked in smooth tones for more help on a business introduction Robert had mentioned at Christmas.

Then there was another one from Cat, rather peevish in tone, suggesting that she had assumed he would be back by now and *had* he heard from Toby? Robert spun the tape on, gabbling through several unconnected messages from political contacts, and reached the end of the tape. So clearly, Toby hadn't been in touch. No surprises there.

But when he listened to the rest of the tape later, after he had unpacked his neat dark leather case, he found that Toby had, in fact, rung. It was too brief to be noticed on fast forward, but between a reminder from the Chief Whip's secretary and an invitation from a charity a familiar voice, familiarly a little drunk, said: "Dad? I'm – oh, bugger it," and hung up.

Of course, Robert did not yet know about Topsy, *née* Teresa, and so it was the next day before he rang Cat and received his share of the family shock. She also, in few and spare words, filled him in on the continuing alienation of Caroline from her baby.

It stirred uncomfortable old memories in him, memories of the only bad times he ever had in his long love of Diana. As clearly as if she were in front of him he saw a fair and fragile mother, drifting around disconsolately in a big house in Washington, disliking a pale, pudgy baby Mark, looking for trouble. He felt a sudden rush of emotion for his elder daughter, a surge of pure thankfulness that she had not allowed Caroline to stay alone with the baby in that smart dull Kensington house with that smooth cold Alan.

"Can you come to lunch?" he said. "Westminster Old People's home, as ever?" Cat, slightly to his surprise, agreed with alacrity to meet him at the House of Lords. Things were easier at home, she explained, than they had been. Caroline seemed rather to enjoy driving people around lost in her own world at the wheel, so there was no trouble about getting to the station. The household was working well, with Martin frying up American breakfasts for everybody and persuading Marianne to come up almost every weekend. Caroline, though silent and depressed, did her share of the cooking and seemed actually to prefer this to the company of her baby. Gary's mother was coming in two mornings a week for the heavy cleaning, glad of the money and the moral support now her son was in prison. Gervase had finished with lambing and was far less tired, and the two boys forever hovered helpfully around the baby. Suddenly, it was easy to get to London. She needed to fix a meeting with Eden anyway. So she would come to the House of Lords the next day at one o'clock.

"Would Caro like to come too, perhaps?" said Robert tentatively. "If there's someone to mind the baby?"

"I have no doubt she would. But she isn't coming, and don't tell her. She can come on her own another time. We've got things to discuss."

By the time Cat stood waiting for Robert under the low stone arches of the House of Lords' lobby, she had one thing more to talk about. Walking out to the car that morning ahead of Caroline, she had intercepted the postman in the lane to see if there were any late amendments from Eden on the spring staff magazine. There were, as she suspected, five bothersome pages of quibbles to read through on the train. But there was also a postcard from Toby.

Standing now near the security desk in the mellow light of the vaulted stone lobby, she pulled it out again. Her father was in sight, but deep in conversation with a thin-faced man in a blue suit. A lord of incredible antiquity shuffled past her, his old back bent, murmuring "Beg pardon, m'dear". His arms did not take to being raised above shoulder height, and he began to make lunging unsuccessful attempts to get his coat on the hook which bore his name. Like nursery-school, really, Cat thought. She stepped forward to help him, dropped the postcard as she did so, accepted his courtly snuffling thanks, and turned to find

Toby's card trapped beneath the tiptoe shoe of a stout peeress. When she retrieved it there was a clear pointed toeprint across the text, which annoyed her immoderately.

She looked for a moment at the picture of Dover harbour, then turned it over again and re-read it. When Lord Gratton extricated himself from the conversation of Lord Gilbrand (with whom, things being tight in the lobby, he shared a coat-peg) she was frowningly intent on the trampled slip of card.

"Lo, darling," said her father. "Sorry to keep you."

"No – it's fine," said his daughter distractedly. "I've been trying to make something out. Toby's writing."

"Oho!" said Robert with something like joviality. "So he's surfaced! Good, good!"

"Not quite," said Cat. "Come on, for God's sake let's go through, before I get trampled by any more of these dinosaurs." Irritably, she hunched her shoulders, jerking her head towards the latest group of elderly men and women arriving for a subsidized Palace of Westminster lunch. "I'm sorry, I know you all do good work and all that, but it gives me the creeps."

"Why, especially?" asked her father, amused. He led the way beneath the vaulting and turned left. "Not that it doesn't take me the same way, some days. But why does it get you?"

"Oh, because of the boys on the farm, I suppose, and how hopeless it is trying to do anything about the way their lives go," said Cat, looking with distaste at a particularly florid hatchment. "Because of Noreen in Hounslow all these years with the planes flying overhead, and Marianne earning peanuts in that psychiatric ward, and Dave having to crawl to some Omani foundation to get his research funded. Just *because*! This building is so fusty I want to turn a hose on it."

"Child of the sixties," said her father fondly. "It isn't turning a hose on things that makes them into new shapes. It's drip, drip, drip that does it. We drip and drip on Parliamentary bills, we improve them, and that improves things for all your Noreens and Garries."

"Oh, I don't too much care about Gary," said Cat, as they turned into the dining room. "You can turn a hose on him, anytime. Do you know his mother got pulled in on Boxing Day for questioning, on suspicion of knowing about his drug stash? Gervase was down at Midholt station with her half the day. She was in tears."

"He's a good man, Gervase," said Robert. "I have no idea how he got that way, given Artemis as a mother. Do you know, she spent all that walk to the Rector's going on about how homeless was only a trendy modern word for "feckless"? On Christmas Eve?"

"Gervase is still rebelling," said Cat. "The world probably owes Artemis a great debt. If it wasn't for her, he'd probably be an ordinary country gent with no imagination."

"What was his father like? Does he ever say?" asked Robert, interestedly.

"Oh, you know. Bless the squire and his relations, and help us keep our proper stations. All that. But look, Dad, I want to talk about Toby. And Caroline. But especially Toby."

She pushed the postcard across the table to him, and he put a pair of wire-rimmed glasses on his nose and frowned at it for a few moments.

"Hmm. Postmark Dover. Picture of Dover. That seems clear."

"It ties in," said Cat. "Mark rang his agent, Louis or whatever his name is, and apparently Toby turned up looking pretty dirty and a bit manic, and asked if there was any money for him. There was two hundred and fifty pounds due, so Louis advanced him that. And he picked up his passport."

"What was that doing there?"

"Apparently he leaves his passport at the agent's, and a few documents – birth certificate, all that stuff Mum made us each take over when we were twenty-one. Toby says he'd only lose them, so he leaves them with Louis."

"So Dover, and a passport," said Robert. "You reckon he's gone abroad?"

"I'd say so. But the thing is, Dad" – Cat's head went forward and her voice broke a little – "none of us have seen him or spoken to him since Topsy – God, that was awful."

Her father looked at her with melancholy understanding. Diana, he reflected, had seen this eldest child as hopelessly prosaic, but as a repressed, discreet diplomat himself, he had always known that behind her calm exterior Cat – like him – suffered from a vivid dramatic imagination. He had hoped she would be an artist or a writer; but maybe the deliberate repression of her romanticism was the reason for her success in writing glib, catchy copy.

Muffled now, her words confirmed his suspicion that she, more than any of them, had suffered some moments of pure horror in the days since she learned about Topsy. "Things falling on your head. I've always been terrified about that. Won't walk under scaffolding. Poor Tops."

"She couldn't have known a thing," said Robert comfortingly. "Not if it fell straight from the overhead grid. There'd be no sound, no rush of air even."

"I think you'd know. A second before. Eyes in the top of your head. You'd know."

There was a silence. The waiter brought them water and took the order. Cat began again: "Anyway, it's Toby I worry about now. I know he and Topsy weren't exactly conventional, but I think he was excited about the baby. He didn't just do his big announcement at Christmas to shock Artemis and annoy Mark."

"Although that was part of it," said Robert gently. "But yes, I know. I wish he'd rung you, or one of the family, when the accident happened."

He looked down at the postcard again, folded up his wire glasses, sighed, and pushed the card back towards his daughter.

"Well, he's an odd one. I remember Diana saying when he was six or seven, when we were on the way to France from Washington, that the reason Toby was so tiring was that you never knew how he would react. You'd be expecting him to be upset and he'd make a joke, and seem quite unconcerned. Like when that dreadful hamster died, in Lille. But at other times, when you thought he'd join in the fun he suddenly wouldn't. Just sit and stare as if he'd seen a ghost."

"I wish he'd rung. I wish he'd come to us," said Cat.

"Yes, but what would he have said, poor devil? He wouldn't have the vocabulary to express something like that. He was never much of what Lord Norwich calls a 'feelings-discusser or a shoulder-leaner-onner'. People like Toby don't start acting conventionally just because conventional tragedies happen to them."

As he delivered this insightful remark, lunch arrived: shepherd's pie for Robert, roast beef for his daughter. They began to eat the comforting nursery food in a gloomy, companionable silence. After a few moments Cat said: "Well, I think he's gone abroad. The postcard."

"It could mean that," agreed Toby's father. "We'll have to think about what he means in that last line. Come back to it. But the other thing. You said Caroline was in trouble?"

Cat had meant to tell him everything, in the hope that her father's concern would be explosively brought to bear on Alan, the son-in-law who admired him – or at least, hoped to trade on his peerage and his influence. She found herself, however, hesitating and qualifying everything. She seemed unable to describe Caroline's problem directly, as she would have to a woman. In these masculine, lordly surroundings, with elderly men of the Establishment tucking into steak-and-kidney pudding all around, it was peculiarly difficult to talk about something as painfully and intimately female as this particular depression and alienation. She stumbled, quite unlike herself, and accordingly became cross and terse.

"Oh, I suppose it's nothing. I daresay she'll be all right. She talks more to Gervase than to any of us. They play chess."

Robert put down his knife and fork and wiped his mouth. "I used to play chess with her in Venice. I taught her when she was five, and we played with the glass pieces Diana bought at Murano." He picked up his glass, and swirled the dregs of the red wine in it.

"What you're saying," he continued after a pause, "is that she doesn't seem to care about the baby."

"I wouldn't put it –" began Cat defensively. Spoken in the House of Lords, masculinity heavy on the air, his words sounded like a harsh condemnation of her sex. "It's sometimes very difficult for new mothers."

"Look," said Robert. "I *know*. I lived with it. Diana really couldn't be bothered with Mark for two years. In Washington. You may even remember that, if you cast your mind back."

Cat flinched. "I remember she cried a lot. And she was always cross. And we had Conchita to help."

"Conchita did all the mothering," said Robert. "It took me a year to realize that. When I tried to talk about you children, your mother always came up with Toby's latest misdeed, or how well you were doing at school. She hardly ever mentioned Mark. Called him 'the baby'. She used to say those words," he continued, after a pause, "rather accusingly. As if he was all my fault."

Cat stirred uneasily. Perhaps, in this new age, one was supposed to talk about these things even with one's own father. Devilishly difficult, it was. Especially cold sober, in the middle of the day. She wished she had arranged to meet him for a drink at his flat. She demurred: "Well, it might have seemed like that. But she had a lot to do. I'm sure she didn't really—"

"She had nothing whatsoever to do," said Robert. "Except cocktail parties in the evening, and spooning with that damn Hungarian count all afternoon."

Cat's embarrassment grew. She steered the conversation back to her own generation.

"It worries me that Caroline was so adamant about not feeding Mary-Annie herself," she began, wildly, although she had not meant to bring this detail up. Robert looked at her and gave a dry, mirthless bark of laughter.

"Diana wouldn't feed Mark. In that Swiss hospital, she took one look and said no. They gave her pills to dry it up. She told me on the phone, after my plane landed in Washington. She'd fed Toby for eleven months. Later on, she fed Caroline for six months."

"Did she feed me?" Cat asked unwillingly.

"Two months. Then she said you were so big you needed solids, you'd wipe her out with the amount you sucked."

Cat could stand this intimacy no longer. She looked at her watch. "Dad, I've got to fly. I've got a work meeting."

Robert, suddenly looking old and tired, reached out a hand and held her arm as she tried to stand up.

"Darling, I wouldn't bring any of this up if I didn't think it might be helpful. I want to know if I should talk to Caroline about all of it, whether it would help her."

"Why might it?"

"Because your mother and I were very happy for ten years, and then again, even happier really, for twenty-seven years.

But there were two years in between the good times which were pretty dreadful. If it had been today, we'd probably have divorced. But people didn't give up so easily, then. I was busy in Washington. I know I didn't do enough for Diana when she was off the rails. We talked about it all, years later. All I'm saying is that Caroline could well be having the same sort of interlude. A new baby, a husband who isn't around or isn't very sympathetic. That's enough to throw someone off the track for a bit. She's lucky to have Knoll Farm, instead of a big stuffy official residence and a Mexican girl."

"But it's different, she's only just married." Cat could not go on. A parallel between her mother's bad time and Caroline's could not be made; Diana had had, and fed, two babies already, and surely, *surely* a well-married woman could not suffer the kind of neurotic physical revulsions which Caroline, almost nightly now, expressed in tears to her sister over their final private tea-drinking session in the kitchen. She looked at her father and blushed. Come to think of it, after three children in seven years there had been a gap of another seven between Mark's birth and Caroline's. Oh God. Why were these things so hard to think about?

In her anxiety to get clear of all this, Cat had lied to her father about her appointment time. When she left the Palace of Westminster, she had an hour and a half to kill before going to Eden, and spent it in a flyblown sandwich bar off Piccadilly, watching skin form on a nasty cup of coffee and re-reading Toby's postcard.

"Tell Caro best of luck to her and the baby," it said. Then in slightly less tidy handwriting: *"Can't seem to get comfortable. Best to go back and start again, I think. Toby."*

What did he mean? She tried to think of Toby, to think like Toby; she conjured up his floppy dark hair, untidy over the collar and treacherously greying round the ears; his humorous, mobile mouth, his arched brows and occasional camp fluttering of the eyelashes to defuse a particularly devastating joke. Because of the uncomfortable talk over lunch, though, this mental Toby kept shrinking and being replaced in her mind's eye by other Tobies. There was the sixth-former, hair down to his shoulders, nonchalantly telling his parents the news that Radley did not want him back at any price but that he had organized a job with Diego at Long Beach. There was the schoolboy Toby who had crossed Europe with her on those rattling, whistling trains, bound for home in Venice; he had once got off at Basle for a dare, and been left on the platform, his white face looking up at her half-scared and half-triumphant in the moments before she pulled the communication cord and started a row with Swiss railways which it took all Robert's diplomacy to cool down ("Herr Hartley, we must insist, if these English children are not fit to travel unaccompanied at this age, you must make other arrangements"). There was Toby in Johannesburg, beaten up at school for telling his Afrikaner classmates that in America and France and "proper countries" black people were considered just as good as white ones. Only Cat knew the reason for the beating-up, and had agreed with Toby that they would not tell their parents because it would only lead to their both being sent straight to English boarding-schools. To avoid this separation brother and sister had conspired to pretend that Toby's fight was precipitated by the usual annoying Toby behaviour. Diana and Robert had accepted this as only too likely.

Sitting at the chipped counter, fiddling with packets of sugar, Cat thought fondly of that Johannesburg Toby. It proved he did have principles, no matter how heavily disguised they might be. Then she thought of him with the nuns, in Lille: cherubic, reciting his nightly *Fable de la Fontaine* by heart, making up the bits he forgot with such panache that sometimes he was not caught out and deprived of his bread-and-chocolate at break-time. She remembered him in Washington, in his Yankee brat baseball hats, running wild and cheeking visiting senators during Diana's bad time; and then saw, as perfect as ever, the moment when she had held the little boy up to see the baby bears in Berne.

God, what a mixture of childhoods they had had, he and she together! What richness of scenery, what poverty of outside friendships, what a crazy claustrophobic bubble they had bounced around the world in, never belonging anywhere! What had he said at Christmas dinner? Something about diplobrats never growing up at all.

Well, she had grown up. If there was one thing her early

motherhood and the poor days in Hounslow had done it was to make Cat renounce childish things. Gervase was grown up, too; that was what she first liked about him when they met. He had lived his childhood, said a polite goodbye to it, put aside play and self-indulgence and shouldered adult responsibilities with a will. She liked that. And Mark had at least covered his continuing childish sulkiness with a façade of dull mercantile respectability, the opposite of his brother's fey irresponsible enthusiasm.

Caroline hardly counted; her life had been different from theirs. Her first memories would be of Venice and she was in Los Angeles until she was eleven; but after that she had become a standard English home counties schoolgirl and then a schoolgirlish habituée of the genteelly English world of art galleries. Caroline was settled, rooted; she belonged clearly in a certain class and in certain very English settings. Not for her that enduring sense that word could come from Whitehall and change your life any day; that nothing would last beyond a three-year posting so you might as well not get too involved.

Cat, fiddling with a plastic spoon at the drab Formica café table, felt a spasm of irritation at her sister. What did she know, her and her day-school friends who spent seven, eight years together and could stay in touch now if they wanted? The effect of foreign postings and a cosmopolitan boarding-school was that the friends of Catherine's childhood and teenage years were scattered across two hemispheres: she had come in and out of their lives like a ghost, and nobody but Toby shared her memories.

Probably, she thought, that lonely fact had actually made her anxious to settle down. She was sometimes conscious of a queer, absurd exultation when somebody – Mr Willetts at the probation service, or Noreen's brother in Hounslow – made a careless remark that indicated that she and they "went back a long way together". She cherished every proof that she, Cat Hartley, had a history of her own now. A personal history, not dictated by the files at the Foreign Office.

This wool-gathering ended as she glanced down again at the postcard, which now bore a dribble of coffee from the unwiped counter as well as the peeress's footprint. *Can't seem to get comfortable. Best to go back and start again.*

• Libby Purves

But where? Cat drank the cold coffee in front of her, grimaced, and set off reluctantly through the darkening afternoon to where, in some neon-lit committee room, the Eden Corporate Outsourcing Motivation Working Party awaited her.

13

"Where?" asked Caroline. "Start again where? What does he mean?" She had been unusually animated since Cat showed her the postcard, with pink spots in her cheeks and a shine in her eyes. "It's such an extraordinary way to express it."

Gervase, Caroline and Catherine were sitting round the kitchen table after supper. The chessboard was out, but for once neither Gervase nor Caroline showed much interest. Cat had work to do upstairs, readjusting her newsletter to be, as the chief nuisance at Eden HQ put it, more "dynamically motivational". Shorter sentences and more buzz words should do the trick, Cat reflected. Perhaps "buzz" itself would be a good buzz word. But she could not bring herself to go up to the study and wrestle with that just now. Caroline and Gervase were anxious to talk. They had both, slightly to her surprise, been fired by Toby's cryptic message into curiosity, compassion and a lust for activity.

"I think he must need help," said Gervase, after first reading it. "You were quite right to talk it over with your father. Where do you think he means when he says 'go back'?"

Caroline chimed in, equally curious. "Do you think he means back to Scotland?" she said. "He met Topsy there, didn't he? When she was up with some Fringe show he wrote, three or four years back?"

"I think so. It was a punk tartan leg-show. KILT WITH KIND-NESS, or something. But that wouldn't explain Dover, would it?" said Cat. "Even Toby wouldn't go to Glasgow via Dover."

Caroline giggled. "He might."

"It's funny," said Gervase. "Here we all are, really rather

worried about the poor sod, and we keep ending up with these surreal Toby jokes."

"It's what he's always been most at home with," said Caroline. But her eye fell on the card, and *Can't seem to get comfortable*. "Poor Toby," she said softly. "It's as if he's never done grief. Doesn't know how to handle it." Cat looked at her sister in surprise. It was the first time she had heard her express pity for somebody else ever since her tearful collapse that night in Kensington.

"How was Toby," asked Gervase awkwardly, "when your mother died?"

Cat frowned, and shrugged. "OK. Fine. Came to the funeral, stayed over with Dad, stayed sober. Didn't say much. He was going around with that group that did his 'Jack and Jill' record, being a publicist I think. Or a roadie, or something. To be honest, I never talked to him about it. You know funerals. All busy and dutiful."

Caroline had risen from the table, and was rinsing the coffee mugs in the sink. She set them to drain and was gone without a word. Gervase looked alarmed. He arched his eyebrows at his wife questioningly.

"*She* was off work for nine months," said Cat quietly. "Remember? You probably don't. We were very busy, we had the bunkhouse full, five boys, everything running full tilt. But Caroline was so devastated when Mum died that she gave up her flat and went to live with Dad in the cottage for nearly a year."

"Oh God," said Gervase. "I put my foot in it just now."

"No," said Cat. "Mark and Dad used to go around carefully not mentioning Mum at Christmas or anything, but I think we ought to. She's always needed chivvying out of her Victorian vapours. She only went back to work in the gallery because Dad got fed up with having her trail around like a pre-Raphaelite maiden, so he sold the cottage and got himself the little flat in Westminster."

Gervase looked unhappy. "Still, poor girl," he said. "It's all a lot to take. Do you know –" his fine features crinkled in concern – "I don't think Alan's really behaving very well. I even wonder if he's the right chap for her."

"Bravo! Give that man a coconut," said Cat rudely, getting up. "I'd better do some work before bed. It's funny, every time today I talk about Toby, in about three seconds flat the subject gets round to dear Caroline's troubles."

She went upstairs, really very angry. Toby was alone somewhere, his lover and unborn baby dead, and still he kept becoming a joke, because Toby had always chosen to be a joke. Whereas Caroline, about whom nobody would dream of joking, had a choice of homes, a beautiful baby she ignored and a rich handsome husband who – Cat disloyally let herself think – she had driven away with her stagey, posed aesthetic coldness. Yet both Robert and Gervase dismissed Toby and fell over themselves to pity and understand Caroline.

"Pah!" said Cat savagely, punching the button on her old word processor. "What I have got, old friend Amstrad, is compassion fatigue. I was a nice person, and no longer am so."

Half an hour later, from along the corridor below her room came a thin, high infant wail. Cat hesitated, then resignedly got up from her desk and went to investigate. Last time she had left Caroline to attend alone to one of the mercifully rare night alarums from the baby, she had followed her into the little bedroom ten minutes later because the screaming did not stop. She found her sister standing over the cot, graceful as an angel in her pure white nightgown and a cashmere shawl, tearfully pleading: "Do be quiet, it's night-time, honestly." Caroline had neither picked up the child nor so much as smoothed the rucked, sweaty sheet and blanket.

Cat had picked up the baby without a word, cuddled her to her tatty flannelette nightshirt and dried the tears. Caroline, also without a word, had vanished back to bed. Something, a sort of horror mingled with a feminine solidarity and reluctant pity, prevented the older sister from telling Gervase about this. But ever since, she had gone to Mary-Annie at night herself.

Cat had no idea how it would all resolve itself. This time the baby, as it happened, only wanted brief assistance to deliver a massive burp. Cat laid her down, kissed the top of the downy head and slipped out of the room. At the end of the corridor the shadowy figure of Gervase was saying goodnight, solicitously, through a doorway to someone who must be Caroline.

Toby walked along the streets of the small, exhausted town,

in the general direction of the Western Docks. His old habit of glancing into shop windows yielded little excitement here in Dover. There was a chip shop, a tired looking wool and haberdashery shop, then two charity shops, another reeking chippie and a heavily barred window behind which radios and cassette machines lay, their casings bleached by too long an unsold exposure to the daylight. Sleet was falling, but he paid little attention to it. He was thinking about death.

He had known deaths in his forty-three years: who could escape it? He faintly remembered a grandfather, seldom seen but mourned at home in an official, embarrassedly British way. News had come to Lille of that death when he was seven, and his mother had taken the three of them to light a candle in the church of Saint-Maurice. "I know it's papist, darling," he had heard her say to his father, "but we expatriate Prods just don't have the rituals available, do we? What do you suppose the Chaplain would recommend? That we drink a glass of sherry in Pa's memory?" Toby had liked lighting the candle and had behaved surprisingly well, hardly needing Cat's restraining hand on his shoulder as they knelt in the side chapel afterwards. Two years later, walking home one evening from the convent, on the corner of the Grand'Place he and Cat had seen a tight crowd and a pair of legs sticking out sideways on the pavement in their midst. The gathering was under a big neon sign of a humped, running ferret which always fascinated him, an advertisement for something called *Le Furet du Nord*. It was Toby who remembered the bang they had heard a moment earlier and tugged Cat's arm.

"Hey, someone's been shot. I bet it's an Algerian." It was a time of Algerian terrorism; Cat's judo lesson with Sylvie and her brother Chrétien was often cancelled because M. Derain was off on a *"cours de déplastiquage"*, learning to defuse the new plastic bombs.

Toby was right. It was an Algerian, a suspect bomber, shot dead moments before by the police. Cat had hurried him past, but the dead feet stayed in his mind. Not unpleasantly: excitingly. Like something in a film.

He walked on. Death as excitement, what a joke. Who could ever have thought that? He, lyricist of the punk anthem "Jack

and Jill they kill for thrill", saw now with awful and private
clarity that there was nothing exciting at all about it. Life was
exciting. Death just stopped you dead. The triteness of the
thought made him suddenly laugh aloud, and the sound of his
own laugh frightened him. He would be shouting philosophical
thoughts at passers-by next, like a bag lady.

There had been other deaths. Later, half a world away, Miguel
had died. His father Diego knew that Miguel and Toby were
beach friends. In fact Toby – a dark, elfin-faced boy who could
in a dim light pass for the paler sort of Mexican – had briefly
lent Miguel his British passport when the cops came, and thus
averted his deportation. That was why Diego and his brother
Pablo gave Toby the job on the burger stand when Miguel died
of the sickness. But that death had not shaken him much, either.
At nineteen, friends come and go for a dozen different reasons,
especially when you have never lived anywhere for more than
three years in your whole life. Miguel had, simply, moved on.
Toby realized with a shock that he had always half expected to
meet the young Mexican again. Probably in a bar in Glasgow.
Most of his old semi-detached friends seemed to turn up there
eventually: it was that kind of city. A hot city, a resurrection
city. Like Los Angeles.

Death, death. It squatted on him now, an idea not so much
horrifying as plain boring. Cat, he knew, believed in something
afterwards, in some sort of ultimate justice, an eventual sorting
out and levelling up of old deserts and old scores. His mother,
Diana, had quite explicitly believed in heaven. "Otherwise, why
would there be all those paintings of it?" she had said flippantly
in the nursing home. When she died, he had not managed to be
as upset as he knew he ought to be; it seemed so obvious that she
had merely moved on to some exquisitely civilized otherwordly
setting, probably a version of the Accademia or the Louvre only
with softer chairs.

But as for himself, he was not sure what he believed or where
Topsy was now. *Whether* Topsy was, now.

Toby found he had stopped again, and that tears were spring-
ing to his eyes. He had no words for this, no words for grief.
Grief was not something in which he had ever had any interest.
Girlfriends had frequently and strongly told him he was an

"emotional illiterate": especially when he burst out laughing at intimate or highly-charged moments in their relationship. Many had left him precisely because of this tendency. The joy of being with Topsy was that there never had been a wrong moment to laugh. She always joined in on a high, glad shriek of merriment.

Toby walked on towards the docks, and the tears on his face mingled with the falling melting sleet. He had obviously missed out learning something, years ago. Whatever thing it was that made other people able to deal with these disasters. That was why he couldn't get comfortable. Best to go back, and start again.

Alan arrived at Knoll Farm one Saturday morning unannounced, his big Saab crunching heavily on the shingle drive. He knocked perfunctorily on the kitchen door and walked in to find a black youth with dreadlocks and scruffy farm clothes playing with a blinking baby in a bouncing chair, which was set in the middle of the large scrubbed wooden table. The boy glanced at him, said, "Hi, man," and continued swinging a red-painted cotton reel on a string just within the baby's reach. "Go on – swipe – yesss!" he crowed. "An' again – backhander – ah, shame!"

"Is Mrs Halliday in?" asked Alan, irritably. This baby was presumably his daughter, although he had only seen her in her first fortnight of life, and mainly asleep.

"Mrs Hartley? Nah. She's gone to Midmarsham, wiv Martin, in the Landy," said the boy, turning his attention back to the baby.

"Not Mrs Hartley. My wife. Mrs Halliday. The mother –" said Alan pointedly, "I presume, of this baby."

"Oh, Caroline. Why din't you say?" said the boy. "She's in bed, I s'pose. Mrs H. got the baby up, and I did her breakfast. She's on a bit of mushed-up stuff now," he added informatively, "only we don't give her eggs because of allergies and bacon's too salty and sausages got additives. So at breakfast she has just milk and a bit of Farex when she's on a growth spurt."

Alan did not reply, but walked through the kitchen, down the stone floor of the corridor and up the back stairs towards the guest bedroom he had occupied at Christmas. Here he found Caroline, apparently asleep. She lay sprawled on her back right across the sagging double bed, her golden hair fanned around her tranquil face, one hand theatrically resting on her breast, and the white broderie of her nightdress parting to reveal a chaste, pale triangle of soft skin at her neck.

He sat down on the bed, heavily. Caroline stirred and rolled her head away from him. Fury filled him, sour and black and sudden. "For Christ's SAKE!" he shouted. "Wake up!"

Caroline hunched, stretched, rolled her head back towards him and opened her eyes. He saw them widen in shock. Heart pounding, she hefted herself up on one elbow and said: "Wha – what 'you doing here? I didn't know—"

"I came to ask you what the hell you're playing at. Seven weeks, you've been here. Do you want a divorce, or what? Your father's been on the phone, it's bloody embarrassing. We're just both making ourselves look silly."

"How you can sit there, after staying away all this time," exploded Caroline, drawing the neck of her nightdress closed, "and coolly ask me if" – she mimicked him "'I want a divorce or what' – you are a shit!"

He glared at her, infuriated by her bleating. "Well, do you?"

"Yes. Since you ask. It hasn't been much of a marriage, has it?"

"Whose fault is that?"

"Yours," said Caroline, promptly. "You only wanted me as a wife for show. Nice blonde art gallery girl, Lord's daughter, suitable for Kensington-stroke-Knightsbridge man on the make. I'm surprised you didn't just order a wife from Harvey Nicks."

"I might as well have," said Alan scornfully. "It always was rather like fucking a shop-window dummy."

"Ohhh!" Caroline fell back on the pillow, tears springing to her eyes. Over the weeks of vague indulged depression, of Gervase's courtly sensitivity and the boys' guileless enthusiasm, she had forgotten how abrasive life with Alan used to be. "I suppose you never thought it was your fault?"

"Couldn't be," said Alan, smugly. "Never had any complaints from anyone else. Still don't have. You've got the problem, sweetie, not me."

"I've had your baby," said Caroline, sniffing.

"Oh yeah. I like your new nanny, by the way," he said sarcastically. "Does he let my daughter chew his greasy dreadlocks?"

"Maria Annunciata is perfectly well looked after," said Caroline. Alan snorted. "Well, I wouldn't know. Bloody typical of you not even to be able to have a boy."

"I want a divorce!" screamed Caroline. "And you'll bloody well maintain me, and her, and keep away from us!"

"That," said Alan coldly, "will be no hardship."

As he passed back through the kitchen, Winston was solemnly peering at the baby over the top of a tin baking tray which he raised and lowered in irregular rhythms. "Peek-a-*boo*!" he said, whereupon Mary-Annie's face broke into a broad, gummy grin and her voice into a crowing explosive laugh. Alan saw only the mess of Farex still hardening on the table, the unwashed breakfast mugs, the wooden stand of socks and underwear airing in front of the range, the cobwebs in the corner, and the scruffy youth making idiot noises at the dribbling infant. He walked past it all and out into the drive. Near his car there was a cloud of snowdrops on the verge and a few crocuses, edges of vivid colour just unfolding from the pale green shoots. He did not see those either, but accelerated his car sharply and drove it hard towards the motorway, London, and his lawyer.

As the grass began to grow, the work of the farm changed. The grazing animals could at last be turned out to fend for themselves, instead of having their food brought to them in heavy bales and buckets. On the other hand, the laborious spring ploughing demanded Gervase's daily attention, and with Martin he walked some ten miles a day up and down the furrows behind the big horses. The two boys, Duane and Winston, could not yet be trusted with a plough except during their two hours' individual daily lesson with Gervase; otherwise they spent the lengthening days mucking out the deep winter litter of the yards with the help of the oldest and most forgiving carthorse. Every two or three days they would break one of the shafts of the cart, and have to stop and mend it. Winston. at least, had been taught carpentry remarkably well at school, so Gervase could leave him to it. All four men came in groaning at five o'clock in dire need of their tea and rest. Martin, whose spirits were high and level, taught them to eat peanut-butter-and-jam sandwiches, and to call the jam jello.

At the beginning of April, Gervase confidently decided there would be no more frost, and made decisions accordingly. After each day's work the three horses were turned out not into the dull yard, but to gallop and roll in soft freedom on the growing grass. The pigs were cleared from the orchard they had reduced to a muddy swamp, and allowed to dig over the turnip and mangel fields for forgotten roots. One of Gervase's small sentimentalities was that he would never ring his pigs' noses to deprive them of the pleasure of digging. The sheep were transferred, in the usual woolly wave of irrational panic, from the barnyard to the hill field.

Cat would take a half-hour break to walk up there in the morning and visit the flock with Mary-Annie on her hip. Every year since her arrival at the farm with her own young children, she had been fascinated by the progress of the lambs. Newborn, they were unsteady and dependent, and stayed close to the mother ewe. Within a week or so, they began to play, jumping on top of the hay in the feeding-rings, butting one another, balancing upon their mothers' placid backs on their sharp little hooves like children on a pile of wobbling foam cushions, legs tense with the effort to stay upright.

Liberated into the field a few weeks later, they would race around in gangs, leaping one another and playing random games which looked deceptively complex. Dave and Marianne used to throw a football in amongst them and watch the group of lambs surge to and fro, knocking it, looking as if they had goals to score. Cat watched the mothers: generally, one or two ewes stayed near the lambs and the others congregated at the far end to graze peacefully in company, ignoring their progeny except when they sauntered back one by one to suckle. "A sure sign," the eighteen-year-old Dave had said when he was considering teaching as a profession, "that school is, in fact, a wholly natural institution."

Then, every year, there suddenly came a day when the lambs stopped frisking. It was as if, Cat thought, the lambs each in turn woke up one morning and said, "Hell, I'm a sheep." What triggered the change she did not know: perhaps it was increasing body weight and the need to feed longer, perhaps the heaviness of a growing fleece. At any rate, when this moment came the young sheep would no longer waste valuable energy in play, nor get stuck in ditches and tangled in wire. Instead they dropped their heads dutifully, grazed, and put on flesh as the farmer would wish.

Their lives, henceforth, would be ruled not by whimsicality or spontaneous surges of life force but by the usual dull ovine exigencies of hunger, panic, flock solidarity, and flight. This regime of dull or frightening imperatives would be, at least for rams and ewes, leavened occasionally by sex; but there was nothing remotely frolicsome about that either. Cat had once been vastly amused by an article entitled "Homosexuality in Farm

Animals: some findings", which she had chanced upon in one
of Gervase's more arcane magazines of alternative agriculture.
The American researcher opined that there were probably a great
many lesbian sheep: but that it proved difficult to gauge because
when a ewe is willing for sex, her behaviour is to stand stock-still
so as to be available for the ram. "So there could," Cat concluded
to Gervase at the time, "be a whole field full of ewes standing
stock-still, lusting after one another and doing nothing about it.
How sad."

Gervase had been passingly amused by the thought – this
was back in the days before the extra land was sold, when
things amused him rather more often than they did now. But
Cat had remembered it, enough to giggle to herself whenever
she passed a field of torpid, stock-still summer ewes. Toby had
liked the joke when she proffered it; Mark seemed slightly
shocked. For some reason she had never felt like telling it to
Caroline.

This year, Gervase's lambing had begun so early that several
of the first lambs had already graduated to being mere sheep. A
few, however, were still young and light, and frisked close to Cat
when she came into the field, unafraid and curious, thrusting
their white noses against her leg. On one such morning, she
knelt upright and set the baby on the grass, supporting its
back against her thighs: the lambs came closer, and allowed
their ears to be assailed by the small fat fists. Cat knelt there
for a while, enjoying the sight of this instinctive baby-to-baby
communication and warding off the bigger lambs from butting
the child. Hearing a sound by the gate she turned, and found
Gervase looking down at her.

"Hi. Look – new stockperson."

He smiled, and stooped to pick up the baby with a practised
movement. Maria Annunciata grasped his nose and ear and
blinked approvingly as he settled her on his arm. It was a
warm day: his shirt was rolled up, and the baby's bare fat leg
lay against his brown, scarred arm. His face, streaked with oil
from the seed drill he had been setting up in the yard, had
more colour and animation than usual. Cat looked at him with
a love which was mixed with a little too much pity. The sight of
Gervase and the baby always filled her with warring emotions.

He should have had one; poor Gervase. He should have let her have one artificially: bloody Gervase.

Her own feelings about the sanctity of natural fatherhood, never as deep as she loyally pretended, had undergone a good deal of change since the outburst of Christmas night. Having Mary-Annie about the house, chuckling and grabbing her toes and beaming toothlessly and falling asleep in positions of comical abandon, had altered all of them to a startling degree. Winston was talking of going to the Midholt FE college to get some GCSEs and study child psychology; Duane seemed to have put on twenty points of IQ in the past month. Martin's repertoire of American hushabye songs was a constant source of general amusement.

Gervase was less effusive about the baby, but took more than his share of her care with ease and grace. He looked younger, and laughed more. Cat herself could bear her work far better now that she could turn gratefully from writing glib management bulletins to the solid benevolent reality of the baby. She no longer saw any attraction in those isolated nights in the London hotel, and only went up by the day, every two or three weeks. Home was where Mary-Annie spent much of the day propped up near her desk, or rolling on a rug, stretching out for rattles and garish plastic squeakers with small, delighted gurgles.

As for the absence of the real father – since his early morning visit to Caroline Alan had sent one cold letter, confirming his wish for a divorce – the loss of him bothered nobody, least of all the baby. The blithe easiness of Mary-Annie's temperament amazed Cat, who remembered the chaos of her own first months with the twins. Indeed in private thought, she had admitted to herself that her passionate Christmas Eve speech in defence of biological fatherhood owed less to rational thought than to her own long-buried resentment of those abandoned days. Tim had left, and there was no man to cheer her and the babies up, only a tearful, staunch but shocked Noreen. Now history had repeated itself and Alan had left; but things were very different. He was replaced by a houseful of men, each more delightedly appreciative than the next, and the baby was thriving on it. Perhaps biological fatherhood was not, after all, so important.

The only cloud over this blessed baby's life, thought her aunt, was that of all the household Caroline was least interested in the child she still formally referred to as Maria Annunciata. She drove her to the local clinic, recorded her weight on the chart provided, and made polite bland conversation when the health visitor called. Beyond that she preferred to spend her day reading, driving around, shopping, helping round the house or drawing at the board she had set up in the guest room. Since the night when Cat had tacitly taken over control by picking up the baby, she had become acutely sensitive to the fact which nobody else in the besotted household had noticed: that Caroline avoided touching Mary-Annie at all.

One evening the sisters had gone together to a free concert by the Midholt Choral Society, where a new arrangement of the medieval carol "I sing of a maiden that is makeles" had been performed. Cat tended to doze in concerts, her mind floating free, solving problems on its own. When the choir sang with sudden a capella clarity the words:

> *Maiden and moder*
> *Was neer none but she*
> *Wel mote such a lady*
> *Goddes moder be*

Cat had jumped, physically jerked, in her seat and turned to the quiet rapt beautiful face beside her. Maiden and mother. Caroline, she suddenly thought, was virgin. This business of not touching the baby's skin, the revulsion she had unguardedly expressed at the birth, was something deeper than mere depression. It was unnervingly odd. *Maiden and mother.* Much could be forgiven a woman whose husband was brutally, insouciantly unfaithful and rejected her so cavalierly at such a time in her life. But all the same, Alan was not the whole explanation. If Caroline had picked the baby up and shaken it, screamed at it, then collapsed in sobbing hugs of remorse Cat could have understood. In all her years of involvement with Gervase's disturbed youths and their womenfolk, she had met across her own kitchen table plenty of stressed mothers. Remembering the worst days in Hounslow, she had been able to sympathize unaffectedly with their mixed feelings about their children.

But this was new and unnatural. Dangerous, even. Caroline should somehow be helped. Often Cat had thought to tackle her on the subject; always her nerve had failed her. A sister was not a good cause, or a client, or a case. And apart from anything else, if they were to quarrel, Caroline might leave and take the baby with her and all this strange new contentment in the farmstead would be gone.

Now, up in the quiet sheep meadow, Gervase finished nuzzling and talking nonsense to the baby and handed her back to his wife as she stood up.

"I was down there loading the pigs," he began. "You know, Sally's litter. They're off, I'm afraid."

He always disliked sending young pigs to the butcher; but these were five months old, and ready. "I kept back one sow, lovely girl, and one pig who might make a boar for Fred Ainsly at Midmarsham."

"Those were the piglets who ran over the Christmas table-cloth," said Cat. "Remember?"

"When Toby and Topsy did their ritual dance? I missed that. I was up the farm."

"I wish we knew where Toby was," said Cat. "I'm still not easy about it." It was the first time in weeks that she had mentioned her brother; Alan's swoop on his wife had taken their attention from the earlier drama. Mark had written to Duncan care of the pub in Glasgow, and received a phone call saying that there was no sign of Toby, but that just after Christmas he had rung up about some clothes and mentioned that he was "shacked up and having a baby". His agent Louis had heard no more since the taking of the passport. Cat thought about him a good deal, but in public the subject had somehow lapsed.

"That's what I came up to talk about," said Gervase, surprisingly. "That and Mary-Annie. It was while I was loading the pigs, Caroline came out to help—"

"She *what*?" Cat was startled. Caroline had never been near the farmyard or any of the animals except to pat a horse cautiously in passing, or admire one of the cleaner-looking lambs.

"Well, she came out just as Martin and I were getting them up the ramp, and I gave her a pig-board to hold."

"Wonders never cease," said Cat. "But what's that got to do with Toby? Or Mary-Annie?"

"Well, I was loading those pigs," said Gervase. "And remembering when they were born, and this year's lambing, and Caroline expecting Mary-Annie. And thinking about young creatures growing up, and – and everything. And it came to me. It's obvious."

"What?" said Cat, although a fluttering, sinking sensation in her chest gave her reason to think that she knew.

"Alan's gone. Caroline's got a lot to sort out, and she isn't well in herself. Alan's put the Kensington house on the market. Suppose Mary-Annie and she just – stayed on here? As their base?"

"With the emphasis on Mary-Annie?"

"Well, yes. Actually, that's what Caroline was really coming out to say. She wants to go to Los Angeles."

Cat moved the baby onto her other arm, and began to walk across the damp grass, towards the gate. Gervase walked with her.

"My sister," said Cat, "wants to go to Los Angeles? Leaving her baby with us. With me. Just like that."

"With us. All of us. She's only going for a week or two. Initially, anyway. There's some Gulbenkian Trust museum conference, and she's got a friend out there who says there could be restoration jobs. The baby would be better off here. Gary's Mum could help. Martin wants to stay till harvest, so he could do the driving while she's away."

Cat was breathing rather heavily. Gervase stopped, reached out in a mute offer to help, and took the baby into his own arms again. Walking on with his long stride down the grassy headland, he continued, half to the baby: "We like having her, don't we? Don't we, beautiful?"

"Of course we do," said Cat at last. "But really, it'll get out of hand. The whole thing, it's weird, it's not right—"

Gervase stopped and turned, barring her way. His face was alight, boyish and pleading, altogether unlike himself. Or, at least, the self she had known for the last decade. So were his words:

"Cat, we made a mistake. I made it. I thought that if I couldn't have a child of my own, and there weren't any babies to adopt, it was more honest and dignified to put all that energy somewhere else. I decided very high-mindedly that I would put all the effort I would have given my own child into helping other people's lost kids. I thought the project and the farm and the charities would be enough."

He eased the baby up his shoulder and rubbed her back. "I thought it would be better to do something honest and useful than having a pretend baby by some pretend scientific method out of a test-tube."

"You're saying you were wrong?" said his wife, slowly.

"I'm saying that there's no such thing as a pretend baby. If the sperm had been from Jack the Ripper, or Robert Maxwell, the baby would have been just as glorious. This one, if you think about it," he kissed Mary-Annie's fat cheek, "is Alan Halliday's. And look at her."

"Yes, but she's not ours," said Cat. She felt dizzy and afraid, not least of her own emotions.

"No," said Gervase. "But she could be." He turned away and began walking down the hill, so fast that Cat, after a moment's astonished paralysis, had to run stumblingly to catch him.

"No!" she said. "We can't adopt a baby! She's Caroline's! Caroline's got to take responsibility! It really is time she thought of somebody other than herself!"

"Oh, she has," said Gervase, slowing down a little as they came within earshot of the yard where Winston and Duane were forking smelly straw into a cart. "That's the point. That's the other thing I was going to tell you. She's also going to Los Angeles because she's convinced that Toby's there."

15

Just as Gervase reached the bottom of the hill, there was a cry of indignation and alarm. Another shaft had broken on the cart, and Duane was blaming Winston. The conversation between husband and wife ended abruptly as Gervase intervened to calm the two boys and the horse. Cat took Mary-Annie back indoors for her nap and returned to her desk. Here, putting aside shock and confusion, she worked steadily at the text of an Eden Welcome pamphlet designed for the induction of young hotel staff. It was to be built, at the Personnel Director's personal insistence, around the buzz phrase: "The Eden Smile".

The Eden Smile tells Eden customers that Eden hotels try hard to be home, she wrote glumly. *Eden people are proud of it: and that pride translates into warmth, consideration, and pro-active efficiency on the customer's behalf.*

She pushed her old kitchen chair back, stretched her arms out as if crucified, and stared critically at the screen. "Translates" would never do for them. Too literary. It would have to go. Pride "turns into" warmth? Or "from that pride springs a warmth", etc?

That might do. On the other hand, the phrase "pro-active efficiency" repelled her so much that she had to avert her eyes from it; but it was the Personnel Director's latest buzz, and must be included. And the pamphlet itself was an extra, paying an extra £500 over and above her retainer. She had insisted on this, in an unwonted burst of commercial hawkishness a few days earlier. Abandoning her normal policy of obliging subservience to paymasters, she had cut up rough, made demands, refused

to come in for a meeting and delivered her financial ultimatum
blithely, by telephone.

Surprisingly, they had met her every demand without a
murmur. Probably she had been undervaluing her services to
Eden for some time, as anxious dependent freelance contractors
often do. It seemed to Cat, however, more as though she had
been magically fortified for the battle by having Mary-Annie on
her knee at the time, pulling at her cheeks and pushing small
intrusive fingers up her nose. Somehow the baby's closeness had
dispelled fear and self-deprecation, and made even dealing with
Eden headquarters into a joke. A surreal, Toby-ish joke. She
had almost said at one point: "I'm sorry, I can't take under five
hundred pounds, I just have too many fingers up my nose."
But the departmental sub-head would probably have thought
this was another of the latest snappy management metaphors,
like "running things up the flagpole" or "going belly-up". In no
time, Eden departmental heads would have been snapping at
one another: "Sorry, JB, scrub round the Stuttgart option – too
many fingers up my nose." Toby would have liked that idea.

"So what the hell," said Cat aloud, squinting at the screen. She
must think of the money and put up with the verbal infelicities
of Eden HQ. She pushed back her dishevelled hair and typed on,
turning out seamless credible glib rubbish, fortified by an infant
niece's innocence and a vanished brother's wayward humour.

Later that day, downstairs in the kitchen, Caroline was scattering
prawns lavishly onto a fish pie. She had offered to make a
financial contribution to the housekeeping, but the Hartleys
had refused it, saying that her willingness to drive the car was
reward enough for her modest keep. Gervase had added that
the small charity which supported the project could always do
with help, if she felt like it.

Cat's housekeeping, however, tended of necessity towards the
plain and plentiful. So it was not long before Caroline had taken
over aspects of the bi-weekly food shopping and begun – with
a personal financial subsidy which was never mentioned – to
introduce her own tastes to the table. Baby corn and mangetout
would appear as vegetables alongside the garden cabbage; stews
would be laced with wine and puddings with Cointreau and

double cream. Cat made fish pies once a week with coley and a great deal of potato: Caroline would volunteer to help, and uneasily insert beneath the potato a layer of fresh giant prawns, sometimes even langoustines, from Tesco's in Midholt. Martha and Gervase would eat the result with enthusiasm, Cat with mild irritation. Duane and Winston would say nothing but just leave their giant prawns on the side of the plate to be devoured later by the aloof, unsociable barn cat.

This particular fish pie, however, was a Caroline creation right from the start: cod, salmon, prawns, mussels, half a bottle of wine, and unseasonal fresh coriander, flown in to the chilly flatlands of Midholt from God knew where. Caroline hummed happily as she made it, for she was thinking of California. The note from her old tutor at the Courtauld, grudgingly forwarded by Alan, had seemed to open a shimmering arch to freedom. Suddenly she realized that from this damp uncertain English spring she could fly in less than a day to all the things she had left at eleven years old. To the dry heat, the long beaches, the palms and the Pacific; the gorgeously arrayed hotel doormen and the general sense of being lapped in relaxed Californian wealth.

She could go now – tomorrow – next week anyway – and be there again, as if the years had never happened. City of the Angels!

Those who knew her in London, through the galleries and the small world of fine-art restoration, would have been astonished to know the fervour with which the refined, gently-spoken, English rose they knew was thinking now of west coast America. They would have understood it better if Caroline had yearned for Prague, or Venice, or Paris. Indeed, she sometimes did: Venice had been the backdrop of her early childhood, and its alleys and prospects and gentle peeling grandeur still lay deep within her and at the root of her career. She had frequently been back there as an adult, first of all at twenty-one as part of her course at the Courtauld, when she gained gratifying kudos among her fellow students for having once properly lived in a flat near the Arsenale. Venice was a continuing part of her life. She had never been back to Los Angeles, or even thought of it.

Yet she thought now that it was LA she had been missing all the time. LA had been the route out of childhood into freedom and a growingly triumphant sense of self. In Venice she had been just the little English girl, obedient to the nuns, kindly treated but not seen as anything remarkable in that city of wonders. In California from the age of seven she had been an exotic: admired and fêted, indulged and listened to. "Hey, honey, sing us that Eye-talian song again! Did you really ride in a gondola?"

In LA it had always been sunny. It had been relaxing, too, to be the only child at home in term-time (except for Toby, somewhere in Long Beach with his illegal Mexican friends). Robert had been busy and important there, so in the house on Las Palmas Avenue she and Diana had become not mother and daughter but sisterly friends, conferring together in cosy girlishness as to how each might best enhance her beauty. There, drifting around the big stores, peering into the windows of Gucci and Cartier and Geary's, Caroline had learnt all kinds of things from Diana: how pale natural blondes should wear black – always with enough glowing skin bare at the neck – how to drape a scarf, how to pause for a heartbeat so that a man could open the door, and smile your thanks without speaking. Here she had absorbed the lesson that a woman, however good her body, looked far, far classier in a one-piece than flaunting it all in a bikini. Here she discovered the woman she would shortly become, a work of art and grace. The child Caroline found a serious joy in the prospect.

That elegant dream had faded with the family's return to the grey UK, and her own enrolment in the dispiritingly prosaic school in Sussex where she wore a hateful grey skirt and square blazer and was expected to play hockey. California became no more than a memory, an atmosphere, a remembered mood. It had never once occurred to her to go back to Los Angeles, any more than it would occur to her that she could be ten years old again. Indeed, it had almost come as a shock, opening the letter so clearly datelined by Marie-Claire, to realize that Los Angeles was still there.

Caroline pushed the pie into the oven, and began to clear up the pans and implements ready for supper. She would go to LA. It would not be self-indulgence; because of course, as she had said on impulse to Gervase, Toby was absolutely bound to have gone there too. In her suddenly exalted mood she knew absolutely that anybody who had once lived in golden California would flee back there if they were in trouble on the other side of the world. Europe was too close, too difficult, too intricate, too unforgiving. California was big and wide and easy. Toby must have gone out there, and got involved as he always did in the rock music business. Marie-Claire lived with a guitarist; she would help to find him, healing his grief by the ocean. Just as she, in that sunny shining place, would get over her own unhappiness. Banging the pots around in the sink, for the first time in months Caroline Halliday began to sing.

Cat came down, pale and stiff from an afternoon at her computer screen, carrying the baby chair and its yawning occupant to the kitchen for her six o'clock milk and stewed apple.

"You sound cheerful," she said. "Have you mixed up Yannie's milk, or shall I?"

Caroline looked down at her baby with hooded unreadable eyes. "Yannie, now?" she said, sombreness overtaking her again. "Yannie?"

"Sorry. It gets shorter and shorter, doesn't it? The boys keep calling her that. Winston says it stops Martin always thinking everybody's talking about Marianne."

"Martin and Marianne. They're quite an item, aren't they?" said Caroline lightly, turning away from the baby to stack some pots in the cupboard while Cat reached for the milk powder and the sterilizer. "She's been up here on nearly all her days off lately. What do you reckon?"

"Well," said Cat, spooning milk into the bottle, "I can tell you one highly significant thing. She's told him her real name."

"Gosh. You mean – er – Mooncloud, wasn't it?"

"Yup. And do you know what he told her in return?"

"No?"

"He told her he is actually christened – wait for it – Martinique. His parents conceived him on a Caribbean cruise."

Caroline straightened up and began to laugh, a carefree new Los Angeles laugh which gave Cat, despite her unease about the baby and the weeks of growing irritation with her sister, a rush of hope and gladness.

"We have to encourage this!" said Caroline. "*I, Mooncloud, take thee, Martinique, to be my lawful wedded husband* . . . wouldn't it be wonderful? Bring the church to a standstill."

"Sssh!" Cat heard the three young men stamping their feet on the scraper outside the kitchen door, and the sound of boots being noisily discarded. She picked up the baby chair and put it on the table. Duane was first in, skidding a little on the lino in his eagerness.

"C'n I give Yan her bottle, Mrs Hartley?"

"Yan, now," said the child's aunt, relinquishing the bottle. "Shorter and shorter." Caroline pretended not to hear this exchange, but concentrated on pulling the film off an expensive pack of imported baby courgettes.

There was no opportunity to talk alone to Caroline that night; she went to bed early, before Martin had gone back to join the boys in the bunkhouse. In any case, neither of the Hartleys wanted to start discussing her future or the baby's before they had talked in private. Gervase abandoned his Rural Housing Trust committee paperwork early to come up to bed when Cat did. She was sitting up against the pillows, waiting for him.

"Did I dream it," she began, "or did you make an extraordinary suggestion up in the field this morning?"

Gervase was silent, pulling off his slippers and socks with exaggerated care.

"Did you," his wife continued remorselessly, "try to suggest that we adopt Mary-Annie as our own?"

"I never said adopt," replied Gervase stiffly, kicking off his trousers and hunting around for the old towelling robe he wore to the bathroom. "I only thought, since it's going so well – blast, where's the belt?"

He struggled for a moment with an inside-out sleeve then resumed, not looking directly at his silent, waiting wife.

"Look, Cat, all through history people have been brought up by their uncles and aunts and grandmothers and cousins. Nineteenth-century novels are full of it. It happened in the war. In Africa nobody thinks twice about it. The Inuit do it. They've got fifteen different words for different degrees of adoption, apparently. All I'm saying is that Caroline needs some time to herself to get straight, and the baby's well off here, and, anyway . . ."

"Anyway?"

Gervase threw his trousers onto a chair and said rather rapidly, staring at the window whose curtain was never drawn. "I was looking at the pigs this morning, and remembering how fast they grew and how important every hour in that orchard had been to them, digging around, having a good life. I thought we ought to do everything we can *now*, for Mary-Annie. She's growing so fast, she's taking everything in. She needs concentrating on. And we—"

"We can do better for her than her own mother?"

"I wasn't going to say that," said Gervase, sharply. "I was going to say, we love her."

Cat was silent for a moment, then: "Yes, we do. I do too. She's the light of my life, if you must know. But it's wrong."

Gervase made a movement but she stilled him, raising her hand and speaking louder. "It won't always be like this. She'll grow up, need to go to school, need all that support. We're both going to be fifty before she's been at primary school a year. We're old farts, Gervase. We're empty-nesters. We're not even all that hot financially, and I don't see Alan paying us child support, do you? Or you taking it, for that matter? And we'll be tired and broke, and she'll be a teenager. It's all just impossible. Caroline is twelve years younger than me."

She paused for a moment, looked at his averted head, and said more softly: "But I do know what you're trying to say about the way she is with the baby. I do love Mary-Annie, and I fear for her. I want to talk about all that."

Gervase grunted, and headed for the bathroom. Cat lay with her hands behind her head, waiting for his return and his reply. When he reappeared, however, she spoke first.

"The thing is that I don't see Caroline staying like this for good. She's had a baby, for God's sake. I don't know what's wrong with her, but she's in some sort of trance. Shock over Alan, probably. Some day the penny's going to drop and she'll want to be a normal mother. Then if we'd virtually adopted Mary-Annie, where would that leave us?"

"Bereft," said Gervase simply. "But it might have been worth it. Specially for Mary-Annie." He pulled back the quilt on his side, and slid into bed beside her, not touching her.

"I didn't tell you," he continued, "but when she said she was going to LA, she had this idea of hiring a Norland nanny and installing her and the baby in this flat in London that Alan's buying her. There's plenty of money."

"Oh, no!" said Cat with real horror. She rolled onto one elbow, looking down at him with widened eyes. "She's just going to – to buy the baby a home and a mother, is she, and bugger off?"

Gervase began to protest, but fell silent. Caroline had in fact made it quite clear that she felt her duty to the baby would be adequately fulfilled by this chilly arrangement. This had shaken him, but for reasons as complicated as Cat's own previous reticence on the subject, he did not want to discuss it.

"Well, if so, she's got us over a barrel," said Cat. "I'm not sending that baby off to some bloody service flat with a hired nanny. We'll formally invite Miss Maria Annunciata Halliday to stay on here. For a bit. As a guest."

"Thank you." Gervase leaned across and kissed her on the temple. "That's as much as it's fair to ask. I am a very foolish fond old man, as King Lear would say. There's something about a baby that is very nourishing, after all these years of young offenders. Perhaps it's the way she doesn't have a probation officer."

"You had Dave and Marianne," said Cat. "They didn't have probation officers."

"No," said Gervase, turning out the light. "But they weren't mine."

Cat opened her mouth to say that this baby wasn't either, but closed it again. She lay awake for some time, listening to her husband's soft regular breathing.

Caroline flew to Los Angeles a week later, having successfully evaded all Cat's attempts to talk seriously to her by a cunning combination of nervous prattle, queenly silence, and sudden gushes of gratitude ("You are super, so kind to look after me like this, I don't deserve it"). As the ground fell away beneath the great aeroplane, she in turn seemed to cast the fetters of earth. It butted through clouds, which skimmed the windows in a confusion of racing mist; then rose triumphantly above them into clear sunshine. Caroline sat back in her club class seat and smiled. Here, up in the sky above the fluffy mattress of cloud, she was whole and pure and clean again, *Maria Assunta*, assumed into the heavens.

Gervase, who had driven her to the airport in Cat's old Renault, was back on the motorway by then and heading for Knoll Farm, her baby and his wife. He found Cat in her attic room, typing furiously with the baby rolling and stretching on a rug alongside. Without turning round, she picked up a postcard from her desk and passed it back over her shoulder to him. It was in Toby's untidy scrawl, bore the words *"Found the way. One way, anyway. Love to All"* and was postmarked Calais. He read it, studied the picture on the reverse, and put it back on the desk.

"What do you think?" he asked doubtfully of his wife's back.

"I think," she said, still typing, "that Dover to Calais is not the most obvious route to Los Angeles."

16

That week, Eden talked of another special commission at a special rate, but could not be diverted from demanding a face-to-face "brainstorming" meeting. Mrs Bird, Gary's mother, volunteered to spend the day at the house so that Cat could go to London without, as she put it, "the whole farm going to rack while a pack of daft men fought over that baby". When her meeting was over, Cat rang Mark on an impulse and asked him to come for a drink with her after work.

They met in a cavernous, mirrored pub two streets down from his office. Mark was looking tense and thin after a period of worsening conflict with Dean Hayes and Melanie Harwood. This time the issue was over whether Eden should emulate Tesco and get the Salvation Army in to run in-store Sunday schools, or whether they should steal a march by employing their own chaplains, in company livery, to counsel shoppers. He was openly contemptuous of Caroline's theory that Toby had gone to California.

"He only had two hundred and fifty quid," he said. "And he hadn't been out there for years."

"Nor had Caroline," objected Cat. "And *she* seems to have decided that LA is the place for her to get over the business with Alan. She's sort of homing there. It hasn't really got anything to do with Marie-Claire's museum conference. Maybe she's right. Maybe Toby went there too."

"Well, I quite liked school holidays in LA," said Mark. "But I certainly wouldn't rush back. If I was going anywhere, I'd go to Johannesburg."

"Good God. Why?"

"See the Kruger National Park again, I really missed those wart hogs when I was back at school. Anyway, I wouldn't go to LA. I don't think Toby was all that smitten with it, either."

"Well, he worked there," said Cat. "Remember all the row about the Mexican boy and the passport?"

"You mean when he was selling greaseburgers? He left that to go and be Pluto. No, Goofy. Didn't he get thrown out of Disneyland?"

"Yes," said Cat fondly. "Disney characters aren't supposed to speak to people when they're in costume. Specially they're not meant to call the customers ignorant arseholes."

There was a faraway, reminiscent, affectionate smile on the sister's face. In the moment's silence which followed this memory, Mark too smiled, but forcedly: the dry mirthless smile of the prodigal son's brother, aware that you are less remembered, less loved, for merely being well-behaved and helpful than you are for being wayward, difficult and charming.

"Well," he said flatly, "for one thing I don't know how Caroline thinks she's going to find him with no clues and no leads, in ten thousand acres of Southern California. She'll probably hardly look. I wouldn't hold my breath waiting for any news. For another thing, I don't think for a minute he's gone that far. He's probably back in Glasgow by now."

"He's not," said Cat bleakly. "I rang Duncan again. Anyway, there was a postcard from Calais."

Mark shifted restlessly on the hard pub bench, and gulped his lager. "Look, Cat, I know you're worried, and I am too. A bit. But he's always been one for wandering around. He's been out of touch for longer than this."

"Not after something like – Topsy dying."

"No." Mark shifted again, embarrassed. "But what can we do?"

"What I wanted to ask you," said Cat, "because you're a bloke, I suppose, is where do *you* think he'd go? Out of all the places we lived?"

"Why would it be somewhere we used to live?" asked Mark.

"Because that's what Caroline did," said his sister firmly, swirling the ice in her whisky. "And the more I think about it, the more I think that's what any of us would do if we were in trouble. We'd run for somewhere we used to live when we were kids. When Tim went—"

Mark looked at her, astonished. Never once had Cat discussed with him the defection of her husband. He thought she never mentioned it.

"When he left, I dreamed about moving to France. To Lille. I kept seeing the old courtyard, and the stone lions, and thinking of the twins in pinafores with the nuns, like me and Toby. I remembered Sunday skating with Sylvie and Chrétien and Thierry and the old gang. It was a sort of hallucination. Sometimes in the night when I was really tired, it felt as if I'd never stopped living in Lille. Just been home on leave."

"You never did go back there, though."

"Never had any money. And I knew that Hounslow was real life. Running off into the past is just a fantasy. I'm a plodder. But Toby isn't, is he? I mean, if he had an idea like that, he'd go."

"Gosh," said Mark noncommittally. "Diplobrat therapy, you reckon? Run back to your favourite post? Tough, if you were in Yugoslavia."

"It's a theory," said Cat stiffly. "Do you want another drink?"

"No thanks," said Mark. "I must get home. Lindy's got the neighbours round for dinner." He stood up.

"Mark," said Cat, as they walked together towards the Underground station. "Where *would* you go? If you ran away?"

"I wouldn't run away," said Mark with finality. "I'm not just home on leave, like you lot. Me and Lindy, we live here."

Their trains went from opposite platforms. Cat turned from his farewell rather brusquely. She crossed the footbridge and moments later looked at him across the grey gap, standing trim and composed in his dark suit and overcoat, waiting for the train home.

As Mark had predicted, there was no word from Caroline, nor any further cards from Toby. Almost a month later, when she had settled the baby after her supper-time romp, Cat was back in the kitchen contemplating the washing-up and picking listlessly at the carcass of an elderly duck culled by Gervase, cooked by herself and eaten without noticeable enthusiasm from anybody. Caroline's exotic enhancements of the farmhouse diet were still missed. The telephone rang and she answered it flatly: "Knoll Farm."

"Hi, it's Caroline!" said a high, distant voice. "How are you all?"

"Fine," said Cat. "Long time no hear."

"Yes. I'm sorry," said Caroline's voice, oddly light and happy. "Only, my therapist said it was better not to. Ring anybody, I mean."

"Your therapist?" Cat snapped the wishbone of the duck, hard, between her greasy fingers. "What therapist?"

"I've been seeing someone. Adeline McGilligan. Marie-Claire knew her. She does this one-month shock programme, not long Jungian stuff. Three sessions a day, and bomb-doses of vitamins. She told me to live inside myself for one month, and make friends with myself. I know," said the tinny voice apologetically, "that it sounds a bit naff, but it's worked. I've even rung Alan, to say I'd like the divorce to be friendly and constructive."

"Christ," said Cat rudely. "What did he say?"

"Well, not much," admitted Caroline. "He just said to talk to the lawyer about the money and leave him alone. But I wanted to say sorry to you, too. I must have been awful to live with all those weeks."

"No need," said Cat, formally. "Glad you're better." Then, on an impulse that had more than a little nastiness in it, "Any sign of Toby?"

Over three thousand miles came a long exhalation. "No. It was a stupid idea. I did put ads in the local paper, the first week. I even had one on the local television, and Marie-Claire's chap has friends in Venice Beach and places like that. But nobody'd heard a thing. The real reason I know he's not here is that there is one guy who knew him, from years ago, and he was positive he hadn't been in touch. He was sure that Toby would have come to him."

"Would Toby have been able to find him?"

"Yes. It's a café. The same one this guy always ran, in Laguna Beach. Toby worked there too. We'd forgotten. And he even wrote occasionally, apparently. He'd written about how he was having a baby. A postcard."

"Oh well," said Cat heavily. "That's that, then. Are you staying out there?"

"No, of course not!" said Caroline, laughing down the wire. "I'm coming home! I'm dying to see Mary-Annie!"

"Oh," said Cat. "Good."

Replacing the telephone, Caroline looked around her at the light, bright, luxuriously simple interior of Marie-Claire's family-room in Pacific Palisades. She would make her new home like this: polished floors, good rugs, Tiffany lamps, no fuss or clutter or stifling British establishment mock antiquity. Los Angeles had not been as rosy as she remembered, not at all: the miles of scruffy run-down housing, car-body shops and hoardings had eclipsed much of the pleasure of seeing Saks again and taking trips to the ocean and the mountains. She had rented a car, remembering happy runs with Diana in the sunshine, but given it up very quickly. She found herself terrified by a new savage aggression in the driving around her: a sense, as Marie-Claire put it, of a handgun in every glove box. She had gone downtown with her friend to the headquarters of the finance company which was backing the museum conference, and hated the glare and the glassiness and the acrid hooting heat of it.

No, she certainly did not want to live here, not geographically. But oh! She did want to live in the private atmosphere which despite the tension on the streets, she had found here. Her newly lightened spirit stretched and basked in a confusion of orange trees and wealth and optimism and expensive simplicity. Her baby, like the Californian babies she had seen, would have a pale carved oak crib on rockers, and simple streamlined cotton clothes, and real diapers for the sake of the planet. Light would flood into their house and their lives. She would paint again, and listen to music, and raise Mary-Annie – she liked the name now – by the precepts of the current buzzing Californian book, *Hey, Baby!*. Phrases – used half-ironically by her Paris-born hostess and more seriously by the therapist Adeline – came to Caroline like clear trumpet calls, summoning her to a simple but rich happiness. *Laid back. In touch. Shiny, happy people.*

She thought with a momentary pang of Cat, up in her cobwebby study at that old computer, supporting a life filled with muck and straw, bounded by intransigent animals with filthy bottoms and marred, inarticulate young men. She thought with a shudder of her own Kensington life, of the stifling traditional pomp of her ill-fated wedding a year ago, of the pointless profusion of General Trading Company knick-knacks in her kitchen, the overcareful clothes in her cupboards and the snobbish chic of Alan's long sitting room. She was out of all that now: renewed, fresh, new from the New World.

Then she thought of Gervase. Oddly, she did not associate her brother-in-law with the muck of the farmyard and the ungainly young men in the kitchen, but with the chessboard, the bookshelves in his study, a restful certainty and quietness, a kind monastic face. Yes, Gervase was in touch with the important things in life. He would understand her transformation. He would be interested in Adeline's book. She would take him one. Cat might laugh at the therapy, but Gervase would not.

Caroline picked up the telephone again to book a flight home. To the new home that she would build, and surprise them all.

17

On a shining Monday morning in May, Martin Szowalski drove the old Renault through the winding lanes that enmeshed Knoll Farm and protected it from the howl of A1 traffic. New green cowparsley brushed against the wheels when he pulled in to let a tractor pass, and the giddy smell of the whitening hedgerows blew through the broken ventilation grid beneath the dashboard, making him sneeze.

Martin felt light-hearted, pleasantly jolted from a long sober routine. Apart from weekend bike rides with Marianne and the regular duty runs to Midholt and Midmarsham, he had not left the farm since Christmas. Mrs Hartley had teased him about it. "You're turning into an Amish recluse," she would protest. "If you want to go to London, or the coast, or Scotland for a few days, for God's sake do. You're a volunteer, not a bondslave. You don't want to spend your whole time in Britain pegged out on the same few acres of Midlands mud."

But Martin never wanted to leave Knoll Farm. For one thing the work entranced him. He had spent months doing hard and mundane tasks on organic farms across Europe, but never before encountered the archaic eccentricity of one worked with carthorses. He was a serious young man, interested in Gervase's theories about how horsepower and human-scale farming could help young offenders regain social balance. He had come to observe this and contribute to the project, but he had stayed out of mere delight. Martin had found a talent: a growing, concentrated, sober pleasure in the big horses, their harness and gear and their time-worn traditional tasks on the land. Never mind what carthorses might do for Duanes and Winstons; they were doing wonders for him.

To begin with he had been allowed only to handle the old horse, Nelson, and a simple waggon: a tumbril, they called it here. But now Gervase let him go harrowing and even ploughing alone with the young pair. He had drilled a field of wheat, four acres of it, assisted only by Duane to fill and check the hoppers as the horses drew them over the prepared soil.

"We'll know exactly how straight you drove them, when that comes up," said Gervase. "The plants will show up every wiggle."

"There'll be a big kink in the line by the hedge," said Martin honestly. "Prince veered off when a pheasant came up under him." He had liked the imputation that he would still be there on the farm, still welcome, in the months when the corn began to sprout. Now, weeks later, there was little doubt that he could stay as long as he wanted, earning pocket money and his keep. Winston was still afraid of the horses, although he would lead the quietest of them if he had to. Duane had improved beyond measure from the gawping idiocy of his earlier self, but was still too prone to panic and confusion for Gervase to risk leaving him alone with a working animal weighing nearly a ton. So Martin evolved into Gervase's head horseman, and took a lot of work off the farmer's shoulders.

His favourite moments came when he was alone under a coppery late afternoon sky, his hands on the plough handles, feeling the living power of the great horses through the smooth worn wood, his arms responsive to every quiver and sway of the willing bodies as they moved along the furrow. At such moments, Martin wanted to stay forever suspended in time, happy in his increasingly ragged working clothes, wedded to these damp brown acres and magically forgetful of the dull realities of finding a living in the late twentieth century. At other times, aware of the financial tightrope the Hartleys walked, seeing Gervase's lined ascetic face bent over his paperwork calculating feed prices and falling markets, he would be chilled by the realization that there were no longer any simple farming idylls. "There never were," Cat would tell him. "Farmers have starved since the beginning of time. Especially small farmers."

But there was Marianne, too. She was on a course, and came home nearly every weekend now. Martin knew, from odd remarks dropped by her mother, that this had not always been so. He and she would talk for hours, casually, out by a hedge or in the barn while he worked. On Saturday he had been laying out sacks and hurdles ready for Monday's shearing, and Marianne had helped him all afternoon. They had hardly touched hands, but both knew that slowly, satisfyingly, things were moving on between them.

Exhausted from stacking hurdles, she had collapsed back on him in the barn, laughing like a comrade, her long hair wild and damp from the drizzle outside. He had set her on her feet and held her shoulders a moment longer than was necessary for balance. When she twisted round to face him she was smiling. He smiled now, thinking how his friends at home – and probably, her friends in London – would despise such a laggard old-fashioned courtship. But for the moment, in the Arcadian dream of those weekends, the pace suited them both very well. "Summer's coming," Marianne had said, stretching and shrugging her thin shoulders. "It gets warmer every day." And she smiled again as, perfectly understanding her, he said, "Yeah, I like the way the warm times come on slowly here. All the better. Back home, the hot wind comes and the land gets scorched, real quick. I like this way best."

As they built the pens of hurdles in the barn, Martin fully expected to be on hand when the shearers came. But on Monday morning Mrs Hartley had opened a telegram, clicked her tongue in exasperation and said: "Caroline's flight gets in this afternoon, two-thirty-five at Terminal Four, she says. I suppose that means she expects to be met."

"Did you say we'd meet her?" asked Gervase absently. He was leaning on the stove and eating a piece of toast while he read a set of committee minutes.

"Not on the phone. But I think she must be expecting it. Come to think of it, I shouldn't think she's ever arrived at an airport in her life and not been met."

Cat was irritable: the baby was teething early, and nights had been disturbed. They moved the cot into their own bedroom so that she and Gervase could get to the child faster; notionally they took turns, but in fact Cat woke at the first whimper and Gervase only at a full-blown wail.

"I'm really sorry, but I think it must be biological," Gervase would say in the morning, waking fresh and untroubled when Cat had been up four or five times, walking the fretful baby up and down the corridor.

"Doesn't matter," she would say. "You've got the farm. I can always nap when she does and catch up on work in the evenings." But she grew daily more tired, and felt her years. Eden were using her services constantly at the moment, squeezing out all her other clients; they were undergoing some kind of corporate restructuring, and Cat was part of the effort to sell the new systems and teams to the fretful workforce. She was earning twice as much as usual, but with the freelancer's insecurity she did not quite dare to turn down any of their demands. Caroline, she thought crossly, could perfectly well take a train up as far as Northampton. Or hire a car and drive to Midholt. On Alan's alimony she could afford a taxi. But instead she sent this peremptory telegram, naming her flight and expecting somebody from a busy household – made extra busy by *her* baby – to drop everything and drive a hundred-and-fifty-mile round trip to collect her and her Gucci luggage.

"Bloody hell then," she said, crumpling the telegram in her hand. "So who's going?"

"We've got the shearers coming at ten," said Gervase. "I really ought to be there. You know how touchy Gerry is, and he's the only one round here who'll do small flocks."

"How many catchers do you need in the barn?" asked Cat. "I'd really rather not get involved with the shearing, if you can spare me. I've got a lot of work I could get done while Yannie flakes out this morning."

She hated catching ewes for the shearer anyway, and Gervase knew it. Cat resented the dreadful irrationality of sheep, the way that right to the end of the shearing day each ewe fought as if her life depended on it, a woolly bundle of panic refusing to be dragged over to the shearing stand even though she could perfectly well see that her sisters had not been massacred, but merely shorn of their uncomfortable coats and left safe and white in the outer pen.

"Oh, don't worry," said Gervase. "Duane and Winston can do it. Then Martin might be so kind as to go and fetch Caroline."

"Winston won't like catching ewes," said Martin. "You know him and animals."

"Sheep won't hurt him," said Gervase. "He can't go on refusing to get to grips with stock."

Duane, who was washing up the porridge-pan, guffawed. "Bet 'e can."

"He can make an effort," said Cat, laughing at the big stolid boy's small joke. "You've all been too soft with him about it. He still says he wants to do NNEB and work in a nursery, you know. There might be rabbits, or hamsters to deal with. Let alone toddlers. He can practise on the sheep." Through the window, she could see Winston's long black clusters of plaits swinging as he carried the baby round the garden, crooning, bouncing her up and down, pointing out colours. "What about you, Martin? It's a boring drive to Heathrow."

"I'd be glad to help, if you think Mrs Halliday wouldn't mind my not being family," said Martin.

"Lucky to get anybody," Cat snorted.

And so it was settled, and later that morning while the baby slept in her carrycot by Cat's desk and Winston nervously eyed his first sheep, Martin drove southward to collect Maria Annunciata's mother from the airport.

The road held no terrors for him, nor the geography of Heathrow airport; but as he came closer he began to feel shy of what he would say to Mrs Hartley's beautiful, cool, distant sister. Despite her friendly condescension to the boys, there had always been something about Caroline which Martin found forbidding. It was a bit like he imagined talking to the Queen. In the kindness of his heart he was quite ready to ascribe all her little coldnesses, even towards the baby, to the bad shock she had received over her husband's leaving. Nonetheless, he did not feel at home with Caroline Halliday and began to wish as the miles reeled on that he had not volunteered so readily.

What would they talk about on the long drive back? Or would she sit silent, criticizing his driving? Should he offer to let her drive? She would have been better off with Gervase. They could talk about chess and art and all that stuff. Even better, of course, with her sister; but then, poor Mrs H. was still banned from driving.

He stood uncomfortably behind the rope barrier as the flight emerged from the baggage hall. Caroline moved towards him, gliding as smoothly as her trolley across the crowded concourse, and after a moment's hesitation recognized his face.

"Malcolm!" she said. "How sweet of you to come!"

"It's, um Martin," he said stumblingly apologetic. "Sorry, but Gervase couldn't come because of the shearing, so I, I—"

"But it's so sweet of you! I wasn't expecting to be met at all!"

Oh huh, lady! thought Martin in sudden rebellion. Oh, huh – so that's why you sent the flight details? Guys who really aren't expecting to be met just say what *day* they'll arrive. Not which *terminal*. This rebellious thought dispelled his uncomfortable sense of awe. Feeling much better, he hefted her two suitcases with a guilelessly friendly grin.

"A OK! Let's get these out to that car park." Caroline followed him, looking around with her new, shiny, happy positive attitude at the ranks of throbbing square black taxis, the pale May sunshine and the faded check shirt across the young man's broad shoulders. She was going home. Home to the country. How comfortable that sounded: she, Caroline, was through with Bond Street and Knightsbridge and crocodile shoes and Alan's dinners in restaurants with the powerful. Off with the old! She was even, she thought, glad for the moment to be away from echoing museums and the thick soundless carpet of Mayfair galleries. She had lived at second-hand for too long: been too fastidious, too frozen. Adeline had told her this and she saw it to be true. Now she would live calmly with her child: near some water perhaps, where she could paint the changing light, heal her inner child and quietly find wisdom, Gervase's kind of wisdom, the balanced pleasure of a simpler, plainer life.

The sight of Cat's old car shook her slightly. Never an elegant vehicle, it had been used this year by a number of drivers – even by Duane, once he got his licence back – and bore traces of farm and family life which jolted her fresh, bright, newly Californian sensibilities. Next to the baby seat (found by Winston for £1.20 at a car-boot sale and dreadfully scuffed) Gervase had left a leather head collar, a drift of files from one of his meetings, and a large spanner. There was evidence on the floor that a feed sack had at some stage split and leaked its floury contents. The outside was spattered liberally with spots of rust and streaks of mud, some of which had unaccountably found its way onto the dashboard. The glove box hung open, spilling cracked cassette boxes. Following her glance, Martin suddenly saw this familiar car with new eyes and flushed.

"Hey – I'm sorry we didn't clean up the car a bit. We only heard this morning."

"No, it's *lovely* to be home. And lovely to be met. I feel as if I was back on the farm already. Mmm, lovely horsey smell." While Martin put her smart suitcases in the boot (with difficulty, as there was an overlooked horse collar and a broken flywheel there already), Caroline surreptitiously dusted the passenger seat with her silk scarf, then slid in, to turn her serenely smiling eyes on him as he climbed in.

"Well!" she said chattily. "Tell me all the news!"

As he manoeuvred from the airport to the motorway, Martin did his best. He began with halting items of farm news, because he felt embarrassed about mentioning the baby, seeing that she had left it behind. Then Caroline gaily asked:

"And how's my daughter? Yannie, you call her, don't you?"

"Uh – yep. She's great. Bigger every day. I guess," he ventured daringly, "she'll be glad to have her Mom back."

Caroline swivelled her big eyes to look at the boy's profile as he drove. Adeline McGilligan was still strong within her as she said: "You must think I'm a terrible woman, leaving her like that. But I needed to get myself strong. Strong inside, so I could be strong for her. I've done that now. I'm ready to be a parent. No pain, no shame, just hope and new beginnings."

This frankness gave Martin considerable discomfort. He had absorbed a good deal of Gervase's reticence along with his farm-lore. Still, it did not seem to need an answer so he drove on silently. After a moment, Caroline began again, apparently without embarrassment: "I can accept your feelings. You're bound to have a residue of your feelings that's hostile to the way I was when I was in grief." She pronounced the word *hostel*, as her therapist so often did. "That's healthy. To reject the manifestations of grief. People in grief give off negativity and danger. But it fades. My job is the same as all of yours: to accept the faults in the person I was, and build on them. None of us is perfect."

"No," bleated Martin, hating this. "Hey, do you mind if I have the *One o'clock News* on? There's some sorta conference about BSE transmission."

"Go ahead," said Caroline, and smiled at him again as he fumbled, rather desperately, with the radio.

When they got to the farm the shearers were packing up their electric tools and stands, and the boys were lugging huge buoyant sacks of fleece up to the end of the barn. Gervase and the old dog could be seen in the middle distance, running the flock of shining white sheep down into the more sheltered of the meadows for their first night of lighter, cooler summer life. The afternoon sun slanted beautifully across the red tiles of the farmhouse roof, and there were pale delicate leaves around the back door. Caroline stood by the car, surveying it all with pleasure.

"Isn't it just gorgeous?" she said. "A place of peace and healing." Martin, who might before that morning have felt much the same way himself, although without saying so, could manage only a surly grunt as he pulled her cases from the boot. "Shall I take these up?" he asked. "Only, I don't know . . ." He lived in the bunkhouse with the boys and, although the rule about not going beyond the kitchen and big sitting room did not strictly apply to him, he rarely penetrated upstairs in the house.

"No, no, you've got work to do, I'm sure," said Caroline graciously. "The lobby will be fine." So she walked alone, through the kitchen and up the stairs, to find her sister and her child.

18

Cat was asleep on the floor of her study, head on a rolled baby
blanket, when the car pulled up. Next to her was a battered
plastic carrycot which the boys had found at yet another car-boot
sale. There were four of these now, each equipped with a clean
ancient flannel sheet and a light cellular blanket from the WI
craft market; Cat hated carrying baby furniture around, and
found it easier to have a number of bases scattered through the
house where the infant could safely be put down to doze. As long
as she had her muslin square to clasp to her face and suck, Maria
Annunciata did not seem to mind a frequent change of bed.

She slept on now, muslin clutched in her small fat fist, while
her aunt raised herself on one elbow and shook her head, trying
mistily to make sense of the sounds on the attic stairs. On the
desk, the old Amstrad screen burned with the words which had
sent Cat to sleep:

Pro-active courtesy, pro-active efficiency – these are the bnechmarks
*of Ened service provisio@ £$^*

The footsteps on the stair became louder and closer, and Cat
sat up, rubbed her eyes, and ran her hands through her hair.
The door opened and she saw her sister: tanned, crisply dressed
in a white blouse and pale linen skirt, golden-haired, clear-eyed
and serenely smiling.

From the door Caroline saw a middle-aged woman in a
tattered tracksuit, with bags under her eyes, her hair a dull
brown birds' nest streaked with grey, sitting on a threadbare
carpet by a cluttered desk and a grimy old computer. Next to
her was a carrycot, its inner walls clean enough but its exterior
a battered nightmare of peeling, fading, hideous orange plastic.

In it, half covered by a clashing blanket in lime green and cherry red, slept a baby dressed in a well-worn towelling Babygro suit, a rag in her fist. Jammed into the corner of the carrycot between the cardboard stiffener and the torn plastic was a twig with many branches, from each of which hung a thread bearing a silver foil milk-bottle top which turned and twisted in the draught from the doorway.

Caroline was silent for a moment, and even through her sleepiness Cat saw why, and was suddenly and deeply angry. It took all her genetic history of circumspect diplomatic repression to say merely: "Hello. Good journey?"

"Fine, thanks," said Caroline, with equal social self-possession. "How is everything?"

"Fine," said Cat. "I was just power-napping. Mary-Annie should be waking up any minute."

"Lovely," said Caroline. Now that she was here, the baby at her feet filled her with frightening, unsayable mixed emotions. She bent with difficulty towards the carrycot, and peered at the small face.

"She's grown."

"They do that," said Cat.

Caroline made a rapid brave decision, went on one knee and picked up the baby, blanket and all. She was not as inept as she might have been before LA: Marie-Claire's best friend in Pacific Palisades had a boy of much the same age, and Caroline had warily handled him a few times as he was passed from one doting woman to another. Besides, she had re-read that encouraging manual *Hey, Baby!* twice all through on the aeroplane.

Upright against her mother's shoulder, Mary-Annie blinked herself awake and burrowed her face, a little snottily, against the white linen of Caroline's Saks blouse.

"That's the girl," said Caroline. "What a big girl!"

Cat watched, half-angry and half-relieved that the baby did not cry at this stranger's embrace.

"Thanks for looking after her so well," said Caroline, not letting her eyes stray to the terrible carrycot and twig. And carefully, step by step, she carried her baby out of Cat's attic and down the stairs.

"She has milk at four o'clock," said Cat to the retreating back.

"Everything's in the kitchen." And, as an afterthought, "Winston will show you where."

The baby was used to many faces, many bodies: from Cat's warm female solidity to Winston's bony energy, from Duane's slow, careful, freckled arms to Gervase's lean tanned ones, from Mrs Bird's dishevelled doughy gentleness to Martin's bristling beard and wiry arms, she knew and rejoiced in the diversity of people. It was rare for her to offer any of them less than a toothless beam of welcome. The smooth, cool, lightly scented bosom of Caroline was new to her but nonetheless agreeable; besides, on reaching the kitchen she found herself in earshot of familiar deep male voices and promising smells of food, and began to crow contentedly.

So it was that Gervase and the two boys, coming in with wisps of oily wool stuck to their jackets and a great thirst for tea, were met by the sight of beautiful Caroline, her face transfigured by a smile of triumphant relief and dawning love, and in her arms little Mary-Annie: grinning and gurgling and waving her fists in an ecstasy of general approval of the world, the company, and – so it seemed to Gervase in particular – her new found mother.

He paused in the door, the boys behind him, and looked at mother and child standing in the dappled sunlight. Then: "Welcome back," he said, and crossed the floor to kiss her smooth cheek with deliberate measured courtesy. "Welcome home."

Cat, descending the back stairs to the kitchen, stepped through the door just in time to see their two bright faces bent together over the baby's head. Looking beyond them, she saw something like dismay in the eyes of Winston and Duane. Things were changing at Knoll Farm; an era ending. Everybody knew it except Maria Annunciata.

The changes were rapid, too rapid for Duane's slow wits to understand. He had never seen much of Caroline except at meal times in the depths of her cold depression, and gaped at this new, swift-moving decisive woman with her steely smiles and cool politeness. She had, being not insensitive to atmospheres, rapidly given up talking like a therapist since the first car ride with Martin, and reverted to her old dainty reticence. Except sometimes, alone with Gervase, when she talked as to a father confessor and he listened gravely.

On the day after her arrival she entrusted the baby – with a slightly absurd formality of gratefulness – to her sister and Mrs Bird, and borrowed the car to drive to Birmingham. In the following days, carriers and parcels arrived in bewildering profusion: a smart new pale walnut cot – "She's outgrowing the carrycots," a modern car seat with a handle, a highchair and harness adjustable for either reclining or self-supporting babies, a changing chest beautifully painted with roses and butterflies, and a snowstorm of new clothes.

Duane had never seen clothes like them. Most were white and many bore discreet frills or embroideries; a few were larkily multicoloured, like tiny chic rugby shirts with strange Italian labels on the chest. There were little silk knitted sweaters and elegantly chunky sheepskin bootees. Some of them did not fit, since Caroline had not taken the baby with her when she bought them; but there were enough good guesses there to transform his familiar little Yannie into another baby altogether. A Kensington baby, beautifully packaged. He would not have attempted to change a nappy now, not with these unfamiliar garments to contend with. But then, he would not have dared anyhow. The baby had suddenly become too close an associate of the awe-inspiring Caroline. He could as soon fumble with her immaculate clothing as with this child's.

Winston was less shy. He was, after all, street-sharp, opinion-ated, and buoyed by his new ambitions in professional childcare. On the third day after her arrival Caroline came into the kitchen one evening – having left the baby to her sister's care while she collected a mended head collar from the saddler in Midmarsham – to find the boy with the long dreadlocks and the single earring spooning puréed apple into her daughter's wide, enthusiastic mouth. A gobbet of it was trickling down her chin, not onto one of the new starched bibs Caroline had bought but onto an old tea towel from Cat's kitchen drawer, which Winston had expertly tied around her neck as he always did.

"Hi," said Winston, concentrating on his task and unable to see the mother's face. "Mrs H.'s gone up the paddock to sort out a sheep. She asked me to do Yan's tea. I usually do anyway."

"Yes, well, I'll take over, thank you," said Caroline.

"S'all right. She's nearly finished, and I've done the milk for after," said Winston, oblivious to nuance. Caroline, however, picked up a white piqué Italian bib from the laundry basket in the corner, and came to stand so very close to him that in a moment he rose, backed away and left her the spoon. Mary-Annie had a second spoon in her hand, with which she was enthusiastically conducting some invisible orchestra, and a third one lay on the table. Seeing the mother's momentary bemusement, Winston kindly explained:

"She likes to 'old the spoon, yeah? In 'er and. So I give 'er one in each hand, and I use the third one. She nearly gets her own ones in 'er mouth, so I dip it in the apple so she gets the idea. She'll be feeding on 'er own in no time."

Caroline did not reply, but went on spooning apple into the baby's mouth, wiping the dribbling lips fastidiously between each mouthful. When the bowl was nearly empty, Winston picked up the bottle from the stove, whipped off its cap and tested the temperature of the milk on his thin dark wrist.

"S'fine. Here you are. She likes to hold the bottle, but she's not too good at it, so you have to watch all the time."

Caroline looked at the white bottle in the boy's black hand, hesitated, then took it and plugged it firmly into the baby's mouth, supporting it with her hand, still not speaking. Only the eager glugging and sighing of the child broke the quiet of the kitchen. Winston watched critically.

"Oughter be tipped up more. Or she gets air in, and burps."

At this point Cat came in to the kitchen, stamping her feet on the mat and shuddering with theatrical distaste. She was holding a bottle of cooking oil.

"I hate capsized bloody sheep. Why can't they get up by themselves? Lying there with their legs in the air. It's a design fault."

"Woss the oil for?" asked Winston, momentarily diverted from supervising mother and baby.

"If they get bloated up from being on their back, you force oil down their throat and it makes them belch and fart."

"Please!" The cry from Caroline was involuntary, and she flushed immediately and pretended to carry on with the baby.

"Saves their rotten life, doesn't it?" said Cat truculently. "And it's all right, it isn't the same bottle of oil we use for cooking." Caroline shuddered. The baby sucked the last centimetre of milk and looked hopefully, dribblingly around for more.

That evening, when the boys had retired to the bunkhouse and Gervase was in his study, Caroline caught her sister alone, peeling potatoes, and said: "Cat, I came into the kitchen tonight and Mary-Annie was alone with that drug boy."

Cat looked at her in genuine astonishment.

"You mean Winston?"

"Yes. The farm boy, the delinquent. He was feeding her."

"He usually does. Him or Duane. They're very careful. They adore her."

"I thought," said Caroline, "that if I left my baby with you . . ."

"That I'd never allow anyone else in the household to touch her? Come off it. You lived here for eight weeks, while we all took turns."

"Well, you and Gervase. And Mrs Bird. I never realized that the farm boys *fed* her."

"They even do her nappies," said Cat brutally. "Always have. If you'd ever bothered to be around your own baby, you'd have known perfectly well that we all help. And don't call them farm boys. You sound like Gervase's mother."

Caroline bridled. Cat had not spoken to her so unkindly since Christmas Eve.

"I really don't think it's unreasonable to be surprised that you leave a four-month-old baby alone to be fed – *God knows what* – by a convicted drug dealer."

"Oh, give me strength!" exploded her sister. "Winston is as safe as houses. Safer than some neurotic anorexic bloody Kensington au pair, I shouldn't wonder. What do you think he does? Spikes her Ostermilk with crack?"

"He's a convicted criminal. Drugs!"

"He has a suspended sentence," said Cat, as if to a three-year-old, "for selling a tab of Ecstasy to an undercover policewoman in a club in Northampton."

"Well? So that makes him suitable to feed my baby?" Caroline was fired up now, angry at the contempt in her sister's voice.

"No," said Cat steadily. "But the person he is now, the person he has become and always was underneath, is a person to be trusted. Within reason, he can be trusted to rejoin mainstream society. That's what we do here. Mary Annie has helped." *Unlike some*, said her tone.

The two women glared at one another, then Cat turned to the stove and, with her back to Caroline lest she be tempted to slap her, continued:

"Do you know how that boy has lived? His mother lost her cleaning job at the steelworks at Corby when it closed. She went on the game and got murdered. He spent three years in a children's home, then was chucked out at sixteen and became a runner for drug dealers. He got caught in his first week and sent to a young offenders' institution. When they let him out he did it again, because he didn't have any other way of affording anywhere to eat or sleep. Mr Willetts the probation officer says he used to look after some of the other younger kids on the street, buy them chips. He's the gentlest thing on earth."

Caroline made a small, dissenting noise. Cat went on, almost pleading now.

"He won't even get tough with the horses, so they haul him all over the place. He's worked here for four months and been good as gold. He's been provisionally accepted at the Midholt FE college to do a course in social care of children. He wants to be a nursery nurse."

Caroline had absorbed Adeline McGilligan's views about the need to be unaggressively assertive. She said, controlledly:

"Well, we shall have to agree to differ. I'm very grateful for all you've done. I won't impose on you much longer. But I am afraid I have a right to say who feeds my baby." Too late, she realized she should not have said "I am afraid". But Adeline, she felt, would have said it was not a bad try.

When Caroline had gone upstairs to check her baby, Cat turned her face to the kitchen door and cried into the roller towel.

19 ʃ

At bedtime, Cat kicked off her old corduroy slippers and told Gervase: "Caroline says Winston isn't to feed the baby."

"She's doing almost everything herself now, isn't she?" said Gervase. "I suppose that's a good thing."

He had been quiet, over the few days Caroline was home. His brief dream of the baby had faded when he saw her in her true mother's arms. He felt a little ashamed of it: this new Caroline was so clearly, so beautifully, the mother. He now felt a chivalrous desire – almost a hunger – that things should go well for her in her state of single motherhood. When they sat together over the chessboard she did most of the talking, her lovely face newly animated, her hair shining in the lamplight. He listened gravely, admiring and supporting her resolve to live well with the child. Now he said to his wife:

"Mary-Annie seems to be doing rather well on it. She's looking very bonny. Caroline says she's slept right through, these last two nights."

The baby's cot was now set up in a separate bedroom, linked to Caroline by a sleek space-age baby alarm system. During Mary-Annie's daytime naps, she carried the receiver clipped unobtrusively to her blouse. She looked (thought Duane privately) just like a TV policewoman waiting for the summons to an affray.

"It's not some magic mother's touch," said Cat, irritably. "The baby's just stopped teething for the moment, that's all. It was very early anyway." She swung her legs onto the bed, wincing at the coldness of the sheet. "If Caroline had been back last week she'd have found it a different game altogether. But never mind that:

what I'm trying to tell you is that she doesn't want poor Winston even touching the baby. Even playing with her. It's because he's black, and he's what she calls a delinquent."

"Oh no," said Gervase, shocked. "I'm sure you've misunderstood. Caroline's really keen on the project, on everything we do here. She was talking about it only tonight. That American doctor seems to have helped her understand a lot of things."

Without answering, Cat lay down on her own side and pulled the quilt around her ears. They did not speak again until morning. But then, Gervase had always been prone to long periods of restful, contemplative silence. It was one of the things which had attracted her to him years before, after living for six years with the nervous chattiness of Noreen and the prattle of the twins. She had loved his quietness, as she loved the quietness of her part-time job at the library. That quietness could harden into silence had never, in those noisy days, occurred to her.

The next day he went out early to the farm as usual, and Cat decided that she should talk to Winston before breakfast. His habit was to walk Mary-Annie round the garden while her bottle was made up, holding her up in his strong dark arms and teaching her the names of plants and colours according to the precepts of the infant development video which Cat had got him from the Midholt library. This excursion must be forestalled, for today at any rate. She must prevent a direct confrontation between the boy and Caroline. If Winston was to take this new situation well, it must be presented to him well, and without exposing him to the reality of the mother's distaste.

When she came down she saw that Caroline had been up since the baby's early milk feed and was in the kitchen, rinsing spoons and frowning at the label of an expensive little jar of organic muesli. Mary-Annie, in her new chair, examined her bare toes and made loud, sociable yarring noises. It seemed to Cat, in her state of heightened sensitivity, as if the baby's eyes kept turning, hopefully, in the direction of the bunkhouse from which every morning her teenage admirers had been wont to emerge, racing to greet her. She nodded briefly to her sister, pushed her feet into rubber boots and went out into the yard to waylay the boys.

It had taken some hours of the night to work out how to put the situation to them. Cat Hartley was no sentimentalist, but in the years of bringing up her own Dave and rubbing along domestically with Gervase's changing entourage of young offenders, she had formed her own view of what lay beneath the showy superficial toughness of the adolescent male. Winston, she felt and feared now, was softer-centred even than most.

Generally, she reflected as she loitered near the bunkhouse door, it was a girl who uncovered the inarticulate warm gooey centre behind a young man's brittle street-wisdom. Sometimes it was an animal. One eighteen-year-old had been on the verge of being sent home as too angry and intractable even for Gervase, until by good fortune a calf had been born too weak to stand. The boy, Mikey, had ended up sleeping in the straw next to the weak animal, while its mother roamed distractedly in the shadows of the barn nearby. He begged an alarm clock from Cat, and four times a night he would milk the cow of colostrum and feed it to the calf through a tube pushed over its rough tongue, while the cow licked the back of his jacket gratefully with her rough tongue. The calf lived; Mikey did not change overnight, but after that he worked his time out at the farm, and left in a better state than he came.

In Winston's case the baby had wrought the change; and to deny him contact with her now seemed a thing more cruel than Cat liked to contemplate. Duane, she thought, would be all right about the prohibition: his obsession with Mary-Annie had faded to a more casual brotherly affection since he began to lavish his inner gooeyness upon the stout, shy new barmaid at the Midmarsham pub. Winston had no girlfriend, and seemed for the moment not to want one.

He erupted out of the bunkhouse, a tall skinny dark figure, and hesitated when he saw her. He glanced back towards Duane who stood, in an ungainly questioning stance, in the doorway. "We late or what? The clock said—"

"No, I wanted to catch you two," began Cat. "It's about Mrs Halliday. Caroline. My sister."

Winston looked suddenly defensive. Maybe, thought Cat, he had understood more of her sister's attitude than she knew.

"She leavin', then?" asked Winston abruptly. "Lives in London, yeah?"

"Not yet," said Cat. "Soon, I daresay. Actually, she's decided to look for a cottage not far from here, rather than go back to London."

The boy's face lightened. Cat dragged herself unwillingly back to the point. "She was ill when Mary-Annie was born, and couldn't look after her much. So she's got a bit of catching up to do. Mothers have to be with their babies a lot."

"Bonding," nodded Winston, more comfortably. "Yeah, obviously." This had been much featured on the video.

Cat looked at the boy's bony, intelligent face and called up all her reserves of the family talent for emollient presentation of hard truths. It was considerable: a talent bred in a dozen diplomatic residences, hammered home from childhood as the central principle of courtesy, and honed on Eden corporate newsletters.

"She's decided," she said brightly, "that we ought to change the way we do things. A little."

The boys looked at her, expectantly. Cat wavered and continued, lying bravely:

"She knows how well you've helped me look after Mary-Annie, and she's really grateful. But now she thinks that it would be better if nobody else did things for the baby – feeding, playing, carrying her around even. Just for a while. So they can get really used to each other. As Winston said, it's a matter of bonding."

It was a brave attempt which fooled nobody. Not even Duane, who looked at his feet and said: "Not even you an' Mrs Bird and Mr H.?"

Cat was thrown.

"Ah – well, mainly – not any of us."

"What about while she does the driving?" persisted Duane, his freckled face creasing in puzzlement. "Shops, an' Mr Willetts an' that. Yan doesn't like being in the car more'n ten minutes, unless it's nap time, an' even then—"

Winston turned on him and broke his silence. "Don't be a stupid dickhead. She just dun't want us two yobs touchin' Yannie, thass all. Innit?"

His challenge was so direct that Cat capitulated.

"OK, all right, that's partly it. She's a bit old-fashioned," she continued wildly. "I suppose she thinks only women should handle little babies."

At that moment Gervase emerged from the kitchen with Mary-Annie cuddled on his arm and Caroline laughing behind him. Winston turned to Duane and said flatly: "C'mon, dickhead. We'll do the pigs before breakfast." Before Cat could speak again, he had vanished into the shadows of the feed shed.

There had been no family gathering back at Easter, because Lady Artemis was staying with friends in Gstaad and Robert was at an aid conference in Rome. Cat had been glad of it. Although Toby had frequently missed family reunions, his absence on this occasion would have had a poignancy she dreaded. Instead, Noreen had come up in Marianne's car, and Dave had turned up for Easter Sunday lunch and fallen as much in love with the baby as any of them. Despite Caroline's frozen listlessness it had been an easy, relaxed Easter. Cat had an obscure, guilty feeling of having somehow got away with it: got past another landmark of the traditional family year without trouble.

Artemis, however, always found that after a gap of a certain number of months her maternal compass-needle fluttered irresistibly back towards Knoll Farm and another visit to her son. This she announced, her high confident voice ringing down the telephone, on the sunny May day after Cat's painful interview with Winston. She was surprised at the unaccustomed warmth with which her daughter-in-law received the notification of her visit.

"That'll be nice," said Cat with sincerity. Indeed, she longed for any dilution of the difficult atmosphere at mealtimes. Winston had spoken to nobody, except in the way of work, since the prohibition. He ate rapidly and left for the bunkhouse. Gervase was believing – or pretending – that there was no problem, and when the baby was at table, exchanged his usual social courtesies with her while Duane and Winston glowered powerlessly, not feeling they could even play peek-a-boo under the cool eye of Caroline. Martin did not really understand any of it, but sensed the new atmosphere of constraint and did not smother Mary-Annie with giggles and tickles or throw her aloft as he had been used to do. Deprived of the element of whoopee in her life, the baby was a little more grizzly than usual; but she was a good-natured creature, and was at least constantly tended by her mother with scrupulous, if slightly mechanical, carefulness.

Only Caroline seemed entirely at peace: in the evenings she sat glowing with such untroubled inner serenity that her sister wanted to shake her as a dog shakes a rat, and with much the same fatal result. Or so she told Marianne, her only confidante in this matter, on the phone one night.

Marianne sympathized wholeheartedly, but could not come to Knoll Farm for several weekends more because of her work. Cat had tried to get Noreen to come, but she was on a coach trip to the Dutch bulbfields. So Artemis would have to do. Any visitor would, at least, provide a diversion. Cat told her:

"Caroline's back. She'll be thrilled to see you. You haven't met the baby yet, have you? She's a darling. Maybe Dad's free too. That would be fun." Robert was indeed free, and when his elder daughter rang him to demand that he help entertain Artemis, he willingly agreed. And on the Friday evening, Lindy rang, sounding a little strained, to ask whether she could come up alone for Saturday night and meet Mark at the farm on Sunday, after his presentation to a sales conference near Kettering.

"Wonderful!" said Cat. "Full house, how nice. Dad'll give you a lift if you don't want to drive."

Caroline had already been to Midholt and bought a great deal of expensive cheese and bread with dried tomatoes embedded in it, and the ingredients for *canard à l'orange*. Gervase had killed and plucked two of the floating population of farmyard ducks and requested this dish, since duck had always been his mother's favourite fowl.

However, when Caroline saw the two grim, scrawny carcasses left for her on the stone slab in the larder, their legs untidy and their skin bagging, she quietly went back to Tesco on Saturday morning on the pretext of dropping Duane at his girlfriend's. Here she bought two corn-fed, butter-plump, oven-ready birds from the Auvergne, rosy and neatly trussed on clean white trays. The old sheepdog was more than pleased to dispose of Gervase's birds and only Martin, passing the kennel, noticed what had happened. Brits, he thought, were sometimes really strange.

None of the visitors was expected before lunch-time. The late morning sun was slanting in through the kitchen window where Caroline stood chopping onions for the *canard*, as Cat came into the room and found herself for the first time in days alone with her sister.

It was a pretty scene, the older sister had to admit to herself. Mary-Annie, in a pale blue smock, lay back in her new soft white padded chair, big-eyed, sucking on an equally new teething ring with bells on it. It was made of some soft smooth plastic but modelled on a Victorian ivory piece. The kitchen was unaccustomedly tidy, and Caroline had found enough primroses to fill a little jug which shone from the centre of the scrubbed table. She herself was wearing jeans and a pale knitted silk sweater, and humming softly as she worked. Her eyes were as big and blue and clear as the baby's.

Cat stood in the doorway for a moment, reluctant to break the picturesque peace of the moment. Then she said:

"Caro." She used the baby name, as she rarely did. "Caro, could I have a word?"

"Of course. I'm just getting the smelly bits of the cooking over with. These onions are strong, aren't they?"

"Organic," said Cat. "Gervase is very pleased with that lot of seed. Small but deadly. Totally pest-resistant."

"They're wonderful," said Caroline warmly. "So are the potatoes. Goodness, they've kept well, haven't they?"

Cat wished that they could continue discussing vegetables and leave it at that. She recognized in herself a strong inhibition against upsetting Caroline, and had decided with dry resignation that it must be a legacy of their youth. When Caroline was the new and precious baby, she, Cat, was a big girl twelve years older who must be gentle and considerate. Even today she could advise and support, counsel and suggest, but rarely rebuke her baby sister. You must not risk making her cry. Old refrains ran through her mind: *She's only little. You should know better! Fancy making poor Caroline cry. Look after Caroline.*

Contemplating beautiful Caroline, beautifully and tearlessly chopping onions, Cat rubbed her forehead in a moment of perplexity. It was a terrible thing, she thought, to recognize an irrational inhibition in yourself and still be its prisoner. Caroline was nearly thirty-three years old now. Not a baby. She had a duty of consideration to other people. She was behaving like a selfish cow. Something had to be said. Cat drew herself together and began:

"I wanted to talk to you about the boys. Winston. And Duane. And this business about Mary-Annie."

"Oh?" said Caroline, not looking at her, chopping with precision.

"I understand about your wanting to look after her yourself mostly. That's great. It's natural. You had a difficult start, you need to make up time." Cat realized that she was repeating to Caroline the half-truth she had concocted for the boys. Well, it would do. She continued:

"But it would be a great help to us – to Gervase's work" – ah, fiendish, diplomatic cunning! – "if you'd just sometimes hand her to one of the boys, quite casually. To Winston, especially. Just for ten minutes. Ask him to take her round the garden, or give her a bottle. He got very fond of her while you were away. And before that, while you were low. Gervase and I think it really helped his growing up to know that we all trust him with something so precious."

It was not entirely true about Gervase. Cat had tried to raise the subject with him once or twice after the first failure, but he had merely spoken gravely about Caroline's need to feel secure about everything connected with the baby, and her right to have reservations about outsiders of a type with which she was unfamiliar. "We're used to these boys. She isn't." As to the effect on Winston, he said, the lad was doing fine as far as the farm went, and had always been a bit moody. He would come round. Attention would make it worse. Meanwhile, he was sure that Caroline did not mean any slight to the boys by her attitude. One must remember she had had a terrible shock, over Alan.

Cat had given up. Gervase, without ever intending to, had a way of making other people feel mean and small-minded.

Now, since Caroline was still chopping and not speaking, she continued: "Winston really is very careful of her. He adores her."

The baby, bored with the rattle, dropped it and began to whicker with frustration. Cat bent to return it.

Caroline put down the knife, and turned, hand on hip. All

Dr Adeline's carefully implanted assertiveness rose to order as she said, in a calm and sweet voice: "I'm afraid I don't think it's appropriate."

Oh God! thought Cat, looking at the beautiful face before her, framed in sunlit, smooth golden hair. Oh God in heaven, was there anywhere a worse torment than being rightly and justifiably infuriated by somebody, so much that you longed to smack her and berate her, and yet to be inhibited from speaking your mind by a lifelong fear of upsetting her? She shuddered a little, put a hand for strength on Mary-Annie's small chubby leg, and said, averting her eyes from her sister's face: "What do you mean, 'appropriate'? You sound like a social worker."

"The other day," said Caroline, "you said I sounded like Artemis. She hardly sounds like a social worker, does she?"

"Let's not fight."

"I'm not fighting," said Caroline, and pulled another peeled onion towards her. The glinting little knife sank into its flesh, and it wept sharp tears onto the board. "I am making decisions about the care of my child. I'm sure Winston will turn out very well, but I don't think it's appropriate or healthy for a boy from that kind of home, with that kind of record, to be handling a baby." She paused. "A baby girl. Or 'adoring' her, frankly."

There was a moment's silence, then Cat, startled by the emphasis of the last words, said in a voice that rose uncontrollably to a squeak: "Are you saying he's some sort of sex abuser?"

The inhibition was fading. She wanted to pique Caroline now, to make her deny any such absurd suspicion, to explain herself. But Caroline only gave an almost imperceptible nod, and pushed a neat pile of onion shavings to the corner of the board.

"She can't speak for herself," she said. "It's up to us to protect her from – emotional abuse and inappropriate relationships. I'd have thought you'd see that. You read the papers."

"She's not five months old yet!" howled Cat, her control now quite gone. "You stupid bloody dirty-minded prig, what fucking nonsense *have* you brought back from America now?"

"I wouldn't have thought," said Caroline, still calm, still chopping, her voice still sweet, "that you'd be so naïve about the things which can happen to children. At any age."

"Winston is *not* a baby-molester!" said Cat. "Ask Gervase! You always seem to believe every bloody thing he says!"

"Gervase agrees with me," said Caroline, "that it's healthy for me to make decisions about Mary-Annie. He doesn't question my judgement. I'm sure nobody questioned your judgement, when the twins were small."

Cat wanted to turn and walk out, but suddenly saw a saving vision of Winston, lanky, bony, grinning whitely at some trick of Mary-Annie's as he expertly tested the heat of her milk on his wrist. He was worth one more try:

"Suppose I promised that I'll always be in sight of him, always in the room, while he plays with the baby? Just to let him down lightly. He's only here another month or so."

"I'm sorry," said Caroline. "I've given it a lot of thought, and anybody who knows about these things" – she meant Adeline, and the author of *Hey, Baby!* – "says that when you're not easy about a relationship in a child's life or an adult's, a clean break is far better."

"But Caro – relationship isn't quite the word—" Cat was still trying, although now she hated herself for it. She ought by rights, she thought, to have thrown a plate at her sister and walked out, telling her to pack her bags and take her dirty prim little mind elsewhere. "Caro, this is a *baby*. She doesn't do relationships yet. She does cuddles and jokes and feeding and pointing at things."

Mary-Annie dropped the rattle again and began to whimper, in earnest this time. Caroline rinsed her hands and dried them carefully on some of the kitchen paper (she used a whole roll every two days in her pursuit of hygiene). The whimpering increased in volume. She crossed to the chair to pick her child up.

"I'm sorry," she said again, "especially as I am a guest in your house. But nothing's changing. Anyway, the boy seems to have lost interest, doesn't he? I don't know what all the fuss is about. I've hardly seen him for two days."

If – and there was no sign of it in her behaviour – Caroline was dismayed by this encounter with her elder sister, the approval she received an hour later from Lady Artemis would have been more than enough to soothe any ruffled feelings. Gervase had sent his mother a Polaroid of his new niece a while back: it showed Mary-Annie staring beadily at the camera in a grubby towelling Babygro and a crudely knitted red woolly tank-top made by Mrs Bird. Artemis had not been attracted by this picture, particularly since the uncleared breakfast-table was all too visible in the background. Anyway, thanks to Martin's camera technique the child appeared to have one ear larger than the other.

She was, therefore, quite unprepared for the beaming beauty and refined wardrobe of this Maria Annunciata. The baby took her unawares, ambushed her with downy wisps of golden hair, wide uncertain smiles and fat waving fists. The old lady capitulated, even risking her immaculate suit by kneeling on the hearth rug where the baby was doing push-ups in the manner of a seal.

She cried, "What a duck!", almost said, "Coochy coo!" and bestowed upon pretty, gentle-mannered Caroline a more wholehearted smile than her own daughter-in-law had ever seen. Cat, after all, had brought into the distinguished Hartley family no such beauty of a baby. When she arrived as Gervase's bride sixteen years earlier, she had been leading two shy, pasty-faced six-year-olds who wore – Artemis shuddered to remember – dreadfully common anoraks.

"Isn't she a gorgeous little one?" she continued, chucking the complaisant Mary-Annie on the cheek. "Looking so pretty! I do love proper broderie. Is it Swiss?"

"Austrian," said Caroline. "I'm afraid I do like little girls in dresses."

"Oh, of course! Sometimes these days you just can't tell, can you? All the children in these *shell suits.*"

Martin came in, shyly, with a basket of freshly split firewood. He was uneasy around Caroline, although since the first effusions of the car journey she had been less ready with the psychobabble. He did not know what had happened between her, Cat, Winston and the baby, but disliked the changed atmosphere. Even the horses were little comfort now that something was askew in the homestead. And Marianne was away on duty for three successive weekends. As for old Lady Artemis, she terrified him. Martin dumped the log-basket and asked diffidently: "Shall I build the fire up a bit?"

"Why not?" said Artemis expansively, turning her big green eyes on him with frightening charm. "Keep us all and baby warm. What a duck!"

"I'll tell Mrs Hartley you're here," said Martin, and immediately regretted it. He sounded like some kinda Jeeves! Why was it, he thought resentfully as he slipped back into the kitchen, that he could be on terms of perfect ease and familiarity with Gervase, Cat, the twins, and everyone else he met in this place from Mrs Bird to Lord Gratton, but still feel like a hick and a stumblebum whenever he was round Caroline or Lady Artemis? No way were they better than the others, not by anybody's standards. Not cleverer, not kinder, certainly not more useful. It was just that in their presence his stature seemed to shrink and his hands and feet to grow huge and unwieldy.

Cat was in the utility room, rinsing out some milk bottles. She looked tired, and her eyes were a little red, but she smiled at Martin.

"Gervase's mother's come," he said.

"I know," replied Cat. "I'm hiding for a moment. You know how it is. Some people make your feet go all enormous, and you just know you're going to be rude."

"Yeah," said Martin, comforted. "Me too."

"I'll go through in a minute," said Cat. "I just had a bit of a shock this morning, that's all. I need a while to get myself ready to face Artemis. It'll be easier when Dad arrives, and

Lindy. You remember from Christmas, Mark's wife. Dad's giving her a lift."

Suddenly she leaned on the drainer, using her two hands to steady herself, and her head fell forwards with a shuddering breath, as if she had been stricken by pain. Martin looked at her with real concern now.

"Shall I get Gervase? He's only cleaning out the vet. cupboard."

"No," said Cat. She straightened up and turned to dry her hands, and Martin saw that she was crying. He started towards her, his hand outstretched to touch her shoulder, then thought better of it. Alone like this, with the colour gone from her cheeks and her hair fluffed out, she suddenly looked too vulnerable – and strangely, too damn pretty – to risk touching. With a small embarrassed "Uh, OK," he backed out of the utility room.

Alone in the room Cat went on staring at the toy which had caught her eye. It was a rag-doll clown with a Velcro tab on it to fasten around a baby's wrist. Winston had bought it at the Midholt toy shop for Mary-Annie, who had spent many hours waving it enthusiastically on her arm. Caroline, although she did not know its origins, had banished it because *Hey, Baby!* said that tied-on toys discouraged babies from correct development of the grasping reflex. Now it was lying, damp and discarded, on top of the pedal-bin with the other rubbish.

In the living room, over a glass of sherry, Artemis solved the problem of Caroline's future dwelling.

"You're absolutely *right* not to go back to London," she said. "It's a *frightful* place to bring up a little gel. What you need is a cottage, and put the rest of your settlement away to pick up some interest for when you and Maria need it most. There are things," she spoke with the wisdom of a woman whose friends numbered many ageing and querulous ex-wives of wealthy men, "things you never *can* get a man to pay for. He'll do school fees, obviously, but there are things like ponies. And decent ski-ing."

"I like the idea of a cottage," said Caroline. "But I haven't seen anything to buy or rent round here, and I'd like to be near my sister and Gervase. I can still help with the driving, then." She smiled, the image of a princess in a story, as kind as she was beautiful.

"Why not the Rectory Cottage?" said Artemis. "Mr Dallway would let you have it for hardly anything. It can't be sold because of some trust or other, and being right against the churchyard. But as rector in charge he's responsible for upkeep, and it's a terrible worry it standing empty."

"Is it up for rent?" said Caroline, interested. "I never knew." The cottage in question, two miles from Knoll Farm on the edge of Midmarsham, was well known to her: tiny, dilapidated pale-pink, with beautiful old oak window frames and a sagging roof of mossy red tiles.

"He had a tenant for ten years, a potter woman, but she left and Mr Dallway just can't bear the idea of putting it on the open market to rent. Not when it's so close to the church. And the Rectory. People have these *sound systems*, you know . . ."

Caroline laughed. "Not me. I like silence. It would be perfect if I could rent it for the moment. Just while Alan and I sort out the money, and I think about the long term. Shall I ask the vicar?"

"No," said Artemis. "*I* shall *tell* him."

She did so before dinner that very evening, making Robert drive her and Caroline down to the Rectory as soon as he arrived, and bursting in on her old friend Mr Dallway's modest evening meal. "All settled then," she said, half-an-hour later, getting back into the car.

"He needs to clear it with the diocese," protested Robert, who was hungry and not a little cross.

"He will," said Artemis. "And it'll be *lovely* for Caroline to have her own little place with her own little baby. I might," she said kittenishly, "come and stay! In that *lovely* little back bedroom!"

"That would be lovely," said Caroline politely. "No, really lovely." Robert, tired of all this ladylike loveliness, put his foot down and sped up the lane to his dinner.

"When shall you move?" asked Gervase later, tackling his duck. "Is the cottage habitable?"

"Perfectly," said Caroline. "Just some decorating, which won't take long, it's so tiny. I've imposed on you for so long, I really feel I should get out of all your hair now, so I'll decamp as soon as possible."

Cat, still quiet and red eyed, looked sharply at her sister but could detect no other meaning behind this. Robert said: "Well, you'll be close at hand. I trust you'll carry on as chauffeur."

"Of course!" said Caroline. "Oh, we'll be in and out of one another's houses all the time! Very Jane Austen! Lovely!" She was gay tonight, a flush in her cheeks, smiling like the little girl Robert remembered. He smiled back. Then his eye caught his elder daughter's face, tired and tense, and he raised an eyebrow in her direction in gentle query. Cat avoided his glance and turned to Lindy, who was also strangely quiet.

"Everything OK?"

"Lovely," said Lindy mechanically, but her enthusiasm was but a pale echo of Caroline's. "Lovely duck. Is it from the farm?"

"Yes," said Gervase, innocently. Martin glanced at Caroline, but she continued demurely to dissect her own portion. He wondered whether it was possible for anybody else to use the word "lovely".

"Lovely and plump," said Lindy to the duck, trying to sound more enthusiastic. "Super."

She fell silent again, and this time Cat made no effort to draw her back into conversation. Robert embarked on some story from his UN aid conference, about a scheme for raising fowls in the Ugandan highlands. Martin asked intelligent questions. Caroline began talking nursery furnishings to Artemis. It was Gervase who looked around, his first hunger assuaged, and enquired: "Did Duane and Winston eat earlier?"

"Duane's at the pub with his girlfriend," said Cat. "Having chips. Winston said he wasn't hungry. He'll be in the bunkhouse."

"I don't think he is," said Martin politely. "The lights are off."

"Perhaps he went to the pub with Duane," said Gervase. He looked at his watch, hesitated, frowned, then explained to the company at large:

"He is supposed to be in by nine, under his probation conditions. Until the end of the month, anyway. Then he has a month without curfews, then he's clear."

• Libby Purves

"I don't know how you live with all this crime business," said Artemis, shuddering. "You must admit, it is rather sordid."

Cat stared at her plate, and the wave of misery which had hung above her all day broke and overwhelmed her. This particular overture from Artemis had been familiar for the whole of her married life. Normally she would have answered, taken issue with the old monster, challenged her on Gervase's behalf while he smiled dryly in his corner. He rather liked being relieved, by his wife's voluble loyalty, of the tiresome need to defend his vocation from his mother. That was the pattern of their relationship as mother and daughter-in-law, and it had been for years a comfortable joke between Cat and Gervase. Years ago Gervase used to laugh about it at bedtime: "Forty-fifteen, I think. My darling, I can't tell you what a relief it is to have you take over the job of arguing social policy with my Mama. I've been doing it for twenty years to absolutely no effect." Cat used to laugh too, and say "You set me up, you bastard. One day I'll teach you a lesson. I'll crack, and agree with her that it's all just too sordid and that they should be locked up and the key thrown away. You wait."

This time, however, she could not respond to Artemis. Tonight the Knoll Farm Project did seem sordid, and pointless, and hopeless. Winston, as she knew perfectly well, had gone to the Midmarsham pub with Duane in her car. He would certainly not be back by nine. It was his first breach of the probation condition since a couple of rebellious evenings early in his stay. Before Mary-Annie came. It would not be the last truancy for Winston was suddenly alone and so – Cat thought with crushing misery – was she.

For it was Gervase's job to keep Winston on the rails, sober and well-governed and up to his work: but only Cat understood the terrible thing which had been done to the boy, and only she feared the terrible consequences. Gervase, for some reason, was wilfully blind to the danger; he could see only Caroline's problems and Caroline's rights. Cat pressed her lips together. She should be angry, but the sensation in her was more like fear. After all these years of living with volatile, angry, damaged, awkward boys and never thinking twice about it, she had for the first time a sense of foreboding.

She realized, with a shock of unwilling admiration, that the reason this sense of dread was so new to her was that Gervase had, quite simply, never been wrong before. He had had failures, like Gary. But he had never misjudged a situation so badly. She, and all of the changing, rolling population of boys and volunteers, had sheltered for sixteen years behind his wisdom and unerring instinct. If his judgement had deserted him, they would all be bare to the winds.

Somehow, nauseous and frightened, she got through dinner, joining in the ebb and flow of spiritless conversation. Once, a dustbin lid blew off outside, and with a twisting pain she remembered Christmas Eve and the racket Toby and Topsy made in the lambing pens. She longed for Toby now as never before. Not for comfort or understanding, for these had never been the currency between them. Rather Cat wanted Toby to bring a joke, a diversion, an outrage; to splash a rude half-brick into the stagnant, reeking pond of family life. But God knew where he was, or whether the sister who wanted him most would ever see him again.

She stood alone in the kitchen at ten, stacking dishes in the sink for Martin to wash up after he had checked the livestock. Winston was not back. Duane was, which made this even more worrying; he had come in for a mug of cocoa and volunteered the information that Winse was "off with some blokes he knows". Robert, Artemis, Gervase and Caroline were gathered round the fire. Lindy, who never spent more time in a room with Lady Artemis than she had to, wandered in to lean on the kitchen stove.

"C'n I help?"

"Martin might like someone to dry for him, in a minute," said Cat shortly. "I'm going upstairs early, got a bit of work to finish."

"Well, the thing is, I did want to ask you something." Lindy twisted girlishly, grinding her pointed toe on the floor, cocking her head on one side.

"Mmm?" said Cat interrogatively. She was scraping some bones into the bucket, not the pig-bucket but a newly installed bucket which fed a green plastic conical composter which Gervase was testing in the orchard on behalf of a recycling campaign. She noted with irritation that there was only one sachet of accelerator chemical left. Why was the simple life so bloody complicated? "Ask away."

"It's about Mark," said Lindy. "I wanted to know if you knew anything about him and kids. He's being funny about our having a baby."

"Ah, babies," said Cat obscurely. "Babies! Cup of instant?" The good coffeepot had gone through to the party in the living room. Gratefully, Lindy received a mug of the powdered variety and sat down.

"I really, really want us to have kids, like really soon," said Lindy. "We've been trying. I've been off the pill for a year."

"And Mark?"

"I thought he was fine at first. But now he won't talk about it."

"Perhaps he's afraid he's infertile? Men really don't like that idea," said Cat. She wondered what she had done to deserve this. Every family gathering ended with her sitting here, looking at poultry bones, drinking nasty coffee and discussing reproduction with a series of distraught female relatives.

"He won't go for tests," said Lindy. "But I don't think he's afraid of firing blanks. I think he's quite bloody *pleased*." The end of the sentence rose: her Birmingham accent and her language always became stronger as she grew more animated. Cat stared at her.

"You mean you think he doesn't actually want a baby?"

"That's it! He doesn't! He went along with me trying, but he keeps saying, ever so cheerfully, that sometimes it just isn't meant to be, and all this fertility treatment is against nature, and how kids aren't everything."

"I suppose they aren't," said Cat slowly. Lindy swept on:

"Then I thought back, and the thing is, he always did go on a lot about me and him being – you know, everything. He always says how he only needs me in the world." She blushed. "He once said his mother never even liked him, and I was the first woman who understood him and so he needs all of me. He doesn't even like me being on the phone when he gets home. I have to be at the door, all lovely-dovey."

Cat, recipient as usual of one confidence too many, squirmed a little. "What I'm getting at, Cathy," said her sister-in-law, banging her mug down on the table for emphasis, "is, I think he might have done something know what I mean?"

"Er—" said Cat. "No, I don't quite get—"

"I'm almost certain," said Lindy, "that sometime, I dunno when, he had the snip!"

"A vasectomy?" said Cat, incredulous. "Why?"

"To not have babies, ever!" said Lindy. "That's why people have it done, right?" And she burst into noisy tears just as the back door opened to admit an instantly embarrassed Martin.

Gervase woke early on Sunday, and found himself looking around the gloom of the curtained bedroom for the baby's cot. Then, shaking off the last soft rags of sleep, he remembered reality and went through his morning drill of composing his mind carefully to understanding, acceptance, and generosity.

Dear little Mary-Annie: she was best with her own mother's arms around her. Her mother, in turn, must be upheld and protected by the family, as all mothers should be supported and encouraged by the wider society. Each of us depends on all the others: the principle of chivalry, the courtesy of the strong to the weak, underlies all civilization. To be in a position to offer protection, support and comfort to those weaker or less fortunate is not a burden but an honour. We share the earth, and owe it, too, a certain courtesy.

Naturally, Gervase did not enunciate all these thoughts and principles as he lay beneath the lumpy duvet beside his sleeping wife. They merely gathered themselves around him, the daytime garments of conviction which he had worn ever since he had found them as an eighteen-year-old student volunteer on a London soup run. He had no need to preach sermons to himself or anybody else. It was not difficult to know what was right.

Sometimes there was even a melancholy beauty in doing right and thinking right, against your own more selfish inclinations. The baby had woken last night and Caroline had brought her down. Seeing them together, both so beautiful in the last flickering firelight, Gervase had been transfixed with an intensity of chivalry he had rarely felt. Or at least not since the day he first saw Cat, coping gracefully with her twin children at the gate of a mean and scruffy West London school where he had come for a City Farms committee meeting.

Cat stirred now, and rolled towards him. Gervase turned and smiled, then laid a hesitant hand on her shoulder. Her eyes snapped open.

"Uurgh," she said. Then, sitting upright, "Oh God. Did Winston get back?"

"Not by the time I came up," said Gervase. "With luck he's here now. I won't ring the Probation service over his breaking one curfew. He's been doing really well."

"You know why he isn't doing well any more, don't you?" said Cat.

"I doubt if it's as simple as you think," said Gervase. "You know my view. Winston's got to respect Caroline's wishes, the same as we do. It's part of learning how to grow up."

"Why shouldn't Caroline respect Winston a bit?" said Cat, wearily.

"I know it's hard for him," said Gervase. "But there'll be plenty more babies for him to play with. A new mother is vulnerable, and deserves support."

"I'm surprised you can't see anything wrong with Caroline's reasons for banning him from the baby," said Cat. "They're very Kensington, you know. Very Artemis."

"I don't presume to know her reasons. You have to make allowances for new mothers. Everyone has to, including Winston."

Cat climbed out of bed. "Well, I put it down to sex," she said rudely. "You can't think of anything but protecting Caroline, and I can't think of anything but how badly she's messing up poor old Winston."

"She can't be expected—" began Gervase, but his wife cut him off.

"No, you're right. She can't be expected to behave like anything but a selfish, snobbish cow. Till last night I never realized who it was your mother had reminded me of, all these years."

Gervase did not answer. It was not in his nature or within his principles to brawl with his wife.

Caroline had provided supermarket part-baked French rolls and croissants for breakfast, and Duane, seeing the prettily laid table, took fright and removed himself and his porridge to the garden on the pretext that it was a beautiful morning. Artemis, admiring the stiff white bib Caroline was tying on the baby, remarked that it was the most civilized breakfast-table she had seen in Knoll Farm for years. Martin, feeling more than ever like some kinda Jeeves, made the coffee. Robert had been out early to collect the Sunday papers from Midholt station and engrossed himself in the foreign news.

Cat picked up the business section and was reading about the corporate reorganization inside the Eden empire: it was a far less flattering version of the new structure and system than she had been writing for their newsletters over the past weeks, and she found herself cringing slightly at her involvement. Just as well Mark was not here until mid-morning to catch her reading it. Lindy was sleeping in, recovering from her cathartic, if inconclusive, storm of tears the night before. Cat, against her will, had promised to ask Mark the big vasectomy question, and was now cursing herself for this excess of helpfulness and wondering whether she could get out of it. Gervase came in from the farm just as the telephone began to ring.

"I'll get it," he said. Then: "Yes. Yes, it is. Oh dear. Are you pressing charges? Good. Shall I come over to collect him? Yes, obviously, the Probation service. Doug Willetts, at Midholt. Speak to him myself. About an hour. Thank you."

He came back to the table. Cat handed him a chipped mug of coffee, without comment. To the company in general Gervase said: "That was the police. I have to collect Winston"

"Really!" tinkled Artemis, mainly to Caroline. "Just like Christmas Day, isn't it dear? Do you *never* get a meal here without the police ringing?"

"Which station?" asked Cat. "Midholt?"

"No," said Gervase glumly. "Much worse. Northampton. He was in a club. It got raided."

Cat rubbed her eyes with the back of her hand. "But no charges?"

"No," said Gervase. "Only the sergeant did say he was apparently back with his old crowd. Two of the men with him were found in possession, and one has been charged with dealing. Luckily he was clean."

"I knew this would happen," said Cat. As Gervase left the room she looked across the table at Caroline, who was spooning apple into the baby's mouth with a neutral expression on her face.

"You did this," she said suddenly. "Caroline, you pushed him back onto the slippery slope. Poor bloody kid."

Caroline put down the spoon, and wiped Mary-Annie's mouth. The child was looking around beadily for the milk which should follow, and gave a little *yarr* of impatience. Caroline reached for the bottle.

"I hardly think that's fair," she said. "I was unwilling to let a farmhand with a drug record associate with my daughter. This morning's news isn't very likely to change my mind, is it?" She shook the prepared bottle of milk, and flipped the cap off.

"He wouldn't have *gone* back there," said Cat, between her teeth, "he wouldn't have *needed* his old friends, if he hadn't been so snubbed. Warned off going anywhere near a baby he'd loved and helped look after for most of her *life*. You did it, Caroline. Whatever happens to him now, you're involved."

"You're entitled to your opinion," said Caroline. "Look, sweetie. Bottle!"

Robert and Artemis found this exchange mystifying, and stared in open-mouthed astonishment at the cold fury which had fallen across this civilized breakfast-table. Martin, however, was overwhelmed by understanding, at last, what was going on. In the bunkhouse Winston had been sullen and angry all week, Duane oddly embarrassed and avoiding the family. He himself had exchanged no more than passing smiles with Mary-Annie, but only because he felt politely constrained in her dazzling mother's presence. The heat rose under his collar: was he, too, banned? Even without criminal convictions, he was, he supposed, a "farmhand".

Gervase reappeared, looked harassed, and saved him from the rising tide of embarrassment. "Martin, I've obviously got to drive into Northampton. Would you mind taking over? Just the horses to do, then the antibiotic shot for that ewe that had the prolapse. I put her in the isolation box. Give her more blowfly spray as well, just in case. There's a lot of stuff round her back end." Artemis shuddered and pushed away her croissant, but Martin gratefully said: "Yep. I'll go right now."

Cat left the table and threw her mug into the sink, where the handle broke off. "I'll be outside," she said to nobody in particular. Then she walked up alone to the meadow where she used to go with Mary-Annie on her hip. There was no frolicking up there now: the last lambs had given up, and become dully grazing sheep.

So solid was Gervase's principle that all should eat together that even on this Sunday, at one o'clock, ten adults were once again grouped around the table eating roast chicken, cauliflower cheese and peas as if nothing were amiss between them. Winston did not speak a word: Cat had tried to talk to him before lunch and got nowhere. Duane gobbled his food and sat, poised for flight, waiting his moment to make an excuse and cycle down to Midmarsham and his girlfriend. Mark had arrived, looking anxious and miserable and unable to keep his hands off Lindy, who fended off his clumsy caresses rather snappishly and flirted with an ever more embarrassed Martin. Artemis and Caroline talked about pelmets and rugs; Robert took in the atmosphere with dismay and escaped between courses, carrying a pile of greasy dishes, to confront his elder daughter in the kitchen.

"What *is* going on?" he asked plaintively. "I'd rather mediate in Sarajevo than your household just now."

"Caroline," said Cat savagely, "is what is going on. And, bloody soon I hope, she is going down the road."

"But I thought she was getting on well," said Robert with a plaintive, injured masculine obtuseness which irritated even his favourite daughter, not least because she knew him capable of better understanding. "I was so pleased when you said she was looking after the baby at last. And she's well rid of that dreadful Halliday man. Did I tell you he still rings me up for contacts? The nerve. Surely everything's on course, now? As far as it can be, with a divorce. Poor little Caro."

"Well, you're wrong. It was better the way it was before," said Cat, taking the plates from him. "Caroline the frigid monster-woman was a bloody sight less trouble than Caroline the Perfect bloody Madonna and child. Believe me. The sooner she goes, the better. I'm sorry Dad: I've had it."

"Well, well," said Robert soothingly. "Diana always said it was asking for trouble when women shared a kitchen. Especially sisters. You've done very well."

His elder daughter made a noise very like "Bah!" Robert continued: "And what about Mark? Does he always come home from sales conferences and maul his wife in public? And why is *she* so grumpy?"

Cat looked at her father, wondering whether to explain the whole thing to him. That day in the House of Lords he had shown unexpected subtlety of understanding: maybe she ought to lay out before him as patriarch all the twisted feelings that lay between his children and their households. But no: she herself could not bear it. That lunch had been embarrassing enough, without her now plunging into some lurid account of suspected vasectomies, quixotic adoption attempts, misplaced chivalry, psychobabble, wilfully provocative designer babywear and an orphan boy betrayed back into a Dickensian life of crime. Instead she just said sadly:

"Sorry Dad. All your little lambs have just grown up and turned into sheep. It happens."

Across both of them, at that moment, fell the shadow of Toby, the black sheep and now the lost one. But neither mentioned him. There was nothing to say.

The task of challenging Mark was not easy. After lunch, he sat next to Lindy on the sofa, holding her unwilling hand. After twenty minutes he finished the last of his coffee and said: "We'd better be off home."

Lindy made a face to Cat and said, "Yeah, OK. I'll get my case—"

"I'll come up," said Mark.

Lindy threw an appealing glance at Cat, who nodded and said: "No, just come through a minute – I've got something to show you."

Unwillingly, he followed her through to the kitchen. Here, weary of diplomacy and subterfuge, she turned to him and said crossly: "Have you had a vasectomy?"

Mark stared at her and took a step back, hitting his head on the low beam by the cooker.

"Why do you ask?" he said stiffly, when he had recovered himself.

"Because Lindy's upset she isn't getting pregnant."

"She could have talked to me about it. These things take time."

"Oh, for God's sake!" said Cat. "I don't want to get involved in your reproductive strategies, I'm sick of the whole bloody subject, for certain reasons I will not bore you with. But Lindy has been weeping half the night about it, and she suspects you're not telling her something. Just go on, spit it out, let's be honest for a change. If you won't tell me, at least have it out with her. Bloody, bloody families!"

She sniffed and, to her horror, began to cry. Mark stood thunderstruck, then seemed to realize that this let him off answering her question, and gave a curious, tight little smile. Cat did not see it but Lindy, who had been lurking behind the door to the backstairs saw the smirk and stepped out to confront him.

"I should've asked you myself," she said. "Cat, I'm ever so sorry. I think I know now, anyway, dunni?"

He was silent. She said again, her voice thick and rough and angry, "Dunni? Mark? S'true, innit?"

"I've already been to the clinic," he said stiffly. "About getting it reversed. They say there's a good chance."

Lindy stared at him a moment, then threw her arms around his shoulders and hugged him.

"Marky! You old fool!" she said. Her tears damped his crisp conference shirt, and she shifted her grip to cling with both hands to his grey suit lapels. "Why din't you tell me?"

Cat recovered herself and said, "Look, you two, get in your car. Drive down the lane, then stop and talk about all this. You don't want Dad and Artemis and Caroline all involved."

But it was too late. Caroline had drifted through with the coffee tray, and to Cat's horror she had lying next to the coffeepot a proof copy of a pamphlet called *Eden PLC and the Millennium: The plan, the prospects, the people.*

"Look," she said innocently. "Artemis found this down the back of the sofa. Don't you work for Eden, Mark? We thought you might be interested."

22

On a grey morning in late June, Caroline moved into the Rectory Cottage. She and Artemis and a bevy of cowed workmen had transformed it from fusty and chintzy neglect into a simple but beautiful interior of Shaker austerity, in keeping with Caroline's new mood of West Coast spirituality. The plank floors were sanded, polished and covered with soft knotted Indian rugs, the sofas draped in expensive cream wool, the matchboarding painted pale blue, the kitchen furnished with two traditional dressers and a deep old stone sink. It was the same sink, but looked quite different now that it was surrounded not by chipped Formica but by a solid oak worktop shaped and cunningly dropped over the previous surface.

"No point spending money on things you can't take away. Not in rented property," said Artemis masterfully. Cat, still low in spirits and reeling from a long, crazy letter from Mark about breach of trust, professional duplicity and wanton conflict of interest, had been glad to have Artemis stay on to help Caroline. Her mother-in-law had at least the gift of being a useful surface irritant, which distracted everybody from deeper pains. During some of her more absurd tirades about the way modern youth "simply don't care", even Duane caught Cat's eye once or twice and almost giggled.

Only Winston remained wrapped up in himself, silent and morose. Martin told her that he had asked for one of the Polaroids of Mary-Annie, and kept it in his pocket. The baby herself he avoided, bolting his food at meal times and leaving early. Cat tried to talk to him once or twice, but whatever

softening of his angry nature the baby had brought about, it
had not yet taught him how to confide.

Thanks to Artemis' relentless bullying of the workmen, on
moving day only the extractor fan in the kitchen remained
to be fitted, everything else being neatly and beautifully in
place. Caroline had not wanted to bring up any household
equipment from Kensington: Alan, she told Gervase with an air
of dignified sorrow, had actually moved in one of his girlfriends.
Accordingly she fetched only the rest of her clothes and a
few personal things in four smart suitcases, and equipped the
cottage kitchen from new. Alan had agreed to settle upon her,
in addition to the maintenance he paid for Mary-Annie, a capital
sum amounting to half the value of the Kensington house. Large
Kensington houses were doing rather well that spring, and Alan's
stockbroker had organized her investments. Caroline would be
comfortable, even without work.

All that had to be done on moving day was for her and Artemis
to bring the cases and Mary-Annie down the lane in Cat's car,
and for Gervase to drive the baby's bulky, awkward-shaped mass
of new equipment in the LandRover. That night Caroline ate
supper and slept in her own cottage home, with her sister's
mother-in-law for company in the spare room.

The weather cleared during the day; at dusk, while Mary-
Annie gurgled herself to sleep in her new pink room and
Artemis telephoned her friends to relate her triumph, Caroline
wandered out into the overgrown little garden next to the
graveyard.

The sky was turning to darker blue above the last red smudge
of sunset, and against it one star shone bright and alone. As she
stood there gently thoughtful, relishing the damp fragrance of
the garden, a footstep crunched on pebbles beside the lane and
made her turn. Gervase stood there, apologetic but smiling, with
a framed picture under his arm.

"I forgot to give you this," he said. "Housewarming." Caroline
took it: behind the glass was a spotted, faded Victorian print,
obviously one of a series of allegorical exhortations to morality.
The picture showed a hooded and skeletal figure at a chessboard,
opposite a young knight; at least, the human player was attired as
a knight but the face was sexless in its purity, and fair hair waved

down its back. Beneath the picture was the legend: *Against the pure, no evil shall prevail.*

"It was in my bedroom when I was a child," said Gervase. "I found it a very reassuring notion. I thought you and Mary-Annie might like it, especially as you'll be teaching her chess before long."

"We'll both teach her." Caroline smiled up at him in the dusk. "But even before that, she's going to need her best uncle nearby. Thanks for everything. It feels funny moving out. But do come and see us. Often."

"I will," said Gervase.

With Caroline and the baby gone, the next few days saw Knoll Farm returning to a semblance of its old normality. Winston in his present surly state was no pleasure to be with, but no more trouble than many other boys had been down the years. Duane had been offered a job on a production line making kits to convert cars for the disabled in a rural industrial unit not far from the Midmarsham pub and his girlfriend. They were, he confided to Cat, keen to "start a family". Cat flinched, but only told him he had plenty of time. A new boy, Terry, was coming in July. Winston's curfew had been extended for another month by Mr Willetts after his escapade in Northampton, but he too was due to leave soon.

Caroline continued to do driving errands and shopping by day, picking up a daily list without much conversation with her sister. Marianne came down for the weekend, to Martin's delight, and the two of them went for a five-hour walk and came back glowing and subtly changed. Next time she came there was no chance for anything but working at Martin's side in the hayfield; haymaking, at Knoll Farm, was deliberately done in an old-fashioned and laborious manner without machinery so that during the weeks of June the farm became hectically busy. The horses were out every day turning or raking the sweet-smelling piles of drying grass, and sweating men built stacks with pitchforks as they would have done a century before.

The idea, as Gervase often told journalists (who ignored it) was not olde-worlde picturesqueness, but to practise his ideas about the dignity and healing qualities of simple manual labour. Nonetheless, amateur photographers and camcorder enthusiasts appeared, as usual, alongside the hedges to record this pastoral poppy-strewn scene with stooks and stacks and horses. One man asked Winston to move out of shot because, being black, he "didn't quite fit. No offence, mate".

Cat, who rarely helped outdoors at this season because of her hay fever, continued desultorily at her desk with the window tightly shut. One morning Gervase came upstairs with her post and stood by her chair holding a letter of his own.

"How about this?" he asked. Despite Cat's visible depression since the affair of Caroline and Winston, his manner towards her was the same as it always was: level, gentle, respectful.

"Just a mo," she said, slitting open her bank statement. "I just want to check this." She looked down at the figures before her, incredulous. "Gosh," she said. "Ta-ra! I'm rich."

Gervase walked over to the window and looked down at the fattening sheep across the lane. Cat continued to stare at the print-out. Since the upheavals at Eden and the removal of her driving duties at home, she had been doing a lot of extra work and logging it hastily in her account book. She had not realized, however, that she was doing so very well. Each month her account automatically fed £750 into the shared account; after she had put away tax money, this rarely left her with more than £120 a month against which she could draw her infrequent personal cheques. Now, although it seemed that the joint account had received its monthly boost, Mrs Catherine Hartley's Private A/C showed a credit of £1893.97. Moreover, another Eden payment was due any day and could well be even bigger than the last few.

"Yup, I'm rich," she said again. Then, looking out through the dusty window at the sunshine: "Shall we have a holiday, for once?"

Gervase began to pace around the room. "You know how I'm placed in summer," he said. "Hay, then harvest. We could go away for a long weekend in September, if I could get cover here and stand down the boys for a few days. I can't just walk out."

"Yes. Silly idea," said his wife, still staring at the statement. "You wouldn't miss me, though, if I went?"

"You do what you like. You work too hard," said Gervase automatically. Then, brandishing his own envelope: "But look at this. Morefield Youth Trust."

"Oh, that bequest thingy? It was in the papers. The millionaire with the druggy son who died?"

"That's him. Anyway, they're really interested in what we're doing. Their senior Trustee is the Prince of Wales. Apparently he told them he was coming here on a private visit. They want to do a fact-finding trip around the time he comes."

"That's nice," said Cat vaguely. "Have they got any spare money?"

"Heaps. But what puzzles me is that they seem to think the Prince is visiting us during haymaking, because they're asking about photography."

"He'd have to get a move on. There's only about a week left, isn't there?"

"Yes. What do you suppose is going on? Do you think they're considering actually supporting the project?"

"Search me," said Cat. She was still looking down at her bank statement. "Interesting, anyway. Well done."

When he had gone she opened the next envelope, the Midholt Choral Society newsletter, which against all reasonable expectation seemed to surprise and interest her almost as much as the bank statement.

At lunch-time she came downstairs. Mrs Bird was dishing out leek and potato soup; she had diffidently asked for more hours' work to cushion the effort and worry of visiting Gary, who had been moved to Littlehey Prison. Cat gladly agreed: there had still been pleasure in cooking when Mary-Annie was all hers, sitting in her bouncy chair, grabbing at her feet and crooning to the birds outside the window. Since she had gone the meals were once again a dull, repetitive chore and she had resolved, at any cost, to pay Mrs Bird and avoid the kitchen.

The boys were already sitting at table, elbows sprawled, eating lumps of bread. Gervase was on the telephone in the hall, but came through, looking almost excited.

"Next Wednesday. It's definite. The visit."

"What visit?" asked Cat, who was reading the Choral Society newsletter again.

"What we talked about. Upstairs. He's coming."

"Old Bat Ears?" said Cat, incredulously. "Here? Wow!"

Sometimes, thought Gervase with a flash of unwonted irritation, his wife sounded just like a cheeky teenage boy. His fault, perhaps, for surrounding her with teenage boys for so many years. Or maybe it was some obscure gesture of solidarity with her favourite, her missing, brother. He recovered his aplomb and frowned meaningly, jerking his head towards the three young men and Mrs Bird.

"Yes. The – er – conservation, bat people. To look at the barn," he improvised. "They think we've got a rare species. Of bat." Cat stared at him in turn. Gervase very rarely lied. It consorted ill with his usual dignity.

Later, alone, he chided her. "We have to keep it quiet," he said. "It's not on the official register of Royal engagements. The boys can know on the day. It's all supposed to be very low-key, but it ties up with the possibility that the Morefield Trust will be quite a lot of help to the project. Financially."

"Aha," said Cat. "Money. Beats royalty, any day."

"They're coming on Monday to look us over," said Gervase. "And if they decide to put themselves behind us, they'll announce it on the day of the Prince's visit, to invited press. It could take a lot of pressure off us financially. Off you."

"Then I'll be even richer." Cat was in a frivolous mood, so strong a contrast to her recent depression that her husband was puzzled.

"Are you OK?" he asked.

"Never better," said Cat. "But I shan't be here to press the royal paw. I'm going on a little holiday. A mission, actually. I'm going to France. I might even track down Toby."

It was curious, she thought in later years, that despite the months of wondering about Toby, and even the abortive discussion with Mark on whether he might have gone to one of their childhood cities, it had never occurred to her to make the journey herself. Partly, it was her habit of dour pragmatism. Cat, since early adulthood, had gone to some lengths to suppress romantic notions in herself. She recognized in her heart a treacherous desire to think of Toby as having fled the world to purge his grief; perhaps to turn up years later like Sebastian Flyte in *Brideshead Revisited*, as a lay-brother in some peaceful Mediterranean monastery. On identifying this wishful, wistful train of thought she had firmly quashed it. Grief or no grief, she cruelly told herself, in spite of the haunting oddity of that postcard Toby was more likely to be off somewhere with another woman, or women, and a great deal of booze. When Caroline had made for Los Angeles claiming to search for Toby, Cat had half-envied and half-despised her sister. It was obviously nonsense: nobody ever found a wilfully missing person just by wandering around looking for them in the right few thousand acres of the globe, even if they could guess where that was. The idea of following the Calais lead had come to her, but been quashed as ridiculous and self-indulgent. There was, after all, Mary-Annie to look after. Then.

The other reason, she saw now, was that in lives such as theirs a kind of curtain fell at the end of every posting, cutting you off from the past. Diplomatic families seemed to know by instinct that it was better that way. None of the Grattons had been back to Lille, nor to Berne or Tel Aviv. Caroline had gone to Venice, but only as part of her fine-art career. Robert travelled to Washington, but once admitted that even then he steered clear of the old house and the old street. Caroline had gone back to Los Angeles, but only because of her abnormal state of emotional turmoil. No, thought Cat: in the ordinary way of things, diplomatic and military families rarely go back. Perhaps they are afraid to acknowledge that they are forever incomplete: that they have left torn-off roots in too wide a spread of alien soil.

But then again, maybe it was this very sense of taboo which had made her wonder if Toby had. Of all of them, he with his perennial perversity was the most likely to break unwritten rules, to whisk aside the curtain and disappear into some corner of the family past. He always liked forbidden thrills. Caroline had shown symptoms of hectic, almost guilty excitement over her return to LA. Now Cat herself was finding that the idea of going to Lille – only an hour beyond Calais on the motorway, for heaven's sake – brought a surprising frisson of joy and fright at her own temerity.

Even the windfall money might not have tripped her into it, were it not for the Midholt Choral Society newsletter and the boxed announcement on the front page.

TWINNING CONCERT WITH SAINT-OMER:
FAURÉ REQUIEM AND CHANSONS CYCLE

We are now travelling to Saint-Omer via the Channel Tunnel! Three 12-seater minibuses will make the journey on 14 June, returning 16 June. On the return trip we are full, as six of our twin-town choristers are coming to swell the numbers for the Verdi Requiem at the Corn Exchange. This means there are six spare seats outbound. Anybody want a one-way ticket to fabulous Flanders? High quality on-board singing guaranteed, a snip at only £22. You could always take the Eurostar back from Lille! and make the whole round trip for £50. We leave at noon on the 14th and get there for dinner and a run-through.

CHOIR – REMEMBER YOUR MUSIC THIS TIME!

Cat was a long-lapsed member of the Choral Society. She had not known about the twinning. So it was thirty-three years since she had read the name of Saint-Omer.

It brought back a cluster of other names on signposts long ago: Béthune, Lens, Douai, Ypres, Roubaix, Armentières: signs from the centre of the northern city of Lille, signs to suburbs and towns of the Pas-de-Calais, long ago and far away in flat homely Flanders where she had been a child. The odd word *Tourcoing* sprang into her mind: where was it? A lit sign on the front of a tram, that was it: *Tourcoing*, suburb of Lille. Her friend Marie-Noelle came in from there, to school with the *bonnes soeurs* at 66 Rue Royale. Cat really liked Sylvie better, and they both came ice-skating on Sunday mornings with Cat and Véronique, her very best friend; sometimes their brothers Thierry and Chrétien came too. Sylvie was the best skater of all, and swung around the rink to the strains of the "Blue Danube" or – better! – Edith Piaf singing *"Je ne regrette rien"*. Cat, at twelve, came alone to the *patinoire* by tram with her own money and her own skates in a smart white plastic boot-bag. By the end of her time in Lille she was enjoying heady freedoms: allowed to walk home from school, alone or in charge of Toby, and to buy a hot *croque-monsieur* in the Place Général de Gaulle on the way. In Lille she found her first near-adult freedoms.

Now she closed her eyes, and saw again for the first time in years the humped, scampering red neon outline of a ferret on the far side of the Grand'Place. Why was it there? Ah yes, the bookshop and stationery supplier where she bought her neat school pencil cases. *Le Furet du Nord*. Why should a ferret be the symbol of a bookshop? Was it still running and writhing up there today?

Lille! God bless it. She would go there and try out her long forgotten French again; she would not kid herself that she would find Toby, but you never knew. Maybe the best way to find a runaway was to run away yourself.

However, as an acknowledgement of the dull middling English-woman she had become Cat would cross the Channel humbly, in a spare seat on the choir bus. All this she had decided, upstairs in her room before lunch. Nothing would now deflect her from it.

"But are you sure you don't want to put it off a few days?" asked Gervase, a little bewildered. "It's not every day we get . . . well, a royal visit."

Cat turned to him and he saw that she was smiling: a mischievous, younger smile. Like her brother Toby's.

"Ah, come on," she said. "You know you're better at selling the project than me. That's why I keep out of these PR things. I'd only say something negative, or flip, or let on about Winston's little outing the other night. Do you really want to let your copy-writing cynic of a wife loose on His Royal Highness's innocent idealism?"

Gervase looked helplessly at her. "Will you at any rate see the Morefield Trust with me on Monday?" he asked. "Please? You are part of the project. For the boys. The family side does matter as well as the work."

"Yes, OK," said Cat. "I'll be good. Whether poor old Winston will be is another matter."

23

Winston, in the event, behaved perfectly, although without much enthusiasm. Perhaps he already knew that the Monday of the Morefield Trust inspection was his last at Knoll Farm. Later that night he went for a walk after supper, hitched a lift into Midholt, and drank six cans of lager with some old acquaintances who by ill-chance he found sitting on the horse trough outside the Corn Exchange with their feet in the Council's prized floral arrangement. He rode with them in a battered Ford van as far as Northampton where, in the clubs and on the streets, he spent the next few days before being picked up by the police in possession of several smiley, sticky dots of Ecstasy and a wad of unearned money.

Cat went to see him in the remand centre on the day before her trip to France. It was a concession, wrenched from the system after several days' hard work by Mr Willetts. He had high regard for Mrs Hartley, and firmly believed that any request she made must have some reason behind it.

"Hello," she said. Winston sat, looking smaller and more defenceless than usual, on a cold plastic chair opposite her.

"Hi," said Winston. He looked away, apparently studying the peeling paint on the small room's door.

"I just came to say something," said Cat. "Do you want to know what it is?"

"Advice to yobs? Come on boy, get yo' act together, society expects it?" said Winston. "OK, might as well."

"No," said Cat. "Not advice to yobs. Three pieces of infor-mation. None of them will be any use when your case comes up, but you might want to know them."

She wanted his attention, and was uncertain whether he had taken any of the fuddling drugs his friends dealt in. She paused, watching him, until unwillingly he dragged his eyes back to her; eyes which, she saw, were perfectly clear and undrugged. He said: "Yeah? What?"

Cat smiled. She had him listening now. She raised three fingers, and counted off her points on them with the other hand.

"Fact one," she said. "My sister, Caroline Halliday, is a silly, snotty, spoilt little cow. None of her opinions on anything – except perhaps Renaissance altarpieces – is worth wasting five minutes on. Got that? She's a silly bitch, and I often want to slap her one."

Winston stared, his attention riveted. Cat continued:

"Fact two. You, Winston Maliba, are one of the best, carefullest, gentlest, most intelligent men with a baby that I have ever known. You are better than an awful lot of women. Your own kids will be really lucky to have you. So will any kids you work with. You did a lot for Mary-Annie, when her bloody mother wouldn't play with her and I was too busy to do much. All the fun that you had together will stay there, inside her, for all her life. Believe me. I know about babies. She'll be a happier and better grown-up because she had you."

Winston sat silent, staring at his thin dark hands on the table in front of him. He was very still. There was a silence.

"Do you want to talk any more now?" said Cat gently.

He shook his head, and a tear fell onto his right knuckle.

"OK," she said, getting up. "So I'll just tell you Fact three. You haven't blown it. Not for always. Even if they send you down, there's life out there waiting. See you."

"That was quick" said Mr Willetts, outside.

"All we needed," said Cat.

The big man sighed. "I've been talking to the solicitor. We might get him another non-custodial sentence. That's what I pray for. If he does time now, he's had it."

"Keep praying," said Cat.

The second minibus in the Choral Society's convoy held five baritones, two basses, four sopranos and Cat. More than half of them had been with her in the choir, for lives did not change fast in Midholt. It was strange to be among them again, and reminded her of more light-hearted days before the Lloyds disaster and the land sale.

When she was first married to Gervase he had a full-time helper on the farm, a woman to cook, and the bunkhouse held five boys at a time. Cat did some part-time copywriting for an advertising agency, raised her own children, and had leisure enough to spend two evenings a week singing in this good-spirited innocent neighbourhood choir. As they teased her now for her desertion, she felt soothed to be among them. They were people from a rare, brief time of undemanding ordinariness in her life: quite different from her spiky cosmopolitan family, from the boys on the farm project and their social workers, and above all from the savage, neurotic working world of Eden PLC. They were kind people, unimaginative, comfortable, sensible provincials who ran shops and banks and builders' yards and channelled their romanticism into the eternal yearnings of song.

"Don't know why you ever left, Mrs Hartley," said the leading bass, gallantly. "Top C's never been the same without you."

"Oooh! cheeky!" said two sopranos in unison. "Not that we don't miss you, love."

"Well, someone has to be in the audience," said Cat. "I'm a very good subscriber."

"Saw you with that sister of yours a month or so back," said a baritone, owner of Midholt's leading fruit-and-vegetable shop. "Gor, that's a beautiful woman. Nearly made me lose my place."

"Pretty, but not flawless," said Cat. "Cracked notes, there. Dissonant intervals." The others laughed. The last musical director had referred to all faults of character by musical similes. Then they teased her until, half unwillingly, she led them off, hesitant but true, into the verse from *Dido and Aeneas* in which she had led the women's chorus thirteen years earlier:

"*To the hills and the vales,*" sang Cat to the speeding traffic on the grey unrolling road,

> "*To the rocks and the mountains*
> *To the musical glades*
> *And the cool shady fountains.*"

The bus filled with sound as the rest joined in, the men improvising themselves a deeper part beneath the soaring sopranos:

> Let the tri-hi-hi-hi-hi-hi-hiumphs
> Let the tri-i-i-umphs
> Of love and of beauty be shown."

Bowling down the A1 they sang on through their common repertoire, the driver – a non-singer, only there for the *hypermarché* beer – smiling indulgently as the women's notes soared and swooped around his ears, and the men's boomed deep enough to rattle the windows on the hired bus.

Back at the farm, Duane and Martin sat a little disconsolately over their mid-morning mug of tea in the bunkhouse.

"Just us, now," said Martin. "And the boss. Weird, huh?"

"I'm off next week," said Duane. "New job an' all. You staying on?"

"Gervase asked me to," said Martin. "I can do some of the driving, and I suppose I'm quite handy with the horses now. We'll have to teach the new boys. I don't need to be home till September."

They looked up as Gervase loomed in the doorway. It was rare for him to come to the bunkhouse unless to sort out a fight: this place, in his system, represented the boys' own territory, a rehearsal for living their own lives. He was smiling.

"Some news. Good news. We are going to be taken over. It's partly thanks to the good impression you gave last Monday."

"Whassat?" asked Duane. Martin, who had taken in more of the import of the Trustees' visit, said:

"They're giving you a grant? The Morefield Trust?"

"Better," said Gervase. "They're employing me. At a salary, to run Knoll Farm more or less exactly the way it is now. Only with a full-time trained care assistant, so we can take people with learning difficulties on day programmes. And we get funding for four places at once in the bunkhouse. And a volunteer, on pocket-money, when we can get one."

"Does it all change, then?" asked Duane, stupidly.

"No, that's the beauty of it. They want the farm to run the way it does now. It's just that we can have more lads. We always used to. And someone to look."

"Will it still be your farm?" asked Martin. He wondered whether he ought to have asked that; Gervase looked embarrassed. But he answered readily enough.

"I make the land over to the Trust," he said. "The house stays mine. The contract is firm for five years, then if I want I can train a successor, sell them the house at market value and sever the link. Or sign for another five."

"Sounds neat," said Martin. "I don't see any farmers back home handing over fifty acres just like that, though."

Gervase laughed, looking twenty years younger.

"I daresay I wasn't ever really cut out to be a landowner," he said. "And I've no one to leave it to but Cat, and she wouldn't want what she calls a load of old mud."

Martin smiled with him, but inwardly marvelled at the unworldliness of some Brits. It was, he knew, quite possible and even likely that the odd, fierce, likeable Cat Hartley would not object to her husband's handing over some hundred thousand dollarsworth of land to a charity in return for being allowed to carry on working as hard as he did now. But he wondered whether Gervase had had a chance to ask her.

Later that day, Gervase took the LandRover past Rectory Cottage, and on an impulse, stopped. Caroline was kneeling on the grass making a daisy-chain. Mary-Annie was sitting up, surrounded by unbleached canvas cushions and wobbling slightly, but nonetheless unmistakably sitting under her own power.

"Look!" said Caroline. "She's almost safe to leave sitting up now. The clinic says her lower back muscle tone is excellent. Really advanced for six months."

Gervase looked fondly at the baby. "Clever girl," he said. Looking up at him, with her lifelong enthusiasm for men, the child crowed and stretched her fat arms skywards. He bent down and scooped her up before the excitement could make her forget her muscle tone and collapse onto the cushions.

"Ooza girl?" he said. "Ooza beautiful girl?" The baby lunged towards him, mouth pursed in goldfish style, to attempt one

of her newly-learnt wet sloppy kisses. Gervase grimaced and
bounced her in his arms, facing him. "Great lump you are," he
said. And to Caroline: "How are things? Settled in?"

"Blissful," said Caroline. "I never knew how good it could be,
living somewhere small and quiet with a child to look after. I
feel as if my whole life has been too complicated." She looked
up at her brother-in-law and smiled, and even with her big eyes
screwed up a little against the afternoon sun she was beautiful.

"I suppose you think I'm a complete escapist. I mean, my life
hasn't achieved nearly as much as yours, and you're still out
there fighting all the dragons."

"No," said Gervase. "I do what makes me happiest. And I
honour your idea of living simply and quietly." He glanced at
the open door of the cottage. At Knoll Farm the view inwards
through the back door showed a jumble of heavy coats flung over
hooks, of rubber boots and boxes and baskets and sometimes the
wheel of a bicycle or a horse collar waiting to be mended. Looking through Caroline's door he saw only a pale clear scrubbed
flagstone floor, a stark Japanese vase with an arrangement of
dried grasses, and a plain but spotless rug in pale restful blue. It
might have been a photograph in an interiors magazine. It was
a door to step through and find rest.

"You've made it beautiful," he said.

"Just a little beautiful. I don't need anything else," she said,
quiet as a nun. Gervase bent down and placed the baby, tenderly,
in her arms. There was a moment's charged silence before it was
rudely broken by a loud burp from Maria Annunciata.

The three buses stopped at last in front of some tall white
gantries and a row of paybooths. Cat had dropped out of the
chorus somewhere on the M20 motorway, when the men began
illustrating a new craze for barbershop harmonies which they
had adopted in order to annoy the chastely minded Musical
Director. To a background of "Shine on Harvest Moon" she
looked around at the Le Shuttle terminus in bemusement.
Holidays with Gervase had been brief and generally Scottish,
but years ago she had crossed the Channel often, on trips
from school to home in Venice or from Lille to grandparents
in England. She knew the Channel crossing: it meant docks,

ferries waiting with wisps of steam coming from their funnels, cars rattling up ramps, foot passengers walking up gangways that swayed, passport and boarding card in their teeth. It meant jokes about the rough crossing, going on deck to see the white cliffs, being glad you were not sick.

This cool sterile efficient approach felt like an anticlimax. "How long does it take?" she asked as the little bus trundled into a steel box of a carriage.

"Twenty-five minutes or so," said the driver casually. "We should be on the Calais bypass by six, well on the way. You want dropping at Calais, though, don't you, love?"

"Mmm," said Cat. She was strangely shaken by this encounter with the prosaic efficiencies and flat unromantic hurry of this modern terminus. It was not a railway station nor an airport nor a harbour, but something new. A processing station for submarine voyagers, each cocooned smugly in their own car, free from the rude jostle of fellow travellers.

It was odd, too, to be sitting in a car seat that swayed and juddered like a train. She had never thought about the safety of the tunnel, regarding the news of its arrival two years earlier as just another echo of a distant changing world, nothing to do with her. Now, forty-five metres below the Channel waves, slightly nauseous from the odd motion caused by the train's swaying and the vehicle's suspension working together, she shuddered for a moment. Had Toby come this way? No, he couldn't have: no foot passengers except on the train, and the train did not run from Dover to Calais and conveniently stop for postcards. He could, of course, have got a lift from somebody in a car. But Topsy's friends had said he would have nothing to do with anybody.

She wrenched her mind back to the present. "Is it easy to drop me at the station, at Calais?" she asked the driver.

"Certainly is. No trouble."

"You're very welcome to come on for the night with us," said Lesley Berrett, a soprano who used to stand next but one to her. "I'm sure the host families would find you a room. You don't want to be jauntering around France in the dark, alone, do you, dear?"

Oh, I do! thought Cat secretly. That is exactly what I want. To jaunter around France in the dark, alone. To be responsible for nobody, to visit my childhood. I shall be in Lille tonight, I shall buy a *croque-monsieur* and take a tram and find a hotel for a couple of nights, and not think of Eden or Winston or Caroline, or babies or meals or family aggravation, or everyone going into a flat spin over Prince Charles coming to frown thoughtfully at muck heaps with Gervase. Instead of all this, she thought with a surge of joy, I am going to jaunter round France alone, in the dark.

Now she was anxious to get out of this coach with her light bag and be clear of these cosy Midholt people whose history had nothing to do with hers. She read the Franglais signs which flickered across the display over their head. *Vous arrivez au destination . . . close sunroofs and vents . . .*

In another moment, the train emerged from the strange subsea hole, the minibuses rolled onto French soil and the driver kept his word and dropped her, fifteen minutes later, at the Calais station. Outside it, though, the first thing she saw was a coach labelled LILLE – ARMENTIÈRES.

She spoke briefly to the driver, surprised that the French words came without effort, and swung her tartan bag over her shoulder to climb up the coach's high step. Catherine Hartley, née Gratton, was on the way home.

24

The coach was three-quarters empty. Cat sat near the front, enjoying through the driver's open window the faint farty, cabbagey smell of French drains. No, surely not drains, not these days. Calais harbour, maybe. Or the chemical plant.

Signs said NORD – PAS DE CALAIS and she smiled, remembering arguments with seven-year-old Toby about the absurdity of calling a region "Not Calais". Or, as Robert more accurately translated it to tease them, "*pas de Calais* – none of that Calais". Then he explained that the "*pas*" had more to do with a step, or a "*passe*", but the children were not listening by then, but shrieking "None of yer Calais!" and swinging on the wrought-iron banisters.

She leaned her head against the vibrating windowpane and watched the signs go by. *Dunquerque*, said the first. How odd, she thought, that she should have heard so many times from Artemis the story of how Gervase's father and his uncle took their little boat to Dunkirk to get the troops off ("Never a thank you, mind, from the common soldiers"). Never once, half-listening to her mother-in-law, had she remembered that once, to her, it was spelt Dunquerque. It was the place where you drove from a camping weekend on the beach at Wissant, to buy the things the little shop did not stock. There was irony in having heard so often of Dunkirk, the episode of British history, and forgotten Dunquerque the peaceable Flemish port town.

Happy, bemused, floating above herself, she leaned back and sat relaxed as the bus thundered on across the great industrial and agricultural plain of Flanders. She read battlefield names which were also childhood Sunday drives: Ypres, St-Omer, Menen. Soon the sprawling industrial conurbation of Lille embraced them. She peered out into the gloom, where rain was beginning to fall. There, there indeed, were signs to *Tourcoing*: that odd name which had come to her when she opened the choral society newsletter in the tumbled attic study so many miles and moods away.

Another name: Lambersart, for heaven's sake. Surely Sylvie Jacob lived at Lambersart, and her brother Chrétien? He came to skating and Judo Club and called her *Chatte*, for Cat, when she was trying hard to be "Catherine" to her schoolfriends. She had retaliated by naming him "Crétin", and to his disgust the name had stuck, as the children swooped and skidded and threw up tinkling showers of ice-scrapings, week after week at the rink.

The coach stopped in the Rue Nationale, and Cat alighted onto the damp glistening pavement. Looking across the road, she felt another jolt of recognition. Above a pharmacist's shop there was a green neon sign: a pulsing, growing then decreasing viridian cross of light. It was a symbol unchanged, somehow overlooked by the bustling decades since she had left Lille. Other forgotten, unimportant signs ambushed her wherever she turned: *La Voix du Nord, Stella Artois, Boulangerie Paul, Défence de cracher*.

Slowly she walked towards the central square: Place Général de Gaulle by name, Grand'Place by popular appellation. Childishly, she very much wanted to see the neon ferret; but stepping out into the pedestrianized square – where were the cobbles? – she saw that while the bookshop was there, vast and prosperous, newly themed with a high artificial rock wall down one side, there was no neon ferret to be seen. What cultural and historic forces, she wondered hazily, preserved a flashing green cross for chemists for a third of a century, yet swept away the clever ferret?

And there was a Metro station. A metro! In Lille? Unbidden, there sounded in her mind's ear the clang of a tram and the rattle of its iron wheels through ankle-twisting tracks in cobblestones. She had not thought of trams much since childhood, but once all postings divided into tram and non-tram cities. Trams in Berne, trams in Lille. No trams, back in London. Trams in Sheffield, though, where Diana's mother lived in a retirement home for her last two years, and where her reluctant grandchildren were once dragged on a visit, only to be consoled by the trams. No trams in Los Angeles – although one holiday trip to San Francisco had caused both her and Toby an adolescent pang of nostalgia at the streetcars. No trams in Venice, obviously. Robert had always promised to take them to Vienna, where the trams were still running in the same rails he had ridden with Diana during their courtship; but they had never quite got there.

So the world Cat grew up in had always divided nicely into the two kinds of cities, trammed and tramless; there was something shocking in seeing that Lille had crossed the divide and proved unfaithful to the clattering lords of the city. No more would their spindly arms draw strength from mazy wires, or flash bolts of escaping electricity against a wet winter's night sky between the tall houses. No more would child Tobies and Catherines swing themselves arrogantly aboard to traverse the city at swaying speed, cutting through the mundane motor traffic. She looked down: the rails must have been long since ripped up, together with the old cobblestones.

Cat stood, feeling queer and cold, looking at the fountain in the centre of the square. Then she slowly turned her head, raised her eyes, and with a rush of relief saw the great vainglorious absurdity of the sky-gesticulating sculpture, the neoclassical stone riot which stands proud of the façade of the Lille Opéra. Yes. She looked around again at the wet stones, the glowering Flemish roofline of steep then shallow pitched housetops with red tiles, like giant cottages. She took in the grand, swaggering, bourgeois confidence of the square and the steamy windows of bistros, *Stella Artois, La Voix du Nord, Le Furet du Nord*, luscious sculptured piles of bread in the *Boulangerie Paul*. The city fell into place again around her, the same old city. It had evolved, that was all.

As she had, too. A grown woman now, with no tea to hurry home to, Cat walked into the first hotel she saw, checked in and rose in the shaking lift to the fourth floor. Opening the door of her room she was met by the stifling tinny smell of old heating in a shuttered room, and looked with recognition at the radiator with its sharp flanges and chased decoration blurred with decades of repainting. The house at Rue du Lombard used to smell like that. There were rounded edges on the dusty panelling of the lobby that led to her shower, and peeling shutters on the windows which she flung open to the damp night air. By the shower was a rectangular and cracked bidet with an elaborate pattern of crazed white enamel foliage around its base.

Recognizing everything, back in the snug idiom of shabby bourgeois grandeur that she knew and had forgotten, Cat smiled through the cloud of irrelevant memory and the long-forgotten props of childhood. Home! The hot, dusty smell of the room mingled with the damp warm breeze that smelt of pavements and dog-dirt and toasted cheese and garlic. She was a little hungry but did not want to go out again. Kicking off her shoes, she lay down on the bed, stretched, and yawned.

Irresistible, inarticulate, more memories closed in. With her eyes shut this could be her bedroom at Rue du Lombard. The year she had the jaundice, perhaps. Any minute M. le Médecin would call with his gold-rimmed specs, speak darkly of the perils of liver ailments, and prescribe vast brownish suppositories and jugs of unsweetened lemon juice. Not a golden memory, exactly, but enough to drift her happily off to sleep.

In the morning, Gervase once again came early to the bunk house. "May I have a word?" he asked, punctiliously. "We've got a bit of an event here today. I wasn't allowed to tell you before."

"Is it about the new lads, Terry and Spider?" asked Duane. "Only we know they're coming on a visit for the day, to see the work, like. Mr Willetts told me at my 'pointment."

"Not just that," said Gervase. "Though actually, we fixed their visit for today for a reason. We wanted to have more of us around to meet our visitor. The Prince of Wales is coming here."

"Cor," said Duane. Martin stood silent at this new turn of events.

Gervase continued:

"He's been interested for quite a time. It's basically a private visit, but there'll also be a couple of press people. The Morefield Trust is going to announce that we are becoming one of their key projects, and that they plan to have more farms."

"Will Mrs Hartley be back?" asked Martin. "I mean, it's a big thing, OK? Wouldn't she be sick to miss it?"

"Oh," said Gervase. "She had something important to do in France. Anyway, it's the farmwork they're coming to see. And you, Duane. Since Winston isn't with us. The Prince will probably want to talk to you about what you feel about being here."

"It's good," said Duane judicially. "But it was more fun with Mary-Annie to look after."

"Well," said Gervase. "Better not go into that with him, perhaps?"

He ran briskly through some arrangements, mainly for animals to be fed later than usual for the photographers' benefit, and asked Martin to look out a particular set of horse harness. There was little else to be done. The security check had been completed yesterday while Martin drove Cat to the bus and Duane to his probation appointment. Gervase would have scorned to do any further prettification of the premises; the farm was, at any rate, always kept neat and workmanlike as part of his ethic.

He paused on the drive and hesitated before going back into the house. It would not be restful in there. Mrs Bird had been summoned early and was cutting bread and emitting little helium squeaks of loyal excitement at the prospect of offering the heir to the throne an egg sandwich. Maybe he should go down to the cottage and ask Caroline if she would like to come up for the morning.

Cat woke to find dusty sunlight streaming through her open hotel window. She lay for a moment and remembered where she was. It felt strange to have no household around her, yet no Eden meeting to go to, either. There was nothing to stop her lying here all day, except that she was very hungry. She had not taken sandwiches on the coach, nor had she bothered with supper. A *café complet* on the corner of the square would do nicely. She sat on the edge of the bed, stretching and looking with disfavour at her travelling clothes, a pair of crumpled, chintzy cotton trousers, grey knitted cotton sweater and black lightweight wool jacket. Very dull, very English. Rooting in her equally dull and English tartan bag she found that some saving instinct had made her throw in a black skirt and green silky blouse. All her clothes came from mid-market mail order catalogues: decent, pleasant, nothing noteworthy, plenty of natural fabrics. Next to Mrs Bird's draggled acrylics she looked almost chic; next to Caroline, irredeemably provincial. Neither of these comparisons had ever bothered her for a moment. Now, however, almost for the first time since her second wedding Catherine Hartley gave ten minutes' serious thought to her wardrobe and decided that at the very least, a trip to *Printemps* could be justified by the health of her bank balance.

First, breakfast. Then a walk. She sat in a bar on the corner of the Rue Neuve and fortified herself with two croissants, half a baguette, and a bowl of *café-au-lait*, remembering how at school breakfasts on Mass days she had learnt to dip the buttered bread casually into her coffee, leaving an oily slick and floating flakes of crust. She did it now, and noted with approval that the barman brought over the jam in a jar and the butter not wrapped in tiny sweaty foil portions, but on a plate with a knife. This homeliness was probably illegal under EC health regulations: it was good to see that France, her almost forgotten second homeland, had not advanced too far along the road of neurotic hygiene. Maybe, after all, it *was* the drains she had smelt through the bus window at Calais.

Looking out through the window, she thought for a second that she could see Toby. But it was another man: as dark as Toby, fine-featured, in a long business overcoat with his hair flopping over his forehead. He was laughing with a square blond friend in an anorak as they walked towards some office with their briefcases. No, nothing like Toby, really: smaller, and smarter. But there had been something. Cat returned, thoughtfully, to her croissant.

Caroline was only too delighted to come up to Knoll Farm for the visit of the Prince and the Trustees. "It's marvellous!" she said. And "I can quite see why you weren't allowed to tell me earlier. How thrilling!"

This, perversely, made Gervase feel guilty that he had not told her. Still, she smiled at him without a trace of offence taken, and put an eager hand on his forearm, on the warm skin beneath the rolled-up shirtsleeve. "Would it be all right if Mary-Annie came up? You know how quiet she is."

"Of course," said Gervase, and smiled down at her. "Nothing's complete without Mary-Annie."

Martin, driving up the lane with the two extra bottles of milk Mrs Bird had demanded he fetch, saw them standing in the cottage doorway, her light hand on his tanned arm, smiling into one another's eyes. He did not like it.

25 ∫

Cat spent all morning walking, refreshed at eleven by more coffee and a *tarte aux fraises* at the *Boulangerie Paul*. She walked to the church of St-Maurice, where she had long ago seen her Catholic schoolmates confirmed by a magnificent purple-and-gold bishop in a waxy haze of candlelight and incense, and envied them in the secret romantic depths of her heart. The smell was unchanged: a cool intoxication.

She stood aimlessly for a moment then lit a candle, knelt before a dim-lit Virgin in a side chapel and improvised a prayer for Toby. He was not here; he never had been. She could feel it. An old priest emerged beaming from the confessional box to greet her as she rose; they exchanged a few words. The old man seemed puzzled and unable to place her, and after a few moments she realized how strange she must sound. She had not been in France for decades, yet in these surroundings her accent and grammar and intonation returned to the old, instinctive, schoolgirl bilinguality while her vocabulary remained comically rusted by years of disuse. She found herself voluble and fluent, thinking in French constructions, dropping slangy, childish French exclamations yet frequently groping for the right word even for simple things like candles – *comment dit-on? flût! aaah ... oui, les cierges* ... To the priest, she must have seemed not like a struggling Anglophone but a French amnesiac. Or a drug-taker.

She walked to the Place de Béthune, and looked for the row of cinemas where she had gone with Toby and Robert on every possible Saturday night, searching out films with English soundtracks and French subtitles. The only one she could remember was *The Long Ships*, a recreation of Viking times so absurd that she and Robert had laughed about its horned hats and fur loincloths all the way home. Toby, still only seven, had been thrilled by the adventure and took offence at their levity.

She walked to the Jardin Vauban and then back to the Grand' Place following a street map, but then decided to fold the map and let her feet take her where they would. After a moment's hesitation she found herself on the Rue Anatole France, heading towards the station and moving purposefully into a quarter of the old town peculiarly rich in sex video shops.

Rue de Roubaix. *Ciné Sex*. Why was she here? Much was unfamiliar, or merely similar to the rest of the town she had walked in all morning; there was a wholly unfamiliar black-glass building, modern and unseemly, in the foreground at one point and yet, sometimes, a smell, a corner, an angle of leprous stone would strike her so forcibly that she gasped.

In a few minutes she turned right at a rusting dark-blue road plaque saying *Rue du Lombard*. This explained at last why she was here. She had meant to visit the old house later, but had convinced herself that it lay over to the west of the Grand'Place. She looked at the great wrought-iron gates of No. 1, and read the newly cleaned plaque on the wall outside, in honour of M. Scrive-Labbé, who *"au péril de sa vie"* brought the first carding machine from England to Lille and founded, presumably, his city's textile supremacy.

How on earth had this crumbling merchant palace, or a corner of it, been acquired for rent by the Foreign Office of the very nation which presumably had imperilled M. Scrive-Labbé's life in the attempt to keep its carding machine? Maybe, though, it was his compatriots who had imperilled his life, in a spirit of machine-wrecking Luddism? Or perhaps it was in a fit of post-Occupation solidarity and gratitude that Madame its owner had permitted M. le Consul Britannique to inhabit it, and his shrill English children to climb on the little stone lions in the centre of the court?

Except that, come to think of it, playing on the stone lions was one thing most definitely not permitted. They were deemed fragile, and Madame the landlady would be out shaking her stick, within seconds of Toby's most furtive approach to them. Cat peered in through the gate. Madame must have been right about the fragility because the lions were gone, only twisted iron fastenings remaining. The place was clearly some government building now: she hesitated to go in to the courtyard, and retraced her steps a little sadly to turn the corner and look for the sweetshop which sold the chocolate mice and Caram'bars. It was the *Video Sexy*. Ah well, evolution.

She walked back, past the Opéra and across the Grand'Place, aiming to go up the Rue Esquermoise past the old Consulate, and beyond it to the Rue Royale and the big wooden doors of the convent at No. 66. How lucky she and Toby had been, compared to her own children with their long dull country school runs by car! She had walked to school, sometimes with her father coming half the distance, to his office, and she had generally walked home. Never mind that there was no garden at Rue du Lombard, and only the forbidden lions for outdoor amusement. That, she supposed with maternal hindsight, must have been hardest on Mark, who was little. But for her and, in his last year at least for Toby, the old city had been freedom itself.

She could not find the Consulate or remember the number where it had been. Baffled, she halted for a moment outside the Banque Jacob. It was Sylvie Jacob's father's bank, as established and honoured a fact of Lillois life as the adjacent Banque Scalbert. When she was going home for tea with Sylvie, they would walk down here together and sit, scuffing their feet and giggling, in the marble foyer while M. Jacob finished his day. He would appear flanked by deferential underlings and wearing a long, smart woollen overcoat, greet the girls politely (*Mademoiselle Gratton! Enchanté!*) and drive them home to the bourgeois decorum of the Jacob townhouse in Lambersart. She looked in: the foyer was lightly modernized now, but the floor she had shuffled her school shoes on was exactly the same. So were one or two of the men's overcoats as they sauntered out for lunch, coats as long and dark and fine as Papa Jacob's used to be, worn even in June in defiance of the age of the anorak.

Watching the men emerge, she saw again the one she had momentarily taken for Toby when she looked through the bar window at breakfast-time. Nothing like Toby, and yet familiar.

It was an idle observation, and she only stood still a moment longer because her feet were tired from long unaccustomed walking on city streets. She did not notice at first that the dark man had turned and was staring at her. Only when he called, his voice echoing in the marble hall, did the shock of full recognition come on her.

"*Chatte!*" said the man in clear, confident tones. "*Chatonne! Méchante Chatte Anglaise! Que fais-tu ici, hein?*"

She stared back from the broad entrance doors. "*Dieu!*" she said, the forgotten exclamation forced from her. "*C'est toi! Crétin!*"

Heads turned in interrogation. The chic receptionist raised a hennaed eyebrow; a young man stiffened as if to hurry to his master's aid. In a second, though, these observers saw that M. le Directeur was laughing delightedly, holding out both hands and advancing on the woman in the doorway. The receptionist gave a tiny shrug and glanced at the younger man. If M. le Directeur was happy to be called a cretin by a rather dishevelled, pink-faced foreign woman of a certain age, that was his affair.

He had her hands now, held firmly in his own. "Where are your skates?" he asked. "Where is your horsetail?"

"Ponytail," said Cat, looking at him with incredulity. "*Dieu*, it really is you! Where is your sister? Sylvie?"

"Bruxelles," said Chrétien Jacob in tones of the profoundest disapproval. "She is a big Euroboss, imagine. Married to an even bigger Euroboss. She was more clever than me, and older, but she would not come into the bank. My father was disgusted. He wanted to make a big modern gesture and be succeeded by his daughter, not his son. But you see how it has ended. Sylvie rejected the Bank, I did not go to St-Cyr, I did not become a general after all. I studied economics." He said the word with vehement comic disgust: Cat could see the boy of thirteen behind the man, and a laugh broke from her. His eyes danced. "Yes, I am Monsieur le Directeur and life is very dull, for a General. It would have been better to stay *un gosse*, with you and Sylvie and Véronique at the ice rink. In fact, even that has closed. There is a trade Expo there now."

He turned to the young man and spoke rapidly. The boy nodded obediently, made a note in a small book, and scuttled off

back into the interior of the bank. Chrétien, still firmly holding
one of Cat's hands, turned back to her.

"*Voilà*. Everything is arranged. I have no important business
lunch engagement any more. *Madame*" – he had glanced foxily
down towards her ring finger and noted Gervase's narrow smooth
gold band – "would you do me the pleasure of accompanying me
to lunch, in some place where my business contact will under
no circumstances see us? A *croque-monsieur*, perhaps, and a bag
of *frites* in the Jardin Vauban?"

"A sausage," said Cat, laughing back at him. "A hot-dog
Americaine, with English mustard to make your eyes weep."

"Ah, memories of childhood," said M. le Directeur, sentimen-
tally. "But I think I can find somewhere with tables and chairs
and a cellar. Viens." The receptionist looked after him as he
swept Cat out through the brassbound doorway into the street.
Not at all his usual kind of little friend. English, too, from one
or two of her words. That would explain the terrible hair.

By this time, events at Knoll Farm were moving along nicely
according to plan. The Prince and the chairman of the Morefield
Trust posed with a cow, then with Gervase and some sheep.
Then the Prince picked up a body brush and groomed a horse for
a while, with Duane; Caroline watched, and was introduced, and
had Mary-Annie duly admired and the importance of "family
atmosphere" spoken of approvingly by another Trustee. More
flashguns crackled for informal pictures. The Prince left. Then
Gervase and the others went to the farmhouse to eat Mrs Bird's
egg sandwiches and talk to the two reporters with notebooks,
and Caroline went with them. Martin said to Duane: "I dunno,
it doesn't seem too right. Mrs Hartley not being here."

"Her sister looks at home, don't she?" said Duane. "Imagine,
little Yannie meeting a Prince."

"I don't like it," said Martin. He did not mean Yannie's exalted
social encounter. He went off to unharness the horses.

Cat had forgotten them all. In a smoky little bistro with
her schoolfriend's brother she was plunged in joyful mutual
reminiscence, each of them capping the other's memories,
forgetful of the present, revelling in detail.

"Remember the Judo tournament?"

"*Re!*" said Cat, and bowed across the table.

"*Hadjimi!*" he replied, and lunged to grab the collar and one lapel of her jacket, knocking over the salt as he did so. "Then I move in – so – and sweep you off balance with a *deuxieme de pied*—"

"But I am too quick for you, and do a Sacrifice," said Cat. "I put my foot in your chest, roll over on my back, and you do a forward roll to the corner of the mat."

"And roll back onto my feet, plunge down, grab you in a neck-lock," said Chrétien, "and immobilize you until you tap—" Cat tapped the tablecloth twice, with a flat hand "For surrender. *Hélas*, superior strength and cunning have defeated you again."

"You never could skate backwards, though, could you?" said Cat. "You used to fall on your head."

"A very necessary apprenticeship for a Lille banker," said Chrétien. "It dulls the sensibilities. *Ah, mais!* It is so good to remember, so dull to be an adult."

"What is your adult life?" asked Cat, attacking a portion of thinly beaten steak and chips. "Do you have a family? Do you live in Lille?"

"I married a Belgian. She lives now in Belgium," said Chrétien carelessly. "I have two sons rising in the Bank, in Calais and Dunquerque, a daughter married, and a little daughter at the Sorbonne. I live mainly in an apartment in Vieux-Lille, not far from M. le Consul's house at Rue du Lombard."

"Oh, I'm sorry," said Cat. "I mean, that your wife—"

The dark man laughed. "After twenty-five years of marriage," he said, "wise married people understand one another very well. *N'est ce pas?*"

He picked up her hand with its wedding ring.

"Where is your husband? I do not see him."

"In England. In Northamptonshire. He is a farmer."

"With sheep?"

"Yes, and cows and pigs and horses."

"Good. He is in England with sheep, you are in Lille. Why?"

"I don't know," said Cat, in genuine astonishment at herself. "*Voyons*, that is true. I don't know. I just got a chance to come."

"Destiny called you," said Chrétien. "*Comme c'est gentil.* Tell me, what does destiny call you to do this afternoon? Does it call you to take a promenade with me, and accompany me to a very poor performance at the Opéra, and dine in some place better than this?"

Cat was silent for a moment. The red wine and the food were making her dazed, groggy and happy and irresponsible. It was a long time since she had wasted a whole day on a whim.

"Yes," she said. "Yes, I feel it calling now."

"To destiny!" he raised his glass.

"To destiny," she said.

She looked across, suddenly uncertain, wondering if she had been misunderstood. French men were famously unschooled in the subtleties of political correctness and sexual harassment. But no! This was no stereotype Frenchman: this was Chrétien, spirited teasing-partner of her childhood, always after her to gang up with him and play jokes on Sylvie. She knew, deeply and instinctively, that she could slap down any silly ideas he might have without even jeopardizing their refreshed friendship. She could keep Chrétien at bay.

If she wanted to.

By mutual silent consent, both fell to talking of other people and places they had known. Chrétien gave her news of Sylvie, of Véronique (now a mother of six living in Orléans, married to a banker he knew slightly). He told her how the Sacred Heart sisters left the convent years before, and how M. Derain the police sergeant who taught them Judo was killed in an Algerian terrorist bombing the year after Cat had vanished to Johannesburg. He told her how the last trams went in the 1980s when the Metro was built, how proud the new Lillois were of their improvements at the centre, how high the crime and poverty rates had grown in the sprawling conurbation all around.

"Could a girl of eleven, as I was, still walk to school?" said Cat.

He considered. "Yes. I think so. In the centre. But too many go by car."

"Could a little girl cross the city to go skating on a Sunday morning?"

"Yes," said Chrétien. "But there might be rude boys. Or rude girls."

"I'm sorry I called you Crétin, in the bank," said Cat, for the first time feeling the awkwardness of that public moment. "I didn't know you were Monsieur le Directeur."

"Pah!" he said. "They have no respect anyway. They know my view of banking. My deputy is excellent, but by great ill-fortune for him and good fortune for me, his family name is not Jacob."

"I didn't recognize you, not completely, until you said my name," said Cat. "How on earth did you recognize me, from a twelve-year-old girl?"

"Round face, English skin, hair that jumps from your head, big green eyes, an expression of hopefulness and worry, a tendency to peer through doors." He reeled his list off, deadpan, then smiled. "*Une petite mine gentille, quoi. Ça ne change pas.*"

"You haven't changed either," said Cat. "You're like my brother Toby, that way."

They wandered out into the afternoon air, and Chrétien asked "What would you like to see? The country, or the town?"

"Town," said Cat. "I wanted to see the old house, but it's a ministry now. Ministry of Culture."

"*Pas de problème.*" He began to walk rapidly down the Rue Anatole France where her hesitant, remembering steps had taken her that morning. "We shall see and appreciate everything. Surely that is the meaning of culture? I have not been inside Numero Un since you left. Anyway, I know exactly how to effect an entrance."

He did. He and his impressive card were greeted with comradely scepticism by the official in charge when he explained that an important client of his bank was Mlle Gratton, who wished to inspect her father's old residence. Together they walked in through the iron-and-glass double doors, together stood for a moment dumbstruck at the way the hall was unchanged even to the way the back stairs oddly began almost next to the grand main staircase. Then they turned with one accord through the curved panelling of the door to their left.

"The playroom! I had forgotten!" said Cat, looking into a dusty meeting room with utility chairs and tables and flakes of plaster off the ceiling. And Chrétien peered in behind her, demanding: "Where is baby Mark's train? The one you can sit on?"

"I expect," said the Ministry official drily from behind them, "that it was considered surplus to cultural needs. This is a monument, *monsieur*. An historic building. Groups come especially, by appointment, to view the remarkable ceiling of the small salon."

"What ceiling?" asked Cat, puzzled. "Oh hang on – a girl sitting on something?"

Together they passed through into what had been Robert and Diana's grandest dining room of all postings.

"Good grief," said Cat. "How could I have forgotten that?"

"No eye for art," said Chrétien. They stared up, Cat wrestling with another wave of the mixed sensations which had assailed her all day. To remember things and then go back and find them a little different, a little smaller, was normal. To be suddenly confronted with things you had utterly forgotten was strange and unsettling. It pushed you helplessly down a slide towards other memories and feelings. Nostalgia, she saw, was not necessarily cosy or voluntary. She was glad that nothing deeply traumatic had happened in her childhood. If it had it would surely rush back now, along with all these other feelings.

Passing back through the double doors to the small salon, she suddenly remembered hiding with Toby in the dark dusty space between the two sets of doors, eating the miniature sausages off a cocktail plate during a party.

Chrétien's best pleadings could not get him beyond the first floor landing: he had, he said, once written *MERDE* on the ceiling of the third attic room by shooting air-pistol pellets into the plaster. It was during a visit when Sylvie and Cat were being dull, with dolls. He wanted to see if it was still there. The official was obdurate, and they left, laughing, pointing at the place where the lions had been and at the cross concierge's little stone hut.

"Extraordinary place to live," said Cat as they passed the barrier into the road. "Scruffy, bit magnificent, all those grand rooms but no garden. The opposite of anything English."

"Not very like my own house," said Chrétien ruefully. "My wife has always been fond of *le style scandinave*. Me, I have an apartment above Rue Neuve, which is entirely Lillois, magnificent and impossible to clean, with shutters which are painted, not naked Scandinavian wood."

"What is Sylvie's house like?" said Cat, wanting to move the subject away from his apartment.

"Rootless Belgian style. Eurosmart. Terrible," said Chrétien, and took her hand. "Now," he said, leading her at a fast pace down the road, "we must understand one another. Speaking of my apartment has made you nervous. You are an English woman now, very respectable, and you think that because I am a French man, I wish to dress you in fur coats and make you my mistress in the middle of the afternoon. You think this. True?"

Cat pulled her hand away, pink-cheeked, and tried to protest. He continued, blithely: "I know this, because my father gave me books to read by Nancy Mitford. He said it was important to understand what English women think about French men, or I would make terrible *bêtises* with the new style of English clients, who are important bank ladies and do not think of making love with business contacts in the afternoon. I know that English women think French men are very, very dangerous and consider themselves invited to bed at all times. This is a very nice idea. But if you think I am an occasion of sin, we shall not have a very amusing afternoon, reliving our youth."

"Hmm," said Cat, recovering her aplomb. "Be honest, then. Be like the chevalier Bayard, without fear or fault. Are you the dangerous Frenchman we are warned about?"

"I am harmless," said Chrétien. He stopped, and turned to face her, grinning. "I promise you. Today I am harmless. In return for my docility, I need stories and conversation and memory. It is terrible, in the bank. Even the women are dull. They want to be respected as bankers and yet admired as women. English women are excellent. They never expect to be respected, and certainly they do not care whether you admire them or not. You can tell by the way they dress. All I want, dear Madame, is to hear the story of your life. It would be delightful if you could include the great influence I had upon you, and the fact that you have never been able to forget me for the last thirty-three years. But, *voyons*, since I had quite forgotten you, I cannot insist on that. *Venez, Madame!* We will walk in the park and you will tell me everything."

26

Hours later, Cat and Chrétien sat opposite one another at a small table in a bistro at the corner of the Grand'Place, laughing. They had abandoned the Opéra after the first act, Chrétien remarking that it was surely enough for a bank to sponsor dreadful modern performances without its director having to watch them. The long-suffering young male secretary was telephoned – he was still working at the Banque Jacob building, apparently – to come "with any woman you can find" and sit in their places so that nobody should remark on his dereliction of duty.

"We shall dine in peace," he said. "And then at eleven o'clock I shall return to the Opéra and mingle with the other sponsors for five minutes." Cat – who had during the afternoon made a hasty dive into Printemps for a black dress, stockings and pumps – pretended to deplore this defection and told him that no Englishman would consider such behaviour.

"You lie," he said tranquilly, breaking his bread and dipping it in the juice of his Chateaubriand. "They are even worse than us. But not as rude and boorish as Belgians. But go on, *allez*! More of this saga."

He had by degrees persuaded Cat to tell him every detail of her recent life. Her fluency grew every minute and she found the act of relating Knoll Farm's domestic travails to this mocking, amused outsider increasingly exhilarating. Chrétien, unaffectedly delighted and entertained, egged her on:

"So he is a philanthropist, a saint, your husband? He cares for *vauriens* and makes young robbers into good citizens, by the care of sheep and pigs? But he earns no money to maintain his beautiful wife? The English! I despair! Then he goes off and looks after *vauriens* while you bravely rescue his sheep from death, and are persecuted by the police. *Aie, aie aie!*"

"No – no," she would protest, laughing at his theatrical display of horror. "It isn't like that. It was my fault about the driving licence. I wouldn't even contest the charge. That was my decision. As for Gervase and me, everything is –" she hesitated, looking for the right word, and hit on the universal French expression – "*bien arrangé*, between us. It works very well. His work with the boys is not unusual, either. You have people here who do the same kind of work, in Paris and Lille."

"Yes," he said smugly. "But they are generally priests, with no wives to distract their attention and make a division of duty. We are more logical, you see?"

Cat had not enough ammunition to argue, and felt too good-humoured and tipsy to protest at the rain of insults he flirtatiously continued to pour on all those who, in his opinion, were failing to look after her properly. She laughed and shrugged her shoulders. The black dress, soft and sheer and short, made her feel like a creature who should, indeed, be looked after. She faintly remembered feeling this before, this relaxed warm sense of being a fragile woman, a precious responsibility. But not for a long time.

Chrétien, more vigilant than his debonair manner betrayed, saw the change in her and enjoyed it. Women, he thought, should be able to slough off this terrible modern omnicompetence, and allow men sometimes to treat them like gossamer. It was an old game, which too many of them (especially Belgians) forgot how to play. Either they refused all care, or began to think themselves entitled to an excess of it. Occasionally, to make Cat laugh even more, he veered off into a description of his own distant wife's exacting standards and material demands, and contrasted them woefully with the neglect women plainly suffered in the wilderness of *l'Angleterre*. Outside the window, it had begun to rain: the neon signs of the Grand'Place reflected in the wet glistening flagstones, making their table seem even more of an intimate island.

On his bantering insistence, she had explained about Caroline, and Alan, and the baby, and the upset over Winston, and how it had all distressed her. Strangely, it was easier to express her own outrage and worry because at this, Chrétien wisely expressed no particular sympathy.

"So – I will just make sure I recapitulate correctly. You see what a good careful banker I have become. I could write a full report on this shocking affair. One: your sister did not like her baby, so you arranged for some criminals to help you look after it. Two: she went to California and a woman called Adeline told her that naturally, she did like the baby after all. Three: she has come home and taken this very important baby away from the criminals, and Monsieur the Saint, your husband, says this is good. Four: you say it is wrong to prevent criminals from feeding babies, and he refuses to listen."

"You make it sound like a bad film plot," protested Cat.

"It is a bad film plot," said Chrétien. "So, to continue: on the side we have another plot, an opera this time, quite terrible enough for the Banque Jacob to sponsor. Your brother Mark has no babies, and his wife suspects he has been cut, so she comes to complain to you. You confront your brother, he admits everything, and they make up the quarrel. End of Act One. In Act Two he discovers that you secretly write a newspaper for this horrible Eden – did you know they have a hotel at Roubaix? Disgusting place, just like America, iced water and no bidets. Because you work for the same company as him he will not speak to you and vows to send his troops to kill you unless the baritone, *votre père*, can prevent him. Correct?"

"More or less," said Cat, pouring herself more red wine. "Except for the troops. And that my father does not play the patriarchal role you suggest. I sometimes think he is still a light romantic tenor at heart."

"Is there a *grand'mère?*" asked Chrétien, interestedly. "In French family battles there is normally a grandmother to arrange things in the end."

"Only Artemis," said Cat. "I suppose she arranged Caroline's house."

"Could she arrange Mark? And the young criminals?"

"No," said Cat. "And don't keep calling them criminals."

"As for the missing Toby," continued Chrétien, "he is obviously the missing voice, the voice from off the stage. Your sister pretends to think he is in Los Angeles because she wanted to go there to cure this strange disease of hating babies. You pretend Toby is in Lille, because your instinct tells you that your fate is to come here and have dinner with a handsome bank director from your distant past. I think this is a very convenient brother." He said thoughtfully, "I wish my sister would disappear, then I could go and search for her for many months – where? The Maldives, perhaps. Or Seychelles. I enjoy scuba very much, did I tell you? I think I could persuade myself that I must search for her on tropical islands. She would, for example, definitely not be in Belgium."

"You have spent so long retelling the opera of my life," said Cat, looking at her watch, "that you have left yourself only two minutes to get back to the Opéra and pretend you enjoyed the real performance."

He glanced at his own watch and jumped up. "Wait!" he said. "I will be back. I will tell them that my important client from England felt faint and had to be escorted to her hotel. I would like a *café noir* and a *Cognac*, and tell Madame Olin that I require petits-fours, not the ones the tourists have, but her own. Then you shall explain properly to me, who is Martin? And why do Monsieur le Saint's sheep need an American as well as all the criminals?"

The rain was heavier now; he hurried across the square, his overcoat held over his head, and Cat looked after him as he ran.

Gervase and Caroline sat either side of the fireplace in Rectory Cottage. Mrs Bird had made Duane and Martin a high tea, while Gervase took one of the Morefield Trustees back to the station. He returned to find them both gone to the pub, and only a crusted portion of shepherd's pie left under an inverted soup-bowl for his supper. He looked at it, but Mrs Bird had a heavy hand with food. The pie failed to tempt his appetite. So he walked out into the warm evening, still elated from the events of the day, and found his steps taking him along the lane towards Midmarsham. There was a light in Caroline's front room, and a welcome met his hesitant knock.

"I wanted to thank you for helping out today. Mary-Annie really broke the ice," he began, awkwardly.

"I was honoured to be asked," said Caroline. "Have you eaten? I was just going to make an omelette."

So, four hours later they were still there, the chessboard between them but the game abandoned, sometimes talking, sometimes falling into warm companionable silences. The apple-wood fire was sinking into low, fragrant embers. Both were sleepy but neither chose to break the peace of the moment. Caroline was filled with a deep sense of contentment. This was her home, her own place; her child slept beautifully upstairs, and the fire she had lit burnt clear and warm and flickered on Gervase's thin, wise, ascetic face. He was deep in thought; a log fell and flared suddenly, and he started out of his reverie and smiled at her. Caroline smiled back, and no words were needed.

Up at the farm Martin made a last tour of inspection of the yard and paddocks, checked the electric fencing round the pigs, and looked despondently at the darkened farmhouse. None of his business, OK? He went to bed, but lay for a long time sleepless, waiting for the sound of a footfall on the drive.

Chrétien came back from his foray to the Opéra after what Cat severely told him was a shamefully short time.

"I told them I was so troubled and moved that I needed time to think alone about the message of this new work," he said. "And I promised them 40,000 francs to fund a feasibility study for an application to Brussels for – for some thing. It was a cheap escape. Now. My coffee? Les petits fours?"

When they could no longer extend their evening by one drop more of coffee or one more sugared grape, Cat reluctantly said:

"I should go to my hotel now. I have had a very long day."

"Indeed. We shall take a little promenade, though. I will show you the new restoration work on the balconies behind the Rue Neuve. See? The rain has stopped. Lille smells and feels at its most beautiful at night, after summer rain." He held out a hand to help her to her feet. "Even that is not terribly beautiful," he admitted. "But it will do."

27

The sympathetic and responsible newspaper which had been invited to take pictures of the Prince's visit to Knoll Farm was not quite so serious-minded as to ignore the potential effect of blondes and babies on circulation figures. Accordingly, the night news editor took one look at the posed pictures of Gervase, Duane, assorted sheep and the Prince of Wales and pushed them aside with a sigh, to spread out the three more informal pictures which the photographer had left on the end of the film. In one of these, the Prince was leaning towards Caroline; in her arms was Mary-Annie in a white puff-sleeved dress and a broad grin, reaching both fat hands towards the red cow which Gervase, laughing, held on a rope halter.

"Aaah," said his secretary, wandering past the desk. "He should have had a little girl, poor old Charles. Look at his face!"

The news editor looked at the enchanting picture, which he now perceived to be full of equally enchanting subtext. Then he looked at the one which lay next to it, the best of the rest. It was a static study of the Prince with his hand on a sheep's head, Duane with his mouth open looking moronic, and Gervase caught at a bad angle and visibly in need of a haircut.

"No contest," he said. "The baby's not really the story, though, is it? Presumably it belongs to the guy who runs it, that Addams Family geezer there. We're doing two-fifty words on the farm and the young offenders, aren't we?"

"Room for five hundred," said his colleague, punching a keyboard. "One or two nice quotes about family life. Tie in with the baby. Family values. All that."

"Great," said the night news editor, and put it from his mind except for the brief, wistful observation: "She's a gorgeous bit of stuff, that wife of his. Wonderful face. Like a statue."

Cat decided to spend the morning on those few things she had promised herself to do to verify that Toby had indeed not been in Lille. The day's and night's events had cleared her mind, and hardened a resigned belief that her search would be useless. Whatever obscure tug of memory and unreason had brought her here was no more likely to be shared by Toby than the motive which had taken Caroline to Los Angeles. Out of their kaleidoscopic early memories each child of the family would have formed a different, private interior pattern, not to be discerned by any parent or sibling. If Toby were alive, he would come back to her one day. If not, she would never know where it was that he travelled after Calais.

Yesterday morning she could not have confronted that thought without succumbing to despair. Today, she could. "*Can't seem to get comfortable. Best to go back and start again*" he had written on the Calais card. At least she knew, now, what he meant by "getting comfortable". She hoped he had succeeded as well as she had, and found the same queer, unexpected peace by going back. She smiled at certain memories of the day before.

During the morning, though, she did the duty she had promised herself to do. She visited every major police station and three of the hospitals, leaving with each the photograph and details about Toby which she had photocopied in Midholt before the minibus left. It was a pointless, lonely task; with a guilty sense of relief she hurried back across town to meet Chrétien for lunch at *La Chicorée* ("*Non, non* – I do not have a business lunch appointment. If I do, it will regrettably be cancelled due to a secret crisis on the Bourse which only I can avert").

Pausing outside the *Furet du Nord*, she saw that the newspaper shop had some English press. She went in and reached for *The Times*, but as she did so glanced down at one of its rivals and saw above the fold the words:

CHARLES BACKS FAMILY FARMS FOR FELONS.

Smiling, she picked up the paper. So Gervase had got his bit of publicity, and presumably his Trust deal as well. Good. She paid for the paper and walked on down the square to the bistro.

Chrétien would not be there for ten minutes; she would sit with a drink and browse idly in the newspaper. Feeling the sun on her back Cat wriggled voluptuously and smiled. The waiter who was laying outdoor tables smiled back, raising an eyebrow.

Wine and good bread on the pavement, diversion in idleness, sunshine, company, male admiration: these were simple pleasures long forgotten. For years she had not had occasion even to flirt, because Gervase was the least flirtatious of men, besides being her husband. Eden meetings were all with men like Mark, their passion focused exclusively on the corporate game and the conquest of markets. At home, living with a volatile floating population of troubled teenage boys had taught her to be consistently wary of giving off the slightest sign of feminine teasing. Out here in the sunshine amid the French smells, such careful inhibition seemed as distant and irrelevant as the dusty Amstrad, the messy kitchen and the skinning of coley fillets for fish pie.

When she had settled down, facing the square across which Chrétien would walk to meet her, Cat unfolded the newspaper. For a few moments she stared at it: then turned it over, took several deep breaths, and turned it right side up again for another look.

It was a long look. Chrétien had crossed the square, entered the restaurant's enclosure and placed both hands on her shoulders before she noticed him. She felt the warmth of his hands through her blouse and turned to him, smiling in spite of herself. When he sat down she pushed the newspaper across, still speechless.

Chrétien, whose English was less good than her French, frowned for a moment or two and then began to laugh.

"Ah, *bien!*" he said. "This is a very good opera now. I begin to enjoy it even more. The younger sister steals the elder one's identity and the husband is wearing an ass's head – no, a sheep's head perhaps – and does not notice. The Prince is deceived."

Cat snatched it back. "You make everything into a joke!" she said, heatedly.

"Everything is a joke, *ma belle*," said Chrétien tranquilly.

Gervase saw the paper at lunch-time, because Martin, back from shopping, had laid the front page accusingly on the table where he could not miss it. He glanced down at the picture, beguiled for a moment by Mary-Annie and irritated by the headline, but stiffened as he read it through.

"CHARLES BACKS FAMILY FARMS FOR FELONS," it said. And under the picture of Mary-Annie lunging for the cow and being laughed at in her lovely mother's arms by the Prince of Wales, the caption:

Mr and Mrs Hartley and their baby daughter demonstrate to the Prince of Wales the family values of Knoll Farm, the latest social project to receive the backing of the Morefield Trust for Youth Reclamation.

The rest of the story was unexceptionable: explaining the takeover of the land, quoting Mr Willetts on the value of Gervase's work and experience, and the Trustees on their pleasure that this innovative social project would at last be put on a secure footing after living for so long from hand to mouth through the efforts of the Hartley family and a small local charity. It even quoted Duane, saying that living in a family and doing a useful job of work had changed his outlook and set him on a new path (Cat, reading that, instantly recognized the coaching of Mr Willetts. Gervase was merely touched).

Martin watched Gervase reading it. When he had finished the young American said: "Whaddya think of that?" and his tone was challenging, less than usually friendly.

"It's a fair account. But a pity about the picture caption being wrong," said Gervase. "Very embarrassing. I must apologize to Caroline for not making it clearer who she was."

Martin, who had not for one moment troubled himself about the embarrassment of Caroline, was momentarily speechless. Then in a queer, rough voice he said: "I need a break. Is it OK if I take off for a coupla days? You did say—"

"Yes, of course," said Gervase absently, still looking at the picture.

"Next week?"

"No," said the boy harshly. "Today." And, an hour later, he left. He did not borrow Cat's car nor the LandRover, but rode the old black bike all the way to Midholt station. It had begun to drizzle: cycling fast through the damp air, pressing the pedals down at each stroke with a controlled, vicious fury, Martin took comfort in one thing only: the prospect of telling Marianne and asking her what the hell to do?

Once Cat was over the first shock she did not know whether to be predominantly angry or amused. Chrétien, addressing his lamb cutlets with gusto, thought the whole thing vastly entertaining.

"This baby which has given 'family value' – what does this mean? – family value to the criminals, and met your future king. This is the same baby which, in truth, is not allowed to be touched by the criminals, because your sister went to California and was cured of hating it?"

"Oh, more or less," said Cat. "Yes, that's a fair summary. Do you think I should be angry?"

"Anger – *un petit colère* – is very good for the complexion. My wife says so," said Chrétien. "It brings up the blood and purifies the pores. *Vas-y*. Be angry." He pulled a mobile telephone out of his pocket and switched it on. "You see, I am truly a modern European banker. Internationally linked at all times." He peered at the display, which seemed unfamiliar to him. "Anatole, my secretary, makes me bring it even to lunch. Go on, ring the saint husband and ask why he is pretending to have another wife. Make 00 44 before the number."

Cat dialled Knoll Farm, giggling slightly. The first glass of wine had begun to work. The answering machine was on, but Mrs Bird picked up the telephone halfway through her message.

"Oooh," she said. She had not seen the newspaper because Gervase had taken it down to Rectory Cottage. "I just took a message for you. That's lucky you rang! Natalie, she said her name was, rang from your office you work for. Eden Pee-elsie, or something. I said you were in France with the music club, and she got very excited and said where? And I said I thought it was right up in the north, not too far, and she said good, because they need a profeel of their new hotel there in a place called –" she checked the message pad again – "Lily. She said they were in a rush, and would you ring her about doing the profeel as an extra?"

Cat thanked Mrs Bird, switched off the telephone and gave it back to Chrétien. He was painstakingly deciphering the newspaper story again, and she waited while he finished.

"I think," he said eventually, "if I am not mistaken, that the opera has gained another new twist. Is this correct, that your husband has given away all your land to this charity for drug-sellers and *vauriens*?"

"Yes," said Cat. "But I'm not at all interested in that. I knew it was on the cards. We keep the house. It's nothing to do with me, the land. It belongs to Gervase's family."

"Then it is your inheritance!" said Chrétien, scandalized. "Wars are fought over land!"

"Not by me," she said. "I pay my own way. Actually, I've just heard I've got a piece of work I can do here, right here in Lille, so I'll feel less guilty. I can even claim my travel expenses back."

"*Fantastique!*" said her companion. "Now you can stay some more days, and we will go back to the Ministry of Culture and this time absolutely demand to look at the ceiling in the third attic."

Caroline gazed down at the newspaper which Gervase brought to her, and looked up at him with beautiful, starry tears in her eyes. "Oh God," she said. "I'm sorry, but seeing it here in black and white like this, all I can think is *why not*? Why does everything work out the wrong way round?"

And she began to cry in earnest, so that Gervase had no choice but to take her in his arms and murmur, to her soft hair, words of comfort. Over her shoulder his eyes were wide with recognition and a look very like horror. Mary-Annie, oblivious to this pretty scene, emitted a loud raspberry, and threw the wooden train she was gnawing into the cold hearth with a crash.

It was a week before Cat came home. She eventually rang Gervase, who sounded constrained and uncommunicative. Despite Chrétien's teasing prompts she did not mention having seen the newspaper, nor did she ask after Caroline. The Eden job provided a good enough reason for her sojourn, a reason which seemed welcome to both of them. Gervase did say, haltingly, at the end of the brief conversation: "I hope you're – having a rest, as well. You deserve a holiday, Cat. It's going to be much easier for you now. Financially."

"Oh yes," said Cat. "Don't worry about me. I'm a new woman."

Putting down the phone, Gervase wondered whether he ought to have told her that Martin had gone for good. He had sent a letter, postmarked (if only Gervase noticed such things) from the street corner nearest Marianne's flat in London. It said that "all things considered" he had decided to go back to the States a month early, and hoped this would not cause difficulty. The clothes he had left in the bunkhouse were all worn out, so it would be fine to burn them or throw them out. The bike was at the station. In formal terms and without warmth, he thanked Gervase for giving him the chance to gain experience with working horses, and said that it would be very relevant to his future career as he had an opportunity to do an anthropological project with the Amish as part of his higher degree. He sent his best to Duane, and to Winston if anyone should see him.

He did not mention Cat. Gervase assumed that, as they had seemed to be good friends, Martin would be writing to her separately. It was a nuisance, he reflected, to lose the lad just now: especially with Cat's driving ban and two new boys, Terry and Spider, arriving any day. But that was the way with volunteers. They always stayed a longer or a shorter time than they originally planned. There was a New Zealander who wanted to come in September and who had ploughed with horses before. As for the driving problem Mrs Bird, who had in the past week been almost continuously at the farm making obscure pickles and rearranging saucepans, had offered to take on the shopping too, if she was given a proper list. Maybe now they could afford more of her time. They always used to have a cook, in the early days of the Project.

And then there was Caroline. But he avoided thinking about Caroline, because it was complicated, and distressed him, and he was too busy organizing the Morefield handover to deal with the implications of it yet. Gervase had always been good at setting priorities. He filed Martin's letter, forgot it, and pulled out a folder marked *IACS returns: 1995–6*.

Eight days after her arrival in Lille, Cat stood with Chrétien, in his long overcoat, on the station platform. She had been back to *Printemps* a couple of times, and was wearing a cotton dress, straight and severe in line and vivid pink in colour, with a white cotton jacket. "*Jolie chatte*," said Chrétien, approvingly, as she came back from buying a magazine. "You look very young. Twelve years old, at most."

"Crétin," replied Cat. "You lie. The very best we can hope is that I look like my mother looked when we were children, and you look like your father. Life does not stand still."

"No," said Chrétien, his arm on hers. "It dances!"

Together, slowly, they walked towards the Calais train. All around her Cat saw other options, blazoned on locomotives and signboards with the devastating casualness of a big continent whose very trains can promise you the world: *Bruxelles, Basel, Strasbourg, Berlin, Milano, Venezia*. Two doors slammed somewhere, echoing under the arches, and another train moved off.

"Are you sure you would not rather take the Eurostar?" said Chrétien. "My London colleagues say it is a marvel."

"No," said Cat. "I'll take the ferry, like we used to. One last indulgence of nostalgia."

She smiled up at him. They had talked themselves out during the first few days: she knew about his formal, property-led marriage, his many mistresses, his arid relationship with his children, his boredom at work and determined frivolity away from it. None of it dimmed her liking for him, only overlaid it with melancholy for the loss of the spirited, hopeful boy he had once been. They had spoken less these last few days, but in the silences between them lay an understanding of one another and of their impending farewell. Only when too much meaning fell into that silence did Cat deliberately stir him to theatrical indignation, generally by mischievously pretending to extol the merits of the Eden-Lille hotel she was profiling.

"*Alors,*" he said now. "This is your train. This is your bag. I think that now we will say *au revoir.*"

"*Adieu,*" said Cat. "A long *adieu*. We agreed that, after international discussions."

"No, *au revoir,*" he said. "There will come a time when even English women will understand how to conduct married life."

Cat leaned across and kissed him, gently, on the mouth. "In another thirty years then, *peut-être.*"

"I shall pass the time in dreaming of your eyes," he said in painstaking English, and bowed theatrically over her hand. "That was a good line, *hein?*"

"Go," said Cat. "Go back to your office! Little Anatole will be worried."

This time Chrétien only raised his hand in ironic farewell, turned, and walked rapidly along the platform. Cat turned also, to climb the high step of the train. When she looked out of the window he was nowhere to be seen.

Mary-Annie was cutting another tooth: it made her angry and fretful, and drove her sleepless mother close to despair. One day, Caroline walked up to the farm with the pushchair in an attempt to pacify the baby, and found not Duane or Martin but two strange boys, with almost shaven heads and enormous boots, staring gormlessly at her from the yard.

"Is Mr Hartley here?" she asked.

"Nah," said one of the boys. "Gonta Mid'olt. Mrs Bird's in."

In the kitchen, Caroline found Mrs Bird scrubbing new potatoes. Mary-Annie began to cry the instant the pushchair stopped, and Caroline almost as soon.

"There there!" said Mrs Bird, flapping round the table in her floral apron. "It can take you hard, looking after a baby all by yourself. You sit down and I'll make you a nice cup of tea. Come on, little darling, none of that noise."

Here Gervase found them, Caroline tear-stained but now composed, Mary-Annie sullenly rolling potatoes round on the floor, Mrs Bird mothering them both.

"Cat's back today," he said baldly. "She said she'd take a cab from the station, since she's on expenses. Could be any time." And Caroline, stumbling to her feet, muttering excuses, stuffed the baby rapidly back into the pushchair with a potato still in her fist and took her leave. Gervase looked helplessly after her and Mrs Bird said, "Well! Making heavy weather of everything today, poor lamb!"

Cat leaned over the rail of the ferry, staring unseeingly back at France. There were new memories there now, three decades newer and many layers shallower than the powerful childhood ones. Petits-fours and laughter; walking on wet pavements at midnight holding a warm dry hand; morning sunshine through shutters, high above the Rue Neuve, and the sleeping body of a man with whom she had no deep or lasting bond nor ever would have.

She wondered why she felt no guilt, she who had always championed fidelity and self-control. Maybe it was part of middle age. Perhaps when you were past child-bearing and knew the value of a long, accommodating, accustomed partnership, these things of the body genuinely could come to mean nothing important. Just an extension of friendship and shared memory, a few nights' defiance of the ageing and stiffening world. "What a Gallic way to think," she said aloud, to the rain. "It must be something in the water."

Turning, she thought for a moment that she saw Chrétien's back vanishing into a staff doorway; but it was another dark, darting figure, one of the stewards by the look of his jacket.

Cat sighed. She would see M. le Directeur, she suspected, a few times more out of the corner of her mind's eye before his image finally faded.

As, of course, it must.

29

Artemis swooped on Midmarsham again the day after Cat came home, and invited Caroline to accompany her on a visit to Gervase's uncle in Scotland for a few weeks.

"You're looking peaky," she said. "And Mary-Annie ought to meet the rest of the family. Heaven knows Gervase is remiss enough about keeping in touch." She seemed, marvellously, to have forgotten that the delightful Mary-Annie and her pretty, well-mannered mother actually formed no part of the Hartley blood line. Senility, as Cat tartly observed to Gervase, is at times a great blessing.

At any rate Caroline gladly went, and Gervase seemed more relaxed after her departure. Cat was in high spirits, fonder and more playful than usual, keeping even Terry and Spider in fits of laughter at meal times with her account of the day when at last – with permission direct from the Minister of Culture herself – she and Chrétien had penetrated into the upper reaches of Rue du Lombard and found the "*Merde*" which the boy Chrétien had spelt in air gun pellets on the plaster ceiling of the third attic room. The punch-line, much appreciated by the boys, was a lively description of the moment when Chrétien had dived behind a water tank, and come up with his dark business suit whitened with plaster and streaked with cobwebs, brandishing the actual gun itself.

"It was not mine, I never said so," he had announced to the surprised and lightly scandalized man from the Ministry. "It was Toby's."

"Toby was never allowed an air pistol," objected Cat. "For heaven's sake, he can't have been more than eight."

"Toby never asked for one," said Chrétien. "He exchanged it for his old ice-skates, at the boys' Epiphany party down at the Jesuit school. How he must have missed it, when I threw it behind the tank."

Whereon he had fiddled with the cocking mechanism for a moment, slipped in a pellet from the old-fashioned holder in its handle, and to everybody's surprise induced the gun to work.

"Pellet went right through the side of the water tank," said Cat. "Mercifully, just on the very top of the water level. But it did drip quite a bit." The boys guffawed. Gervase was quiet, wrapped in his own thoughts.

Marianne rang after a few days, asking whether she could come down for the weekend. Cat was so pleased at the prospect of seeing her daughter that she met her on the drive; the day was fine and they left Marianne's bag in the car and walked together up to the top pasture. When they were a good distance from the house Marianne said: "Mum, two things I have to talk to you about. The first one is me and Martin."

"Yes?" said Cat, with what she dryly recognized as breathless, middle-aged maternal anticipation.

"We're getting married," said her daughter. "We would have liked to tell you together, because I'm going to the States with him, to work wherever he ends up. It might not even be nursing. I've said I don't mind, it'll be an adventure. But he wouldn't come up this weekend, because of the other thing."

Cat frowned, not understanding. "But it's wonderful. He's a nice boy, a gem, just right for you. You know my views on early marriage and I suspect you do right to ignore them. I would have loved to see him and tell him that. Does he think Gervase and I are going to disapprove?"

Marianne flopped down on a convenient log. "Oh no, no. It isn't that. It's worse. It's something he's got a bee in his bonnet about. About Gervase."

"Oh?" Cat was still at sea. Marianne drew a deep, rough breath.

"About Gervase and Caroline. While you were away. He thinks Gervase and Caroline . . . oh, you know. He was so angry that he left. He thinks the world of you, Mum. He did think the world of Gervase, too, but now he's just spitting mad about it all."

Cat was silent, taking it in.

"Well," she said finally. "I'm really touched that he cared that much. But I don't believe it."

"I don't know what I believe," said Marianne cautiously. "But I promised him I'd tell you. He says he saw them, more than once, looking exactly as if . . ."

She avoided her mother's eye but doggedly continued: "And he says that one night Gervase wasn't back until the small hours. He was angry because it was just after you went away, after Caroline moved to the cottage, and it looked as if it was planned. Gervase didn't have supper with the boys. He wasn't here most of the night. Martin lay awake. He's from a very moral Catholic family."

"Marianne," said Cat. "I have lived with an unfaithful man before, remember. I know the scenery. I really don't think I'm living with one now. And I don't think Caroline would do it either."

There was a pause, then:

"I do," said Marianne flatly. "She's been jealous of you and Grandad all her life, hasn't she? Because Grandad prefers you, even though she's prettier. It could have been a great chance for her to steal an older man, a father-figure-type, off you. To prove she can beat you."

"You," said her mother, "have been mixing with psychiatrists for too bloody long. Get out west with Martin and rope some steers, why don't you?"

But later, when Marianne had gone upstairs with her bag, Cat sat down suddenly at the kitchen table as if she had been winded.

On stage, for dramatic convenience, people tend to confront one another immediately about such allegations. In real life it can be harder to find the moment. Cat, at any rate, so steadfastly did not believe that her husband had slept with her sister that she was inclined for a while to ignore the whole thing. Caroline, after all, was in Scotland; all the evidence suggested that Gervase was actually much happier since she left. He was busy with the paperwork for the Morefield Trust handover, and kept optimistically, and rather touchingly, she thought, returning to the fact that with farm costs paid and himself on a small salary, her own financial responsibilities would dwindle.

"You could write something of your own," he said hopefully. "Not always have to do commercial work."

Cat only laughed at him. "I'm not a thwarted poet, you know. There isn't a burning work of art in me, waiting its chance to get out. It's nonsense about all copywriters having a novel in their bottom drawer: some of us are just copywriters."

"But you must want to do something of your own," he would persist, disappointed.

"No," she said. "Sorry. No soul, you see. The only thing I quite fancy is doing some soap opera scripts. Winston and I used to have some great ideas about what to do next in *Coronation Street*."

She was unsure, even as she spoke, how much of this statement was manufactured for the sheer pleasure of seeing his shocked face. Fleetingly, she thought of Toby.

There had been a postcard from Artemis at the end of the first three weeks saying that Caroline was a "huge success" and that Mary-Annie was being taken on long moorland walks with her mother by a neighbour, a distant cousin called Roddy who carried the baby in a backpack and was teaching Caroline to fish, up at the Castle.

"*Roddy*," said Cat. "Wouldn't you just know that Artemis would find someone called Roddy, in a Scottish castle, and foist him on Caroline? That woman belongs in a P G Wodehouse novel. Aunt Agatha."

"It sounds as if it's doing them all good," said Gervase, flatly. "I think it was time Caroline got away for a bit."

Cat hesitated then, as if to speak; but in fact it was another three weeks, and the eve of Caroline's return, before she at last raised the matter of Martin's suspicions. She had come back on her old black bike from a visit to the doctor's Friday afternoon surgery in Midmarsham. Mrs Bird had gone home early, and Terry and Spider were cutting thistles in the lower pasture. She found Gervase in the workshop by the yard, shaping a new shaft for a tumbril. As usual he straightened, put down the spokeshave and gravely saluted his wife.

"I don't know how to lead up to this," she said. "But Marianne has told me why Martin left. It was because he thought you were having an affair."

Gervase looked at her in silence, impassive. "An affair with Caroline," she continued. "And Gervase, we're both grown-up people. We've been through a lot together, so it seems simplest if I just ask you, and we can go from there. OK?"

He did not answer, but went on looking at her, troubled.

"Is it true? Have you slept with Caroline?"

Gervase cleared his throat.

"No," he said. "No."

"Did you want to? Was it going to happen? Is it going to happen?"

He hesitated, searching for words: "No, it wouldn't have happened. Ever. I mean, not for me. I am afraid that Caroline may have got the wrong idea."

"I see," said Cat, remembering Marianne's theory, and pressing her lips together. Gervase saw her expression and hurried on:

"She has been in a vulnerable state. It was probably all my fault. I am naïve about women, I always have been. You know that."

"Did you make yourself clear?" asked Cat.

"Yes," he said in a low voice. "It was a dreadful thing to have to do. I never knew that doing something right could feel so cruel and sad. But the truth is, I have not been unfaithful to you. Not ever."

"Ah," said Cat. "I didn't really think you had, actually. But it makes it harder for me."

"Why?" asked Gervase. Suddenly the infuriating innocence of his look was too much for her: the same look, she thought suddenly, that a far younger Gervase had given her on her wedding day. She ducked her head, and hurried on blindly, wanting it all over and done with, out in the open, whatever might be the result.

"The reason it makes it harder is that I have to tell you that *I* have been unfaithful to *you*."

The stableyard was quiet. A bird twittered suddenly; a horse, inside the shelter, scraped an iron-shod hoof on the concrete.

"I'm not as honest as you are," said Cat. "And I probably

wouldn't have told you, because it meant nothing important. But I have to, because I'm now pregnant."

Gervase looked at her incredulously. His first thought was for her protection: she was cracking up, suffering delusions, and it was his fault for imposing such years of strain on her in this odd life. His fault for not being able to give her babies.

"Sit down," he said, pulling over a low workbench. "You're tired. It's my fault."

"It's not your fault, you *gummock*!" said Cat, who read his reaction only too well. "And I'm not a crazy menopausal woman. It's true. I had a brief fling in France. With a childhood friend. The one who found the air pistol behind the water tank, remember? I was telling the boys the story at supper when I came back. It never occurred to me I could get pregnant. Not for a minute. I must have been out of my head."

The corroborative detail about the air pistol seemed to clear Gervase's perception, and he looked at her with new eyes.

"You'll have to forgive me. It'll take a while to sink in," he said formally. And then, in a different voice, which shook a little:

"Are you sure you're pregnant?"

"Yes. I did a test two weeks ago, and the doctor's done an official one. He says it's a bit late over forty, but everything's fine and there's no reason I shouldn't have it. No physical reason."

Gervase picked up his spokeshave again and began stroking the wood of the cart-shaft.

"Are you going to go?" he muttered. "To France? Are you and the baby going to live with him?"

"No!" shouted Cat. "I told you, the affair was irrelevant. It was – I don't know, think of it as therapy. Like a health farm, a massage, physiotherapy, all mixed up with childhood friendship and old jokes and a couple of good dinners with too much wine." She ran her hand through her hair, half-embarrassed, half-perplexed.

"It was just very French, the whole thing. I can hardly believe it now. It's not real. Except that there is this baby."

"He'll want it," said Gervase in a low voice, scraping the wood. "Of course he will."

Cat went over to him, took the tool from his hand, and led

him to the bench. Her arm was round his shoulders, his head in her neck. She felt his tears warm on her skin.

"No, he won't," she said. "Anyway, tough shit if he does. It's ours, Gervase. Ours, if we want it. I do."

They sat for a long time in the yard together, and their talk was quiet and private and deep. When at last they came indoors, Terry and Spider were finishing their high tea under the eye of Mrs Bird, and there were two messages on the answering machine. One was from Caroline, in a high, light, happy voice, announcing her return. The other was from Artemis, who usually refused to use such machines, saying in conspiratorial tones that Caroline had some very good news to tell them. Gervase must, she said, ring his mother straight away once Caroline had explained, and she would fill in all the background. It was perfectly suitable, she said, and he need not worry.

"It'll be about *Roddy*," said Cat. "I bet you."

It was about Roddy, inevitably. Caroline shyly told her sister all about it the next day when she arrived home, and asked her to tell Gervase. If all continued to go well, she would probably move to Scotland.

Nothing more was said between them about what could have happened during Cat's trip to France. The sisters returned gratefully to their old status of non-confiding but vaguely benevolent relatives, each with her own busy and perfectly satisfactory separate life. So did Lindy, who rang up a few weeks later with some anodyne chat and said brightly to Cat, as if none of the awful intimacies of past months had ever been shared:

"Mark and I are thinking of starting a family, did I tell you? I had a bit of trouble, but I've been to a clinic and we've got the all-clear now."

Cat, the diplomat's daughter, responded with suitable surprise and pleasure, just as if the subject had never been raised between them before. Mark, said Lindy airily as she rang off, sent his love. Cat conveyed hers back in an equally light tone, wondering as she did so whether she had destroyed the crazy accusing letter Mark had sent her or whether it still lay incriminatingly on her

desk under a grimy pile of Eden faxes and induction leaflets.
She must look it out and destroy it. Every home should have
a shredder, she thought. There was no point in preserving the
past if it was only going to cause trouble.

30

Toby Christian Hartley, immediately nicknamed TC, was born in March. He weighed seven and a half pounds and looked, all the family said, startlingly like his uncle and namesake: dark, elfin, with a weirdly amused air even on his third or fourth day of life.

His uncle Mark stood as godfather, and spent most of the ceremony gazing tenderly across the font at his own pregnant wife. Gervase stood as close as he could get, maintaining a jealous vigilance as his son – oh yes, his son! – lay whickering in protest in Mark's unskilful arms. The service was Anglican, traditional and soothing; outside Midmarsham church a gale bent the trees and blew stinging sleet and occasional hailstones. Mark and Lindy had wanted to delay the gathering until spring and were backed up by Artemis, who detested travelling in winter; but Cat had insisted on an early christening so that the baby's half-sister Marianne could be there before her departure to Texas. Caroline invited her Scottish cavalier, who came rather shyly because it was his first appearance at a Gratton family gathering.

After the ceremony, they drove through the darkening gale in their various cars to a tea at Knoll Farm laid out by Mrs Bird. Roddy lugged from his car a christening present of a case of vintage port. This, said Roddy, would come of age in the same year of the 21st century as Toby Christian did.

"If it's lucky," Cat muttered. She had eschewed all alcohol in her pregnancy, and was beginning to recover a taste for it. Gervase laughed, and assured Roddy that the port would be properly hidden from the owner's mother.

"Well," said Cat. "It'd only be family tradition if I did drink it. Dad, isn't it true that Mum borrowed my silver-and-glass christening necklace I got from my godfather in Murano, and lost it?"

"That's right," admitted Robert. "She lost it at a cocktail party in Tel Aviv. She was conscience-stricken. She bought you a silver spoon instead."

"Which she also lost, in the move from Washington," said Cat. "Nothing like a good grudge, is there?"

Robert had grown suddenly old, bent and small, with a new translucence to his skin: a winter of chest infections and stiffening limbs had given him what the French would call a *coup de vieux*. In spite of it he felt now a sense of completion, of resigned contentment. He was tired and had scaled down his public work, so that the family seemed suddenly to have swum into clearer focus. They were more important to him than at any time since Diana's death. And the family, with one exception, seemed to be flourishing.

The dimness and conventionality of Caroline's new man friend had shocked him for a while, but now he reflected that perhaps the best régime for his younger daughter was precisely what Roddy could offer: uncritical adoration and rolling acres. She seemed calm and blooming, if a little chilly towards her brother-in-law Gervase. Mark was less tense than usual, his wife pink-cheeked and clinging; and above all, this new grandchild filled him with particular joy. Looking around his burgeoning family the old man said quietly to Cat:

"Happy day. But you mustn't think we've all forgotten who's missing. Do you know, Mousie, I sometimes work out how old Toby and Topsy's child would have been now. About eight months, I reckon."

Cat was touched. "Oh Dad!"

"It's another grandchild of mine," he said gruffly, touching the new baby's cheek. "And of Diana's."

Cat looked down at her infant lolling off to sleep in a wicker basket at her side. She fended off Mary-Annie, who was crawling to investigate her squashy new cousin, and as Caroline hurried up to suppress her daughter, she turned back and said abruptly to Robert:

"Do you think we ought to stop hoping now, Dad? Admit that TC here has only got one uncle?"

Robert put his hand on hers, briefly and gently. "Yes, I do. I have a feeling about it. He would have been in touch, wouldn't he? If . . ."

Cat leaned over the baby, and smoothed the white blanket. Then she pushed away a tear from the corner of her eye, angrily, with the back of her hand. "You're right. It's better to accept it," she said after a moment. "I suppose I will, one day."

Against Gervase's inclination, there was now a portable television in the corner of the kitchen. Cat, bored in the later months of her pregnancy, had pleaded its case: there was a General Election campaign, and she always found them, for perverse and cynical reasons not shared by Gervase, irresistibly entertaining. Sometimes, watching a particularly shrill altercation between two political popinjays who reminded her of puffed-up Eden executives, she would feel the baby move in her womb in sympathy as she laughed, and knew for certain that it was a boy. A bad boy like Toby or Chrétien, with whom one day she could laugh at otherwise unshareable jokes.

After tea in front of the fire, the family drifted back in chattering groups to the kitchen to prepare for their journeys home. Mark switched on this small television. He had been looking anxiously out of the window, and at Lindy, and at his watch.

"The weather's getting a lot worse. Cat, do you mind if we watch the forecast at twenty to six? If there's snow on the motorway, we might stay over tonight at the Lion."

"Stay here," said Cat. Toby Christian woke up in his basket in the corner and gave an ear-splitting wail. "No, on second thoughts, get your sleep while you can, Lindy. Go to the Lion."

"We still might go home," said Mark. "Let's see if it's going to get any worse."

He turned the sound up and straddled a chair. Cat stood behind him, and the others glanced indifferently towards the screen. The news was still on. Lindy yawned: since her pregnancy she had slowed down, grown sleepier and pinker in the cheek.

"*Finally, back to this afternoon's fire on the cross-Channel ferry,*" said the newsreader. "*Latest reports suggest that in spite of early fears, there were no fatalities. Of the fifty passengers who were taken to hospital, all but five have now been sent home after treatment for*

shock and bruising. Three men, believed to be cooks in the galley area
where the fire broke out, are said to be in a stable condition, and five
other crew members are undergoing treatment for smoke inhalation."

"God," said Robert. "What a terrible day to be on a ferry."
Outside the wind was howling, an empty Arctic sound in the
darkness, and now it was howling on the screen as well, blowing
the sleet horizontally across the blackened upper decks of a small
ship. The family were all watching now, gripped by the brief
distant drama: Caroline and Roddy, Robert, Noreen, Marianne,
Dave, Gervase and Cat, Mark and Lindy. Only Artemis was
wholly uninterested; she darted a freezing look at Randy, the
latest graduate of the farm regime, who had come shyly into the
kitchen in search of tea. He stood awkwardly in the doorway,
unsure of what was going on. Noreen moved silently to the stove
and poured the boy a cup of tea.

"*A company spokesman,*" said a reporter, over pictures of
firefighters moving through twisted and blackened plastic tables,
"*praised the quick thinking of staff in this cafeteria.*" The film cut to a
man in a suit and a hard hat, saying:

"*Once the chefs had been pulled out, the fire doors which cut off the*
kitchen area worked as designed. This is a very modern ferry, and the
technology didn't let us down. However, fire doors have only a limited
life and it was essential that the passengers should be moved out onto
the open deck area very quickly indeed."

The reporter took over. "*In these conditions, smoke travels very fast*
once it has an outlet," he intoned, "*and the company says there would*
have been many more cases of inhalation, and possibly some fatalities,
if the cafeteria stewards had not achieved the evacuation very rapidly
indeed."

A passenger appeared on the screen, dishevelled and intense,
in a padded anorak.

"*We couldn't see any smoke,*" he said. "*And frankly, a lot of people*
didn't want to move. Not while their food was hot."

"Right," said Marianne, watching, interested. "God knows
how you'd get the stupid berks moving, especially out into
the cold in weather like that. I did a fire drill when I was a
waitress at the holiday camp, and you have no idea how stupid
people are. Nobody on holiday ever believes anything bad can
happen to them."

"*One of the stewards, the older one, was amazing,*" said the man on the screen. "*At first, I have to admit we all thought he'd flipped, he was being that abusive. But he got everyone out bloody quick. Fair play to him, I say. When we looked back that place was solid smoke.*"

The reporter appeared in person now, frowning responsibly. "*Questions will be asked,*" he said sententiously, "*about the speed with which the smoke spread. But on this occasion, at least, it seems that the nightmare of a fire on a crowded ferry, in bad weather, did not claim any lives.*"

Mark glanced at his watch, impatient. "They're overrunning the weather," he said. Cat and Robert, however, as lifelong Channel travellers, were animatedly interested in the drama.

"I wonder what the steward actually did?" said Robert. "He obviously got dozens of dozy people on their feet and out onto the deck."

"Perhaps he was ex-army or something," said Cat idly. "Habit of command. Like Gervase when he does his Cadet Force bark, at the boys. At the double, now, chaps!"

Gervase, holding the baby, gave a small smile. Randy sucked at his tea, not knowing whether to seem amused.

"I want the *weather forecast,*" said Mark, fretfully. The newsreader had taken over again, but seemed to be listening to a message through his earphone.

"*We go back live now –*" he said uncertainly – "*to – Marcus Jordan, at the Dover hospital where victims of the ferry fire are still being treated.*"

"Oh, for God's sake," said Mark. "They play it for everything it's worth, don't they?"

And at that moment, onto the screen came the unmistakable face of his elder brother, albeit topped with a turban of bandages and framed in the head of an iron hospital bed.

As the viewers stared disbelievingly at the shimmering little glass rectangle of the screen, the mirage was confirmed.

"*Toby Gratton,*" said the reporter "*is the steward who is credited with evacuating the cafeteria in record time when the fire was first detected. His voice may be hoarse now, as he recovers from the effects of smoke inhalation, but according to his colleagues he made good use of it at the height of today's crisis.*"

The camera panned to the next bed, where a younger man sat up, his hair scorched.

"People weren't moving," he said. *"Most of them just sat there. I have to admit, I was on the point of panicking, I knew the doors couldn't last. Then Tobe comes up and starts shouting at the punters – the passengers I mean – yelling the odds. He slapped a couple of them, which I have to say we are definitely not trained to do. It worked, though."*

"God Almighty," breathed Cat. It was the first time anybody in the kitchen had spoken since the silent, ghostlike figure of her brother had appeared on the screen. There was a woman speaking now, a middle-aged dumpy figure with her arm in a sling and the caption "PASSENGER" printed across her image. *"He called me a stupid fat tart,"* said the woman, giggling a little. *"But I have to say I forgive him. I suppose it was shock treatment, to get us moving. He told my husband to – well, move his pansy arse. There was another man he prodded with a cake-slice and called a stupid suicidal git."*

This outbreak of overfrank reportage caused the correspondent abruptly to cut in with an improvised sign-off. *"So – er – unconventional heroism perhaps, and hardly by the book. But nonetheless, it may be due to Steward – er – Gratton, that lives were not lost in the Channel today. Marcus Jordan, at Dover."*

Mark never saw his weather forecast. Cat leapt up as the news ended, pushed the off button and turned, radiant with an almost frightening energy, to face her family.

"He's alive!" she said. "Toby's alive. Did you see? It was him. It was, wasn't it? Today. Alive."

"I wouldn't have believed it, if it weren't for the bit about him insulting people," said Robert wonderingly. "That's what he got sacked from Disneyland for, remember?" Mark shook his head, speechless.

"What the hell is he doing working as a waiter on a ferry?" asked Dave. "Why didn't he tell anybody where he was? What a berk! Look what he's put everybody through!" His voice shook with anger, and Marianne put a restraining hand on his shoulder.

"Some form of breakdown?" murmured Gervase, appeasingly. "Lost memory?"

"He knew his bloody name," said Dave. "It's unforgivable.

Mum!" For Cat was crying now. He crossed to her side. "Mum,
I'm sorry, but Uncle Toby really is a selfish bastard."

"Hear, hear," said Marianne. "And I speak as a member of the
caring profession. He needs kicking. Mum!"

She too went to her mother, and took her other arm.

"Well," said Robert. "Never mind all that. Who's going down
to Dover, then?"

Against the howl and crash of the wind outside, there was
silence in the kitchen. From between her elder children, Cat
looked defiantly at Gervase. Gervase held the baby close and said,
"It's a bad night for driving. Darling, please don't. Not tonight.
We'd have to take TC with us, for feeding. It's too big a risk for
both of you." Cat bowed her head in acknowledgement.

Then Robert made as if to speak, but everybody had seen the
exhaustion in the old man's face from the drive to Northamptonshire that morning. Mark shook himself out of his stupor, looked
despairingly at his own wife and said:

"I suppose it's me, isn't it? Perhaps if Lindy stayed here."

"No," said Dave. "That's not fair, Uncle Mark. I'll bloody well
go. With Marianne, if she wants to come and be psychiatric."

Marianne nodded. "We'll take my car. Better on the ice."

Dave continued, looking at his mother, "But I'm warning you,
Ma, I'm going to demand a doctor's certificate with three rubber
stamps on it, saying he was too bonkers even to drop anybody
a postcard in a whole bloody year. If he can't produce one I am
going to punch him on the nose. OK?"

"OK," said Cat, sniffing away her tears to smile at her indignant
elder son. "You do that."

31

By great good fortune, the Ward Sister in charge of the smoke-damaged ferry passengers had trained with Marianne. To her brother's admiration, the latter skilfully parlayed her way into the hospital when they arrived shivering off the road at half-past ten, and revived her old acquaintance to such an extent that nurse Natalie allowed her to peep into the side-ward where Toby lay asleep.

"We had to put him there," she murmured. "After the television report we had newspaper reporters trying to get in."

"Why is his head bandaged? Is there concussion?" asked Marianne in a low voice as they turned away.

"Nope. Just a couple of cuts."

"And can he talk? They didn't interview him."

"It was a problem earlier. Now he's a bit croaky, that's all. Doctor reckons he can go tomorrow, if there's anywhere for him *to* go where the reporters won't harass him."

"Oh, there is," said Marianne a touch grimly. "I'll tell you all about it, if you promise not to tell the reporters."

"Promise," said Natalie. And later, "What a business! Do you and your brother want to spend the night in the Relatives' Room? There's two beds from people who went home earlier, but I can't offer clean sheets. It's all locked up."

Dave rang his mother from the lobby to confirm that it was definitely Toby, and that there was nothing much wrong with him. When she had taken the call, Cat came up to bed and rolled happily into Gervase's waiting arms. Next to them, young Toby Christian snuffled contentedly in his basket, and after a while his mother trailed a hand to stroke his hair as he slept.

"You've got two uncles after all," she whispered. "A very respectable one and a naughty bad one. He's coming to see you, tomorrow."

When Toby woke in the narrow hospital bed there was a nurse leaning over him, gently removing his bandages, and at the foot of his bed two tall, healthy, broad-shouldered and somehow accusing figures. He closed his eyes again and groaned theatrically.

"Family!" he said. "How lovely!"

"Why did you do it?" asked Dave. "It's well over a year. And not a word. Mum's been frantic. And Grandad. Even Uncle Mark was looking for you. Auntie Caroline went to Los Angeles!"

"Silly cow," said the figure in the bed. Now that the bandages were off the young people saw, with a start, that he had a swath of grey hair in his dark forelock, and that his face too had suddenly aged and sagged. He looked as old as Uncle Mark, now; which he well might, considering he was nearly five years older.

"Uncle Toby," said Marianne with deadly firmness, "everyone thought you were dead. You sent two cryptic postcards, then nothing for fifteen months. Why did you do it? I could understand a few weeks, after poor Topsy, but it's been so *long*."

Toby moved restlessly in the bed while the nurse, listening agog to this confrontation, made slow work of dabbing his forehead and putting on plasters instead of the cumbersome strapping. His voice was hoarse, but managed at the same time to be flippant. It was a striking combination.

"For a start, I never dreamed it was that long. Time does fly, when you're serving chicken and chips to fat wallies. Anyway, I didn't have anything else to say. I was thinking."

"What about?"

"Which side of the Channel to get off. To and fro, to and fro, equally crummy seamen's hostels either side. Keep travellin' on. You know."

"Well, you're bloody well travellin' on to Knoll Farm when they chuck you out of here," said Dave. "We're standing guard.

You won't get away again until you've explained yourself properly to poor Mum."

He never did, and nor did Cat expect it. The ferry company was thankful enough to discharge their abusive tabloid hero with more money in his pocket than he had had since his first hit song in the 1970s. "Funny, how rude words earn me money," he said. He began writing lyrics again after a while, heartbreaking love songs this time, which like all good lyrics sang better than they read. They caught the fancy of a new boy band and propelled him back to comparative prosperity. He even bought a flat in Brixton, where the sight of his housekeeping arrangements upset Caroline so much on her one visit there that she would not allow Mary-Annie even to drink a glass of water from his kitchen tap.

Sometimes his elder sister would hunt through Toby's new lyrics for clues as to what the lost year on the Channel had meant to him. But she never came to any firm conclusion, even about "Sail away Sian, over the ocean". Mostly she neither asked nor wondered, but accepted his shuttered, shadowy corners as she accepted her own, and was content that he resumed his visits to the farm. He came more often now: teased Gervase, mocked the staidness of Cat's neighbours, and played delightedly with his namesake nephew.

"Why Toby *Christian*, I wonder," he once said, in a silly falsetto, to the baby. "Why such a funny name? Nobody *else* in the Choral Society has a baby with such an exotic foreign-sort-of-name, do they, brat?" He sounded so like Artemis that his sister giggled. Then with a swift sidelong glance, catching her off-guard, he added in his own voice:

"Does Farmer Daddy know why? Such an unusual name. In England, anyway."

"He does," Cat replied. "Gervase knows everything that I know."

Toby nuzzled the baby and said, as if it were a dreamy non sequitur: "I don't suppose the bastard ever will send my air gun back."

"Which bastard? What do you know about air guns?" said Cat, defensively.

"I met your Duane helping out in the Lion. He's not bad behind the pumps. Just gets a bit flustered when the froth keeps on coming."

"And?" said Cat, recovered now.

"And," said Toby, "Duane told me this shocking story Spider told him, about rude French words on ceilings, and water tanks in attics, and European merchant bankers. That's the trouble with you solid respectable citizens. You may have clean kitchens but you have absolutely no morals, when it comes down to it."

The mother's help had just come in to the room, carrying a pile of folded baby clothes. Cat, in her new modest prosperity, had decided that she could afford a helper to look after baby TC at times of tight deadlines or London meetings, and to take him to Midmarsham toddler group when she could not face the chatter of very young mothers.

"Isn't that right, Nanny?" said Toby, using Artemis' voice again. "These modern young mothers have no idea how to carry on, have they?"

"Don' call me nanny, man," said Winston, irritated.